KING PENGUIN

THE DEATH OF ARTEMIO CRUZ

Carlos Fuentes was born in Mexico City in 1928 and educated at the University of Mexico and the Institut des Hautes Études Internationales, Geneva. He was a member of the Mexican delegation to the International Labour Organization in Geneva (1950–52). In 1954 he was appointed Assistant Head of the Press Section in the Ministry of Foreign Affairs, Mexico, and the following year he became Assistant Director of Cultural Dissemination at the University of Mexico. In 1957 he returned to the Ministry of Foreign Affairs as Head of the Department of Cultural Relations. Carlos Fuentes has held various editorial posts and since 1960 has been Editor of *Siempre* and *Politica*. In 1974 he became a Fellow of the Woodrow Wilson International Center for Scholars, Washington, D.C., and he has served as Mexico's Ambassador to France.

Among his other books, published and acclaimed in many countries, are the novels *Where the Air is Clear*, *The Good Conscience*, *Aura*, *A Change of Skin* and *Terra Nostra*.

CARLOS FUENTES

THE DEATH OF
ARTEMIO CRUZ

TRANSLATED BY SAM HILEMAN

A KING PENGUIN
PUBLISHED BY PENGUIN BOOKS

Penguin Books Ltd, Harmondsworth, Middlesex, England
Viking Penguin Inc., 40 West 23rd Street, New York, New York 10010, U.S.A.
Penguin Books Australia Ltd, Ringwood, Victoria, Australia
Penguin Books Canada Ltd, 2801 John Street, Markham, Ontario, Canada L3R 1B4
Penguin Books (N.Z.) Ltd, 182–190 Wairau Road, Auckland 10, New Zealand

First published as *La Muerte de Artemio Cruz*
in Mexico 1962

This translation first published in Great Britain by
William Collins Sons & Company Limited 1964
Published by Martin Secker & Warburg 1977
Published in Penguin Books 1978
Reprinted as a King Penguin 1984

Reproduced, printed and bound in Great Britain by
Hazell Watson & Viney Limited,
Member of the BPCC Group,
Aylesbury, Bucks
Set in Monotype Plantin

The premeditation of death is the premeditation of freedom.

MONTAIGNE, *Essays*

Men who come to the surface
Cradled by ice
Who return through graves
See what you are ...

CALDERÓN, *The Great Theater of the World*

I alone, I know what I can do. To others I am only a perhaps.

STENDHAL, *The Red and the Black*

... of myself and of Him and of we three, always three !

GOROSTIZA, *Death without End*

Life is cheap, life is worth nothing ...

Mexican Popular Song

I wake . . . the touch of that cold object against my penis awakens me. I did not know that at times one can urinate without knowing it. I keep my eyes closed. The nearest voices cannot be heard: if I opened my eyes, would I hear them? But my eyelids are heavy, they are lead, and there are brass coins on my tongue and iron hammers in my ears and something, something, something like tarnished silver in my breathing; metal, everything is metal; or again, mineral. So I urinate without knowing it: maybe during these hours – for it comes to me that I have been unconscious – I have eaten without knowing it: for hardly had it lightened when I stretched out my hand and, without wanting to, pushed the telephone off on the floor, and there I lay face down on the bed with my arms dangling, a tickling tap in the veins of my wrists. And now I am awake, but I don't want to open my eyes. Just the same, although it is not desired, something shimmers insistently near my face, something seen through closed eyes in a fugue of black lights and blue circles. I tighten the muscles of my face and open my right eye and see it reflected in the squares of silvered glass that encrust a woman's purse. I am this, this am I: old man with his face reflected in pieces by different-sized squares of glass: I am this eye, this eye I am: eye furrowed by roots of accumulated choler, old and forgotten and always present; eye green and swollen between its lids: lids, eyelids, oily eyelids. And nose: I am this nose, this nose, this earth-brown baked nose with flaring windows; and I am these cheeks, cheeks, cheek-bones where the white whiskers are born. Are born. Face. Face. Face, grimace, face that has nothing to do with the lines of age or the grimace of pain; face mouth-open and the eyeteeth darkened by tobacco, tobacco, tobacco. The moist air of my breathing fogs the mirroring glass. A hand removes the purse from the night-table.

'Look, Doctor, he's ...'

'Señor Cruz ...'

'In the very hour of his death he had to trick us!'

I won't speak. My mouth is full of old brass: the taste of it. But I crack my eyes and through the lashes see the two women and the doctor who reeks of antiseptic: from his sweaty hand, inside my shirt now palpating my chest, evaporating alcohol rises like a spasm. I try to remove that hand.

'Come, now, Señor Cruz, come ...'

No, no, I won't open my lips. Or, rather, I won't open that straight lipless line of mouth that appeared in the reflection. I will keep my arms stretched out over the sheets. The covers reach to my belly. My stomach ... ah! And my legs remain spread with that cold object between my thighs, and my chest continues sleeping with the same dull tick-tick-tickle that taps in my wrists and that I have felt ... have felt before, at other times, after sitting too long in a movie: poor circulation, that's what it is, that's all it is. Nothing worse. Nothing more serious. Just poor circulation. One is forced to think about one's body. But it tires a man to think about his body. His own body, that is, the only single body he has. It's tiring. Don't think. Enough that it's there: I think, witness: I – am – body, I. Body that lasts. Body that goes away, that leaves, that dissolves in nerve-ends and scaling skin and cells and globules: my body, upon which this doctor lays his fingers. Fear. I feel the fear a man feels when he thinks about this own body. And my face? Teresa's purse is gone, she took it away; I try to remember my reflection: face cut up by unsymmetrical facets of glass, the eye very near the ear and very far from its mate: a face distributed among three shimmering mirrors. Sweat trickles down my forehead. I close my eyes again and I ask, I beg that my face and my body be returned to me. I ask: but I feel the hand that is caressing me, and I would like to escape it but don't have the strength.

'Do you feel better?'

I don't look at her. At Catalina I do not look, but farther: Teresa sitting in the big armchair, a newspaper open in her hands. My newspaper, I'm sure. It's Teresa, all right, but she has her face hidden behind the spread pages.

'Open the window.'

'No. You might be chilled and get worse.'

'Leave him alone, Mother. Can't you see what he's pulling?'

Ah: I smell incense. Ah! His murmur in the door. Now he enters with the holy water held in front, with his black skirts and the smell of that incense, to say farewell to me with all the rigor of a sermon. So: they have fallen into the trap.

'Has Padilla come yet?'

'Yes. He's waiting outside.'

'Tell him to come in.'

'But the fath . . .'

'Have Padilla come in first.'

Ah, Padilla. Come closer. Did you bring the tape-recorder? If you knew what is to your advantage, you would bring it here just as you brought it every night to the house in Coyoacán. Today, more than ever, you ought to want me think that everything goes along the same as always. Don't break our routine, Padilla. Ah, you are beside me now. And the women don't like that.

'Go near, child, so that he can recognize you. Tell him your name.'

'I am . . . I am Gloria.'

If I could only make her face out better. If I could only be sure of her expression. She must notice this stink of dead skin; she has to see my sunken chest, the gray tangled beard, the fluid dripping from my nose, these . . .

They draw her away from me.

The doctor has been counting my pulse.

'I must consult with my colleagues.'

Catalina's hand just touches mine. What a futile caress. I can't see her clearly, but I try to fix my eyes in hers. There, I have her now. I take her cold hand.

'That morning I waited for him with happiness. We rode our horses across the river.'

'What are you saying? Don't talk. Don't tire yourself. I can't understand you.'

'I'd like to go back there, Catalina. But how useless.'

Yes: the priest kneels beside me. He murmurs, as Padilla plugs in the tape-recorder. I hear my voice, my words. *Ay*, with a cry.

Ay, I cry out! *Ay*, I survived! Two doctors appear in the door. I survived. Regina, I hurt. I hurt, Regina, I discover that I hurt. Regina, soldier: I hurt, embrace me. They have nailed a cold long dagger in my stomach. And someone, someone else has driven a spike into my guts. I smell that incense and I'm tired. I let them do what they will, let them lift me heavily while I moan. I don't owe life to any of you. I can't stand it, I can't, I didn't choose this, my feet are cold, the pain doubles me up, I don't want these dying fingernails, these blue fingernails. But aaahhh, aaaahhh, I survived! What did I do yesterday? If I think about what I did yesterday, I'll stop thinking about what is happening now. That's a lucid thought. Very lucid: think yesterday. You're not so crazy, you don't suffer so much, you can think yesterday, yesterday, yesterday. Yesterday Artemio Cruz returned to Mexico City from Hermosillo. Yes: yesterday Artemio Cruz ... before becoming ill, yesterday Artemio Cruz ... no, he didn't become ill, no, not Artemio Cruz. No: someone else, someone different, someone in a mirror in front of his sickbed, the bed of someone else. Artemio Cruz: his twin. Artemio Cruz is sick, he does not live. No, he lives! Artemio Cruz did live once. He lived several years. Years, not yearns. No, he lived several days. Days, not daze. His twin, Artemio Cruz, his double. Yesterday Artemio Cruz, he who lived only a few days before dying, yesterday Artemio Cruz, who is ... I am I, and yesterday

You, yesterday, did the usual things, just as any day. You don't know if it's worth remembering. You would prefer to remember, there lying in the half-darkness of the bedroom, not what has happened already but what is going to happen. In your half-darkness your eyes would prefer to look ahead, not behind, and they do not know how to foresee the past. Yes: yesterday you will fly home from Hermosillo. Yesterday, the ninth of April, 1959, you will fly back in the regular flight of the Compañia Mexicana de Aviación, leaving Sonora's capital and its infernal heat at exactly nine-fifty-five in the morning, and arriving in Mexico

City at exactly four-thirty in the afternoon. From your reclining seat in the four-motor plane you will look down on a gray flat city, on a belt of adobe walls and galvanized steel roofs. The stewardess will offer you chewing gum wrapped in cellophane, and this you will recall because she will be a very lovely girl, and you will always have an appreciative eye for a trim figure, though your years condemn you to merely imagining things rather than doing them (the words are wrong: clearly, you will never feel 'condemned' even though all you can do is imagine). The luminous words – NO SMOKING, FASTEN SEAT BELTS – will just have come on when the plane, entering the Valley of Mexico, will abruptly drop, as if suddenly it has lost the power to sustain itself in that thin air, and then, immediately, will dip sharply to the right, and coats and jackets and bundles and bags will cascade down and there will be a common cry, a common shout cut off by low sobbing as flames will begin to hiss from the outside right motor; and everyone will shout again and only you will remain calm and motionless, chewing your gum and observing the stewardess's legs as she runs down the aisle trying to quiet the passengers. The fire-suppressors inside the motor will operate, and the plane will land uneventfully, and no one will have noticed that only you, an old man of seventy-one years, that only you maintained composure. You will feel proud of yourself without showing it. You will reflect that you have done so many cowardly things in your life that now courage has become easy; and you will smile and tell yourself that no, no, that isn't a paradox: it is true and almost universally true.

You will have made the trip to Sonora by car – 1959 Volvo, Federal District plates 712 – because several gentlemen in the state government there have decided to become difficult. That is why you will have to make that long hurried trip, to secure the situation again, to reestablish loyalties already bought and paid for: yes, bought, for you will not deceive yourself with ceremonious words: and the gentlemen will be convinced again, persuaded again, that is, bought again, receiving their bribes, another unceremonious word, as levies on the shippers of fish from Sonora and Sinaloa to the Federal District: ten per cent to each inspector, and the fish will arrive at the capital made strangely expensive by the chain of graft along the way, but you will receive more than twenty times their value in 'loyalty.' You will take satisfaction in thinking about this little arrangement, though at the same time it will seem possible material for a short red-ink exposé story in the newspaper you own, and now you tell yourself that thinking about it is really a waste of time. But you will insist just the same, go on thinking about it just the same, because there are things you do not want to think about, things you want to forget by remembering something else; and above all, you want to forget yourself, the man you find yourself to be now. You will exonerate yourself. You cannot find yourself. But you will meet yourself. They will take you home fainting. You will collapse in your office; the doctor will come and will say that he can't make a diagnosis for several hours; other doctors will come; they won't know anything, they won't understand anything, they will mouth long difficult words. And you will become the images of your imagination, like an empty wrinkled wineskin. Your chin will tremble. There will be a dirty smell in your mouth, a bad smell at your armpits, and above all your crotch will stink. And there you will be thrown to lie, without shaving or bathing, a collection of sweats, a residue of irritated nerves and unconscious physiological functions. Yet just the same, you will go on insisting on remembering what will happen yesterday.

From the airport you will go to your office, crossing a city impregnated with tear-gas because the police will have just finished breaking up a demonstration in the Caballito plaza. You will meet with your editor-in-chief and discuss the front page heads, the editorials, and the cartoons, and you will feel pleased. You will receive a visit from your Yankee associate and you'll make clear to him the clear danger in these misnamed 'reform' movements to clean up the unions. Afterward your administrator, Padilla, will come to your office and report that the Indians go on agitating, and you, through Padilla, will send sharp word to the manager of the *ejido*, telling him to clamp down on them, for that's what you pay him for. Oh, you will work hard yesterday in the morning. The representative of a certain Latin-American benefactor will call on you, and you will persuade him to step up the subsidy he gives your newspaper. You will phone your gossip columnist and tell her to light some squibs under that Couto who has been waging war on your interests in Sonora. You will do so much! And later, you will sit with Padilla and go over your accounts, which will be very entertaining. One whole wall of your office is covered by the map that shows the sweep and inter-relationships of your business network: the newspaper in Mexico City, and the real estate there and in Puebla, Guadalajara, Monterrey, Culiacán, Hermosillo, Guaymas, and Acapulco. The sulfur domes in Jáltipan, the mines in Hidalgo, the timber concessions in Tarahumara. The chain of hotels, the pipe foundry, the fish business. The financing operations, the stock holdings, the administration of the company formed to lend money to the railroad, the legal representation of North American firms, the directorships of banking houses, the foreign stocks – dyes, steel, and detergents; and one little item that does not appear on the wall: fifteen million dollars deposited in banks in Zurich, London, and New York. Yes: you will light a cigarette, in spite of the warnings you have had from your doctor, and to Padilla will relate again the steps by which you gained your wealth: loans at short terms and high interest to peasants in Puebla, just after the Revolution; the acquisition of land around the city of Puebla, whose growth you foresaw; acres for subdivision in Mexico City, thanks to the friendly intervention of each succeeding president; the daily newspaper; the purchase of mining stock; the formation of Mexican-U.S. enterprises in which you participated as front-man so that the law would be complied with; trusted friend of North American investors, intermediary between New York and Chicago and the government of Mexico; the manipulation of stock prices to move them to your advantage, buying and selling, always at a profit; the gilded El Dorado years of President Alemán, and your final consolidation; the acquisition of *ejido* farm lands taken from their peasant occupants to project new subdivisions in cities of the interior; the timber concessions. Yes, you will sigh, asking Padilla for another match, twenty good years, years of progress, of peace and collaboration among the classes; twenty years of progress after the demogoguery of Lázaro Cárdenas; twenty years of submissive labor leaders, of broken strikes, of protection for industry. And now you will raise your hands to your stomach and to your head of grayed chestnut hair, to your oily face, and you will see yourself reflected in the glass top of your desk, the image of your sick twin, as all sounds will suddenly flee, laughing, from your hearing, and the sweat of men will swirl around you and their bodies will suffocate you, and you will lose consciousness. The twin in the glass will join the other, who is yourself, join the seventy-one-year-old old man who will fall, unconscious, between the swivel chair and the steel desk: and you will be here and you will not know which events of your life will pass into your biography, or which will be suppressed and hidden; you won't know. They are vulgar facts and events, and you will not be the first man with such a page to his credit or discredit; but after all you will have enjoyed yourself, and you will not forget this, though you will be remembering other things, other days, you will have to remember them: days near, far, pushed toward forgetfulness or brought up by recollection, days of encounter and rebound, of fugitive love, of freedom, rancor, failure, of will, days that were and will be more than any names you can give them: days when destiny will sniff after you like a bloodhound and will find you and frighten you and embody you in words and actions: your complex, opaque, adipose solidity bound forever to that other, impalpable stuff that is your soul absorbed by your solidity: love of fresh quinces, ambition of growing fingernails, tedium of progressive baldness, melancholy of the sun and desert, debility of dirty plates, distraction of tropical rivers, fear of sabers and gunpowder, loss of the wind-fresh sheets, youth of dark horses, old age of abandoned seashores, meetings with envelopes bearing foreign stamps, repugnance of burning incense, nicotine sickness, pain of red earth, tenderness of an afternoon patio, spirit of all matter and stuff of all souls: the cutting edge of memory that separates the two halves; life's solder that welds them together again, joins them and dissolves them, follows and finds them: fruit with two halves that today will be made one again, and you will remember the half you left behind: destiny will meet you, and you will yawn: you won't have to remember now, and you will yawn: events and their feelings stand clear and free of each other and fall broken beside the long road: there, behind, there was a garden – if you could only go back to it, if you could only find it again at the last; but you will yawn: you have always held your ground, you will yawn, and so you are in the garden, but the pale leaves deny the fruit and the dusty gullet denies the water: you will yawn: days will be different and the same, distant and present, soon they will forget their necessity, their urgency and terror, and you will yawn: you will open your eyes and see the women there with their false solicitude: you will whisper their names: Catalina, Teresa: they will not cease to hide their true feelings of betrayal and violation, their irritated disapproval transformed now by necessity into a mask of worry, affection, and sorrow: that mask will be the first sign of the transition that your illness and the presence of the doctors will impose upon them: you will yawn. You will close your eyes and you will yawn. You, he, Artemio Cruz, who will believe in your days without seeing them

[1941: July 6]

He rode by limousine toward his office. The chauffeur was driving, and he went on reading the morning paper but at that moment and quite casually he happened to look up and he saw the two women entering a shop. He watched them and wrinkled his eyes, and then the car moved on and he continued reading the news from Sidi Barrani and El Alamein, looking at the photos of Rommel and Montgomery. The chauffeur was sweating in the heat of the sun and could not turn on the radio. He, in back, reflected that he had not done badly in associating himself with the Colombian coffee-growers when the war in Africa began, and the two women entered the shop and the shop-girl asked them please to be seated while she advised the proprietress (for she knew who they were, this mother and daughter, and her instruc tions were to inform the proprietress the moment they entered): the shop-girl walked silently over the carpets to the room where the proprietress was addressing invitations spread on a green leather table, and she, when the shop-girl entered and said that

the señora and her daughter were there, let fall the spectacles
that hung from a silver chain, and sighed and said: 'Ah, yes, ah,
yes ... the date is nearing now,' and she thanked the girl for
having informed her, and patted her violet hair and pursed her
lips and put out her mentholated cigarette, and in the shop salon
the two women had taken seats and they did not speak until the
proprietress came into sight; then the mother, who had this
notion of appearances, pretended to be carrying on a conversation
that had never been begun, and said in a loud voice, but that one
seems to me much the more beautiful. I don't know what you
think, but that is the one I would choose if the choice were mine.
Really, it's very lovely. Her daughter nodded, accustomed to
these conversations that were not directed to her but to the person now entering, who took the daughter's hand but not the
mother's – because the mother did not offer her hand – and
greeted them with an enormous smile and with a bob of her
violet head. The daughter started to slide to the right so that the
proprietress might sit on the sofa too, but the mother stopped
her with a glance and a finger wagging near her chest, and the
daughter looked with sympathy at the woman with violet hair
who had remained standing and now was asking them if they
had decided yet. No, said the mother, no, they were still un-
decided, and for this reason they would like to see the gowns
again ... on this choice so much depended, everything else, such
details, that is to say, as the colors of the flowers, the gowns of
the ladies, and all that, but I'm sorry to cause you so much work.
I would like ...
    'Please, señora. We are happy to serve you.'
    'Yes, we would like to be sure.'
    'Naturally.'
    'We don't want to make a mistake, and then later, at the last
minute ...'
    'You are right. It's wise to choose slowly and calmly, and
not, later ...'
    'Yes. We want to be sure.'
    'I'll go to tell the girls to get ready.'
They were left alone and the daughter stretched her legs and
the mother looked at her with alarm and wagged all her fingers

at once, for she could see the girl's garters, and at the same time she gestured for her to put a little spit on the left stocking: the daughter looked and found the place where the silk had broken, and she wet her index finger in her mouth and touched it to the budding run. She stretched again, explained I'm a little sleepy, as the señora touched her hand and they continued sitting on the rose brocade cushions, without speaking until the daughter said that she was hungry, and the mother replied that afterward they would go to Sanborn's and have breakfast, although she, the mother, would not eat because recently she had been putting on too much weight, a problem the girl did not have to worry about yet.

'No?'

'No, you still have your girl's figure. But later, watch out. In my family we all have good figures when we are young, but after forty ...'

'You're doing very well still.'

'You don't agree, that's what happens, you never agree. Besides ...'

'I woke up hungry this morning and had a good breakfast.'

'You don't have to worry now. Later, yes, be careful.'

'Does child-bearing make us very fat?'

'No, that isn't the problem, that isn't really the problem. A ten-day diet and you'll be just as you were before. The problem is after forty.'

Inside, preparing her two models, the proprietress knelt with a mouthful of pins and moved her hands nervously and grumbled at the girls for having such short legs, how were they going to glow like ladies of fashion with such short legs? They needed to exercise, she told them, tennis and equitation and all those other activities that serve to improve the race; and the models told her that she seemed irritated, and she said yes, those two women were very irritating indeed, the señora never gave her hand to anyone and although the daughter was friendlier, she was also a little distracted, as if no one else were there; well, to be brief, she did not know them well and so could say nothing, and as the Americans put it, the customer is always right. Now, they had to enter the salon smiling, saying cheese, chee-eese, cheee-eeese.

She was forced to work, even though she had not been born to work, and she had grown accustomed to today's rich women. Fortunately, she and her friends could still get together Sundays, the girls she had grown up with, and she could feel herself a human being at least once a week; they played bridge, she concluded, and she clapped her hands seeing that the models were ready. Carefully she removed the pins from her mouth and stuck them into the little velvet cushion.

'Will he come to the shower?'

'Who? Your fiancé or your father?'

'Papá.'

'How should I know?'

He saw Bellas Artes pass, orange dome and thick white columns, but was looking higher, straight overhead where the electric cables joined, separated, moved – not they, he with his head back against the soft gray wool cushion – parallel or at angles or connected with the tension distributors: the ocher Venetian façade of the Post Office Building, the leafy sculptures, distended teats and empty cornucopias of the Banco de México; he rubbed the silk band of his brown felt hat and with the point of his toe rocked the folding seat in front of him: Sanborn's blue tiles, the carved and darkened stonework of the Convent of St Francis. The limousine stopped at the corner of Isabel la Católica and the chauffeur, removing his cap, opened the door and he put on his hat and his fingers combed the thick locks along his temples. Vendors of lottery tickets, bootblacks, women in rebozos, children with their upper lips smeared with mucus swarmed around him as he moved towards the revolving door and passed into the vestibule and adjusted his necktie in front of the glass and through it, in the second glass, which looked out on Madero, saw a man identical to himself, wearing the same double-breasted suit, but colorless, tightening the knot of the same tie with the same nicotine fingers, a man surrounded by beggars, who let his hand drop at the same instant he in the vestibule did, and turned and walked down the block, while he, for the moment a little disoriented, looked for the elevator.

Again the outstretched hands of beggars disheartened her, and she squeezed her daughter's shoulder to hurry her into the artificial coolness and the scent of soaps and cosmetics. She stopped in front of a counter to look for a moment at the beauty articles displayed behind the glass, and she found herself looking at herself, then through herself, narrowing her eyes the better to see the rows of bottles and jars on a strip of red taffeta. She asked for a jar of 'Theatrical' cold cream and two lipsticks of that same color, the color of that taffeta, and looked without success for money in her crocodile purse: Here, find me twenty pesos. She received her package and change, and they entered the restaurant and went to a table for two. The waitress appeared, a woman wearing a Tehuantepec native costume, and the daughter ordered nut-waffles and orange juice and the mother, unable to resist, asked for raisin bread with melted butter; and then they both looked around for familiar faces until the daughter asked permission to remove the jacket of her yellow suit, because the sun that fell through the skylight was too intense.

'Joan Crawford,' said the daughter. 'Joan Crawford.'

'No, no, it isn't pronounced like that. Crow-fore. Crow-fore. They pronounce it like that.'

'Crau-fore.'

'No, no. Crow, crow, crow. The "a" and "u" together are pronounced like "o." I believe that's how they pronounce it.'

'I didn't enjoy the picture much.'

'No, it's not very good. But she was lovely.'

'I was just bored.'

'But you insisted on going ...'

'They told me it was good. But it isn't.'

'Well, it passes time.'

'Crow-fore.'

'Yes, I believe that's the way they pronounce it. Crow-fore. I believe they don't pronounce the "d."'

'Crow-fore.'

'Yes, I think so. At least, unless I'm mistaken.'

The girl poured honey over her waffles, and when she was sure that every little cranny had its share, she cut them into small bites. Each time she filled her mouth, she smiled at her mother. The mother was not looking at her: one of her hands played with the other, the thumb rubbing the pads of the fingers and seeming to want to lift the fingernails; and she was looking at another pair of hands near her, without wanting to see the faces: how slowly he took her hand and explored it, touching every pore. No, they were not wearing rings. They must be sweethearts or something. She tried to look aside at the puddle of honey in her daughter's plate, but involuntarily her eyes returned to the hands of the couple at the next table; she could avoid their faces, but not their caressing hands. The daughter's tongue played between her lip and her gum capturing bits of waffle and nuts, and then she cleaned her lips, staining the red napkin; but before she put on lipstick, the tip of her tongue searched for last crumbs and she asked her mother for a bite of raisin bread. She didn't want coffee, she said, though she loved coffee, because it made her nervous and she was nervous enough already. The señora touched her hand and told her that they must go, for they still had so much to do, and paid the check and left the tip, and they both rose.

Boiling water would be injected into the deposits, the North American explained, and would dissolve the sulfur, which would be carried to the surface by compressed air. He explained the process again, while his compatriot said that they were quite satisfied with the exploration, cutting the air with his hand, waving his hand very near his sunburned red face, repeating: Domes, good; pyrites, bad. Domes, good; pyrites, bad. Domes, good ... He, at his desk, tapped his fingers on the glass and nodded, accustomed to the fact that when they spoke Spanish to him they believed he did not understand, not because they spoke it badly but because he would not understand in any language. Pyrites, bad. The North American spread the map on the desk as he removed his elbows, and the other explained that the zone was so rich that it could be exploited to the limit until well into the twenty-first century, to the limit, he repeated, until the deposits ran dry; to the limit, to the limit, to the limit, removing the fist he had pounded down on the area of green, dotted with little triangles, that indicated the geologist's findings. The North American winked an eye and said that the timber, cedar and mahogony, was also an enormous resource and in this he, their Mexican partner, would have one hundred per cent of the profit;

they, the North Americans, would not meddle, except to advise continuous reforestation; they had seen good timber-land made worthless by foolish cutting; didn't men know that trees meant money? But that was his affair, for with or without the timber, the sulfur was there. Then he, behind the desk, stood and smiled, hooked his thumbs in his belt and rolled his cigar between his lips waiting for one of them to cup a burning match and hold it to him, his lips forming an 'o' until the cigar glowed. He demanded two million dollars immediately. They questioned him: to what account? For although they would cheerfully admit him as their Mexican partner for an investment of only three hundred thousand, he had to understand that no one could collect a cent until the domes began to produce. The North American geologist took a small piece of chamois from his shirt pocket and began to polish his glasses, and the other paced from the table to the window and from the window to the table, and he repeated quietly, those are my conditions, and let them not suppose that they would be paying him an advance or anything of that sort: it would merely be what they owed him for trying to gain the concession for them, and indeed, without that payment, there would be no concession: in time they would make back the present they were going to give him now, but without him, without their front-man, their figure-head – and he begged them to excuse his frank choice of words – they would not be able to obtain the concession and exploit the domes. He touched a bell and called in his secretary, who read, rapidly, a page of concise figures, and the North Americans said okay a number of times, okay, okay, okay, and he smiled and offered them whiskies and told them that although they might exploit the sulfur until well into the twenty-first century, they were not going to exploit him for even one minute in the twentieth century, and everyone exchanged toasts and the North Americans smiled while muttering that s.o.b. under their breath.

The two women walked slowly, arm in arm, with their heads bent, stopping in front of every shop window to say how pretty, how expensive, there's a better one farther on, look at this, how attractive, until they grew tired and entered a cafe and looked for a good table, one far from the entrance, where vendors of lottery tickets could be seen and the dry thick dust swirled, far too from the restrooms, and ordered two orange Canada Drys and the mother took out her compact and powdered her nose and in the small mirror saw the two soft folds of skin that were beginning to form around her eyes, and with a snap closed the compact. They watched the bubbling of their drinks of soda and aniline, waiting for the gas to escape in order to sip small swallows, and the daughter secretly removed her shoe and rubbed her cramped toes, and the señora, seated before her glass of orange pop, thought of the separate bedrooms at home, separate but adjoining, and the sounds that succeeded in passing through the closed door every morning and every night: occasional coughing, the fall of shoes on the floor, the clink of the keyring on the dresser-top, the creaking of the unoiled closet door, at times even his breathing as he slept. Her back felt cold. This very morning, walking tiptoe, she had slipped close to the door and felt a chill down her back as she had reflected with surprise that all those sounds, loud or soft, were secret sounds; and then she had returned to her bed and wrapped herself in the covers and fixed her gaze on the clear sky, where a few shimmering fugitive lights played, spangled through the shadows of the chestnuts. She had drunk the remains of a cup of tea and had gone to sleep again, until the daughter came to wake her, reminding her that they had a busy day before them. And only now, with the cold glass between her fingers, did she remember her chilled back, those first hours of the day.

He leaned back in his swivel chair until the springs creaked, and asked his secretary: was there any bank that would be willing to take the risk? Was there any Mexican who would trust him? He pointed the yellow pencil at his secretary's face: one thing was true and he, Padilla, could confirm it: not a damn soul in Mexico wanted to risk anything, and he was not going to let that wealth rot in the southern forest. If the gringos were the only ones willing to finance the exploration, well, what could he do? The secretary looked at his watch. He sighed and said, all right, it's all right, I invite you to lunch, they could eat together: did he know a new place? Yes, the secretary said, a new and very nice lunch place, very good fritters, of squash blossoms, of cheese, and of corn fungus; it was just around the corner. They could go together, then. He felt a little tired, he did not want to return to the office that afternoon; in a manner of speaking, they ought to celebrate. Well, why not? And besides, they had never eaten together. They descended in silence and walked toward Avenida Cinco de Mayo.

'You're very young. How old are you?'

'Twenty-seven.'

'When did you receive your degree?'

'Three years ago. But . . .'

'But what?'

'Theory and practice are different.'

'And that amuses you? What did they teach you?'

'A lot of Marxism. So much that I even wrote my thesis on surplus value.'

'It ought to be good training.'

'But practice is different.'

'Is that what you are, a Marxist?'

'Well, all my friends were. It's a stage one goes through.'

'Where was that restaurant?'

'Close, right around the corner.'

'I don't like to walk.'

'It's not far now.'

They divided up their packages for easy carrying and walked slowly toward Bellas Artes, where the chauffeur was waiting. Their heads were bent and they watched the shop windows as if with antennae. Suddenly, trembling, the mother clutched the daughter's arm and let one of the packages drop: just in front of them were two snarling dogs; the dogs separated, still snarling, and then suddenly leapt at each other, biting necks until blood flowed; they ran down the street and stopped and fought again, viciously, with cold fury and razor teeth, two street dogs, a male and a bitch, mongrels. The girl recovered the fallen package and led her mother to the parking place. They sat in the car and the chauffeur asked if they wished to go back to the Lomas, and the daughter said yes, some fighting dogs had frightened her mamá, and the señora said it was nothing, just so unexpected and so close; they would return downtown that afternoon, for they still

25

had many shops to visit, many purchases to make. There was plenty of time, said the girl, more than a month, but the mother said time flies and your father is not doing anything about your wedding, he leaves it all to us. And you have to learn to hold yourself more aloof. You can't go around shaking hands with the whole world. I want the wedding to hurry up and be over, because I believe it may make your father realize that he is now a man of responsible age. I hope it will do that. He doesn't seem to notice that he is fifty-two now. I hope that children come quickly. At any rate, he will have to stand at my side during the civil and religious ceremonies, and receive the congratulations, and see that everyone treats him like a respectable middle-aged gentleman. Maybe that will make an impression on him. Maybe.

I feel a hand caressing me and would like to escape its touch, but I don't have the strength. What a useless caress, Catalina. How useless. What are you going to say to me? Do you think that at last you have found those words you have never dared to pronounce? Today? How useless. Don't let your tongue move, don't permit it the luxury of an explanation. Look: learn from your daughter, Teresa. Our daughter: and how difficult, what a pointless possessive, 'our'. Teresa does not pretend. Teresa has nothing to say. Teresa sits, look at her, with her hands folded, in her black dress, and she waits, she doesn't pretend. Earlier, out of my hearing, she must have said to you: 'I hope it ends quickly. He is capable of making himself sick just to mortify us.' She must have said something of that sort to you, I heard something of the sort when I woke from that long and gentle sleep. I remember, vaguely, the injection last night, the narcotic. And you must have responded, for you would have wanted to give her words a different twist, 'Dear God, that he doesn't suffer long.' And now you do not know what twist to give the words that I murmur:

'That morning I waited for him with happiness. We rode our horses across the river.'

Ah, Padilla. Come closer. Did you bring the tape-recorder? If you knew what is to your advantage, you would bring it here just as you brought it every night to the house in Coyoacán. Today, more than ever, you ought to want me to think that everything goes along the same as always. Don't break our routine, Padilla. Ah, yes, you are beside me now. And the women don't like that.

'No, Licienciado. We can't allow it.'

'It's a custom we have had for many years, señora.'

'Don't you see his face?'

'Let me try. Everything is ready. All I have to do is plug the machine in.'

'Then you must take the responsibility.'

'Don Artemio ... Don Artemio ... I brought the recorder this morning ...'

So I scored a bullseye. I try to smile. The same as always. A man to be trusted, Padilla. Clearly, he merits my trust. Clearly he deserves a good part of my estate, and its administration in perpetuity. Who, unless he? He knows everything. I must pay you well. You inherit my reputation.

Teresa sits with the newspaper opened, concealing her face.

And I feel him arrive with that smell of incense, with his black skirts and holy water, to say farewell to me with all the rigor of a sermon. So: they have fallen into the trap. And that Teresa continuously weeping, now taking her compact from her purse to powder her nose in order to be able to weep again. I imagine the last moment, when the casket goes down, a multitude of women will be weeping and powdering their noses over my tomb. Well, I feel better. I would feel perfectly all right if it weren't for the stink rising from the folds of these sheets that I have stained with such ridiculous splotches. Is that spasmodic snoring my breathing? Is that how I am going to receive that black-skirted dolt and confront his office? Aaaaah. I have to control my breathing. Aaaah. I tighten my fists, the muscles of my neck, and next to me is his floury face come to assure the veracity of the formula that tomorrow or the next day will appear in every newspaper: *with all the comforts of Sacred Mother Church*. And he puts his shaved face close to my cheeks, boiling with white hairs, and he crosses himself and whispers the 'I, a sinner,' and all I can do is turn my head and groan while my imagination draws images I would like to throw in his teeth: the night when that poor dirty carpenter gave himself the luxury of lying upon the terrified virgin who had believed the stories and cozenage of her family and had kept the little white doves locked between her thighs, believing that doing so, she would give birth, the little doves hidden in the virgin garden, between her legs, under her skirts, and now the carpenter mounted her full of a very justified desire, justified because she must have been lovely, lovely, and he climbed upon her to the crescendo of protesting whines from that intolerable Teresa, that pale woman who gleefully desires my final rebellion, that it may be the pretext for her final indignation. And it seems incredible to see them seated there, quiet, without recriminations. How long will it last? I don't feel so bad now. Maybe I'll recover. What a blow that would be, wouldn't it? I will try to look better; to see if you two will take advantage of it and forget these gestures of coerced affection and for the last time empty your hearts of the diatribes and insults that you carry choking your throats, that you carry in your eyes and in that ugly humanity into which you have both been converted. Poor circulation. That's what it is, that's all it is. Nothing more serious, just poor circulation. It bores me to see them sitting there. Something more interesting than they ought to be within the sight of half-open eyes that are seeing things for the last time. Ah: they brought me to this house, not to the other. Hah! How discreet. I will have to rebuke Padilla one last time. Padilla knows which house is my true home. There, in the other, I would be able to enjoy myself now looking at things I love: I would open my eyes and see a ceiling of warm old beams; the gold chasuble that covers the headboard would be within reach of my hands, and the candelabra on the night-table, the velvet of the chairs, my Bohemian glass. And I would have Serafín near me smoking and I would breathe her smoke; she would be neat and calm, as I have always insisted, calm and neat, no black mourning rags, and there I would not feel old and tired: everything would be arranged to tell me that I am still a living man who rules a home, the same as before, the same, the same. Why are they sitting here, ugly sloppy false old women, reminding me that I am not what I have been? There everything is ready and there they know what to do. Here they prevent my remembering, they tell me only what I am now, not what I was. No one tries to explain anything before it is too late. Bah! How can I escape anything here, escape myself here? Yes: and now I see that they have taken pains to make it appear that I come to this room to sleep at night: in the half-open closet I see the outlines of jackets I have never worn, neckties I have never wrinkled, new shoes. I see a desk where books no one has read have been placed, papers that no one has signed. And this elegant vulgar furniture, when were its dust covers pulled off? Ah ... there's a window. There's a world outside, there's the high wind, wind of the high mesa, wind that shakes the dark trees. I have to breathe it.

'Open the window.'

'No. You might be chilled and get worse.'

'Teresa, your father doesn't hear you.'

'He hears me. He closes his eyes, but he hears me all right.'

'Shhhhhh.'

'Be quiet.'

They are going to be quiet now. They are going to move away from the head of the bed. I keep my eyes closed. I remember that I went out to lunch with Padilla that afternoon. Now I remember. I've beaten them at their own game. Everything stinks, but I'm warm. I've beaten them all. Yes: the blood flows warm in my veins, soon I'll recover. Yes, it flows warm, still giving heat. I forgive them. They haven't hurt me. It's all right, let them talk, let them chatter, I don't mind. I forgive them. What warmth. Soon I'll be well. Ah!

You will feel satisfied to have imposed your will upon them – confess it: you imposed your will so that they would admit that you are their equal: seldom have you felt happier. For ever since you began to be what you are, to learn to appreciate the feel of fine cloth, the taste of good liquor, the scent of rich lotions, all those things that in recent years have been your only, isolated pleasures; ever since then you have lived with regret for the geographical error that has prevented you from being one of them. You admire their efficiency, their comforts, their hygiene, their power, their strength of will; and you look around you and find intolerable the incompetence, misery, dirt, the weakness and nakedness of this impoverished country that has nothing. You ache because you know that no matter how hard you try, you can never be what they are but can become at most only a pale copy, a near approximation. For after all – confess it – has your vision of things, in your best and worst moments, ever been so simple as theirs? Never. Never have you been able to think in terms of blacks and whites, goods and evils, God and the devil. Confess that always, even when it has seemed otherwise, you have found in black the germ of its opposite; your own cruelty, when you have been cruel, has it not been tinged with a certain tenderness? You know that every extreme includes its contrary: cruelty, tenderness; courage, cowardice; life, death. In some manner, almost unconsciously, by being who you are and where you are and what you have lived, you know this, and therefore you can never be like them, who do not know it. Does that disturb you? Yes, it's troubling. How much more comfortable to be able to say: this is the good, and this is the evil. Evil: you will never be able to point it out because we, less protected than they, do not wish to lose our intermediate zone of ambiguity between light and shadow, that zone where we can find forgiveness, where you could find forgiveness. Who would not be as capable as you, if for only one moment of his life, to embody good and evil at the same time, to let himself be guided simultaneously by two mysterious threads of contradicting colors that are born of the same egg, the light thread rising, the dark descending, and that nevertheless and in spite of everything both finally meet again in the same fingers? You will prefer not to think about this. You will detest the I, the part of your you, that calls it to your attention. You would like to be like them, and now, an old man, you have almost accomplished it. But only 'almost,' no more than 'almost.' You yourself will make forgetfulness impossible. Your bravery will be the brother of your cowardice and even its twin; your hatred will be born of your love; all your life will have contained and promised your death. You will not have been either good or evil, generous or selfish, faithful or traitorous. You will allow others to establish your good points and your defects; for you, yourself, how will you be able to deny that each of your affirmations will deny itself, and each of your denials affirm itself? No one will really be aware except you yourself, that your existence will be woven of all the threads in the loom, exactly as are the lives of all men. There will not be lacking, nor will there be more than, one single opportunity to make your days what you want them to be. And if you become one thing rather than another, that will be because in spite of everything you will have to choose. Your choices will not negate the possibilities remaining to you, or anything that you will leave behind by the act of choice: but those possibilities will be weakened, attenuated to the degree that today your choice and your destiny will become the same: the coin will no longer have two faces: desire and destiny will be one. Will you die? It will not be your first death: you will have lived enough dead life, enough moments of mere gesticulation, to assure that. When Catalina puts her ear to the door that separates her from you and listens to your movements; when you, on the other side of that door, move without knowing that someone hangs upon the sounds and silences of your life: who will live in that separation? When both of you know that one word would be enough, yet both hold silent: who will live in that silence? No, no, this is not what you would like to remember. You would rather remember something else: the name and face that the passing of years will wash away. But you will know that if you remember only this, though you will save yourself, your salvation will be too easy. First you must remember what condemns you, and then, saved by condemnation, knowing that the other, the apparent savior, will be the real condemnation; then, having done this, you may remember what you will. You will think of Catalina young and will compare her with the vapid woman of today; you will remember, and will remember why. You will embody what she and everyone thought then: you won't know it, you will just embody it; for you will never be able to hear, but you will always have to live, others' words. You will close your eyes: yes, you will close them. You will not smell that incense, nor hear those sobs, you will think of other things, other days, days that come by darkness to your night of closed eyes and that you recognize by voice, never by sight. You will have to trust your night blindly, without seeing and recognizing it, as if it were the God of your days: your night. And now you will be thinking that merely closing your eyes will be enough to hold your night. You will smile in spite of the pain that begins to return, and you will try to stretch your legs a little. Someone will touch your hand but you will not respond to that ... what? Caress? Act of attention? Anguish? Guile? No: for you will have created night by closing your eyes, and from the bottom of that inky ocean there will sail toward you a stone ship that the noon sun, hot and drowsy, will comfort in vain: ship of thick blackened walls raised to defend the Church against the attacks of pagan Indians and to unite the military and religious conquests. Toward your closed eyes they will advance, the rude Spanish, Isabelline soldiers, with a rising sound of fifes and drums; and you under the sun will cross the spacious esplanade where a cross stands in the center and open chapels, theatrical projections of the Indians' native cult, occupy corners. On the height of the church at the end of the esplanade *tezontle*-stone vaulting will repose above the forgotten Mohammedan, Christianized cutlasses, sign of a different strain of blood imposed upon that of the conquerors. You will walk toward the façade, early Baroque, Spanish but rich in vine columns and aquiline-nosed keystones: the façade of the Conquest, severe yet jocund, with one foot in the dead Old World and the other in the New, which did not begin here but on the other side of the ocean: the New World arrived when they arrived; façade of austere walls to protect their avaricious, sensual, happy hearts. You will enter the nave, where all that was Spanish will be conquered by the macabre smiling lavishness of Indian saints, angels, and gods: one single enormous nave that will lead to an altar of withered gilt leaves, to the opulent shadows of masked faces and lugubrious, festive, and always compelled prayers, and also to the freedom, the only freedom granted, to decorate a church and fill it with tranquil horror and sculptured resignation and hatred of simplicity, with the dead time that had been prolonged by the deliberate delay of free craftsmen with cunning tool, and by their moments of independence in color and form far from the exterior world of whips and shackles and pustules. You will advance down the nave to the conquest of your own New World. Heads of angels will pass, prodigal grapevines, many-colored flowers, red globular fruits captured in gold nets, mortised white saints, fright-faced saints of the heaven the Indian created in his own image and likeness: angels and saints with faces of the sun and moon, with harvest-protecting hands, with the index fingers of guide dogs, with the cruel, empty, useless eyes of idols and the rigorous lineaments of the cycles. Faces of stone behind kindly rose masks, ingenuous and impassive – dead, dead, dead. Create the night. Swell the black sails with wind. Close your eyes, Artemio Cruz

[1919: May 26]

He related the story of Gonzalo Bernal's last moments in Perales, and the doors of the home opened to him.

'He was always so pure,' said the father, Don Gamaliel Bernal. 'He always believed that action contaminates us and obliges us to be false to ourselves unless it is presided over by very clear thinking. I believe that that was why he left home. Well, I think that was part of the reason, for certainly the storm sucked in all of us, including those of us who never left our places. No: what I'm trying to explain is that my son felt it was his duty to take part in the Revolution in order to offer explanations, coherent ideas; yes, I believe he went away to prevent that cause from failing, like so many causes, to stand the test of realization. I don't know. His thought was complex. He preached tolerance. I am glad to know that he died bravely. I am glad to see you here, sir.'

It was not without preparation that the stranger had gone to call on the old man. He had visited certain places in Puebla, talked with certain men, learned what it was necessary to learn. This was why now he could listen to Don Gamaliel's disjointed remarks without moving a muscle of his face. The old man's head leaned back against the polished leather of his chair, presenting his profile to the yellow light that filtered through the dust of the closed library. The high shelves were heavy with volumes bound in calf and sheepskin, and a ladder's small wheels had scarred the yellow-ocher floor. Thick books in English and French, geography, belles lettres, the arts, the natural sciences, whose perusal required the use of the magnifying glass that Don Gamaliel held motionless between his silky veined hands without noticing that the afternoon sun was shining through the lens and focussing hotly on a fold of his carefully ironed striped trousers. The visitor watched the spot of light. An uncomfortable silence separated the two men.

'Pardon me ... can I offer you a drink? Or better: you will stay and dine with us.' He spread his hands in a gesture of invitation and pleasure, and the magnifying glass fell upon his lap. A thin old man, tight flesh stretched over brittle bones, yellowish white hair flowering around his head, at his chin, above his lips.

'These changing times don't alarm me,' he had said earlier, his voice always precise and well-bred, modulated always within the range of courtesy. 'What purpose would my education have' – he indicated the book-shelves – 'if not to assist me to accept the inevitable nature of change? Things change, in appearance at least, whether we want it or not – why should we obstinately persist in not seeing this and in sighing for the past? Or shouldn't we term it that? You, sir – pardon me, I forget your rank ... yes, colonel, lieutenant colonel ... You, sir, I say, I don't know your origin nor your vocation – I esteem you because you shared my son's last hours – but what I mean is this: you, who took part, could you foresee everything? No, and neither could I, who did not take part. Perhaps engagement and detachment are equally blind and helpless, and in this ... Although there must be, of course, some difference. In short ...'

The stranger watched the old man's amber eyes fixedly, eyes too bold to induce an atmosphere of cordiality, too confident behind their paternal graciousness. Perhaps those seignorial movements of his slender hands, that constant nobility of his profile and neat goatee, that attentive inclination of his head; perhaps these were natural: just the same, even naturalness too could be pretended: a mask might at times feign too well the expressions of a face that existed neither outside it nor under it. And certainly the mask of this old man was so like his true face that only a thin line, a quite impalpable shadow, demarcated them. The stranger reflected that some day he might be able to tell Don Gamaliel this without subterfuge.

All the clocks in the house sounded at the same instant and Don Gamaliel straightened to light the acetylene lamp that stood on the roll-top desk. He raised the top of the desk slowly and fingered several sheets of paper. One of these he took between his hands, and he half-turned toward his guest. Then he smiled, wrinkled his brow, and smiled again as he deposited the paper on top of the others. Gracefully he lifted his index finger to his ear: a dog was barking and scratching on the other side of the door.

The visitor continued his scrutiny while the old man's back was turned. Not a single penstroke broke the harmony of the whole picture: erect shoulders moving with elegance, the white slightly disheveled hair, the air of gentility. It was a too-perfect picture. Possibly his courtesy was only the natural companion of his ingenuousness. But this was irritating: the conquest would be too easy, it would lack savor. Don Gamaliel's slow progress reached the door and he paused. He looked back over his shoulder, his eyes amber, one hand on the knob and the other lightly caressing his beard. His eyes seemed to fathom his guest's thoughts, and his smile, slightly twisted, was that of a magician about to reveal the unexpected. If the stranger could sense and respond to an invitation to complicated silence, yet Don Gamaliel's gesture and movement were so artful and elegant that there was no opportunity to return his glance and so seal their tacit pact.

Night had fallen and the uncertain light of the lamp hardly illumined the gilt spines of the books and the linear silver pattern of the wallpaper. As the door opened, the stranger thought of the long string of rooms that led from the entry of the mansion to the library, room after room above the patio of enamels and blue tiles. The dog entered, jumping with happiness and licking its master's hands. Behind the dog appeared the girl, dressed in a white gown that stood out sharply against the darkness.

For a moment she waited in the shadow outside the door. The

dog jumped toward the stranger and smelled his feet and hands. Laughing, Señor Bernal grasped the red collar. He murmured some apology that the stranger, standing now, buttoning his jacket with the precise movements of a soldier, smoothing out its folds as if he were wearing his campaign tunic, did not hear: he stood motionless before the beauty of the young woman who had not yet entered.

'My daughter, Catalina.'

Still she did not move. Her smooth chestnut hair fell long over a long, warm neck; her eyes were at once both liquid and hard, with a trembling expression, yellow like those of her father but less accomplished in pretense, franker: two bubbles of glass that were repeated in the other dualities of her full young body, in the half-open moist lips, in the high constricted breasts: eyes, lips, and breasts all soft yet hard, combining helplessness with rancor. Holding her hands clasped in front of her thighs, she advanced with her gown swaying to the movements of her hips, a body whose pale gold was revealed in the color of her forehead and cheeks. The stranger took her hand and sought to find in it, but did not find, the betraying dampness of emotion.

'The señor was with your brother during his last hours. I told you about him.'

'You were fortunate, señor.'

'He spoke about you and your father. He asked me to come to see you. He was a brave man to the end.'

'No, he was not brave. He loved all this' – her hand touched her breast and then described an arc in the air – 'he loved all this too much.'

'Idealistic, yes, very idealistic,' Don Gamaliel said softly. He sighed. 'The señor will dine with us.'

The girl took her father's arm and with the dog at his side he led them through narrow damp old rooms full of porcelaine and vases, clocks and glass-fronted cabinets, antique furniture, and religious paintings of ample proportions and slight value. The gilt feet of the chairs and small tables rested on the same floor of uncarpeted painted planks, and the lamps were unlit until they reached the dining room, where a large cut glass chandelier shone down on mahogany furniture and on a painting in which glowed the earthenware vessels and flaming fruit of the tropics. With his napkin, Don Gamaliel waved away the mosquitoes whirling around the real fruit dish, less abundantly heaped than the painted one. His hand invited them to take seats.

Sitting in front of her, the stranger could at last fix his gaze on the girl's motionless eyes. Did she know the purpose of his visit? Could she see in his eyes the sense of male triumph that her physical presence now crowned? Did she recognize the confidence in his light smile? Did she feel the assertion of possession that he scarcely disguised? Her eyes returned only that strange message of hard fatality, as if she would show herself disposed to accept everything, yet would convert her resignation into an opportunity for her own triumph over the man who already, silently, smilingly, had begun to make her his.

She, for her part, was surprised by the strength of her weakness, by the rapidity with which she was succumbing. She looked up from the table to observe, without false modesty, the stranger's strong features, and she could not avoid meeting his green eyes. He was not handsome – no, but his olive skin and the sinuous strength of his lips and the pulsing of a nerve in his temple promised that his touch would be virile if not gentle. Under the table, he stretched his foot and nudged her toe. The girl lowered her eyelids and glanced toward her father. She drew her foot back. Her father, perfect host, smiled as benevolently as always, and toyed with his glass.

The old Indian servant-woman came in with the bowl of rice. Don Gamaliel observed that the dry season was ending a little late this year. Fortunately, rain clouds had begun to mass over the mountains now, the harvest would be good, not so rich as last year but good just the same. It was strange, he went on, how this old house held dampness, dampness that stained the shadowy corners and gave life to ferns and mosses in the patio. Perhaps that was a propitious symbol for a family that had grown and prospered thanks to the fruits of the soil: that had been settled here in the Valley of Puebla – he ate his rice, picking it up on his fork with precision – since the beginning of the nineteenth century, and had proved itself stronger than the absurd events of a land incapable of tranquility, enamored of convulsion.

'At times it seems to me that the absence of bloodshed and death drives us desperate, as if we feel ourselves alive only when surrounded by firing squads and destruction,' the old man's voice continued cordially. 'But we go on. We always go on, for we have learned how to survive . . .'

He filled his guest's glass with dark heavy wine.

'But we have to pay a price for survival,' the stranger said drily.

'Ah, but an acceptable price can always be negotiated . . .' When he filled his daughter's glass, he caressed her hand. 'It's all in the elegance with which it is done. There is never any need to alarm anyone, to wound feelings. Honor must remain intact.'

The stranger touched the girl's foot again. This time she did not draw back. She raised her glass and observed him without blushing.

'One must make distinctions,' said the old man as he dried his lips with his napkin. 'Business, for example, is one thing, and religion is another.'

'So he seems so pious, going with his daughter to take communion every day? Well, remember, my friend, when you see him there, that all he has got by robbing priests back when Juárez put the church property up for sale and every drummer with a few hundreds in cash could buy up whole plantations.'

He had spent six days in Puebla before presenting himself to Don Gamaliel Bernal. His cavalry troop had been disbanded by President Carranza, and then he had recalled his prison conversations with Gonzalo Bernal. He took the road to Puebla. It was a matter of simple instinct, and a matter too of his confidence that in the destroyed and confused world that had been left by the Revolution, to know so little – the name of a family, their city, their address – was to know much. The irony that he was he and not Bernal who was going to Puebla amused him. It was, in a sense, a masquerade he was undertaking, a substitution, a joke he would be able to play with perfect seriousness; at the same time it was his certificate of life, of his capacity to survive and to fortify his own destiny with that of others. When he reached Puebla, when he could see the red and yellow mushroom church domes scattered across the valley, he felt that he was arriving not as one man but two, with Gonzalo Bernal's life added to his own, as if Bernal when he died had transferred to him the possibilities of his own interrupted existence. Maybe, he thought to himself, the deaths of others is what lengthens our own life. But he had not come to Puebla to think.

'This year he hasn't been able to buy even seed. His debts have gone on building up, what with the peasants turning against him and seizing those fields he never planted. They said if he didn't give them that unused land, they would not work the cultivated land. Out of pure pride he refused, so he did without a crop. Before, the rural police would have come to his help and made short work of the *campesinos*. But now a different rooster crows.'

'And not only that. The people who owe him money have been defying him too. They don't want to pay, they say that with the interest he has taken from them, they have already paid much more than they owe. So you see, Colonel. Everyone has so much faith that things are going to change now.'

'Ah, but the old man is as slippery as ever. He would rather die than give men what's coming to them.'

He threw down the dice and shrugged his shoulders, and signaled to the bartender to serve another round of drinks, a gesture that pleased them.

'And who owes this Don Gamaliel?'

'Who doesn't is more like it.'

'Does he have a close friend? A confidant?'

'Sure, Father Páez.'

'He doesn't use his tricks on the priest?'

'Oh, the little Father takes care of Don Gamaliel in heaven, so Don Gamaliel looks out for the little Father down here.'

The sun blinded them as they stepped out on the street.

'There she goes, proud and sassy.'

'Who is she?'

'Who do you think? The old bastard's daughter.'

Studying the points of his shoes, he walked along the old chessboard streets. When his heels no longer sounded on the paving stones and his steps raised dry gray dust, he lifted his head and eyed the ported walls of the old fortified church. He crossed the wide esplanade and entered the long, silent, gilded nave. Again his heels echoed. He advanced toward the altar.

Father Páez watched, his coal-black eyes burning between his inflamed cheeks. He was hidden in a high passageway to the old choir of the nuns who had fled Mexico during the liberal Republic, and from the moment he had first seen the stranger at the far end of the nave, he could distinguish in those distant movements the unconscious martial bearing of a man accustomed to a state of alert, to command, attack. It was not the slight bowing of his cavalryman's legs. It was the nervous force of a fist in daily contact with reins and pistol. Even when, as now, the stranger walked with his hands closed, the priest could recognize the power and confidence in those hands. Elevated in the nuns' secret place, Father Páez reflected that such a man had not come to his church to make acts of devotion. He raised his cassock and slowly descended by a spiral stairs that led to the abandoned convent: skirts tucked up, shoulders hunched as high as his ears, black body and red yet bloodless face, penetrating eyes: carefully he made his way down. The stairs urgently needed repairs; in 1910 his predecessor had lost footing on them, with mortal consequences. But Remigio Páez, like a black bat, seemed able to see all the invisible obstructions and dangers in the black descent. And the darkness and danger alerted his senses. A soldier in mufti in his church, without company, without escort? Ah, that was novelty enough to have passed unnoticed. Fortunately, he had seen him. The battles, the violence, the acts of sacrilege – he remembered the troop who only two years ago had carried off the chasubles and all the sacred objects in the church – were behind now, and the enduring Church, founded for the centuries of centuries, again would achieve an understanding with the powers of the terrestial city. A soldier in mufti . . . without escort . . .

He went down with his hand just touching the swollen wall. A trickle of water wet his fingertips. He remembered that the rainy season would begin very soon. And he had charged himself to make clear, with all his powers, from the pulpit as well as in the confessional, that it is a sin, a heavy sin, a sin against the Holy Spirit, to refuse to accept the gifts of heaven. No one can dare oppose the designs of Providence. Providence has ordered things as they are, and as they are, so must they be accepted: men must go out and labor in the fields, gather in the harvest, render the fruits of the earth up to their legitimate owner, a Christian owner who pays the obligations of his stewardship by punctually remitting his tithe to Holy Mother Church. God punishes rebelliousness, and Lucifer is always conquered by the archangels – Rafael, Gabriel, Michael, Gamaliel ... Gamaliel.

'And justice, Father?'

'My son, final justice is imparted above. Do not look for it in this vale of tears.'

'Words,' muttered the priest as he rested, finally, on the ground floor and shook the dust from his skirts. Words, damned sparks of syllables that set fire to the blood and dreams of honest men who should content themselves with passing swiftly through this short life to enjoy, in exchange for their mortal test, life eternal. He crossed the cloister and walked along an arched passageway. Justice, indeed! For whom, and for how long? When life can be so pleasant for all, if all merely understand the fatality of their destiny in life and do not try to avoid it by stealing land, dodging debts, becoming ambitious ...

'I believe, yes, I believe,' he repeated under his breath, and he opened the sacristy door.

'Admirable piece of work, isn't it?' he said as he approached the tall man standing in front of the altar. 'The friars showed the native craftsmen sketches and engravings – and the Indians gave Christian forms to their native taste. They say that an Indian idol is hidden behind every altar. If this is so, they must be good idols, that do not demand blood the way the ...'

'Are you Páez?'

'Remigio Páez,' said the twisted smile. 'And you? General, Colonel, Major ...?'

'Plain Artemio Cruz.'

'Ah ...'

When the former lieutenant colonel and the priest said goodby outside the church some time later, Father Páez doubled his hands upon his paunch and watched his visitor stride away. The clear blue morning sharpened and brought nearer the lines of the two volcanoes, one the silhouette of a sleeping woman and the other that of her solitary guardian. He blinked his eyes: he could not bear the brightness of this transparent light. With gratitude he observed the advance of the black clouds that soon would dampen the valley and put the sun out, every afternoon, with their punctual torrential gray.

He turned and went into the shadow of the convent. He rubbed his hands. Little did it matter to him, that rascal's haughtiness and insults. If that was the way to save the situation and permit Don Gamaliel to pass his last years secure from all danger, it would not be Remigio Páez, minister of the Lord, who would interfere with a display of indignation and crusader's zeal. Quite the contrary. He took relish in recalling his wise humility: if pride was so important to the man, then Father Páez would listen to him with lowered head both today and tomorrow, even nodding affirmatively from time to time as if sorrowfully accepting the justice of the accusations the powerful ape leveled against Mother Church. He took his black hat from its hook, fitted it carelessly over his mop of hair, and directed his steps toward the residence of Don Gamaliel Bernal.

'Yes, he can do it. Why not?' said the old man after his conversation with the priest that afternoon. 'But I ask myself: what pretext will he use to enter this house? He told Father Páez that he is coming today. No ... I don't quite understand, Catalina.'

She raised her eyes. Her hand rested on the stretched cloth upon which she was with careful attention drawing a floral design. Three years ago they had received the news of Gonzalo's death. Since that time father and daughter had drawn together to make the slow passing of their afternoons seated on the wicker patio chairs into something more than a consolation – into a custom that, according to the old man, would be maintained until he himself died. Small importance had it that yesterday's wealth and power were being dismembered. Possibly that was the tribute exacted by old age and time. Don Gamaliel resisted only passively. He would not venture out into the countryside to dispossess the campesinos of the land they had seized, but neither would he accept their seizure. He did not require his debtors to pay either principal or interest – but from now on they would never borrow another cent from him. He hoped that some day, when need forced them to abandon pride, they would come to him on their knees. Meanwhile he held himself firm in his own pride.

And now ... and now this ex-soldier had appeared and had promised to lend at a rate of interest much lower than that the old man imposed, and had dared to propose, moreover, that the paper Don Gamaliel held should pass into his fresh hands quite gratuitously ... with no more recompense than the fourth part of what might be recovered. Take it or leave it.

'And I don't think that will be the end of his demands.'

'The land?'

'Yes. He will urge some sort of surrender, depend upon it.'

She rose and moved among the red-painted patio birdcages covering them with canvas hoods after watching the birds' nervous movements as they went on pecking their birdseed and chirping for the last time before the sun disappeared.

The old hacienda owner had not expected to have to pay so heavily for survival. The last man to see Gonzalo alive, his cellmate, the bearer of his last words of love to father and sister, wife and son.

'He told Páez that Gonzalo thought about Luisa and the child just before he died.'

'Father ... we don't talk about that.'

'I don't say anything. He did not know that she would marry again, that my grandson would bear a different name.'

'You haven't mentioned him for three years. Why now?'

'You are right. We have forgiven him, haven't we? I have thought that we had to forgive him for passing over to the enemy. I've thought that we had to try and understand him.'

'I think we have been forgiving him in silence all these afternoons.'

'Yes, yes, that's right. You understand me without words. How comforting! You understand me ...'

That was why when their guest arrived, feared and expected – for someday someone had to come and say: I knew him. I saw him. He thought of you – and set his perfect trap in motion without even mentioning the real problems of the campesinos' revolt and the suspended payments; that was why Don Gamaliel, after showing his guest to the library, excused himself and walked hurriedly, slow old man who identified leisurely movement with elegance, to Catalina's bedroom.

'Get ready. Take off that black dress and put on something bright. Come to the library when the clock strikes seven.'

That was all he said. He knew that she would obey him: this moment would be the test of all the melancholy afternoons. Yes: she would understand. There remained that card to be played. And to Don Gamaliel it had been enough to feel the stranger's presence and strength of will, to understand, and to tell himself, that any delay would be suicidal, that opposition would be difficult, and that the sacrifice demanded would be slight and, in a certain sense, by no means repulsive. He had already been alerted by Father Páez: a tall man, full of force, of few words, with hypnotic green eyes. Artemio Cruz.

Artemio Cruz. So that was the name of the new world that had risen from the ashes of civil war. So that was the name of the newcomers who had appeared to dispossess the old order. Unfortunate land, said the old man to himself as he walked slowly back to the library, unfortunate land where each generation must destroy its masters and replace them with new masters equally ambitious and rapacious. The old man thought of himself as the final product of a peculiarly indigenous culture: that of illustrious despots; as a kind of father, at times hard, in the end a good provider, and always the custodian of a tradition of good taste, gentility, and culture. That was why he had taken the stranger to the library. In that room the venerable, almost sacred character of what Don Gamaliel was and represented was more evident. But the stranger did not allow himself to be impressed. This did not escape Don Gamaliel as he rested his head back against his leather chair and half closed his eyes, the better to study a rival who came armed with a new and hammer-forged experience, who was accustomed to gambling for everything because he had nothing. The true purpose of the visit was not mentioned. Don Gamaliel accepted this as best: perhaps the stranger understood matters as subtly as he did himself, though his motivation was more powerful: ambition. Ambition. The old man smiled as he silently repeated a word that for him was no

44

more than a word. Ambition, the urgent drive to claim what he had gained in battle, by his sacrifices and his wounds, that saber-scar across his forehead. And in the stranger's eyes was written what Don Gamaliel knew how to read.

He went to his desk and drew out the sheet of paper on which his debtors were listed, and the stranger did not move a muscle. Better so. By this road, they would understand each other clearly. Perhaps it would not be necessary to mention unpleasant details; perhaps everything would be resolved more elegantly. The young ex-soldier had quickly grasped the style power should adopt. This, the sense of an heir, made what lay ahead easier.

'Didn't you see the way he was looking at me?' cried the girl when their guest had said goodnight. 'Didn't you notice what he wanted ... the indecency of those eyes?'

'Yes, yes,' said the old man, calming his daughter with his hand. 'It's only natural. You are very beautiful, you know, and you have seldom left the house. It's natural.'

'And I'll never leave it again!'

Her father slowly lit the cigar that had yellowed his mustaches. 'I thought you would understand,' he said, smoothing his beard. He rocked his wicker chair and looked at the heavens. It was one of the last nights of the dry season. The sky was so clear that by squinting he could perceive the true colors of the stars. The girl hid her flashing cheeks between her hands.

'What did Father Páez tell you? That he's a heretic! A godless man, who fears neither ... And did you believe that fairy-tale he told us about Gonzalo?'

'Easy, easy, my dear. Fortunes are not always made in the shadow of divinity.'

'Did you believe that fairy-tale? Why did Gonzalo die and this señor live, if they were both condemned and in the same cell? Why didn't both die? I know one thing, I know it: what he told us is not true. He made that story up to humiliate you and so that I would ...'

Don Gamaliel stopped rocking. Things were resolving themselves so well, so tranquilly. And now Catalina, with her woman's intuition, was bringing up the arguments that he had himself already considered, measured, and discarded as pointless.

'You have the imagination of your youth, my dear.' He stood and extinguished his cigar. 'But if you want frankness, I will be frank. This man can save us. Every other consideration must be put aside.'

He sighed and stretched out his arms to touch his daughter's hands.

'Think about your father's last years. Don't you think he deserves a little . . .'

'Yes, papá. I don't say any more.'

'And think about yourself.'

She bent her head. 'Yes. I've known, since the day that Gonzalo left home, that something like this had to happen sooner or later. If Gonzalo were only living.'

'But he isn't living.'

'I'm not thinking about myself. Who knows what I'm thinking about?'

Don Gamaliel held the lamp high and they followed its circle of light through the cold old halls. The girl's mind filled with confused memories. The tense, sweating faces of Gonzalo's school friends gathered for long discussions in the back room. Her brother's own obstinate, illuminated, anxious face, his nervous body that had seemed at times to exist outside reality, his love of comfort and good meals and good wine and books, which in wrenching times of anger he had repudiated. The coldness of Luisa, her sister-in-law, and the violent quarrels that had been abruptly silenced when she, then only a small girl, entered the living room. The sob drowned in laughter with which Luisa had received the news of Gonzalo's death. Luisa's silent departure one cold dawn when she believed the house to be asleep. But the girl, now an adolescent, had been watching from behind the living room blinds and had seen the hard hand, the derby and cane, of the man who had taken Luisa's hand and helped her and the baby up into the dark carriage that was already loaded with her widow's trunks.

She could avenge her brother's death – Don Gamaliel kissed her forehead and opened her bedroom door – only by embracing this stranger, embracing him but denying him the tenderness he would like to find in her. She would murder him living, distilling bitterness until he would be poisoned. She inspected herself in the mirror, seeking in vain the changes that her change of purpose should have brought. And in the same way her father and she would be avenged also for Gonzalo's abandonment of them, for his idiotic idealism: by delivering up her girl's body of only twenty years – why was she weeping tears of self-pity for her youth? – to the man who had shared Gonzalo's last hours, hours she could not think of without rejecting self-pity; by whirling her toward her dead brother without the softest whimper of fury or even the least movement of her face; and if no one explained the truth to her, she would seize what she believed to be the truth. She took off her black stockings. As her hands rubbed her legs, she closed her eyes: no longer did she have to admit the memory of the rough crude foot that had sought hers during the dinner and had filled her breast with an unknown feeling that could not be suppressed. Well: perhaps her body was not the work of God but that of other bodies, but – she bowed and pressed her laced fingers above her eyebrows – her spirit was God's. She would not allow her body to take a road of spontaneity and delight, hungry for caresses, if her spirit dictated otherwise. She raised the sheet and slid into bed with her eyes closed, reached out and extinguished the lamp, and pulled the pillow over her head. She did not have to think about that. No, she didn't have to think, and that was all there was to say. She would pronounce that other name now ... she would tell her father about him. No, no: it was pointless to humiliate her father. Next month, or maybe before, the stranger would enjoy their money, their land, and her own body, Catalina Bernal: what more was there to say? Ramón? No, not that name now. Not now. She slept.

'You have said it yourself, Don Gamaliel,' said the stranger when he returned the next day. 'You cannot stop events. Let's go on and give up those fields to the peasants. After all, it is land that can only be dry-farmed. You will lose very little. We give it up, so that the Indians will go on raising only patch-crops. And you will see that when they are obligated to us, they'll leave their patches to be hoed by their women, and return to working our irrigated fields for wages. Look: you pass for a hero of the agrarian reform, and it costs you nothing.'

Amused, the old man smiled behind his beard, and observed him. 'Have you spoken with my daughter yet?'

'Yes, I have talked with her.'

She could not control herself: her chin trembled when he moved his hand near and tried to raise her bent head and closed eyes. For the first time he was touching that creamy smooth skin. They were surrounded by the penetrating scents of the patio, by the smells of plants and herbs suffocated by dampness, the smell of rotting earth. He would love her. When he touched her, he knew that he would love her. He would have to make her understand that his love would be real, though appearances were against him. He would be able to love her as he had loved before, the first time: he was master of that proven tenderness. He touched her hot cheek again. She felt his strange hand upon her skin, and her rigidity was not enough to prevent tears from appearing between her lashes.

'You will not be disappointed. You'll have no reason to complain,' the man murmured, putting his face near lips that avoided contact. 'I know how to love you.'

- 'We must be grateful to you . . . that you have favored us with your presence.'

He opened his hand and stroked her long hair. 'You understand, don't you? You are going to live at my side. You must forget many things. I promise to respect your concerns. You, for your part, must promise that never again . . .'

She raised her head and her eyes became anguished with a hatred she had never felt before. The saliva dried in her mouth. Who was this man? Who was this monster who knew everything, who seized and destroyed everything?

'Be quiet!' the girl said, freeing herself from his hand.

'I have talked with him. He's a weak kid. He would never really love you. He let himself be frightened very easily.'

'No – he isn't strong like *tu*! He isn't an animal like you.'

He took her arm, smiled, and squeezed her fist.

'Little Ramón is leaving Puebla. You will never see him again.'

She twisted free. She ran to the red birdcages: the birds were singing, and one by one, while the man watched impassively, she opened the small doors. A cardinal appeared and tried to fly. The lark, accustomed to its water and birdseed, refused. She lifted the bird to her little finger, kissed its wing, and tossed it into flight. The last bird flew away and she closed her eyes and let the man take her arm to lead her to the library, where Don Gamaliel was waiting, as always patiently.

I feel hands at my armpits moving me to lie more comfortably against the soft pillows, and the new position is cool, like balsam. I feel hands. But when I open my eyes, I see the newspaper whose spread pages hide its reader's face. There, I think, is *Vida Mexicana*, and it will be there every day, no power on earth can prevent that. Teresa – it is she who is reading – drops the paper with alarm.

'Is something wrong? Do you feel worse?'

I reassure her with my hand and she picks up the paper again. No, I don't feel worse. I feel contented, the maker of a good joke. Perhaps, perhaps it would be a real master joke to leave a private testament to be published in my newspaper, the truth about my experiment in freedom of the press. No: I am exciting myself too much, the stabbing is in my guts again. I try to stretch my hand toward Teresa, asking her help, but she is lost in her reading. Earlier, I watched day fade beyond the wide windows and heard the pious rustle of curtains. Now, in the half-light of this bedroom with bowl ceiling and oak closets, I cannot easily distinguish the faces at the other end of the room, for the room is large, but her I can see: she is here, seated, stiff, with her lace handkerchief between her fingers and her face colorless. Perhaps she does not hear me as I murmur:

'I waited for him with happiness that morning. We rode our horses across the river.'

And that stranger, he of shaven cheeks and black eyebrows, is beside me begging an act of contrition of me, offering me the keys to heaven while I think of the carpenter and the virgin.

'What are you saying? Punch-drunk and yet contrite?'

I have startled him. And Teresa has to spoil everything by saying bitterly: 'Then let him be, Father, let him be. Don't you see we can't do anything? If that's what he wants, then let him die the way he has lived, cold and mocking everything.'

The priest motions her back. He puts his lips near my ear, he almost kisses me. 'There is no reason for them to hear us.'

I manage to grunt: 'Then be brave and go try to save those bitches.'

He stands up and the voices of the two women are indignant as they take his arm. Padilla approaches, and the women don't like that.

'No, Licienciado. We can't allow it.'

'It's a custom we have had for many years ...'

'Then you must take the responsibility.'

'Don Artemio ... Don Artemio ... I brought the recorder this morning.'

I nod. I try to smile. The same as always. A man to be trusted, Padilla.

'The outlet is next to the dresser.'

'Thank you.'

Yes, that's my voice, my yesterday voice – yesterday, or this morning? I can't remember now. I am talking with Pons, my editor – ah, the tape garbles, adjust it well, Padilla, run my voice backward cackling like a parrot. There I am again:

How do you see the situation, Pons?

Ugly, but easy to take care of, for the moment.

Well, now we push it in the paper. Hit 'em hard. Don't hold anything back.

Whatever you say, Don Artemio.

It's better if we get the public ready.

We've been plugging at it for so many years.

I want to see page one and all the editorials. Get me at home, no matter what time.

Everything will be coordinated. Unmask the red plot. Foreign infiltration perverting the essentials of the Mexican Revolution.

That good old Mexican Revolution!

Labor leaders manipulated by foreign agents. Tambroni comes out hard. Blanco gives us a pretty column identifying the union head with Antichrist. Blistering cartoons . . . How are you feeling?

Ay, not so good, not so good. My monthly. It'll pass. How we'd like to be the men we once were, eh?

Yes, we once were.

Tell Mr Corkery to come in.

I cough from the magnetic tape. I hear the hinges of a door that opens and closes. I feel that nothing moves inside my belly, nothing, nothing, the gases don't go out for all that I strain. But I see the women. They have returned. The door closes behind them and their steps are silent on the thick carpet. They have closed the windows.

'Open the window.'

'No. You might be chilled and get worse.'

'Open . . .'

Are you worried, Mr Cruz?

Plenty. Sit down and I'll tell you. Something to drink? Pull that cart over. I don't feel so good.

The rolling of the little wheels. The clink of bottles.

You look okay.

Ice falls into a glass. Soda hisses.

Look. I'm going to explain this situation to you in case they haven't understood. Tell them at the central office that if this so-called movement to clean up the union goes through, we can cut off our pigtails.

Our pigtails?

'In plain Mexican, we'll be fucked.'

'Stop that machine!' Teresa cries, going to the recorder. 'What kind of vulgarity . . .!'

I manage to move a hand, make a face. I lose some of the taped words.

. . . is it that the railroad union men propose?

Someone sneezes nervously. Who?

. . . explain to the companies that they better not believe innocently that we are dealing with a democratic movement to get rid of corrupt leadership. No, sir.

I'm all ears, Mr Cruz.

Yes, it must have been the gringo who sneezed. Hah-hah.

'No. You might be chilled and get worse.'

'Open . . .'

I, but not only I, other men too, can breathe in the perfumes the wind brings, the air-carried aromas of other noons: I can smell, I can detect scents far removed from this cold sweating, from these damned gases. I make them open the window. I can breathe in what I want to, entertain myself choosing among the odors that the wind brings: yes, autumn forests; yes, burned leaves; ah, yes, ripe plums; yes, yes, the rotting tropics; yes, salt flats; pineapples slashed open by a machete; tobacco hung in the shade; the smoke of locomotives; waves of the open ocean; snow-covered pines; ah, metal and manure: so many smells, brought to me by that eternal current. But no, no, they won't let me breathe as I wish. They sit down again, they stand and walk about and then sit together, as if they were one shadow, as if they cannot think and act separately, they sit again, at the same time, backs to the window, to shut me off from the fresh air, to suffocate me, to force me to close my eyes and remember because they will not let me smell. Damned women, how long did you wait before fetching a priest, before trying to quicken my death by having him drag confessions from me? And there he goes on, on his knees, with his scrubbed face. I try to turn my back to him, but I can't because of the pain in my ribs. *Ayyy.* Now he will have finished, I will have been absolved. I want to sleep. There comes the stabbing in my belly again. Ahhh – And the women, the women, those who rule. Yes. No. I don't know. I have forgotten your face, who loved. Oh, God, I have forgotten that face. No, I don't have to forget it. Where is it? Ah, that face was so beautiful, so beautiful, how can I forget it? It belonged to me, how am I going to forget it? Ahhhh. I loved you, how can I forget you? Who are you? Please, who are you? I want to believe in you, sleep with you, where are you, how can I summon you up to be with me here? What? Why? Another injection? But why? No, no, let me think of something else, quick, something else, for that hurts, it hurts, it

You will close your eyes aware that the lids are not opaque, that though they are folded down, light still reaches your retinas, light of the sun that will remain framed in the open window at the height of your closed eyes that, being closed, blur all details of vision, altering shadow and color but without eliminating vision itself; the same light of the brass penny that will spend itself toward the west. You will close your eyes and you will see again, but you will see only what your brain wants you to see: more than the world, yet less: you will close your eyes and the real world will no longer compete with the world of your imagination. You will close your eyes and the motionless, unvarying, repeating light of the sun will create a new world for you, one in motion behind your eyelids, moving light that can tire you, frighten you, confuse you, make you happy or sad. Behind your closed eyelids you will know that the intensity of the light penetrating to the back of your eyes is able to provoke feelings strange to you and far from your will; yet nevertheless you will close your eyes and create a transient blindness. You cannot close your ears to create deafness; you cannot cease touching, even if you touch only the air; you cannot imagine a complete loss of all sensation, nor can you stop the trickle of saliva across your tongue and palate, nor can you escape smell, nor can you stop the laboring rise and fall of your chest that gives life to your lungs and blood: you cannot seek a tentative and partial death, you will always see, always touch, taste, smell, hear. You will have cried out when they pierced your skin with a hollow needle flowing with narcotic liquid: you will have cried out long before you felt pain. The news of the pain will travel to your brain in advance of the pain itself, to prepare you for the pain, to alert you against it so that you will be more sensitive to it, more aware of it: for awareness weakens us, we are changed into victims by awareness when we become aware of the pain that never consults us, being unaware of us;

and you will feel yourself split into two men, one who will

receive messages and one who will act upon them: man sensory and man motor, man of sentient organs that will transmit feeling by millions of tiny fibers that wend toward your cortex, toward the wrinkled surface of the upper half of your brain where for seventy-one years the world's colors, touch of flesh, earth savors and scents, flavors, sounds of the wind, have been received, collected, expanded, stripped and restored and transferred dance by dance to the frontal lobes, the motor area, to the net of nerves and glands and muscles that moves your body and transforms the little face of the world that happens to be looking at you;

but in your half-sleep, the nerve that conveys light impulses will not connect with the visual area of your brain; you will hear color rather than see it, just as you will taste touch, touch smell, smell sound, and you will open your arms wide to avoid toppling into chaos, to recover the familiar regular order of sensation, the order of the simple received event simply transmitted by nerve to brain and returned by nerve to muscle, to become effect once more, an action, another event. You will open your arms and behind your closed eyes you will see mental colors, and at last, without seeing, you will feel the origin of the touch that you hear: it is the rub of the bedsheets between your twitching fingers. You will open your hands and become aware that your palms are damp and maybe you will remember that those palms were born empty of lines of life and luck and love; you were born, you will be born, with your palms smooth; but just that you will have been born will be enough for those blank surfaces to fill, in a few quick hours, with lines of portent and significance. And you will die with the lines in your palms clear and deep, but just that you will have died will be enough to wipe those surfaces empty again in a few quick hours and leave your palms with neither past nor future;

chaos: it has no plural

order, order: you will pull yourself together on the bedsheets and in silence, within yourself, will repeat the sensations that the ordering and clarifying power of your mind will sort out for you. With a strong effort you will locate the parts of your brain that announce hunger, thirst, sweat, goosepimples, balance, vertigo: you will locate them in the lower half, the servant half, the domestic who carries on the immediate tasks and thus frees the other, higher part for thought, imagination, and desire: child of artifice, of necessity and accident, the world will not be easy for you, you will not be able to know it passively, but will always have to think, to prevent the clustering of dangers from destroying you; you will always have to imagine, to prevent mere guesswork from denying you; you will always have to desire, to prevent the weaving of the unpredictable from swallowing you up; and you will survive:

you will recognize yourself:

you will recognize others and will let them, let her, recognize you; and you will know that you oppose everyone because everyone will be one more obstacle confronting your desire;

you will desire, and how you will wish that your want and its object might be one and the same; how you will dream of instantaneous fulfillment;

you will rest with closed eyes, but you will not stop seeing and you will not stop desiring. Desire will send you back into memory and you will remember, going back, back, never forward, in order to be satisfied:

for memory is desire satisfied:

and with memory you will survive, before it becomes too late before chaos prevents memory

[1913: December 4]

He felt the moist hollow of her knee upon his waist. That was how she always perspired, freshly, lightly: as he moved his arm from around her, it came away dampened too. He extended his hand to stroke her back slowly, indolently; he could stay that way for hours, doing nothing except caressing her back. As he closed his eyes he thought of the amorous infinity of that young body clasped to his. A whole life would not be long enough to survey, discover, explore that soft curving geography with its touches of black and rose. Her body waited beside him and he, without speaking or looking, stretched until he touched the bed's iron bars with his toes and the tips of his fingers. Dawn was still far off. They lived only within night's black crystal. The mosquito net isolated them and they were together within it. He opened his eyes. The girl's cheek touched his and his tangled beard scratched her skin. Darkness was not enough to prevent her long eyes from shining, half-open. He breathed deep. Regina's hands joined behind the nape of his neck and the length of their bodies touched again. The heat of their thighs melted into a single flame. He sighed: bedroom of starched blouses and skirts, of sliced-open quinces on the walnut table. The unlit night candle. And beside him, the sea scent of a woman moistened and soft. Her fingernails scratched between the sheets, her legs rose again, lightly, and grasped his body. Her lips sought his neck. The nipples of her breasts trembled as his lips and beard came near them, the tangled beard separating. If she spoke, he covered her lips with his hand and felt her breath. Without tongue, without eyes, only the mute flesh abandoned to its own pleasure. She understood. She pressed against him. Her hand went down to his genitals and his to hers, hard, almost hairless, the pubis of a child, and he remembered her standing naked before him, young and hard so long as she was still, but undulant and soft when she moved to wash herself in secret, to draw the curtains, to fan the fire in the brasier. They went back to sleep. Only their hands, one hand, moved in the smiling dream

I'll follow you.

Where will you live?

I'll slip into each town before the fighting, before the town is taken, and wait for you there.

Will you leave everything behind?

Everything except a few clothes. You'll give me money to buy fruit and meals, and I will wait for you. When you enter the town, I'll already be there. With a dress I have.

That skirt now lay over the chair in this rented room. He liked to touch it when he woke, and to touch her other things as well, the combs, the little black shoes, the small earrings left on the table. At such moments he wanted to offer her more than these fleeting days of difficult meetings and inevitable separations. And at other times they would not be together for weeks: some sudden order, a chase in pursuit of the enemy, or some defeat that forced them back to the north. Like a gull, she seemed able to sense the movement of the revolutionary tide despite the quick ebb and flow of battles, and she would go patiently from pueblo to pueblo, asking for the battalion, listening to the replies of old men and old women who had remained at home:

They went through here about two weeks back.

Not a man was left alive, it's said.

Who knows? Maybe they'll be back. They forgot some of their cannon.

Watch out for the Federals. They're picking up everyone who has anything to do with the Rebels.

And so they would meet once more, as now. She would have the room ready, with fruit – fresh quinces – and their meal, and the skirt flung over a chair, everything ready so that no time need be lost. He would watch her walk about the room, make the bed, loose her hair. Then he would take off her last garments and, kneeling while she stood, kiss all her body, running his lips over her, tasting her skin and her pubic down, the moisture of her genitals, gathering the throbbings of that standing, excited child into his mouth until at last she would take his head between her hands and hold it to make him stop, rest, leave his lips in one place. He would stand while she still held his head. She would sigh, and when she became limp, he would carry her to the bed.

Artemio, will I see you again?

Never ask. Just remember that at least once, we met.

And she never asked again. She was ashamed of having asked even once, of having thought that their love might have an end, that its time should be measured as any time is measured. It was unnecessary to concern herself with anything except love. They met during the rare days of rest when a pueblo had been taken and the battalion had halted to recover, to show an armed presence where the dictatorship had ruled before, to resupply and make plans. And thus they decided it, the two of them, without ever saying anything, without ever thinking of the dangers of the war or of the time when they would not meet again. If one did not appear at the next place of assignation, each would go his way without a word, he south to the capital, she back to the north, to the coast where he had met and loved her.

Regina . . . Regina . . .

Do you remember the rock that thrust into the sea like a stone ship? It must be there still.

That was where I met you. Did you use to go there often?

Every afternoon. There's a pool among the rocks and you can see yourself in the still water. One day I was looking in the water, and your face appeared too. At night, the stars shone in the sea, and by day, the sun burned.

I didn't know what to do that afternoon. We had been fighting sort of quietly, and suddenly they collapsed, they surrendered, and between one minute and the next it was peaceful. I began to remember peaceful things, and I went to the sea and found you sitting on that rock. With your legs wet.

And I wanted it too. There you were near me, beside me, reflected in the same water. Didn't you notice that I wanted it too?

Dawn was slow, a gray veil lightening to discover their sleep, sleep joined by their hands. He awoke first and he looked at her. Her sleep was the centuries' frailest spider web. Sleep, death's twin. Her legs were drawn up, her free arm was over his chest, her lips were moist. They liked dawn love, to make of it a celebration of the new day. Gray light just touched her silhouette. In an hour they would hear the noises of the pueblo; now there was only her breathing, she was the only thing that lived. Nothing had a right to awaken her except another happiness greater than the serene happiness of her slumber, her body dark, just outlined against the white sheet, wrapped in the sheet and wrapped in herself. Did he have the right to waken her? His imagination leaped past the act of love and he looked at her as if she were already sleeping afterward. When is happiness greatest? He stroked Regina's breast, imagining what their waiting union would be, the same union, joy wearied of memory, desire and love for a new act of love: happiness; and he kissed her ear and with his eyes near saw her first smile. Her hand played with him again. Under his fingers, her desire flowered and flowed wet, and her legs again sought his waist. Her hand knew everything; his erection slipped from her fingers and came and went with their pressures. Her thighs spread trembling and full and the erect flesh entered the open, entered caressed, surrounded by an eager pulsing, squeezed within a universe of soft and amorous skin: they were reduced to an earthly conjunction, to reason's seed, two voices that call in silence naming everything: he thought about everything except this, thought, counted, thought of nothing, so that this would not end, tried to fill his mind with seas, sands, winds, fruits, houses and beasts, fishes and sowings, so that it might not end: and then he lifted his face with his eyes closed and the veins of his neck swollen and strained, and Regina lost herself and answered with thick breath as she tightened around his penis, then with her lips smiling yes, yes, she liked it, yes, she was ready, don't stop, yes, go on, go on, let it never end, yes, and then the awareness that everything had happened at the same moment for both of them and neither could look at the other because both were the same and were saying the same words.

'Now I am happy.'

'Now I am happy.'

'I love you, Regina.'

'I love you, my husband.'

'Did I make you happy?'

'It never ends. It lasts and lasts. How you fill me.'

And out in the streets of the pueblo the sloshing of a bucketful of water thrown to settle dust, and by the river the wild ducks passed gabbling. A whistle set in motion the events that no one could stop: boots dragged jangling spurs, hooves pounded. The smells of lard and oil entered. He stretched his hand out for the cigarettes in his shirt pocket. Regina went to the window and opened it wide. She stayed there, breathing deep with her arms spread, standing on toe-tips. The circle of brown mountains advanced with the sun. Bread smells came from the town bakery, and from farther, the scent of myrtle mixed with the stink of the rotting *barrancas*. She was nude. She wanted to grasp day by the shoulders and drag it inside to the bed.

'Do you want your breakfast?'

'It's early. Let me finish my cigarette.'

Her head lay on his shoulder again. Her long strong hand rubbed his hip. They both smiled.

When I was a little girl, life was full of beautiful moments, vacation, holidays, summer days, games. I don't know why I began to wish for what I didn't have, when I grew up, for as a girl I never did. That's why I went to the beach. I told myself that I ought to hope. I changed so much that summer. I was no longer a child.

You're still a child. Did you know that?

A child, after what you and I do together?

He laughed and kissed her, and she drew up her legs, a bird with folded wings, and nestled against his chest with laughing and little mock cries.

And you?

I don't remember that far back. I found you, I love you very much.

Tell me: how did it happen that the moment I saw you, I knew nothing else would matter? I told myself that in that very moment I had made a decision. I knew that if you should pass me by, all my life would be lost. And how was it with you?

With me it was the same. Didn't you think I might be just one more soldier out for a good time?

No. I didn't even notice your uniform. I saw your eyes in the water and I knew that from then on, when I saw my own eyes, yours would be beside me.

'Lovely: my love ... go and see if we have coffee.'

When they separated that morning, a morning like all the others of the seven young months they had loved each other, she asked whether the column would be leaving again soon. He said that he did not know what the general planned. Some defeated Federals still remained in the region, roaming in bands, and they might have to go out to disperse them once and for all. In any case, the pueblo would remain their base, for here there was plenty of water and livestock, it was a good place to rest for a while, and they had arrived from Sonora very tired and needed a rest. At eleven, everyone had to report to headquarters in the plaza. In every pueblo they passed through, the general investigated working conditions and issued decrees reducing the workday to eight hours and distributing land among the campesinos. If there was a hacienda in the area, he sent a detachment to burn its store. If there were money-lenders – and there were always money-lenders – he declared all debts void. The rub in this zealous reform program was the unfortunate fact that everyone was always off fighting on one side or the other, so no one was left at home to execute the general's decrees and to benefit from them. Under these circumstances the general found the best policy was to take immediately what money there was from the wealthy who were to be found in every pueblo, and to leave to the final triumph of the Revolution the details of the land and workday reforms. Now they had to get to Mexico City and chase the drunkard Huerta, the murderer of Don Panchito Madero, out of the presidency. What changes! the young officer murmured as he stuffed his khaki shirt inside his white pants: what changes! From Veracruz, his own region, to Mexico City, and from there to Sonora, because his teacher Sebastian had asked him to do what an old man could no longer do: go north and take arms and fight to liberate Mexico. He had been just a kid then, though at that almost twenty-one. Word of honor, he had never even slept with a woman. But how could he refuse and fail his *maestro* Sebastian, who had taught him all he knew: to read and write and to hate priests.

Regina set the coffee on the table.

'How hot it is!'

It was early. They went out on the street, she in her starched skirt, he in his felt sombrero and white tunic. They lived near the barranca: bell flowers hung over its void, and a rabbit killed by the fangs of a coyote was rotting in the foliage. At the bottom flowed a little stream. Regina tried to see the water, as if she hoped to find again the reflection of her make-believe. Their hands joined. The street climbed to the edge of the ravine and from the mountains came echoes of thrushes. There was suddenly a sound of hooves that galloped up in a cloud of fine dust.

'Lieutenant Cruz! Lieutenant Cruz!'

The horse reared back with a single dry whinny. It was Loreto, ever-smiling, the general's adjutant. 'Come, quick,' he panted, wiping his face with a kerchief. 'We're pulling out right away. Have you eaten? They're serving eggs at the barracks.'

'I've eaten,' he said with a smile.

They embraced as the dust-cloud rose again.

'Wait for me.'

'What do you think has happened?'

'Nothing serious. Probably some marauders in the neighborhood.'

'You want me to stay here?'

'Yes. Don't do anything, just wait. I'll be back tonight or tomorrow morning at the latest.'

'Artemio . . .'

'Yes?'

'Will we go back there someday?'

'Who can say? Who knows how long it may last? Don't think about that. Do you know that I love you very much?'

'And I you. Very much. I think for always.'

The troops had already received their new orders and in the stables and the central patio of the barracks were making ready with the calm of ritual. They moved the cannon into line, pulled by white hollow-eyed mules, then the limbers, down the spur that led from the gun-park to the station. Cavalrymen checked reins, took down feedbags, checked girths, fondled the hairy manes of their war horses, so gentle and slow with these skilled riders: dusty horses with tick-infested bellies, two hundred of them moving deliberately in front of the barracks: sorrels, roans, blacks. Infantrymen oiled rifles and filed before the grinning dwarf who passed out cartridges. Northern sombreros of gray felt with rolled brims. Neckerchiefs. Cartridge belts looped around waists. Occasional boots; yellow leather work-shoes, often sandals; denim pants. And here and there – in the streets, the park and yards, the station – were *Yaqui* Indian sombreros adorned with green sprigs. Musicians with music staffs in hands and the metal instruments on shoulders. Last gulped swallows of warm water. Plates heaped with bean fritters and *ranchero*-style eggs. From the station shouting rose: a flatcar packed with Mayan Indians was puffing into town with a sharp beating of drums, shaking of colored bows and crude arrows.

He made his way through. Inside, before the map carelessly tacked on a wall, the general was explaining. 'The Federals have opened a counter-offensive at our rear, in territory already liberated by the Revolution. They want to cut us off. This morning one of our mountain lookouts saw heavy dust clouds in the direction of the pueblos occupied by Colonel Jiménez. The Colonel has arranged a system of signals, piles of wood to be burned in case he is attacked. We must divide ourselves. Half will go back across the mountain to help Jiménez. The other half will go out to give hell to those bands we defeated yesterday and to make sure no new trouble comes at us from the south. Only one company will remain in this pueblo. But it seems unlikely that they'll get this far. Major Gavilán ... Lieutenant Aparicio ... Lieutenant Cruz: you three go back north.'

The signal fires were burning when, toward noon, he passed the lookout post in the mountain cut. Below he could see the combat train; it ran silently and was loaded with their cannon, mortars, and machine guns, and with boxes of equipment. The cavalry troop went down the craggy slope with difficulty. From the railroad, the cannon began to shell pueblos they could suppose the enemy had reoccupied.

'Speed it up,' he ordered. 'That shelling will last about two hours and then we'll have to go in and see what we find.'

The hooves of his horse touched the flat. The young officer never knew why at that moment he lowered his head and forgot all about the task with which he had been charged. The presence of his men vanished, along with the firm intention to carry out his orders, and in its place came a strange tenderness, a silent lament for something lost, the desire to return to Regina and forget everything in her arms. It was as if the blazing sun had burned the slate clean of everything, words, thought, duty, men, even the distant cannonading. In place of the real world appeared a dream world in which only he and his love had a claim on life and a reason to preserve life.

Do you remember that rock that thrusts into the sea like a stone ship? It must be there still.

He was looking at her again, wanting to kiss her yet fearing to wake her, sure that merely by looking at her he was making her his. Only one man rules her secret fancies, he thought, and that man possesses her and will never give her up. In looking at Regina, he looked at himself. His hands dropped the reins. All that existed, all his love, was buried in her flesh, and it contained both of them. He wanted to go back and tell her this and how much he loved her, so that she would know.

The horse whinnied and reared. He fell from the horse on stone-hard spined ground. Federal shells rained down on his cavalrymen, and when he stood, through the smoke he saw the chest of his horse burning and the bodies of forty or fifty horses scattered around. There was no light overhead. The sky was dust and smoke, no higher than his head, and he ran toward the cover of the low trees whose branches were hidden by the smoke. He reached a dense thicket. Meaningless shouting reached his ears. A riderless mount came by and he leapt up and swung his leg across, and hiding his body behind the horse, spurred until they were galloping. Desperately, his head and shoulders hanging, he gripped at the horn and the bridle. At last noon's brilliant light disappeared; he was in shadow and could open his eyes, drop from the horse, roll until he came up against a tree trunk.

There he felt it again. He was surrounded by the confused racket of battle, but lying between him and the noise was an uncertain distance; he could even hear the slight swaying of the trees and the furtive scurry of lizards. Alone, propped against the tree trunk, he felt again the sweet life that flowed languidly through his veins, the physical well-being that opposed itself to all rebellious intents of his mind. His troopers? His heart beat evenly. Would they be looking for him? His arms and legs felt tired and contented, limp. What would they do without his orders? He looked up through the leafy ceiling at a flight of birds. Would they lose discipline; would they run, they too, to hide in this blessed thicket? But on foot one could not cross the mountain again, so he ought to wait here. And if he were captured? He could think no longer: someone moaned near his face, a body dropped into his arms and threw him off balance. A red rag hung from one shoulder and the wounded man said softly:

'We're ... givin' ... 'em ... hell.'

A shredded destroyed arm hung down the young officer's back dripping blood. He tried to push away that pain-twisted face with open mouth and closed eyes, tangled mustache and beard no longer than his own. With green eyes, the man could be his twin.

'Ain't there ... any way out? We're gettin' licked ...'

'Have we retreated?'

'Retreated? Hell ... no, we gone ... forrard.' With his good arm he tried to point. The terrible expression on his face never altered.

'Forward? How?'

'Gave 'em ... Water, water, buddy ... bad ... ver' bad ...'

He fainted, clasping the officer with strange force, and the young lieutenant slowly eased himself free and lowered the leaden body that was so like his own. A faint uncertain breeze rustled the tree tops. Silence, broken by shelling. He took the wounded man's good arm and stretched him out on the ground of knotted roots. He opened his canteen, drank from it, and held it to the wounded man's lips until water ran down the blackened chin. His heart beat evenly still, without jumps, and as he knelt there, he asked himself: how long will this man's heart go on beating? He loosened the heavy silver buckle of the man's belt and turned away from him. What was happening out there? Who was winning? He got to his feet and walked deeper into the little woods, away from the man on the ground.

It was very brushy and he had to feel his way, keep his head down to protect his face, work branches out of the way by touch. He was not wounded, he did not need help. At a spring, he stopped and filled his canteen. A tiny stream flowed still-born: it soon dried, beyond the thicket, under the burning sun. He knelt and took off his tunic. With both hands he bathed his chest, his armpits, his hot shoulders, the dry and taut muscles of his arms, his greenish, sun-scaling skin. He wanted to see himself reflected in the water, but the bubbling prevented him. His body was a blur. Not his body: Regina's, she had taken his, giving hers in exchange; yet with every caress he had claimed his body back again. Not his body, but hers, and for her that body must be saved: they did not live isolated and each alone now, they had broken the wall of separateness; they were two but really one. Forever. And ever. The Revolution would pass; pueblos and lives would come and go; but that would remain, forever. He rinsed his face, buttoned his tunic, and walked out of the thicket onto the plain.

Rebel cavalry galloped toward his place of refuge and the mountain. Quirts slapped haunches, hooves galloped, there were sharp rifle cracks, and then he was alone. He did not understand: what were they doing? They were charging toward the mountain, while he was walking toward the pueblos. Were they fleeing? He was disoriented and turned in a small circle with his hands to his head. It was vital to decide on a fixed destination and never to lose that golden thread: then he might be able to understand. One minute of confusion was enough to change war's chess-like precision into a jumble torn in tatters and pieces, lacking all rationality. That cloud of dust . . . those fierce horses rushing toward him . . . that rider shouting and brandishing a bare saber . . . the train stopped in the distance . . . the dust storming every second nearer . . . and the bitter sun every second nearer too, confusing him . . . blade gashing his forehead . . . charging horses sweeping past as he rolled on the ground . . .

He stood and lightly touched his wounded forehead. He ought to go back to the wooded thicket, there he would be safe. He staggered. The sun dissolved and the horizon, the line of plains and mountains, broke into segments. He reached cover and grabbed a tree trunk and hung on until his head cleared. Then he unbuttoned his tunic and ripped a strip from the shirttail. He spat on the cloth and bound it around his forehead. Twigs near him cracked under boots, and he started violently. His anguished eyes traveled up the stranger's legs. It was a Rebel carrying a body on his shoulders.

'Found him near the edge of the thicket, sir. A-dyin'. They shot his arm clean off. I think he's done died on me' – he squinted to make out the pips of the young officer's rank – 'Lieutenant. He heists like a dead one.'

The tall soldier put the body down, propping it against the tree, just as Artemio Cruz had done half an hour, fifteen minutes earlier. He put his face near the wounded man's face.

'Yeah, he's gone now. If I'd got here a little sooner, maybe I could of saved him.'

With his square hand, the tall soldier closed the dead man's eyes. He fastened the silver belt buckle. As he lay the head down, he said between his white teeth:

'Shit, Lieutenant, if they wasn't a few men with guts like this bastard, where'd the rest of us be?'

Cruz turned away and ran, turned away from the corpse and tall soldier and ran toward the open plain.

He stumbled over a body. He knelt beside it, without knowing why. Then a voice cut through the din:

'Lieutenant Cruz! Lieutenant!'

A hand touched his shoulder. He raised his face.

'You're wounded, man. You're hurt bad. Come along with us. The Feds have taken off! Jiménez held the plaza. Come along with us back to the barracks at Río Hondo. What a fight the cavalry put up! They outdid themselves, they sure outdid themselves! Come on, man. You don't look good.'

He leaned on the officer's shoulder. He murmured:

'To the barracks? Yes, let's go home.'

The thread was gone: the thread that had led him, without getting lost, through the labyrinth of war, without getting lost and without deserting. He lacked strength to grasp his mount's reins, so a halter was tied to Major Gavilán's saddle. Long slow ride across the mountain that separated the battle plain from the valley where she waited. The thread remained behind. Far below, Río Hondo had not changed: the same cluster of houses with broken roof tiles and adobe walls, earth-red, pink, white, ringed by cactus. He thought he could see the window, close by the green lip of the barranca, where she would be waiting for him.

Gavilán trotted in front of him. Afternoon shadow threw the mountain over the two weary men. The major pulled up for a moment, waiting for him to come abreast, and offered him a cigarette and held a match. As the match went out, he spurred to a trot again. Gavilán's face was pained. The lieutenant dropped his head. I deserve it, he thought. So they knew the truth, his desertion during battle, and would rip off his pips. But they did not know all the truth. That he had wanted to save himself so that he could return to Regina's love; and they wouldn't understand, not even if he explained. Neither did they know that he had abandoned a wounded comrade, a life he could have saved. But Regina's love would pay for his guilt. He lowered his head until his chin touched his chest, and for the first time in his life felt ashamed. Shame: but it wasn't shame that showed in Gavilán's clear direct eyes. The major raised his free hand and stroked his blond beard, stiff now with dust and sweat.

'We owe you fellows our lives, Lieutenant. You and your men stopped them. The general will receive you as a hero . . . Artemio. May I call you Artemio?'

Gavilán tried to smile. He placed his hand on the other's shoulder and with a dry chuckle went on:

'We've served a long time together, yet look, we don't call each other by our first names.'

Gavilán's voice and glance asked for a response. Desert night fell clear as glass and day's last color silhouetted the mountains, distant now, shrunken and flattened by darkness. Flames they had not been able to see earlier were visible in the pueblo.

'Dog bastards!' said the major in a choked voice. 'They surprised us. Certainly they could never get as far as the barracks. But they did their damage, they took their revenge. They have promised to punish every pueblo that aids us. So they took ten hostages. They sent word that they'd hang them if we didn't surrender the plaza. The general answered them with mortars.'

The street was full of soldiers and civilians, stray dogs and stray children who cried in doorways. Several fires had not yet burned out and the women were sitting on rescued furniture piled in the street.

'Lieutenant Cruz,' said Gavilán, bending to reach the ears of some of the men. 'Lieutenant Cruz.'

'Lieutenant Cruz.' The murmur ran from the soldiers to the women and on through the crowd.

Way was made for the two horses, the major's bay, nervous in that press of people, and the other's led black. Hands reached in greeting, cavalrymen who squeezed his leg and pointed to the blood-stained rag around his head. He was congratulated on his triumph. They rode on, through the pueblo. The barranca dropped away and trees moved in the evening breeze. He looked up: the familiar white house. The window, but it was closed. Candlelight brightened far-apart doors. In others, dark groups of shawl-wrapped figures squatted.

'Leave them hanging!' shouted Lieutenant Aparicio. He

wheeled his horse and with his quirt pushed aside imploring hands. 'Let everyone see and remember! So you'll know the kind of men we fight against, men who kill their brothers. Look well! This is how they murdered the whole Yaqui tribe, because the Yaquis wanted to hold on to their land. This is how they murdered the workers at Río Blanco and Cananea, because hunger made them resist. And this is how they'll kill all of you if we don't beat hell out of them! Look, people, look!'

Trees near the barranca: coarse hennequin ropes, crudely made, drew blood still from the crooked necks. Open eyes, purple tongues, motionless hanging bodies now and again gently swayed by the wind that came from the mountains. Their expressions: some lost, others infuriated, most gentle and uncomprehending, speaking quietly of pain. Their muddy sandals, a child's bare feet, a woman's black slippers. He dismounted and went near. With a broken cry he embraced Regina's starched skirt. For the first time since his manhood, he wept.

Aparicio and Gavilán took him to the rented room. They made him lie down while they cleansed his wound and changed the dirty rag for a bandage. When they left, he pressed the pillow close and hid his face. He wanted to sleep, sleep, just sleep; and he told himself that maybe sleep would make it the same again, join them again. On the bed surrounded by the yellow-white mosquito net he smelled her damp hair, smooth body, and warm thighs. She was there more real than she had ever been in life. She was more herself, in his fever, more his, made vivid by memory. During the brief months of their love he had never looked at her eyes with such feeling. Black gems, deep sea quiet under the sun, depth of time-stirred sand, dark cherries from the tree of her flesh and his hot heart. He had never told her that: there had not been time. There had not been time for so many unspoken words of love; there had not been time for the last word. If he closed his eyes, maybe she would come back whole and alive, summoned to life by the eager caresses that pulsed in his fingertips. Maybe to think of her would be enough to have her always beside him. Maybe memory may really prolong life, lace their legs together, open the window to the dawn, comb out her long hair, bring back the sound, the smell, the touch. He sat up. In the dark he felt for the bottle of mezcal. But it would serve not forgetfulness but to quicken memory.

He would return to the beach and the rocks while the white alcohol burned inside him. He would go back: where? To that make-believe beach that never existed anywhere? To her child's lie? To their sea fiction that she had conjured up that she might feel clean and innocent and sure of love? Liquor was good for the exploding of lies, pretty lies.

Where did we meet?

Don't you remember?

Tell me.

Don't you remember that beach? I used to go there every afternoon.

Now I remember. You saw my face reflected next to yours.

Remember that I never wanted to see myself without you beside me.

I remember.

He ought to believe her pretty lie forever, until the end. It had no trace of truth. Neither did the truth: it was not true that he had gone into that Sinaloan pueblo just as he had gone into so many others, ready to grab the first woman who incautiously ventured outside. It was not true that a girl of eighteen had been thrown helplessly across his horse and carried back to the officers' dormitory to be violated in silence. It was not true that her honesty had silently forgiven him: her resistance melted into pleasure and arms that had never touched a man before crept around him with joy, and her moist mouth had repeated, as last night, that yes, yes, she had liked it, with him she had enjoyed and loved it, she wanted more, she had been afraid of such happiness. Regina: drowsy, excited: Regina. She had quietly accepted the fact of her pleasure and had admitted that she loved him. The story of the sea and their faces in the still water was invented to forget what might later, when he loved her too, shame him. The woman of a lifetime: Regina. Zestful filly. White witch of surprise. Woman without excuses, without words of self-justification. Never bored, never weighting him with complaint, always there, if not in this pueblo, in the next. It was fantasy, that stiff body hanging from a tree; it would go away, and Regina would be waiting in the next pueblo. The same as always. She had left and gone south. She had slipped through the Federal lines and rented a room in the next town. Yes: he was sure: because she could not live without him, nor he without her. So the thing to do was to move on. Take his horse and grab his pistol, get on with the fighting, so that he could meet her at the next place of rest.

He put on his tunic in the darkness and hung the crossed cartridge belts over his chest. Outside, the quiet black horse was tied to a post. People still clustered near the hanging bodies, but he did not look at them. He mounted and rode to the barracks.

'Where'd the sons of bitches go to?' he shouted at one of the barracks guards.

'They're on the other side of the barranca, dug in near the bridge, waiting for reinforcements to come up. Looks like they want to try taking the town again. Come on in, sir. Eat something.'

He dismounted. Unhurriedly he walked across the patio to the cooking fires, where clay kettles swung from crossed sticks and women's hands slapped wheat tortillas. He dipped a wooden spoon into tripe soup, took an onion and sprinkled it with powdered chile and oregano. He chewed the northern-style tortillas, firm and fresh. Pigsfeet. He was alive.

A torch in a rusty iron ring lit the barracks entrance. He jerked it out and carried it with him. His spurs dug into the black's belly. Men still in the street leaped out of the way. The black reared as he jerked hard on the reins and raked again with his spurs. Then the horse understood. It was no longer the horse of a wounded deserter, the doubt-filled man who had crossed the mountain as darkness fell. He pulled on the horse's mane to make it understand. For now he had to have a war horse, an animal as furious and swift as himself. He held the torch high and rode toward the barranca bridge.

A bonfire burned at the end of the bridge. The bastards' kepis shone pale. His black horse drove forward, hooves pounding grass and dust and thorns, and sparks streamed back from the torch as he rode straight at the fire and leaped it, emptying his pistol at their stunned eyes, their dark backs, the spinning figures who did not know and could not understand what was happening. They dragged the cannon hastily back, unaware that the attack was a single horseman who had to head south, get to the next town, where she waited.

'Out of my way, you bastard sons of bitches!'

Voice of pain and desire, voice of the pistol, voice of the torch flung at the limber ammunition cases. Then the powder was exploding and their teams were stampeding, a chaos of shouts and whinnies and crashes that now found echo sounds from the pueblo, where the bells in the flame-lit pink tower were clanging. Other hooves came crashing across the bridge and found the destruction, the flight, the burning fires, but did not find either Federals or Lieutenant Artemio Cruz, who was galloping south with the retrieved torch over his head, over the sparking eyes of his horse, riding south following the thread in his hands, riding south.

I survived. Regina. What was your name? No: just Regina. Nameless soldier, what do you call yourself? I survived. All the rest of you died, but I survived. Ah: they have left me in peace, they think that I am sleeping. I remembered you, remembered your name. But you have no name. And they both come toward me, one leading the other, with their empty eye sockets, believing that they are going to convince me, rouse my pity. Ah, no. No, I don't owe either of you my life. I owe it to my pride. I challenged, I dared. Virtue? Humility? Charity? Pah: one can live without all that, one can live, but you can't live without pride. Charity? Why: would it have done any good? Humility? Why: you, Catalina, what would you have done if I had been humble? You would have conquered me with contempt, if I had been humble. You would have left me. And imagining the sanctity of that sacrament, you forgive yourself: ha! if it hadn't been for my money, you would have divorced me quick enough, sacrament and sanctity not withstanding. And you, Teresa, though I support you, you hate me, you insult me: how would you have managed to hate and insult me if I had let you be miserable and penniless? Hah: imagine yourselves, both of you, stripped of my pride, you hypocrites, lost in the multitude with your feet tired and swollen, forever waiting on corners to catch buses, working in a shop or an office, running a machine, wrapping packages, saving penny by penny to buy a car on time, lighting candles to the Virgin that she preserve your dreams, making little monthly payments on some scrubby lot somewhere, sighing for a refrigerator, sitting in a cheap neighborhood movie every Saturday eating peanuts and popcorn, afterward trying to make a taxi stop for you, eating out once a month: imagine yourselves subscribing to all the phoniness I have made unnecessary for you: having to shout, Why, there's no place like Mexico! in order to feel alive; having to be proud of serapes and Cantinflas and mariachi and *mole poblano* in order to feel alive! Imagine yourselves having to depend in all reality upon the munificent Church, upon fasts and pilgrimages, upon prayer ... in order to remain alive!

'Domine, non sum dignus ...'

Cheers. First, they want to cancel all the little loans US banks have made to the Pacific Railroad. Do you know how much interest the railroad pays on those little loans every year? Thirty-nine million pesos, my friend. Second, they want to eliminate those of us who have been guiding the rehabilitation of the railroad. Do you know how much we are paid? Ten million a year, ten million. Third, they want to get rid of the go-betweens who arrange the US loans. How much did you and I make from that last year, my friend?

Three million each.

To the peso. And they don't stop there. Do me the favor of wiring National Fruit Express that these Red leaders want to cancel the refrigerator car leases that bring the company twenty million pesos a year, and give us a good commission. Cheers.

Haaaa, that was neatly explained. Blockheads. If I didn't look out for your interests for you, you blockheads. Oh, get the hell out of here, all of you, let me listen! I want to see if they understand me. To see if they understand that a finger up means ...

Sit down, honey, I'll be right with you. Díaz: watch very carefully that not one single line gets into print about what the police have been doing to put down those rioters.

But apparently a man was killed, sir. Right in the middle of downtown. It won't be easy to . . .

Pah. Orders from above.

But I am sure that one of the workers' sheets is going to run the story.

And you are just sitting there? Don't I pay you to think? Don't they pay your informant to think? Get in touch with the D.A.'s office and have them shut that press down.

How little is needed to start thought: a spark, one little spark to energize the whole complex and enormous network. For man. Lesser beings need a lightning jolt that would kill us. But we thrive on difficulty and I must have white water to navigate, distant targets, enemies to repel. Ah, yes. In the eye of the whirlwind. No: calm doesn't interest me.

Maria Luisa. This Juan Felipe Couto, as usual, wants to be known as sharp. That's all, Díaz. Pass me that glass of water, Luisa, doll. I was saying: he wants to be known as a wheeling and dealing operator. Like Federico Robles, you remember him. But I'm not going to let him push me . . .

When, chief?

It was with my help that he got that highway contract in Sonora. I was able to arrange to have his bid approved when it was a good three times more than the job could possibly cost, for I knew that the highway would pass through some irrigated districts I picked up from ejido farmers. Now I've just found out that the shrewd bastard has bought land himself in that area and is planning to detour the highway so that it will go through his property, not mine . . .

Why, but what a swine! And he seems so nice.

So there you have it, little doll. Now I want you to write a few little rumors in your column, just hinting at our friend's imminent divorce. Very smooth, nothing crude, just enough to let him understand we mean business.

Chief, we have some shots of Couto in a cabaret. With a tall blonde who very plainly is not Madam Couto.

Hold them for the present. We won't use them unless we have to.

They say that the cells of a sponge are in no way united, yet the sponge itself is clearly a united whole: that's what they say, I remember they say that if you pull a sponge apart, the pieces

74

will come together again, it will never lose its unity. It will always find a way to join its scattered cells again. It never dies . . . never dies.

'That morning I waited for him with happiness. We rode our horses across the river.'

'You ruled him and ruined him and took him from me.'

He stands up and the voices of the two women are indignant as they take his arm and I go on thinking about the carpenter and now about the carpenter's son and all that we would have avoided if he had just been left free with his twelve press agents, free as a goat, living upon the fame of his miracles, drawing free meals and free quarters reserved for the sacred magicians, until old age and forgetfulness would have ended him forever; and Catalina and Teresa and Gerardo sit in the arm chairs at the far end of the room. Damned women, how long did you wait before fetching a priest, before trying to quicken my death by having him drag confessions from me? Ah: you would all like to know things. How I am going to enjoy myself. And you, Catalina, you are capable of telling me now what you never told me because you were afraid to; you can know now, and I know what you would like to know. And the sharp face of your daughter does not hide her hunger to know, too. And her husband: it won't be long before the poor devil comes to inquire, to weep, to see if at last he isn't going to get something out of it. Ah: how little you know me. Do you think I will let my fortune pass into the hands of three hypocrites like you three, three blind bats who don't even know how to fly? Three blind wingless bats. Three blind mice. Who despise me. Yes. Who can't avoid feeling the hatred beggars feel. Who detest the furs they wear, the mansions in which they live, the jewels with which they adorn themselves, because I have given them these things. No, you are not going to touch me now . . .

'Let me be.'

'But Gerardo has come . . . Little Gerardo, your son-in-law. Look.'

'Ah, the poor devil.'

'Mamá, I can't stand it, can't stand it, can't stand it!'

'He's sick . . .'

'Bah. I'll get up. You'll see now . . .'

'I told you what he's doing.'

'Let him rest.'

'I tell you what he's doing! He's faking like always, to make fools of us like always, always.'

'No, no, the doctor says . . .'

'What does the doctor know? I know him better than any doctor. It's another trick.'

'Don't say any more.'

Don't say any more. Now, the oil. He anoints my lips. My eyelids. My nostrils. No, they don't know what I have had to pay. My hands. My cold feet, which now have no feeling. These women do not know, they have never had to risk everything. My eyes. They spread my legs and he rubs my thighs with oil.

'Ego te absolvo.'

They don't know. She hasn't spoken. She did not talk.

For seventy-one years you will have lived without awareness: of the flow of your blood, the beat of your heart, the yellow liquid dripping from your gall-bladder, the bile secreted by your liver, your kidneys' work in producing urine, the labor of your pancreas as it maintains your blood-sugar; your mind will never have ruled these functions of your body, you will have known that you breathed but you won't have thought about it, because your breathing did not depend upon your thought: you will have paid no attention and you will have gone on living: there were many things you could not do: sleep on a bed of jagged glass, walk on fire, feign death, and control your body's autonomous functions: you will simply have lived, letting your body take care of itself. Until today. Until today, when the autonomous functions of your body will force you to be aware of them: they will dominate and master you: every breath that passes laboriously toward your lungs will make you know that you are breathing, every throb of the arteries in your abdomen will make you painfully aware of the circulation of your blood: your autonomous functions will master and conquer you because they will require you to notice life's processes, instead of merely living. You will try to imagine – such is the lucidity that obliges you to take note of the slightest palpitation, the least movements of juncture and separation, and what is more terrible, even the movement of what no longer moves – you will try to imagine your belly, the serous membrane that will line your abdominal cavity and enfold your intestines and with a double fold woven of tissue and blood and lymph vessels will join your stomach and intestines to the abdominal wall; a double-fold of adipose cells that will be supplied by the celiac river, which carries nutrition to your viscera and stomach and which, penetrating the root of the double-fold of the membrane and obliquely descending, reaches to the beginning of the middle intestine after having passed behind the pancreas; and that other artery with origin below the celiac, which carries blood to a third of your duodenum and the head of your pancreas, and which crosses the duodenum, passes beside the aorta, the inferior vena cava, your right ureter, your genito-femoral nerve, and the veins from your testicles: for seventy-one years that artery will have been unknown to you, flowing heavy and red, but today you will know it, for today the flow will stop, the river will dry. For seventy-one years your mesenteric artery will have performed perfectly: but there is a point in its descent where, touched by a segment of your vertebral column, the vessel must go down and forward at the same time, and then abruptly backward again; for seventy-one years the blood will have flowed swiftly past this point of compression without difficulty, until today: today it cannot, the artery will no longer be able to withstand the pressure, today the swift movement of the piston down and forward and then to the back will be detained by congestion, a paralyzed mass, a brown stony mass of blood that will obstruct the circulation to your intestine. You will feel the throb of the growing pressure: you will feel it: that throb will be your blood, blocked for the first time in seventy-one years, no longer able to course smoothly and quickly to the shore of life, blocked, congealed within the hot cavity of your guts, rotting, stagnant, no longer able to reach the shore.

And it will be now that Catalina will come to the bed and will

ask if there is anything she can do for you, for you who can do
nothing except struggle against the sharpening pain, try to will
it away by willing yourself to sleep or rest; and she will not be
able to refrain from that gesture, that tentative hand touched
forward and then quickly withdrawn, afraid, to be joined to the
other hand on her matronly breast, only to reach out a second
time and tremblingly touch your forehead; she will stroke your
forehead, but you will not notice: lost in the stabbing of your pain
you will not notice that for the first time in decades Catalina has
put her hand to your brow, is stroking your forehead and brushing back the sweaty mop of hair, caressing you with a fear that
tenderness has gratefully overcome, shamed tenderness that is
shamed by the certainty that you do not even know she is touching you; and perhaps with the stroke of her fingers there will
come to you words that will mix with that recurrent memory
which, lost in the depths of these hours, unconscious, beyond
your will, returns involuntarily to slip through the chinks in the
wall of pain and repeat to you, now, words you did not hear then.
She too will think about pride. And thus the spark will be born.
You will hear her, in that mirror the two of you share, the water-
mirror that will reflect both of your faces and that will drown
you both if you try to kiss your liquid reflections: Why do you
not just turn your head and look at her directly, in the flesh? Why
must you kiss only her cold reflection? Because, like you, her
face is deep in the stagnant water, she repeats to you, now that
you do not hear her, 'I let myself go.' Her caressing hand tells
you of the excess of liberty by which liberty is destroyed: the
liberty that raises a tower that rises forever, but that does not
reach heaven, a tower that quarters the abyss and divides the
earth: you can give it its name: separation. And so with pride you
will deny yourself, and you will survive, Artemio Cruz, surviving
by exposing yourself to the hazards of liberty, taking the risk
successfully until no enemies are left: and then you will become
your own enemy, that the proud battle may go on: all others
conquered, there will remain only yourself to be conquered: you
will step from the looking-glass of still water and lead your last
attack against the enemy nymph, the nymph of passion and sobs
who is daughter of the gods and mother of the goatlike seducer,

mother of the only god that has died in man's time: from the
looking-glass she will step too, mother of the Great God Pan,
nymph of pride, and again your double, your double, your last
enemy in the depopulated land of the victims of your pride: you
will survive: you will discover that virtue is merely desirable and
sovereignty merely necessary: and the hand at this moment
stroking your forehead will come at last and with its small voice
silence the bark of challenge and remind you that at the end,
because it is the end, arrogance is not needed and humility is
appropriate: her pale fingers will touch your fevered forehead,
they will want to still your pain, they will want to say to you
today what they have not said for thirty-four years.

[1924: June 3]

He did not hear her say, as she woke from her insomnia: *I let
myself go.* She lay back beside him. Her long chestnut hair
covered her face and in all the folds of her body she felt that
tired dampness, that summer weariness. Her hand covered her
mouth, and she saw the day reaching before her, the vertical sun,
the rainy-season afternoon downpour, the night change from
sweltering heat to freshness. She did not want to remember what
had happened during the night just ended. She hid her face in
the pillow. 'I let myself go, I let myself go,' she said.

Dawn wiped away night's remnants and entered, cold and
clear, through the half-open window. What night had blurred
began to take definition again.

I'm young, after all. It's my right ...

She put on her wrapper and fled from the man's side before
the sun climbed over the mountains.

*Oh, what weakness! To wake up always with this weakness and
hatred. The disgust I feel ...*

Her eyes met those of the smiling Indian moving along the
edge of the orchard. Ventura removed his straw sombrero and
bobbed his head to her.

... when I wake and see him lying beside me.

The Indian's white teeth glistened as he came nearer.

Does he really love me?

The man stuffed his shirt into his tight trousers. Ventura walked past the window where the woman sat.

It's been five years now . . .

She turned her back on the window and the fields.

'What brings you so early, Ventura?'

'What my rabbit ears tell me. May I use the dipper?'

'Is everything ready in the pueblo?'

The Indian nodded. He walked to the reservoir pond, buried the gourd dipper in the water, drank, filled the dipper again.

. . . maybe he himself has forgotten why he married me . . .

'So what do your rabbit ears tell you, Ventura?'

'That old Pizarro hates your guts, boss.'

'That's news?'

'And that he is planning to use the cover of the rally today to even things with you once and for all.'

'Ventura, blessed be your ears.'

. . . and now, maybe, he really loves me . . .

'Blessed be my mother, who taught me to keep them clean and the wax out of them.'

'Well, you know what has to be done.'

. . . loves me, admires my looks . . .

The Indian laughed soundlessly. He touched the unraveling brim of his straw sombrero and glanced toward the tile-roofed terrace, where the woman had seated herself in a rocking chair.

. . . my beauty and my passion . . .

He could remember her seated there at other times during the past five years, now with her belly swollen and round, now thin and silent, but always beautiful and always remote from the passing laden grain-carts, from the bellowing of steers being branded, from the dry summer withering of the *tejocotes* in the orchard that the boss had had planted around the buildings of the hacienda.

. . . what I am . . .

She watched the two men for a moment with the eyes of a rabbit measuring the distance that separates it from wolves. Her father's death had stripped her, abruptly, of the proud defenses of the first months. He had presented a continuation of the old order, the old hierarchies. At the same time, her first pregnancy had given her a pretext for withdrawal and aloofness.

But dear God, why I can't be at night the way I am during the day ...

And the man, turning to follow the Indian's eyes, saw his wife's immobile face and reflected that during those early years he had been merely indifferent to her coldness. He himself had lacked time and will to concern himself with her world, that secondary world he owned but into which he had never fitted, where he had not formed himself or found his place, or known himself except as he had been known by her.

... as cold at night as I am during the day ...

Another and more urgent world had needed him.

('The governor doesn't bother with us, Señor Artemio. That's why we have come to you.'

'What I'm here for, boys, what I'm here for. You'll have your new road, I give you my word. But on one condition: that you no longer take your grain to Pizarro to be milled. What land has that old miser ever divided up with you? So why go on doing him favors? You bring me your grain, I'll mill it and market the flour.'

'Señor, you're absolutely right. It's just that Don Pizarro will have us killed.'

'Ventura: pass out rifles among the boys, so they can take care of themselves.')

She rocked slowly back and forth, remembering the days and even months during which her lips had not opened.

But he's never reproached me for the way I treat him during the day ...

Everything had seemed to move along without her participation. And he dismounted at night with his hands calloused and his face smeared with dust and sweat, and whip in hand hurried past her to fall on the bed, only to be up again before sunrise, off again on the exhausting round of the land that had to be made to produce, to render up, to become his pedestal ... :

... the passion with which I accept him during the night seems to be enough, to satisfy him.

. . . the corn fields in the small irrigated basins that surrounded the ruins of the old haciendas: Bernal, Labastida, Pizarro. Maguey and pulque fields off farther, where the hard-packed clay began again.

('Well, Ventura, is there any grumbling now?'

'You know, boss. They hide it, for after all, things are better now than they used to be. But they realize that you have parted with only dry-farm fields, that you've kept the irrigated land for yourself.'

'What else?'

'Well, they say that you go on charging interest on the loans you make them, just like Don Gamaliel used to.'

'Look, Ventura, you go and tell the boys that the steep interest is not what they pay but what I charge the businessmen I lend to, and the landlords like Pizarro. You tell them that if they feel they're hurt by the loans I make them, okay, no more loans. I thought I was doing something they needed done. But if . . .'

'No, that's not what they want.'

'Tell them that before long I'm going to foreclose on old Pizarro, and once I get my hands on his land, I'll split with them. We'll divide the irrigated fields as well as the dry-farm. Tell them that. Tell them to hang on and have faith in me, and they'll see how things turn out.')

He was a real man.

But his tiredness and his worries kept him far away from me, and I never asked for the frenzied love-making he gave me night after night.

Don Gamaliel, loving the society and comforts and promenades of the city of Puebla, forgot his hacienda affairs and let his son-in-law run things just as he wanted to.

Father asked me to accept him, so I did. With neither doubts nor pretexts: I knew I had been bought. And had to stay.

It was not so bad, the country, so long as her father lived and she could go see him every two weeks, spend the day with him, load the sideboard and cupboards with rich chocolates and cheeses, make her devotions with Don Gamaliel in the church of St Francis, prowl the Parián market, take a turn around the armory plaza, cross herself in front of the cathedral's great stone fonts, or simply sit in the patio and watch her father's coming and going.

Of course I obeyed him: hadn't he protected me, reared me, sheltered me?

So long as she could do this, the possibility of a better life was kept alive, and the loved familiar world of her girlhood was real enough for her to return to the country each time, to return to her husband, without sharp regret.

I was bought. Without voice, will, bought, a mute witness to his stone purposes.

And she could think of hacienda life as a kind of vacation to be spent in a strange world that his strength had raised from the dust, while her real home was in the city, the patio of the old mansion there, and her real pleasure was the fresh linen spread on her father's mahogany dining table, the feel of the hand-painted plates and the polished silver, the smells.

Sliced pears, quinces, peach preserves.

('I know that you have ruined Don León Labastida now. Those three houses of his you got in Puebla are worth a fortune.'

'Well, you know how it came about, Pizarro. Labastida wanted one loan after another and paid no attention to the interest. He himself wove the rope that hung him.'

'You think it's a good joke to see the proud old names come tumbling down. But you're not going to push me around, Cruz. I'm not one of those elegant city sops like Labastida.'

'You meet your payments on time, Pizarro, and you don't over-extend yourself.'

'Nobody is going to break me, Cruz. So help me God.')

Don Gamaliel felt the approach of death, and himself arranged the obsequies with care and luxury. His son-in-law could not refuse the thousand ringing pesos that the old man required. His chronic cough worsened. Soon his chest clogged and he had to labor to draw thin air into his lungs through a hardening mass of phlegm, mucus, and blood.

Source of a man's casual pleasure …

The old gentleman ordered a hearse with silver fittings, a black velvet pall, and eight horses shining in silver harness with black feather-plumes over their foreheads. He had his wheelchair rolled out on the living room balcony while the hearse and the richly caparisoned horses passed back and forth before his feverish eyes.

A mother ? Who gave birth with neither happiness nor pain ?

He asked his daughter to take the four tall gold candelabra from the glass cabinets and have them polished: they had to surround him during the wake as during the Mass. He beseeched her to shave him herself, for his beard would go on growing for several hours: the neck and the cheeks only, with a little trimming for the goatee and mustache. She must dress him in his stiff-fronted shirt and his morning coat, and have the dog poisoned.

Motionless and mute even when giving birth. From pride.

He wrote his will, leaving Catalina everything and designating her husband as the administrator. Those last weeks he treated her more than ever like a little girl, the child who had grown up beside him while he was growing old. He never mentioned Gonzalo's death, nor his son-in-law's first visit: it seemed that death was providing an occasion to put those events piously out of the way forever, and at last to restore, in some sense, the world that had been lost.

Do I have the right to destroy his love, if his love is true ?

Two days before the end, Don Gamaliel abandoned the wheelchair and took to his bed. There, propped up against a heap of pillows, he maintained his erect elegance, his fine aquiline profile. At times he reached out to assure himself that Catalina was with him. The dog lay under the bed, whimpering. Then the old man's lips parted in a spasm of terror and he could no longer reach, his hand lay still on his motionless chest. Catalina sat beside him staring at that hand. It was her first experience of death, for her brother had died far away and her mother when she was a baby. So this is what it is, she thought: this close quietness, and that unmoving hand.

Very few families accompanied the hearse to the church of St Francis first and afterward to the cemetery. Perhaps people were still afraid of the old man. Her husband ordered the mansion rented.

How lonely I felt then. That the child was there was not enough,

84

Lorenzo was not enough. And I thought how it might have been, life with that other man, Ramón, the life he prevented.

('Boss, old Pizarro stays at the hacienda all day, sitting in front of the ruined buildings with a rifle in his hands. He never leaves the ruins.'

'Those ruined buildings are all he has left.'

'Oh, they say there are still a few men faithful to him. And brave men, at that.'

'I know, Ventura. Remember their faces.')

One night she realized that without meaning to, she was watching him when he did not know she was looking at him. The unaffected indifference of the first years was being little by little forgotten as, during the brown hours of evening, she began to be alert to his glance, to his deliberate movement as he stretched his legs on the leather footstool, to the way he knelt to light the fire laid in the old fireplace during the cold country winter.

Ah, it must be a look of weakness, full of pity for myself and asking pity of him; and restless, too, for I can't overcome the sadness and loneliness death has left me. I believed that that restlessness was only my ...

She did not notice that, at the same time, the man with her was a new man who looked at her with different eyes, as if wanting her to understand that the time of difficulties had passed now.

('Well, Boss, they're all asking when you're going to divide up Don Pizarro's land with them. Everyone.'

'Tell them to hold on. Don't they see that Pizarro hasn't quit yet? Tell them to hold on and to keep their rifles ready in case the old man dares to tangle with us. Then when things quiet down, we'll divide up the land.'

'I know your secret, Boss. I know that you're already selling off Don Pizarro's best land to small farmers in exchange for building lots in Puebla.'

'Small landowners will give work to the campesinos too, Ventura. Here, take this. And don't get excited.'

'Thank you, Don Artemio. You know I'm ...')

A new man who now, assured of material well-being, was disposed to prove to her that his strength could also serve acts of kindness. The night when his eyes finally stopped and gave her

85

a moment of concentrated attention, she thought, for the first time in a long while, of how her hair looked, and she lifted a hand to check.

... while he smiled, standing by the fireplace, with ... with a new kind of frankness. Do I have the right to deny myself possible happiness?

('Tell them to bring back their rifles, Ventura. They don't need them, every man has his own piece of land now. And the larger farms are either my property or the property of my friends. There's nothing to be afraid of now.'

'Sure, Boss. They're willing, they appreciate the way you have helped them. Of course, some of them were dreaming of a lot more. But they're resigned now. They say things could be worse.'

'Pick ten or twelve of the toughest men and let them have rifles. We want to be able to take care of malcontents on either side.')

Later I was resentful. I let myself go ... And I enjoyed it. How humiliating.

He wanted to erase the memory of how their life together had begun; he wanted her to love, without thinking of the act that had forced her to take him as her husband. Lying beside her, he silently asked, and she was aware of it, that the interlaced fingers of that hour be something more than merely an immediate response to their hunger.

Maybe if I had married the other, I would have felt something more. I don't know, I've known only my husband. Carried away by passion, as though he can't live a moment longer without knowing that I feel it too.

She reproached herself by thinking that the facts were otherwise: how could she believe that he had loved her from the moment he saw her pass on a street in Puebla, before he even knew who she was?

And when we draw apart, when we go to sleep at last, when we begin to live the new day, it's all gone, not even a gesture remembers the love we knew at night.

He could have told her. But one explanation would require another, and all would lead to one day and one place, a jail and a night in October. This he wanted to avoid; to do so, he knew, he had to make her his without words, and he told himself that his body and tenderness could speak without words. But then he was attacked by a new doubt. Would this girl be able to understand all he wanted to say to her by the act of taking her into his arms? Could she interpret his tenderness? Was not her sexual response too strong, too resonant? Would she not lose, in the strength of her own passion, the possibility of understanding what his passion meant?

Maybe it was shame that made them put the nights behind them like something not to be touched during daylight. Or maybe it was a desire to set their nights apart from the rest of their life, to make them more important because isolated.

He did not dare to speak, to ask. He went on, hoping that truth would finally impose itself upon her. And custom and need and inevitableness as well: for where could she look? Her only future was at his side. This blunt fact might itself be enough to make her forget that other, the man who had preceded him. He went to sleep beside his wife with this hope, now become a dream.

I beg forgiveness for having forgotten in my pleasure the reason for my hatred. Dear God, how can I help but respond to such strength, to the force in those green eyes? What can my own strength be once that ferocity and tenderness turn upon me without asking whether I welcome them, without asking pardon for the guilt I could throw in his face? And it has no name. Things happen before one can give them a name . . .

('You are so quiet tonight, Catalina. Are you afraid to break our silence? Does it say something to you?'

'No . . . don't talk about it.'

'You never ask for anything. I'd like it if you would sometimes . . .'

'I leave the words to you. You know about . . . about these things that I . . .'

'Yes. You don't have to talk. You give me such pleasure, such pleasure. I never dreamed that . . .')

By night she would let herself go, let herself desire and respond to desire. But when she woke in the morning, she remembered the beginning, and once again would oppose his strength with her silent rancor.

I won't tell you; at night you conquer me, but I defeat you during the day; I won't tell you that I never believed that story you made up for us. Father knew how to hide his humiliation behind dignity and breeding. For me there is secret revenge, as long as I live.

She got out of bed, braiding her loose hair, without looking back at the tumbled bedclothing. She lit the candle and in silence prayed, as in silence she tried to assert, during daylight hours, that she had never been conquered, even though every night and her second pregnancy said otherwise. And only in moments of real solitude, when neither her hatred from the past nor shame about her present pleasure occupied her thought, could she tell herself honestly that he, his life and strength, made an invitation . . .

I am offered this strange adventure and it fills me with fear.

.An invitation to the unknown, to plunge into an uncharted future where nothing was made safe by familiarity. He created everything afresh and new, as if there were no precedents: fatherless Adam, Moses without the Law. This was not how life in Don Gamaliel's orderly world had been.

Who is he? How has he sprang from within himself? No, I am not brave enough to be his partner. I have to control myself: I mustn't cry remembering my girlhood.

She compared the tranquil days of her girlhood with the present gallop of hard faces, ambition, shattered fortunes and fortunes created from nothing, foreclosed mortgages, towering pride.

('Your husband has reduced us to misery. We can't have anything to do with you any longer. You are part of what he has done to us.')

It was true. That man.

That man.

That man who had come to destroy them: now he had succeeded, and she had saved her body by selling it to him, but not her soul. She spent long hours at the window looking out over the valley shaded with wild-pear trees, rocking the child's cradle from time to time, waiting for the second act, trying to imagine the future that this adventurer would offer her. He took the world as he took her body, cheerfully overcoming shame, breaking all the rules of decency with gusto. He sat at the same table with his hacienda foremen, peons with quick eyes, men who knew nothing of good manners. The old home became a stable inhabited by field hands who talked of things that she could not understand. He began to receive delegations of neighbors and to hear flattery: he must go to Mexico City, to represent them in the new Congress. They would nominate him. Who could really look out for their interests, if not he? If he and his señora would care to ride through the pueblos of the district next Sunday, they would see how popular they were and how confident he could be of election.

Ventura bobbed his head again before putting on his sombrero. The buggy was brought around to the door by a peon. The man turned from Ventura and walked toward the rocker where the pregnant woman sat.

Or is it my duty to go on hating to the end?

He held out his hand and she took it. The rotting *tejocotes* opened beneath their feet, barking dogs jumped around the buggy, the plum branches were still wet with dew. As he helped her up, he involuntarily squeezed her arm. He smiled.

'Have I done something to offend you? If I have, please forgive me.'

He waited for a moment. If she would at least show some feeling, that would have been enough. Some sign, not even of affection, that might hint weakness, softness, the desire to be protected.

If I could only make my mind up. If I only could.

As when they had first met, his hand moved to her palm and found no response. He took the reins. Without looking at her husband, she opened her blue parasol.

'Take care of the boy.'

I have split my life into night and day, as if I had to satisfy two separate reasons for being. Dear God! Why can't I choose one or the other?

He drove the buggy east. Cornfields ran beside the road,

watered by irrigation streamlets that the campesinos channeled with their hands, protecting the seeded hills. Hawks floated in the distance. The green spikes of maguey plants emerged. Machetes were at work making cuts in the trunks. That rich sap. Only the hawks, high above, could measure the extent of the moist and fertile lands that now belonged to him, Bernal land, Labastida, Pizarro.

Yes: he loves me. He must love me.

The silver lines of the irrigation ditches ended and the land took its usual aspect: lime-white maguey flatland. As the buggy passed, workers left their machetes and mattocks, drovers whipped up their burros. Clouds of fine dust floated over a parched unbroken land. Ahead, a slow religious procession was winding along like a black swarm. The buggy caught up with it and could not pass.

I want to go over why I think he loves me. Doesn't his passion prove it? Don't the words he says when we make love, and his impetuousness, and his obvious pleasure, don't these prove it? Even as I am, pregnant, he can't leave me alone. Doesn't that prove it?

Children dressed in white tunics trimmed with gold, some of them with halos of silver paper trembling over their heads. Leading the children, shawled women with red cheeks and glassy eyes who were crossing themselves repeatedly and murmuring old litanies; they were on their knees and bare-foot, and their hands clasped their rosaries. Some of the women supported the man with crippled legs who was going to fulfill an oath; others whipped the sinner, the lawbreaker, who wore a belt woven of thorn branches and received their lashing with satisfaction. Thorn crowns opened wounds on dark foreheads, cactus scapulas pierced the penitent skin of bare chests. Indian murmuring, not Spanish. The ground spotted with drops of blood their feet trod upon; crusted, calloused feet. The buggy could not pass.

Why can't I accept it without feeling wrong, without reserve? I want it to be proof that he cannot resist my body, but I take it as only proof that I have overcome him, that I can evoke love from him every night and freely deprecate it the next day with my coldness and distance. Why can't I decide? Why do I have to decide?

The sick pressed onion poultices to their temples or let themselves be brushed by the women's palm fronds. Hundreds, hundreds: an unbroken moaning and murmur of prayers: even the mangy curs slunk low with their heads down. The procession crawled toward distant pink towers, a tiled façade and yellow mosaic cupola. Gourds were lifted to thin lips and the phlegmy white of pulque dripped down chins. White eyes, ring-worm eaten faces, the shaved heads of sick children, noses pitted by smallpox, eyebrows erased by syphilis: the marks of the *conquistadores* on the bodies of the conquered. They crawled, barefoot, on their knees, on all fours, toward the sanctuary erected to honor the god of the Spanish, hundreds, hundreds, bare feet, calloused hands, the sign of the cross, sweat, moaning, welts, fleas, mud, lips, teeth: hundreds.

I have to make my mind up. I have no other choice than to be this man's wife until I die. Why not accept it? Yes: easy to think, hard to do. It is not so easy to forget why I hate him. God. God, tell me if I myself am destroying my chance for happiness. Tell me if I ought to put him above my duty as a sister and a daughter . . .

The buggy moved forward with difficulty through the dust, passing bodies that knew no haste, that moved on knees toward the church. The rows of maguey plants prevented their driving around the procession. The woman held her parasol against the sun and it swayed gently above the shoulders of the penitents. Her eyes were wide, her earlobes pink, her skin white. She held her handkerchief over her nose and mouth. Breasts high under the blue silk, belly swollen. Small feet crossed, satin slippers. Hands . . .

We have a son. My father and brother are dead. Why does the past hypnotize me? I must look ahead. I don't know how to make my mind up. Am I going to sit still and let what happens decide for me? That may be. God. I am expecting another child . . .

Hands stretched toward her: the scarred arm of a grizzled old Indian man, the bare arms of the women. There was a mumble of admiration and affection, a wish to touch her, voices: 'Little mother . . . little mother.' The buggy came to a stop and the man jumped down. He shook the whip over their dark heads, shouting for them to make way. He was tall, dressed all in black, with his sombrero cocked over his eyebrows.

God, why have you put me in this conflict?

She picked up the reins and jerked the horse violently to the right, knocking down penitents, until the horse reared and struck out with his forefeet, broke red clay jars, tumbled crates of cackling chickens, grazed the heads of fallen Indians. The horse whirled and she felt oppressed by the sweat and sores of those dark bodies, their muffled shouting, the insects, the pulque fumes. She stood, balanced by the weight of her belly, and snapped the reins over the animal's haunches. The crowd tumbled out of the way with little whimpers of innocence and fright, their arms up as they fell backward toward the wall of maguey. The buggy dragged around and she flew homeward.

Why have you made it necessary for me to choose? I wasn't born for this.

She panted as the horse galloped toward the houses hidden by the fruit-trees he had planted.

I am a weak woman. All I want is a life of peace, one in which others will make my choices for me. No, I can't decide . . . I can't, I can't . . .

Long tables were placed in the sun around the church. Clouds of flies buzzed over the great pots of beans and over the hard tacos piled in mounds on spread newspapers. There were large jars of berry-flavored pulque, dry ears of corn, three-colored almond *jamoncillos*. Presently the mayor of the district climbed a little platform and eulogized him, and he quietly accepted his nomination for Federal Deputy, a nomination that had been arranged months before in Puebla and Mexico City, by a government that recognized his revolutionary merits, his excellent example in retiring from the army to carry out the program of agrarian reform, and his outstanding services in establishing, in the absence of regular authority and at his own risk and expense, a proper order in the district. Around him rose the persistent babbling of penitents on their way into, or out of, the church, crying loudly to God and the Virgin, wailing, drinking from pulque jugs. Someone suddenly shouted, and several shots were fired, but the new candidate did not lose his composure, and the Indians went on stolidly chewing their tacos. He turned the speech-making over to a native who could read and write, as the Indian drum hailed him and the sun hid itself behind the mountains.

'Like I told you,' said Ventura as the punctual afternoon rain began. 'Don Pizarro's killers. They were drawing a bead on you before you sat down on the platform.'

Hatless, the man pulled a cornshuck raincoat over his head. 'How are Don Pizarro's killers now, Ventura?'

'Cold as ice, Boss. We had them surrounded since before the rally began.'

He put his foot in the stirrup. 'Throw them in the old man's goddamn doorway.'

He hated her when he came into the bare, whitewashed room and found her alone, rocking in the chair and rubbing her arms as if his arrival had chilled her, as if his very breath, the dried sweat of his body, the hesitant tone of his voice caused a cold wind. The nostrils of her thin straight nose quivered. He threw his sombrero on the table and walked toward her, his spurs scarring the tile floor.

'They . . . they frightened me.'

He did not speak. He removed the raincoat and hung it close to the fireplace. Rain flowed noisily down the roof tiles overhead. It was the first time she had attempted to excuse herself.

'They asked for my wife. This was an important day for me.'

'Yes. I know . . .'

'How can I make it clear . . . we all need . . . we all need someone to see and know our life, so we can live our life.'

'Yes . . .'

'But you . . .'

'But I didn't choose the life I live!' she said sharply, gripping the arms of the rocker. 'If you force people to do your will, then don't ask them later for gratitude or . . .'

'Against your will? Why do you enjoy it so, then? Why do you moan and scream in bed if you're just going to go around with a long face afterward? Shit, who can understand you!'

'Wretch!'

'Go on, answer me. Why?'

'I would be the same with any man!'

She raised her eyes to face him. Now it was said. She had

preferred to put it coarsely. She went on: 'What do you know about it? I could give you a different face and name . . .'

'Catalina . . . I have loved you. Nothing has been lacking on my part.'

'Leave me alone. I'm in your hands forever, you have what you wanted. Be satisfied with what you have and don't ask for the impossible.'

'Why are you complaining? I know you enjoy it . . .'

'Leave me alone. Don't touch me. Don't throw my weakness up to me. I swear I'll never let myself go with you again. Not that way again.'

'You're my wife.'

'Don't come near me. Oh, I'll sleep with you, you won't lose anything, you'll have what belongs to you. But that's all.'

'Yes, what belongs to me. And you'll just have to stand for it.'

'I know how to console myself. With God at my side, and with my children, I'll be all right.'

'And why do you mention God?'

'Your insults don't matter now. I know how to console myself.'

'For Christ sake, console yourself for *what*?'

'As if you didn't know. For knowing I live with the man who betrayed my brother and humiliated my father.'

'You're going to have hard going, Catalina Bernal. You're going to make me think of your father and your brother every time you spread your legs for me . . .'

'You can't offend me anymore.'

'Don't be so sure.'

'Do what you will. Does the truth hurt you? You killed my brother.'

'Your brother didn't have time to be betrayed. He wanted to be a martyr. He didn't want to save himself.'

'He died and you are here, alive and enjoying his inheritance. That's all I know.'

'Then burn, Catalina, and remember that I will never let you go, never, not even when I die, because I too know how to inflict humiliation. You're going to regret not having taken into account . . .'

'Do you think I can't see the animal in your face when you tell me you love me?'

'That was not the only way I loved you. You were a part of my life . . .'

'Don't touch me. There are some things you will never be able to buy.'

'Catalina, let's forget this day. Remember, we are going to live all our lives together.'

'Get away from me. I know about that, I've thought about it.'

'Then forgive me. I ask you again.'

'Would you forgive me?'

'I have no reason to need to forgive you.'

'Will you forgive me because I cannot forgive you, because I can't forgive myself for forgetting him, the man who really loved me? If only I could remember his face . . . I blame you for that too, you know. You've made me forget his face. If only I had known love from him before knowing it from you, then I could say that I had lived. Try to understand: I hate him even more than I hate you, because he let himself be frightened away and never came back. Maybe I say these things to you because he isn't here for me to say them to him. Yes, tell me that's cowardice. Maybe it is, I don't know, I'm weak . . . and you, if you want to, can have many women, but I am tied to one man, to you. If he . . . if he had taken me by force, today I wouldn't need to think about him, I wouldn't have to hate him without even being able to remember him clearly. But he didn't take me. I was left unsatisfied, forever . . . do you understand? And I blame you for everything, because I'm not brave enough to blame myself and because he isn't here for me to hate. I hate you, and you are strong enough to stand it. Tell me: can you forgive me all this? Because I can't forgive you as long as I don't forgive myself and him, who was so weak, who ran away . . . But I don't want to think about it. I don't want to talk, just let me live in peace, let me ask my forgiveness of God, not of you . . .'

'You're through? I think I prefer you silent.'

'Well, you know now. You can hurt me all you want to, I've given you your weapon. And I want you to hate me too. Let us put away our illusions, both of us, once and for all.'

'It would be simpler to forget everything and start over.'

'No, we aren't made that way.'

She remembered, as she sat motionless before him, her first decision, the afternoon Don Gamaliel told her what was happening: to accept events and bide her time; to let herself be sacrificed now, in order to avenge the sacrifice later.

'You can't stop my hating you, don't you see that? Tell me one reason to stop.'

'Hatred is too easy.'

'Don't touch me! Take your hands away!'

'Too easy. Love is what is hard. It demands more, it . . .'

'Hatred is natural, it's what I feel.'

'And it requires no cultivation, no care. It just comes out by itself.'

'Don't touch me!'

She did not look at him now. Silence erased his presence, tall, wearing black, mustached. His head felt compressed by stone pain. And his wife's beautiful cloudy eyes continued speaking to him, her tight-closed mouth, almost smirking with contempt, threw at him the words her lips would not utter:

Do you think that after doing all that you have done, you still have a right to love? That life's law can be changed now so that with everything else you will have love too? You lost your innocence in one world, you can't reclaim it in another. Maybe you had your garden. I had mine, too, my little paradise. Now we have both lost. Try to remember, for you can't find in me what you have lost forever and by your own action. I don't know where you came from, or what you did. I only know that your life lost before I knew you what you made mine lose later: the dream, the innocence. We will neither of us ever be the same again.

He wanted to read her immobile face. In spite of himself, he felt himself drawn by the explanation she had not spoken. The word came back, dark and awful: Cain: that terrible word must not ever come from the lips who, even if all hope of love was lost, would be his witness, mute, distrustful, the rest of his life.

He tightened his jaw. There was only one thing he could do to break down this wall of separation and bitterness. Certain words must be said now, or never said. If she accepted them, they would be able to forget and begin anew. If she did not . . .

Yes: I am alive and beside you now because I let others die for me. I can tell you of those who died, for I have washed my hands of their death and shrugged my shoulders. Accept me thus, with this guilt, and look at me as a man with needs . . . Don't hate me. Have compassion for me, beloved Catalina. For I love you. Weigh my guilt against my love and you will see that my love is the greater . . .

He didn't dare. He asked himself why: why did not she demand it from him, the truth he was incapable of revealing . . . aware that this cowardice separated them further and made him also responsible for the shattering of their love; why didn't she insist, so that they might cleanse themselves of the guilt that he wanted to share in order to be redeemed?

Not alone, alone I can't do it.

I am strong now. My strength lies in accepting this destiny without resisting.

During that brief moment, intimate and silent, he, too, accepted the impossibility of trying again, of going back. She rose saying that the child was sleeping alone in the bedroom. Alone, he imagined her on her knees before the ivory crucifix, completing the ultimate act of separation from his destiny and from his guilt, which was tied to her personal salvation, rejecting that which might have been theirs, rejecting it whether or not he might offer it to her silently. She would not return to him.

He crossed his arms and walked out into the country night. He lifted his head toward brilliant Venus, first star. On another night long ago he had looked up at the stars. Nothing was to be gained by remembering: neither he nor the stars were what they had been then.

The rain had stopped. From the orchard came the heavy scents of guava and tejocote and plum and pear. He had planted those garden trees. He had raised the hedge that separated the house and orchard from the fields, creating thus his personal domain. Wet earth sank beneath his boots. He drove his hands into his pockets and walked slowly to the gate. He opened it and went on toward the nearby group of small houses, where lived the young Indian girl who, during his wife's first pregnancy, had accepted him occasionally, with a total absence of questions or thought about the future.

He went in without knocking, pushing open the door of the dilapidated adobe hut. He took her by the arm, pulled her from sleep, and felt the warmth of that dark drowsy flesh. The girl looked at him fearfully, at the curly hair that fell over his green eyes, at his thick lips and bristly mustache.

'Come,' he said. 'Don't be frightened.'

She raised her arms to slip on her white blouse and reached for her rebozo. He led her outside. She moaned softly, like a roped calf. He raised her head toward the sky.

'Do you see that big star? Looks as if you could reach out and touch it. But you'll never touch that star, will you? What we can't reach with our hands, we better say no to. Come along. You're going to live with me in the big house.'

The girl walked, head down, through the orchard. Trees washed by the rain shone in the darkness. The ripe earth was deep-scented.

And above, in the bedroom, the woman left the door ajar and lay down. She lit the candle. She faced the wall, crossed her hands behind her shoulders, and drew up her legs. A moment later she stretched her legs down and felt for her slippers. She got up and walked the length of the room, raising and lowering her head. Unconsciously she hummed to the child asleep in the crib. She rubbed her belly for a little, and lay down again, and remained there with her eyes open and the candle lit, waiting to hear his footsteps in the hall.

I let them do what they will, I can neither think nor desire; I begin to be used to the pain, for nothing can go on forever without becoming simply customary, the pain that I feel under my ribs, around my belly button, in my guts; now it has become my pain, a pain that gnaws rather than stabs: the vomit taste on my tongue is my taste, the swollen hump of my belly is the baby I carry, which makes me laugh. I try to touch my baby, and run my hand from my umbilicus to my crotch. New. Round. Clammy. But the cold sweat has stopped. The colorless face that I see briefly reflected in the glass facets of Teresa's purse as she passes beside the bed. She never lets go of her purse; there must be thieves in this bedroom. I have suffered a collapse, that is all I know, the doctor has gone, he said that he was going to get more doctors. He doesn't want to take the responsibility for me. That's all I know. But I see them. They have come in. The mahogany door opens and closes and their steps are silent on the thick carpet. They have closed the windows. They have run the gray curtains shut, with a hissing noise. They have come in. Ah, there's a window. There's a world outside, there's the high wind, wind of the high mesa, wind that shakes the slender dark trees. I have to breathe . . .

'Open the window.'

'No. You might be chilled and get worse.'

'Open . . .'

'Domine non sum dignus . . .'

'Shit on God.'

'Because you believe in Him . . .'

Very sharp. That was very clever. It calms me. I won't think about those things now. Yes: why should I insult Him, if He doesn't exist? That seems right to me. I am going to permit all this to continue, because to rebel is to concede that those things really exist. That's what I am going to do. I don't know what I was thinking about. Excuse me. The priest understands me. I am not going to offer the proof of rebellion. This way is better, I shall put on an expression of boredom, that's best. How much importance he is giving to all this, to an event which to me, the most interested party, means the end of importance. Yes: now we are on the right road. The straight road. I realize that everything will cease to have importance, and for them, that becomes what is most important: pain itself and the salvation of a man's soul, not their souls but mine. I breathe through my nostrils with a hollow snoring, and I let them do what they will, and I cross my arms over my stomach. Get out of here, all of you, and let me listen. To see if they don't understand me. To see if they understand that a finger up means ...

... they hold that those refrigerator cars can be manufactured here in Mexico. We have to prevent that. Twenty million pesos is one and a half million dollars ...

Plus our commissions.

That ice isn't going to do your cold any good.

Just hay fever. Well, I'll be ...

I'm not through. Furthermore, they claim that the rates the mining companies pay for freight from the central part of the country to the border are extremely low and in fact amount to a subsidy. They say it costs more to ship vegetables than ore.

Nasty, nasty ...

Sure. And you know that if the freight rate goes up, it will become impractical for us to work our mines.

Less profits, sure. Lesprofitsureleslesleslesles ...

What's wrong, Padilla? Padilla, man. What is that damn noise?

'The end of the reel. Just a moment. The other side follows.'

'He isn't listening, Licenciado.'

Padilla must be smiling, for he knows. Padilla knows me. I am listening, all right. Oh, I am listening. And that noise fills my brain with static, that sound of my own voice, my voice in reverse squealing as it speaks backward, chittering like a squirrel, voice like the eleven letters of my name, which can be written a thousand ways Amuc Reoztrir Zurtec Marzi Itzau Erimor, but which has its key, its pattern, Artemio Cruz: ah, I hear my name squeak, run backward, stop:

So be so kind, Mr Corkery, and wire what I tell you to the interests in the United States. So that they will move the press against the communistic railway workers of Mexico.

Sure. If you say they're commies, I feel it my duty to uphold by any means our ...

Yes, yes, yes: how fortunate that our ideals coincide with our interests. And another thing: speak with your ambassador and ask him to put some pressure on the Mexican government. They are new in office and still green.

Oh, we never intervene.

Excuse me. I meant: recommend to the ambassador that he study the situation calmly and offer our government his disinterested opinion, influenced only by his natural concern for the interests of American citizens in Mexico. Let him explain that a favorable climate for investment must be maintained, and that with these riots . . .

Okay, okay.

Oh, what a barrage of meanings, implications, words: oh, what fatigue: oh, what language without language. But I said it, it is my life, and I must hear it. They won't understand my gesture, my fingers can hardly move: but let it be shut off now, I'm bored with it, it means nothing, just crap, crap . . . I have something to say to them:

'You ruled him and ruined him and took him from me.'

'That morning I waited for him with happiness. We rode our horses across the river.'

'I blame you, only you. You are the guilty one.'

Teresa lets the newspaper fall. Leaning close to my bed, Catalina says, as if I can't hear her: 'He looks very bad.'

'Has he said where it is?' Teresa's voice is low.

Catalina shakes her head. 'The lawyers don't have it. He must have written it himself. But he is quite capable of dying without one, just to make life complicated for us.'

I listen to her with closed eyes, pretending, pretending.

'The Father couldn't get anything out of him?'

Catalina must have shaken her head. She kneels by the head of the bed and I hear her voice, quiet and broken: 'How do you feel? Don't you want to talk a little? There's . . . Artemio, there is something very serious. We don't know whether you've left a will. We'd like to know where . . .'

My pain is passing. They fail to see the cold sweat on my forehead, and my motionless tensing. I hear their voices; now I can distinguish their silhouettes. Everything comes into focus and I can see them, their faces, their bodies. I wish the pain would come back into my belly. I tell myself, very clearly I tell myself that I do not love them and have never loved them.

'We'd like to know where . . .'

So: let them go on thinking that they are dealing with a shopkeeper who doesn't give credit, the bitches. A forecloser of mortgages, a crooked lawyer, a quack doctor. Let them think they belong to the chickenshit middleclass, the bitches. Standing in line, getting into line to buy watered milk, pay land taxes, get an appointment, obtain a loan; standing in line to dream that they can get ahead, envying the wife and daughter of Artemio Cruz as they pass in their automobile, their house in the Lomas de Chapultepec, their mink coats, emerald necklaces, trips abroad. Yes: let them imagine that they belong to the world that is empty of my pride and decisions, the world they would know if I were virtuous and humble: down in that world that I know and have risen from. Or up here where I am now: only here, I tell them, is dignity possible, not below in the middle of envy and monotony and standing in lines: all or nothing: do they know that that is how I gamble, all or nothing? All on the red or all on the black, if you have balls. With your balls hanging exposing yourself to be shot by those on top of you, or those below you. That's what it is to be a man, the kind of man I have been and not the kind you wanted . . . half-man, man of petty sulking and confused anger and whorehouses and bistros, postcard virility. Not me! I haven't needed to yell at you, to get drunk so I could frighten you, to beat you in order to have my way. I have never needed to humiliate myself to beg affection of you. I gave you wealth expecting nothing, neither affection nor understanding, and because I demanded nothing of you, you have not been able to leave me; you have clung to my luxuries, cursing me as you would never have cursed my shitty manila pay-envelope; yet forced to respect me as you would have respected my mediocrity: assholes, presumptuous, helpless cunts who have known all the advantages of wealth yet have never lost the sticky souls of the middle class, if you had at least used your advantages, at least understood what wealth is for: while I have had everything, do you hear me, everything that can be bought and also what cannot be bought. I had Regina, I loved Regina, her name was Regina and she loved me, she loved me when I had nothing, she followed me, she gave me life down there, below: do you hear me? But I heard you, Catalina, I heard what you said one day:

'Your father . . . your father, Lorenzo, do you think . . . do

you think God can possibly . . .? I don't know, the holy men . . .
the true martyrs . . .'

'Domine non sum dignus . . .'

Even in the depth of your pain you will smell that incense that
continues to float toward you, and behind your closed eyes you
will know that the windows have been closed, that you are no
longer breathing the fresh afternoon air but are breathing only the
incense, the stink of the priest who will come to give you absolu-
tion, an office you will not request of him and that you will
nevertheless accept in order not to gratify them by a show of
rebellion during your last hours: you will want everything to go
on without your owing anyone anything, and you will want to
remember yourself in a life where no one will owe anything: she
will prevent this, her memory – you will name her: Regina; you
will name her: Laura; you will name her: Catalina; you will
name her: Lilia – will sum all your memories and will force you
to recognize her: but even that gratitude you will transform –
and will know it, behind each cry of biting pain – into self-pity
for the loss of your lost one: who will give you more, to take
more away from you, than that woman, the woman with four
names whom you have loved: who will give you more?

You will resist yourself for you will have made a secret vow,
not to recognize your debts: you will have wrapped Teresa and
Gerardo in the same oblivion, a forgetting that you will justify on
the ground that you will really know nothing about them, the
girl will grow up at her mother's side, far from you, who will
have life only for your son, and she will marry that young man
whose face you will never quite be able to fix in your memory,
that vague grayish young man who must not take up and waste
the grace-time given you for remembering: and Sebastián, you
will not want to remember your schoolmaster Sebastián, those
hands that will lift you by the ear, whack you with a ruler: you
will not want to remember your aching knuckles, your chalk-
whitened fingers, your hours at the blackboard learning to write,

103

to multiply, to draw houses and triangles and circles: you will not want to remember, for these are your debts:

you will groan and arms will hold you down as you try to get up and walk, in order to dull your pain

you will smell the incense

you will smell the closed garden

you will tell yourself that one cannot choose, that one does not need to choose, that on that day you didn't choose: you merely let it happen, you were not responsible, you created neither of the two possibilities that called to you for choice: you could not be responsible for options you did not create: and rising from your writhing body and the machete that stabs your guts until your tears run, you will dream of that arrangement of life, made by you, which you can never reveal because the world will give you no chance to but will offer you only its established commandments, its warring codes, which you will not live and about which you will neither dream nor think:

the incense will be an odor that measures time, a smell that means something:

Father Paéz will live in your home, he will be hidden in the basement by Catalina: and what will happen will not be your fault, it won't be your responsibility:

you will not remember what you and the priest say to each other that night in the basement, whether it was you or he who said it: what can you call a grotesque who of his own free will dresses like a woman, castrates himself, and voluntarily becomes drunk on the fake blood of a God, but who loves, I swear it, the love of God being great and deep and the tenant of all our bodies, giving them their apology for being: it is by God's grace and blessing that we have these bodies and can offer them the moments of love of which life always wants to despoil us: you don't feel ashamed, you don't feel anything, but indeed will forget your agonies, which cannot be sins because all the words and acts of our hurried brief love, always today's love and never tomorrow's, are only a consolation that we ourselves give ourselves in acceptance of that necessary evil that justifies our contrition: for how can we be contrite without recognizing the evil in us? how can we kneel and beg forgiveness for sin unless we have sinned? forget your life, let me put the light out, forget everything, and later we will pray together for forgiveness and will beg that our moments of love be erased, that we may consecrate this body which was created by God and speaks of God in every desire satisfied or frustrated, in every secret caress, in the ejaculation of the semen that God Himself planted:

to live is to betray your God: every life-act, every act that affirms we are living beings, requires the violation of your God's commandments;

and that night you will talk with Major Gavilán in a whorehouse, with all your old comrades, and you will not remember what was said, or whether they said it or you said it, speaking with a cold voice that will not be the voice of men but of power and self-interest: we desire the greatest possible good for our country, so long as it accords with our own good; let us be intelligent and we can go far: let us accomplish the necessary, not attempt the impossible: let us decide here tonight what acts of cruelty and force are needed now to make it possible for us to avoid cruelty and force later: let us parcel out well-being, that the people may have their smell of it; the Revolution can satisfy them now, but tomorrow they may ask for more and more, and what would we have left to offer if we should give everything already? except, perhaps, our lives, our lives: and why die if we thereby do not live to see the benificent fruits of our heroic deaths? we are men, not martyrs: if we hold on to power, nothing will not be permitted: lose power and they'll fuck us: have a sense of destiny, we are young and we glitter with successful armed revolution: why have we fought, to die of hunger? when force is necessary, it is justified: power may not be divided:

and tomorrow? tomorrow we will be in our graves, Deputy Cruz, leaving those who follow to arrange the world as best they can:

domine non sum dignus, domine non sum dignus: yes, a man who can speak sorrowfully with God, a man who can forgive sin because he has committed sin, a priest who has the right to be a priest because his human wretchedness allows him to effect the redemption of his own body before he grants redemption to the rest of us: *domine non sum dignus:*

you will reject your guilt; you will not agree to be judged by a law you did not create but found already made: you would have loved
loved
loved
loved
oh, how happy were those days with your teacher Sebastián, whom you will no longer want to remember, seated at his knee learning those elemental principles that you must abandon to become a free man rather than a slave to commandments which were written without your participation: oh, how happy were those days of apprenticeship when he gave you what you needed to make your way in life, days of forge and hammers when Sebastián came home already tired but gave you solitary instruction, so that you might amount to something and make your own commandments: you, the rebel, you free, new, unique: you will not want to remember that: he sent you and you went, to the Revolution: and this memory does not come from me and will not reach to you:
you will have no reply to the codes, one opposing and the other imposed;
you innocent,
you will want to be innocent,
that night you did not choose,
you did not choose, that night.

[1927: November 23]

His green eyes looked toward the window and the fat man asked him if he didn't want something to drink and he blinked and his green eyes looked toward the window. Then the fat man, who until that moment had remained very, very calm, jerked a pistol from his belt and slammed it down on the table: he heard the bang and the rattle of the glasses and bottles and he stretched out his hand but the other was already smiling, smiling even before he could identify that abrupt gesture, explain the noise and the shaking of the blue crystal glasses and the white bottles, and name the sudden sensation in the pit of his stomach. The fat man smiled, and a car raced down the alley to shouts and curses of alarm, and the headlights flashed across the fat man's round head. The fat man spun the cylinder of the revolver and indicated that it held only two cartridges; spun it again, cocked it, and put the muzzle to his temple. He tried to fix his eye somewhere but the tiny room offered no point of focus: bare walls, painted blue, and the bare stone floor, the two tables, the two chairs, the two men. The fat man waited for his green eyes to finish their circuit of the room and return to his fist, the revolver, the side of his head. The fat man was smiling but also sweating, and he was sweating too. He tried to hear the tick of the watch in his vest pocket. Perhaps it was not so loud as his heart. Anyhow, the report of the pistol was already in his ears; yet at the same time the silence was like wire and drowned out all possible sound, including a pistol shot. The fat man waited. He watched. The fat man pulled the trigger. A dry metal snap lost itself in the silence, and outside, night went on just as before, moonless. The pistol was still pointed at the fat man's head and the fat man began to smile, to laugh, to guffaw: his fat body shook from inside, like a custard, from the inside of flesh that did not even quiver. For several seconds they remained so and he did not move; he was smelling the scent of incense that had gone with him everywhere since that morning, and looking at the fat man through imaginary fumes of incense; the fat man continued laughing from inside before putting the pistol on the table again and with stubby yellow fingers slowly pushing it toward him. The confused happiness in the fat man's eyes might mean held-back tears; he did not want to know. His stomach still tightened at the memory, not yet a memory, of that obese figure with the pistol pointed at its thick head; the fat man's fear, above all the way that fear was controlled, cramped his guts and kept him silent: it would be the end if they should find him in this room with the fat man dead, if they should know there had been a quarrel: he had already recognized that the pistol was his own, kept always in a drawer of the chest, and now he saw that the fat man's stubby hand was not touching the metal, a handkerchief was wrapped around the butt, so that perhaps he could have knocked it out of his hand in time: but if he had tried to knock the pistol down and failed, the suicide would have been obvious. Obvious to whom? A police commandant dies in an empty room faced by his enemy. Who disposed of whom? The fat man loosened his belt and drank off his glass at one gulp. Sweat stained his armpits and ran down his collar. Those stubby, cut-off looking fingers kept pushing the pistol nearer. What should he say? That everything had been proved, the fat man went on, on his part: so, was he going to switch? He asked what had been proved, and the fat man said, that about himself, on his part, no doubt remained: as he had just risked death, so he was not going to chicken out; one did not go on flying the same kite forever, that's the way things go. If this doesn't convince you, then I don't know what will. So, he said to the fat man, that was a proof that he should join them: that one of them had demonstrated at the cost of risking his life that they wanted him? He lit a cigarette, offering one to the fat man and then striking the match and holding it toward the fat man's coffee brown face; but the fat man blew the match out, and he felt surrounded. He picked up the pistol and left the cigarette balanced on the lip of his glass without noticing that ashes fell into the tequila and sank to the bottom. He pressed the muzzle against his temple and the metal had no temperature at all, though he thought it ought to feel cold, and it came to him that he was thirty-eight years old but that this fact was not very important to anyone, and less important to the fat man and even less important to himself.

And that morning he had dressed before the big oval mirror and the thick smell of incense had reached his nostrils and he had stopped for a moment. From the garden, from the clean dry November earth, came the scent of the chestnuts. He looked at himself in the glass: a strong man with strong arms and a flat lean belly where hard muscles were plaited below the dark umbilicus. He ran his hands over his broken nose, smelling the incense again. He took a clean shirt from the chest of drawers and did not notice that his revolver was gone, and finished dressing and opened the bedroom door, thinking: I don't have time, I don't really have time. I tell you that I don't have time.

The garden had been planted with decorative rose-bushes and shrubs laid out in horse-shoes and fleur-de-lis, a green border around the house, which was two-story, Florentine, with slim columns and plaster friezes at the porch entrance. The outside walls were pink. In the rooms, as he passed through that morning, the early light outlined gilt candelabra, marble statuary, velvet drapes, high brocaded chairs, glass cabinets, the gold filets in the love seats. He stopped at the side door at the back of the living room with his hand on the doorhandle. He did not want to open it and descend.

'He was one of those who went to live in France. We bought it for little or nothing, but the restoration was expensive. I told my husband: let me take care of it, just let me handle it, for I know how ...'

The fat man jumped from his chair and knocked the pistol aside: no one heard the shot, for the hour was late and they were alone; yes, probably that was why no one heard it: the bullet buried itself in the blue wall and the commandant laughed and said enough of games now, and especially of dangerous games: why? when everything could be so easily arranged? Why? So easily, he thought; this is the age of easy arrangements. Will I never live peacefully?

'Why don't they leave me be? Why don't they?'

'But that is obvious, you're important. It all hangs upon you.'

'Where are we?'

He had not come, they had brought him; and though he knew that they were downtown in the center of the city, the driver had bewildered him, right, left, right, had changed the simple Spanish rectangular system of streets into a labyrinth. It was all bewildering, like the short stubby hand of the man who had knocked the gun away and was now sitting down again still laughing, again heavy, fat, and sweaty, with his eyes sparking.

'And aren't you and I the sons of bitches?' the fat man chuckled. 'Eh? Always make sure your friends are sons of bitches, then you know your friend won't fuck you. Let's have a drink.'

They drank and the fat man said that this world is divided into sons of bitches and poor bastards, and you choose which you want to be. He added that it would be a shame if the deputy –

if he – did not know enough to choose in time. They, the fat man and his fellow sons of bitches, were honest and very gentlemanly, they offered everyone his choice, but not everyone was as smart as the deputy, some were stubborn and thought they were tough and tried to make trouble ... when it was so easy to change horses, to wake up on the right side of the bed, who shouldn't prefer that to ...? Nor will it be the first time you have changed sides, will it? Eh? Pah, where have you been these past fifteen years! The voice lulled on, as heavy and oily as the fat man himself: a buzzing snake throat of fat rings lubricated by alcohol and Havana cigars: would he care for one?

He continued to rub his silver belt buckle abstractly, while the other watched him with fixed eyes, until the metal reminded him of the cold or warmth of the pistol.

'The priests are going to be shot tomorrow. I tell you this as another proof of our friendship, and because I know you aren't a blabbermouth.'

They pushed their chairs back. The fat man went to the window and rapped on the glass sharply, and made a sign, and then held out his hand to him. He left the fat man in the doorway and went down a stinking dark shaft of stairs; he had to step over a garbage bucket, and everything smelled of rotting orange peels and wet newspaper. The man standing beside the street door raised a finger to his white sombrero and pointed the way to Avenida 16 de Septiembre.

'Well, what do you think?'

'That we damn well better change sides.'

'Not me.'

'And you?'

'Not me.'

'And you?'

'I'm listening.'

'Is anybody else listening?'

'Saturn can be trusted and she doesn't let gossip leak out.'

'If it does, I'll gossip and leak her too.'

'We made it with the Chief and they'll break us with him.'

'He is through. The new man has a good organization, a good team.'

'Well, what do you propose?'
'Answer "here," I say.'
'I'll let them cut my ears first! What the hell are we?'
'What?'
'There are ways and there are ways.'
'But right now, not so easy to find.'
'No. Whoever quits . . .'
'No, no, I don't say that.'
'Like maybe yes and maybe no at the same time.'
'Bullshit. I say play it like men, one or the other, the old man
or the new man.'
'General, wake up. It's getting light.'
'So what's decided?'
'Well, it's like this. Every man knows where he stands.'
'I would say . . .'
'Then you really think the Chief won't come through this?'
'I think so, I think so.'
'What?'
'No . . . I'm not sure, but that's what I think.'
'And you . . . have you decided?'
'That's how it's beginning to look to me too.'
'Just keep in mind when the time comes that we never talked
it over.'
'One can forget what never happened.'
'I mean, just in case there's any doubt.'
'Those goddamn doubts.'
'Ah, shut up. Bring us a drink there.'
'Those goddamn doubts, monsieur.'
'Together? Yes or no.'
'Together, yes, but each little goat by his own little road.'
'So that at the end they can go on sharing the acorns where
they always did.'
'Right. That's it.'
'Aren't you going to eat something, General Jiménez?'
'Every man knows his own story.'
'And if anyone talks . . .'
'Shit, what are you thinking about, brother? Aren't all of us
here brothers?'

'I might say yes. But then one thinks of the little mother who gave birth to all of us, and one begins to wonder.'

'Those goddamn doubts, as Saturn says.'

'These double goddamn doubts, Colonel Gavilán.'

'And all you can do is agree, or . . .'

'You go alone and you decide alone. That's it.'

'Still, one would like to preserve his hide intact.'

'And his honor, Señor Deputy. Always his honor.'

'Honor, General. I wouldn't want it otherwise.'

'So . . .?'

'Nothing, we haven't said a word.'

'Nothing, nothing.'

'Are they really going to wipe out the Chief?'

'Which Chief, the present or the former one?'

'The old one, the old one . . .'

Chicago, Chicago, that toddlin' town . . .

Saturn lifted the needle from the phonograph and clapped her hands.

'All right, girls, quiet down.'

He put on his flat straw hat and opened the curtains, laughing, and saw them out of the corner of his eye reflected in the room's dirty mirror, brown-skinned girls whitened by powder, with beauty-spots penciled on their cheeks, their breasts, beside their lips; satin and patent-leather slippers, short skirts, blue eyelids; and Cerbero, powdered and madeup too, holding out his hand and saying:

'My little present, sir?'

And it would work out very well, he reflected as he rubbed his belly and paused in the small garden in front of Saturn's house of assignations and breathed the soft, fresh mist from the water in the fountain of velvet slime, very well: General Jiménez by now would have taken off his blue spectacles and would be knuckling his dry eyelids as the scales of his conjunctivitis dropped slowly down on his beard: he would be asking someone to pull his boots off, for he was tired and used to having his boots pulled off for him, and they would all laugh because when the girl bent over to tug, the General would hoist her skirts and show her round dark buttocks covered by lilac silk, and some would be looking not at the girl's butt but at the rarer sight of the General's always hidden eyes open for once like fat insipid oysters; and all of them, comrades, brothers, colleagues, would hold their arms out and have their coats removed by Saturn's young roomers, who would buzz like bees around the men in uniform as if there were some mystery about what is beneath a tunic, the buttons with eagle and serpent, the gold rank pips: he had seen them like that, still wet behind the ears, fluttering like that around him too, with their mestizo arms high and the powder and the puff in their hands, whitening the heads of their good friends, their wonderful friends the comrade brothers lying on the beds with their legs apart and their shirts splotched with cognac, their heads running sweat but their hands dry, while the beat of the Charleston throbbed and the girls slowly undressed them, kissing each part as it was bared and squealing when the men grabbed at them: he looked at his fingernails with the white tips that are called proof of lies, and the half-moon of his thumb, and very near him, the dog barked. He turned up the collar of his coat and walked homeward, though he would have preferred to return to the whorehouse and sleep with powdered arms around him and free himself of that acid that gnawed his nerves and made him stand there with his eyes wide staring purposelessly at the files of low, gray houses with balconies loaded with vases of porcelain encrusted with glass, the rows of dry palms that dustily lined the avenue; staring, smelling: cobs from roast corn, enchilada scraps, vinagrettes.

He ran his hand over his bushy beard, and looked through the keyring. She would be there in the basement at this moment: she who went up and down the carpeted stairs without the least sound and was always startled to see him enter: '*Ay*, what a fright you gave me. I didn't expect you. No, I didn't expect you so soon, I swear I wasn't looking for you so soon.' He asked himself why she made his arrivals so much a sort of secret plot . . . he came home too soon always, which was always his fault. Their meetings, the attraction opposed even before he started to respond to it, the mutual rejection that at times drew them together, was nameless before and nameless after: both acts were the same, approach and withdrawal. Once in the dark their fingers had touched on the banister and she had squeezed his hand and he had turned on the light; she was coming down the stairs as he was going up; her face was not like her hand and at once she snapped the light off; he wanted to call it perversity but that was not the word either, for what is habitual, neither premeditated nor unusual, is not perverse. Yet as a woman he knew her still: soft, wrapped in silk and soft sheets, to be touched rather than seen because at such times the bedroom lights were always off: one moment when their hands had touched and she did not hide her face or put on a mask. Just once, so there was no reason to remember it, yet his stomach warmed with the bittersweet desire to repeat that moment. He thought about it and told himself that it had been repeated this morning; in the dark of dawn on the rail of the basement stairs, her hand had touched his and she had said, though no light was burning, 'What are you looking for here?' before correcting herself and saying in an even voice: '*Ay*, what a fright you gave me! I didn't expect you. No, I didn't expect you, I swear I wasn't looking for you so early.' Her voice even, without mockery, and he merely stood there smelling that almost incarnate odor of incense, that odor with a voice and singsong words.

He opened the basement door and at first could not see him, because the incense smoke was so thick, and she took the black arm as he tried to hide the folds of his cassock between his legs and to disperse the holy fumes by waving his arms, until suddenly he realized the futility of this, of her protection and his black and exaggerated fear; then he lowered his head in a gesture of completion, as if to assure himself comfortingly that he was successfully adopting, for his own satisfaction if not for the satisfaction of his two witnesses, neither of whom was looking at him, they were looking at each other; that he had adopted successfully the consecrated attitude of resignation. The priest pleaded with the man who had just entered to see him, to recognize him, but out of the corner of lowered eyes saw that he could not take his gaze from the woman, nor she hers from his; the more she tried to conceal and protect her minister of God guest, the more her eyes were gripped by these of her husband; and the priest felt his stomach churn and the veins of his eyes yellow and his tongue become thick with the promise of the terror that, when the moment came – the moment before the moment, for there would be no other – he would not be able to hide. Only this moment remained, he was thinking, to accept his fate, but in this moment he had no witnesses. The man with green eyes was asking his wife to beg, that she dare to ask, risking the chance of his yes or no, and she could not respond, she could not answer. And that day when she abandoned the possibility of responding and asking, the priest reflected, she had sacrificed him, his own life. The candlelight was caught by the transparency and glow of her skin; the candlelight threw black shadows that repeated the profile of her face, her throat, her arms. The man waited for her to speak, to ask, and saw the tightening of that throat he would have liked to kiss. The priest sighed: she was not going to ask anything and so for him, standing before the man with green eyes, there remained only this one moment in which to express his resignation, because tomorrow he would not be able to, it would be impossible, resignation would forget its name and would be called guts and guts don't know the words of God.

He slept until noon. An organ-grinder in the street woke him with an intermittent song that the silence of the night before – or its memory, which was the night and silence – broke into, and then the melody would start again with a slow melancholy that floated up through the half-open window, until noiseless memory made a new interruption. The telephone rang. He picked it up and heard the fat man's laugh, as controlled as the laugh of an actor, and:

'Hello.'

'We have him in the precinct station, Señor Deputy.'

'Yes?'

'The President has been informed.'

'So ...?'

'You know. Some little gesture. A visit. You don't have to say anything.'

'When?'

'Drop by today about two.'

'Good, I'll see you.'

In the adjacent bedroom she had been listening with her ear

glued to the door and she began to cry. Then she did not hear anything. She dried her cheeks before sitting down in front of her mirror.

He bought a paper from a newsboy and tried to scan it as he drove, but could read only the headlines announcing the execution by firing squad of those who had made an attempt upon the life of the candidate. He thought of the old man, his chief, in the great moments, during the campaign against Villa, in the presidential palace when they all swore their loyalty; his eye caught a photograph of Father Pro collapsing, with his arms spread, before the execution volley. Beside him ran the white canvas tops of new automobiles; women's short skirts and cloche hats were passing, and the balloon trousers of elegant young men; bootblacks squatted on their heels around the frog fountain. But it was not the city that his glassy and fixed eyes saw, but the word: he savored it, saw it in the quick looks that crossed his from sidewalks, in the postures, the shrugged shoulders, the coarse finger-signs. He felt himself dangerously alive, gripping the steering-wheel, intoxicated by the faces, the gestures, the fuck-fingers of the streets, caught between two swings of the pendulum. Today you fuck them because tomorrow, fatally, those you have fucked today will fuck you. Light shining back from glass blinded him and he lifted his hand to his eyelids: he had always known how to choose well, to turn to the rising sun and away from the descending. The immensity of the Zócolo opened before him, street-merchants' little stands set up among the arcade pillars, the cathedral bells intoning two in deep bronze. He showed his credentials as a Deputy to the guard at the entrance on Moneda. Crystalline winter air of the high plateau sharpened the silhouettes of old ecclesiastical Mexico, and groups of students in examination time came by from Argentina and Brazil streets. He parked in the wide patio. He went up in the elevator cage. Rooms of purple rosewood and bright chandeliers. He took a seat in the anteroom. Very low voices became louder only when unctuously pronouncing one word:

'The President.'
'The Prahsahdunt.'
'The Pressadint.'

The fat man grabbed his arms and they embraced, pounding each other on the back and ribs, and the fat man was laughing from inside as always and made a gesture with his finger of shooting himself in the head, and again laughed silently with that silent shaking of belly and dark cheeks. With difficulty the fat man buttoned the collar of his uniform, and he asked whether he had read the papers; yes, he said, he had, and now he understood the game, but this had no importance, he had come only to reiterate his loyalty to, his unconditional support of, the President; and the fat man asked him if he had anything in mind and he said yes, there were certain vacant public properties, just fields, on the outskirts of the city, which now were worthless but in time might perhaps be subdivided. The fat man agreed to take care of the matter, for after all, they were brothers now, they were practically twins, and the good Deputy had been fighting the good fight since . . . oh, way back in '13, and now had a right to live in security, far from the shifting sands of politics; he said this and slapped him on the arm and the back and the buttocks to seal their friendship. The gold-handled door opened and out came General Jiménez, Colonel Gavilán, and other friends who the night before had been at Saturn's; they passed without looking at him, with their heads down, and the fat man laughed and told him that many old friends of his seemed to have felt the urge to come put themselves at the President's disposition in this hour of national unity, and by an extended arm he was invited to enter.

At the other end of the office, by a green light, he saw those eyes, those eyes of a tiger in ambush. He lowered his head and said:

'I am yours to command, Señor President. To serve you unconditionally, I assure you, Señor President.'

I smell the oil they smear on my eyes, my nose, my lips, my cold feet and blue hands, my thighs, around my genitals, and I ask them to open the window: I want to breathe. I breathe through my nostrils with a hollow snoring, and I let them do what they will, and I cross my arms over my stomach. The sheet-linen, its freshness. That is something important. What do they know, Catalina, the priest, Teresa, Gerardo?

'Let me be.'

'What does the doctor know? I know him better than any doctor. It's another trick.'

'Don't say any more.'

'Teresita, don't contradict your father ... I mean, your mother. Don't you see that ...'

'Ha. You're just as responsible as he is. You for weakness and cowardice, he for ... for ...'

'Enough, enough.'

'Good afternoon.'

'Here.'

'Enough, for God's sake.'

'Go on, go on ...'

What was I thinking about? What was I remembering?

'... like beggars. Why should Gerardo be forced to work?'

What do they know, Catalina, the priest, Teresa, Gerardo? What importance are their boasts going to have, or the statements of sympathy that will appear in the newspapers? Who will have the honesty to say, as I say now, that my only love has been material possessions, sensual acquisition? Property, that is what I want. The sheet that I touch. And everything else before me now. A floor of Italian marble veined green and black. Bottles that preserve distant summers. Old paintings with scaling varnish that recapture the light of sun or chandeliers, that invite slow perusal by sight and by touch, seated on a sofa of white leather touched with gold, with a glass of cognac in one hand and a cigar in the other, dressed in a light, silk smoking jacket and soft patent-leather slippers, on a deep soft wool carpet: and there a man owns the landscape or the faces of other men, there, or seated on a terrace facing the Pacific, watching the sun set and allowing one's senses, the tautest of them, the most delicious of them, to repeat the back and forth slide of the silvered waves on the wet sand. Land. Land that can change itself into money.

Land laid out in city blocks over which rise the forests of construction's reinforcing steel. Yellow and green country acres, always the richest, near the dams, worked by growling tractors. Vertical land beneath ore-rich mountains. Machines: the delicious smell of the rotary press spitting sheets with an accelerated rhythm . . .

Eh, Don Artemio, aren't you feeling good?

No, it's the heat. This damn sun. What's new, Mena? Mind opening those windows?

Right away . . .

Ah, the street sounds. All together and at once: one cannot be separated from another.

What did you want, Don Artemio?

Mena, you know how enthusiastically, right up to the last moment, we defended Batista here. But now that he is no longer in power, it's not so easy; and it's less easy to defend General Trujillo even though he is still in power. You represent both of them and you must understand . . . It leaves little . . .

Well, now, don't worry about it, Don Artemio, I'll find a way to take care of things, even in spite of all the hooting. And speaking of this, I have some copy here explaining the work of the Benefactor . . . If you will . . .

Certainly, leave them with me. Ah, look, Díaz, how fortunate that you've come. Run this on the editorial page with a fictitious signature. Well, good day, Mena. I'll expect your news.

Your news. News. I will expect your news. News of my white lips . . . *aaay*, a hand, give me a hand, *aaay*, somebody else's pulse to revive mine, white lips . . .

'I blame you, only you.'

'Do you feel better? Do it: Let us ride our horses across the river. Let us return to where I was born. My birth-region.'

' . . . we'd like to know where . . .'

So at last and at last they give me that pleasure: they come on their knees, physically on their knees, to ask me. The priest beat them to it. Some disaster must be very close when the women too come to the head of my bed like a little earthquake I can't help noticing. They are trying to see through my joke, this final travesty that I have enjoyed so much alone, this final humiliation the last consequences of which I will not be able to enjoy, but whose initial spasms delight me now. Perhaps this will be the last little triumph ...

'Where?' I murmur with such sweetness, such dissimulation. 'Where ...? Let me think ... Teresa, I think I remember ... Isn't there a little mahogany case ... where I keep my cigars ...? It has a double bottom ...'

I don't have to finish. The two women jump up and run to the enormous horseshoe table where they think that I sometimes, at night, pass hours of insomnia reading: they wish that were what I did then. They force the drawers, scatter papers, and at last find an ebony box. Oh, so it was there. There was, I thought, another. Now they have found the other. Their fingers open the double bottom in haste, twisting it off. Nothing there. When did I eat last? I urinated, but not for some time. But to eat. I vomited. But to eat.

The under-secretary on the telephone, Don Artemio.

They closed the curtains, right? It is night, right? And there are plants that must have the light of darkness in order to flower, they wait until darkness comes out, the moonflower, it opens its petals in the evening. The moonflower. There was a moonflower vine on that hut near the river. It opened its flowers in the evening.

Thank you, señorita. Hello ... Yes, Artemio Cruz. No, no, no, no worthwhile conciliation is possible. It's a clear attempt to over- throw the government. They have already managed to pull the union out of the official party, in mass. If this continues, how will you people sustain yourselves, Señor Under-secretary? Yes ... That's the only way: declare the strike non-existent, draft them into the army, destroy them at one clean blow and jail their leaders. It will be as if it hadn't happened, Señor ...

Mimosa, too, I remember that mimosa also has feeling: it can be sensitive and modest, aristocratic and trembling, it lives, mimosa ...

... yes, certainly. And something else, to speak plainly: if you gentlemen show yourselves weak, my associates and I will of course have to remove our capital from Mexico. We need some guarantees.

Listen, what would happen, for example, if two hundred million
dollars were to leave the country in the space of two weeks? Eh?
No, not if I understand you. That's all that is needed!
There. The tape has ended. Ah. That was all of it. Was that
all of it? Who knows, I don't remember. For quite some time I
haven't been listening to those taped voices, I've just been pretending to listen, really I have been thinking about other matters,
things I like to eat: it is more important to think about food, for
I haven't eaten for hours; and Padilla disconnects the recorder
and I have kept my eyes closed and don't know what they are
thinking, what they are saying, Catalina and Teresa and Gerardo
and the girl – no, Gloria left, she left some time ago with Padilla's
son, they are necking in the living room, enjoying the chance to
be alone together – what they are saying, because I keep my eyes
closed and think only of pork chops, prime ribs, barbecued goat,
stuffed turkey, about the soups I like so much, almost as much
as I like desserts; yes, I was always one for sweets and here the
desserts are delicious, desserts of almond and pineapple, coconut
and clotted milk, ah, ah! and burned milk too, *chongos* as they
make them in Zamora, glazed fruit, and red snapper, sea bass,
flounder, oysters and crabs
    'We rode our horses across the river. And we went as far as
the sandspit and the sea. In Veracruz.'
    gooseneck barnacles, octopus and squid, *ceviches*, beer as bitter
as the sea, beer, Yucatán venison, and I am not old although once
in a mirror I was old, and the old cheeses, how I love them: I
think, I want, and it makes me feel better, how boring to listen
to my own voice, precise, authoritative, insinuating, always playing the same role, always, what tedium, when I could be eating,
eating, eating: I eat, I sleep, I fornicate, and the rest, what?
what? what? Who wants to eat sleep fornicate and the rest with
my money? you Padilla and you Catalina and you Teresa and
you Gerardo and you Paquito Padilla – is that your name? what
are you doing chewing my grand-daughter's lips in the living
room, you who are still a kid, because I don't live here, you are
all young but I know how to live well and that's why I don't live
here, I'm an old man, am I? an old man ridden by manias, who

has the right to his manias because that night he fucked them, he fucked them all, he chose in time, and like that other night, ah, now I have remembered her, that night, that word, that woman: damn it, have them bring me something to eat: why don't they bring me something to eat: out, get out: *ay*, pain: get out, out: fuck your mothers:

You will say it, it is your word and your word is my word: word of honor, man's word, word that lasts, coin word that everyone spends: imprecation, snapping greeting, life word, brother word, memory, voice of the hopeless, man's extravagance, boss word, invitation to a brawl, call to labor, epigraph for love, bastards' word, threat, mock, oath, comrade word at fiesta and binge, claim to guts and balls, magic saber, height of chicanery, white word and nigger word, frontier barrier, resumé of our history, Mexico's saint and countersign, your word and my word
  Fuck your mother
  Fuckin' bastard
  We fuck 'em all
  Quit fucking around
  And I'm really going to fuck him
  Come on, you little fucker
  Don't let them fuck you
  I fucked the bitch
  Fuck you
  Go fuck yourself
  Get a fucking move on
  I fucked him out of a thousand pesos
  Break your fucking ass but don't give up
  My fucking kids
  I was fucked on that job
  Don't fuck up the whole day
  We're all fucked
  The bitch fucked him
  I fuck around but I'm no quitter

The Indians got fucked, and the Spaniards fucked us
I don't like fuckin' gringos
Viva Mexico, you fuckin' fucked up fuckers frigging forking fugging firking mucking screwing plowing plugging screwed up fouled up: the word's offspring. Born of fucking, dead from fucking, living fucked: pregnant belly and winding sheet, hidden in the word. It faces you everywhere, it deals your hand, cuts your deck, covers your bet, disguises reticence and the double-cross, reveals cowardice and bravery, intoxicates, shouts, succumbs, lives in every bed, presides over the ceremonies of friendship, of hatred, and of power: our word, you and I, members of the lodge, the fraternity of the fucked: you are what you are because you knew how to fuck 'em without letting them fuck you; you are what you are because you didn't fuck around: chain-gang of the fucked, linked before and behind, joined to all who have lost and preceded us, to all who will lose and follow us: heir to being fucked by those who stand above you, inheriting the right to fuck those who crawl below you: child of the children of the word, father of sons of the word: our word, looking out at us from every face, behind every gesture, yet an outcast: prick, shit, ass-hole, schmuck, the word provides your promises, secures your sacrifice, and you fuck yourself: lonely foreskin, you have no mother but you have your word: mother-fucker, you have your buddy: ass-hole buddies, you have your wives or your fists, your old women and your office chippies, and you have the word: with the word you rattle closet skeletons, with the word you feel fine and with the word you fart around and with the word you grow old; you advance with the word and with guts, you are as truthful as the word, you hang to the tit of the word

And where do you go with the word?

oh, mystery, oh, deception, oh, nostalgia: you think that the word will carry you back to your beginning: but to what beginning? Not yours: no one wants to return to the lie of a Golden Age, to illegitimacy, the animal moan, the struggle for bone and the cave and flint-stone; to the sacrifice and the madness, the nameless terror of that beginning, to the consecrated fetish, to fear of sun, storm, eclipse, fire, to fear of masks and idols, fear of puberty, of water, hunger, helplessness, cosmic terror: the word, the pyramid of your negations, the bloody altar of your fright

oh, mystery, oh, deception, oh, mirror facing a mirror: do you believe that you can go forward with the word, that you will affirm yourself? Forward to what future? Not to yours: no one wants to go on to damnation, suspicion, frustration, resentment, hate, envy, rancor, despight, insecurity, misery, abuse, insult, intimidation, false pride, bravado, with the fucking corruption of your fucking word

leave the word behind you, kill it with borrowed arms, destroy it: murder the word that stands between us, makes stone of us, rots us with its poison mixed of idolatry and the cross: so that it cannot be either our reply or our destiny

pray, while the priest anoints your lips, your nose, your eyelids, your legs, your penis, with the last unction: pray, that the word be neither our answer nor our destiny: word, children of the word, the word that poisons love, breaks friendship, hardens tenderness, the word that divides, destroys, envenoms: cunt friezed with serpents and obsidian; drunken belch of the priest on the pyramid, the lord on the throne, the princes of the church in the cathedral: smoke, Spain, and Anáhuac; smoke, payments on the word, excreta of the word, the word's highlands, the word's sacrifices, honors, slavitudes, temples, and tongues: and who will you fuck today in order to exist? and who tomorrow? who will you fuck, who will you use: the sons of the word are those beings you will change into objects for your employment, pleasure, mastery, despight, victory, your life: the son of the word is a thing you use: better than nothing

you tire

you never beat it

you hear the murmur of other prayers that do not listen to your prayer that the word be neither our answer nor our destiny: cleanse yourself of the word

you tire

you never beat it

you made it your life road

you too are a son of the word

of betrayal absolved by your betrayal of others

of the oblivion you have needed in order to remember
of the endless chain of our injustice
you tire
you tire me and conquer me: you force me down to that hell
with you: you want to remember other things, not this: you
make me forget that nothing is, that nothing has been, yet something will be: with the word you defeat me
you tire
rest, then
dream about your innocence
say what you have tried and what you will try: say that one
day rape will pay you back in your own coin, will reveal its other
side: when you as a young man will want to betray what as an
old man you have had to be grateful for: the day when you will
notice something, the end of something: a day when you will
wake – I conquer you – and will look in the mirror and at last
will see that you have left something behind: you will remember
it, that first day stripped of your youth, that first day of a new
time: think of it, for you will think of it, solid as a statue in order
to be seen in all dimensions: you will push aside the curtains so
that the early breeze can enter: oh, how it will empty you, and
you will, ah, forget that smell of incense and the smell that
follows where you lead, oh, how it will cleanse you: the breeze
will not let you think of any doubt, it will not lead you to the
thread

[1947: September 11]

He pushed aside the curtains and breathed the clean air. The
early breeze came in, rippling the curtains. He looked out: these
hours of dawn were the best, the most serene, in a spring that
was repeated daily. Before long the drumming sun would suffocate them. But at seven, the beach before the balcony shone with
peaceful freshness along its silent curve. Waves scarcely murmured and the voices of the few bathers were not enough to
disturb the ritual encounter of the morning sun, the tranquil sea,

and sands combed by tides. He pushed aside the curtains and breathed the clean air. Three very small children were going along the sand with their buckets, gathering the treasures left by night: starfish, shells, bits of polished wood. A sailboat rocked close to the coast. Transparent sky reached over the land through a filter of the palest green. Not a single car moved on the avenue that separated the hotel from the beach.

He let the curtain drop and walked to the bath with its moorish tiles. In the mirror he saw his face swollen with sleep that, nevertheless, had been short and so different. He closed the door softly. He opened the taps and stopped the basin, and threw his pajama top over the cover of the toilet seat. He got out a new blade, removed the waxed paper wrapping, and fitted it into the gold-plated razor. He dropped the razor in the hot water and soaked a towel and covered his face with it. Vapor rose from the basin and steamed the glass, and he wiped it clear with his hand. He snapped on the fluorescent tube over the mirror. His shaving cream was a new product from the United States, brushless. He smeared the white, refreshing cream on his cheeks, chin, and neck. Taking the razor out of the hot water, he burned his fingers, and he shook them in irritation for a moment and then raised his left hand to stretch the skin of his cheek; he began shaving, downward, carefully, twisting his mouth. The steam made him sweat, he felt the drops running down his ribs. Now he shaved close; he rubbed his chin to assure himself of the smoothness, and opened the taps and soaked the towel and covered his face with it again. He wiped off his ears, then doused his face with an astringent lotion that made him exhale with pleasure. He washed the blade and dried it and put it back in the razor, and the razor back in the leather case. Gray soapy water swirled down the drain, sucking the whiskers with it. He observed his face in the mirror: he wanted to find it the same as always, for as he wiped the glass clean again he felt, without being clearly aware of it in this early hour of insignificant, merely necessary chores, of slight indigestions and vague hungers, of undesired smells that rise from the unconscious life of sleep; he felt that for a long time he had been looking at himself every day in the bathroom mirror without really seeing himself. Rectangle of glass and quicksilver, the only truthful portrait of his face with green eyes and energetic mouth, wide forehead, prominent cheekbones. He opened his mouth and stuck out his white-spotted tongue; then he checked the gaps of the missing teeth. His bridges were at the bottom of a glass of water in the medicine cabinet; he took them out, rinsed them quickly, and, turning his back to the mirror, fitted them in. He squeezed greenish paste on the brush and cleaned his teeth, gargled, loosened his pajama pants, and turned on the shower, testing the water with his hand. The uneven spray splashed on his back as he rubbed soap over his lean body, the ribs, soft belly, the muscles that still kept a certain nervous tension but now tended to sag inward, in a way that seemed grotesque to him, if he didn't keep a close watch on his posture, especially when he was observed, as during these days, by impertinent glances around the hotel and the beach. He held his face in the spray, shut the water off, and rubbed down with the towel. Again he felt pleased when he dashed his chest and armpits with lavender and ran the comb through his curly hair. He took a pair of bathing trunks and a white polo shirt from the bathroom closet. He slipped on his Italian beach sandals and cautiously opened the door.

The breeze was still swaying the curtains and the sun was hot and bright: it would be a shame, a real shame, to let such a day be wasted ... in September one never knew. He looked over at the wide bed. Lilia was still sleeping, like a graceful ragdoll: her head over on her shoulder, one arm thrown up across the pillow, her shoulder uncovered and one knee drawn up, free of the sheets. He went over to that young body on which the early light played charmingly, catching the golden down on her arm and the moist corners of her eyelids and lips, her straw-colored armpits. He leaned down to look closely at the tiny beads of sweat on her upper lip and to feel the warmth that rose from her, sun-browned young animal, innocently shameless. He wanted to turn her over and see the front of her body, and for a moment his hand reached out. The half-open lips closed and the girl sighed. He went down to breakfast.

When he had finished with coffee, he wiped his lips on the napkin and looked around. At this hour the children always seemed to be eating, shepherded by their nanas. The sleek wet heads of those who had not resisted the temptation to take a swim before breakfast and now were already ready to return, in their wet suits, to the beach where only the imagination of each child would give rhythm to the hours, long or short, of sand castles and forts, sand burials, tar-stained walks, tumbling games, bodies tossed timeless beneath the time of the sun, squealings in soft formless water. It was odd to watch them searching the wide sand for the special spot where there was buried treasure, to watch them building their palaces. Now the children left and adult guests started coming in.

He lit a cigarette and felt the slight dizziness that during recent months had accompanied the first deep drag. He looked toward the curve of beach that wound from the open sea to the inner half-moon of the bay, now dotted with sails and an increasing bustle of activity. A couple he knew passed and greeted him with a gesture. He nodded and took another slow drag.

Noises of the dining room: silver on plates, spoons in cups, bottles being opened, the bubbling of mineral water, chairs scraped into position, the chatter of couples, of groups of tourists. And the surf's increasing sound, not to be drowned out by mere human noises. From his table the new, modern face of Acapulco could be seen, hotels built hurriedly to accommodate the great numbers of American travellers kept by the war from Waikiki, Portofino, and Biarritz, and also to hide the grubby, muddy yards of the nude fishermen, the huts crawling with big-bellied children and mangy dogs and trichina and bacilli, the open sewers. Always two faces in this Janus-town, so far from what it was, so far from what it wanted to be.

He smoked. There was a slight swelling in his legs, which could not tolerate, even at eleven in the morning, his light summer clothing. Sunburn. He rubbed his leg. There must be a chill inside him. Yet the morning was aburst with light and the round sun burned with orange arrogance. And Lilia came in, her eyes hidden behind dark glasses. He rose and held her chair for her, and beckoned a waiter. The couple he knew were whispering. Lilia ordered papaya and coffee.

'Did you sleep well?'

The girl nodded, smiled without showing her teeth, and touched his hand, brown against the white tablecloth.

'Shouldn't the papers from Mexico City be here by now?' she asked as she sliced her fruit. 'Why don't you see.'

'All right. But hurry. The yacht is coming for us at twelve.'

'Where will we lunch?'

'At the club.'

He walked toward the hotel desk. Yes: it would be a day like yesterday, one patterned by difficult conversation, idle questions and idle replies. Why did he want more? Their tacit agreement did not call for love, not even for a semblance of real interest. He had wanted a girl for his vacation. Monday everything would be over, he would not see her again. Who could ask for more? He bought the newspapers and went up to put on flannels.

In the car, Lilia buried herself in the papers. She read bits of movie news aloud. She crossed her bronze legs and let one shoe fall off. He lit the morning's third cigarette, did not tell her that he owned the newspaper, distracted himself watching the signs on the tops of new buildings and that strange transition from fifteen-story hotels to hamburger stands to the torn mountain excavations toothed by steam shovels, the pink interior of the earth exposed above the highway.

Lilia jumped gracefully to the deck. He tried to balance himself and finally stepped aboard. The other man was already there, ready with his hand extended, almost nude, a brief pair of trunks, dark face oily around the blue eyes and the heavy, expressive eyebrows. He extended his hand, to help them aboard, with a movement like an innocent wolf: audacious, candid, yet secretive.

'Don Rodrigo said you won't mind sharing the boat with me.'

He nodded and sought a place in the shadow. Adame was continuing, to Lilia:

'... the old man invited me over a week ago, then forgot all about it.'

Lilia smiled and spread her towel out on the sunny afterdeck.

'Would you like something to drink?' he asked Lilia when the steward appeared.

Lying down, she made a negative gesture with one finger. He

129

left his shade and went over to the steward's cart and picked up some almonds while the steward made him a gin and tonic. Xavier Adame had disappeared on the roof of the cabin. His firm footsteps could be heard, a rapid dialogue with someone on the dock, then the sound as he lay down on the roof.

The small yacht moved slowly out of the bay. He put on his cap with the transparent visor and lay back to drink his gin and tonic.

Lilia lay in the sun before him. She undid the knot of her halter and sunned her back. Her whole body spoke of pleasure. She raised her arms and tied her loose, bright copper-colored hair at the back of her neck. Delicate perspiration ran down her throat and neck, lubricating the round soft flesh of her arms and her smooth back, the sharp cleft between her breasts. He watched her from the depth of the cabin. She slept now in the same posture she had had this morning, lying on her shoulder, with a leg doubled up. He saw that she had shaved her armpit. The motor became louder and the waves opened before them in two divided crests of spray that fell on Lilia's body. The water wet her shorts, splashed on her thighs, and the cloth clung close across her buttocks. Gulls swung down, screaming at the swift boat. He sucked his drink slowly. That young body, far from exciting him, was making him irritable, filling him with a feeling of a kind of malevolent austerity. Seated in the shadow of the cabin, slumped in a canvas chair, he played with the thought of how he would satisfy his desire upon her tonight, of what he had stored up for that silence and solitude when their bodies would disappear in darkness, and his could not be an object for comparison. In the night he would offer her his experienced hands that loved patience and also surprise. He looked down at his hands, the prominent greenish veins that had replaced the strength and impatience of an earlier time.

They were out of the bay. The uninhabited coast, tangled shrubs and great towering bastions of rock, made a shimmering reflection of itself in the heat waves above it. The yacht changed course abruptly in the choppy sea and a wave broke over them, soaking Lilia. She squealed happily and lifted her bust with a deep gasp, those firm breasts with their pink nipples. She lay down again. The steward came with a fragrant tray of soft plums, peeled peaches, and oranges. He closed his eyes and let a forced smile escape, wrung from him by his thought: her sleek wet body, that tight body of full thighs, also carried hidden in it the miniscule cell of time's cancer. Ephemeral marvel,. what will remain of you in twenty years? Sun cadaver, sweating oil and water and your fleeting youth, lost in the wink of time's eye. Thighs that will compress and spread with births and your simple, anxious stay on earth, the earth's elemental routines, repeated and repeated over and over, exhausted of originality. He opened his eyes and looked at her.

Xavier Adame came down from the roof. He saw the hairy legs appear, then the brief trunks with the knot of genitals, finally the bronzed chest. Yes, he moved like a wolf. Adame ducked to enter the cabin and took two peaches from the ice-bedded platter and smiled toward him and went out, and squatted in front of Lilia, his legs apart in front of the girl's face. Adame touched her shoulder. Lilia smiled and took one of the peaches with some words that he, in the cabin, could not hear, they were lost in the sound of the motor, the wind, the fast-slapping waves. Now both of them were chewing in unison and the juice ran down their chins. If at least . . . yes. The young man closed his legs and lay down, stretching out on the port side. His smiling eyes looked up at the white sky and he wrinkled his forehead. Lilia looked at him and her lips moved, and Xavier said something, moved his arm and pointed toward the coast. Lilia tried to look toward the coast too, holding her halter in place over her breasts, and Xavier moved closer to her and they both laughed as he tied her halter and she sat up with her wet breasts sharply outlined, and shaded her eyes with her hand and stared at the little beach he was pointing to beyond the distant line of surf. It lay like a yellow shell against the thick jungle. Xavier stood and shouted an order. The yacht turned toward the beach. Lilia lay down and pulled her bag over to offer Xavier a cigarette. They were talking.

He saw them: two bodies side by side, equally dark and equally smooth, a single uninterrupted line from head to stretched toes, motionless but tense with clear expectation, joined by their newness with each other, by their scarcely veiled eagerness to try each other and themselves. He sucked his drink and put on his dark glasses; with the visor of the cap just above, his face was hidden.

Xavier and the girl talked. They had eaten their peaches down to the pits and were saying:

Tastes good

or perhaps,

I like

something that no one had said before, something that is said by the bodies of those just beginning life. They would be saying ...

'Why haven't we seen each other before. I'm always around the club ...'

'No, I'm not ... Come on, let's throw the peach pits. One, two ...'

He saw them throw the pits with one movement of two arms, with a laugh that did not reach inside the cabin. He saw the strength of Adame's arm.

'I beat you,' said Xavier as the pits dropped far from the yacht. She laughed. They lay down again.

'Do you like to ski?'

'I don't know how.'

'I'll teach you ...'

What would they be saying? He coughed and went over to the cart to make himself another drink. Xavier would be finding out the relationship between the girl and him. She would tell her sordid little story. He would shrug his shoulders and make her prefer his wolf body, for one night at least, for a change. But love? to love ...

'It's all in keeping your arms straight, see? Don't bend your arms.'

'First I'll watch how you do it.'

'Sure. Wait till we get to the beach.'

Ah, yes. To be young, to be young and rich.

The yacht stopped some yards off the remote beach. It rocked tiredly and gave off a breath of gasoline that stained the sea of green glass and white bottom. Xavier Adame took the skis and threw them into the water. He dove and came up smiling and slipped the skis on.

'Throw me the line!'

The girl found the grip-bar of the tow line and threw it down to him. The boat moved powerfully forward and Xavier Adame rose out of the water, following the wake with one arm raised in salute, while Lilia watched, and while he drank his gin and tonic. The strip of sea that separated those two youngsters joined them in some mysterious way: it united them more closely than the embrace of sex, it fixed them in oneness that was as motionless as if the yacht were not furrowing the Pacific, as if Xavier Adame were a statue, forever marble, forever drawn by the boat, as though Lilia had stopped upon one of the waves, the waves that seemed to have no substance of their own, rising, falling, breaking, dying away, forming again, forming others that were just the same, always moving, always the same, removed from the world of time, the image of themselves, of the primal wave, the lost millenium and the millenium to come. He sank back in his low comfortable chair. What was he going to choose now? How could he escape that crowning happenstance of needing what fled from his control?

Xavier Adame let go of the tow-line and sank into the water off the little beach. Lilia dove into the sea without looking at either of them. An explanation would come, and which would it be: would she explain him to Xavier, would Xavier ask such an explanation, or would she explain Xavier to him? Lilia's head and face rose glistening in sun and water near Xavier's head, and he knew that no one, except himself, would dare ask for any explanation; that down there in the water, no one was looking for reasons and the fatal encounter could not be held off, no one would corrupt what not only was but must be. What had come up between these two young people? What had come up: his body huddled in the chair, polo shirt and flannels, visored cap? His impotent stare? Down in the water, two bodies swam in silence and the rail prevented his seeing what was happening. Xavier Adame whistled. The yacht moved off again and Lilia appeared for an instant, standing on the surface of the ocean. She fell, the boat stopped; full, open laughter reached his ear. He had never heard her laugh like that. As though she were born anew, as though there were no past, no millstones of history and no stories, no plunder, no pillage, no shame committed by her, or by him.

By everyone. That was the intolerable word: everyone. His bitter tightening of lips and eyes could not prevent the word from breaking into speech, from breaking through all roads of power and guilt, breaking through his domination of others, of someone, of a girl he had bought: the word threw them into a horizonless world of common actions, similar destinies, experiences beyond the etiquette of proprietorship. He had not branded her forever: she would not be, forever, the woman he would occasionally take and enjoy: that would not be her limit, her destiny: to be what she had been ... because in a given moment she had been his. Well: but could she love as if he had never existed?

He went to the stern and shouted:

'It's getting late. We have to get back to the club for lunch.'

He was aware of his own face, his whole figure, rigid and starchy pallid. For no one had noticed his shout. Two light bodies gliding alone together beneath the opaline water could hardly hear, moving side by side without touching, as though floating through a second layer of air.

Xavier Adame left them on the dock and returned to the yacht: he wanted to ski some more. He waved goodbye from the bow. The breeze rippled her blouse and in her eyes was nothing of what he would have preferred to see. Xavier had not asked. Lilia had not told him that sad little melodrama. He savored it as he enjoyed, at the edge of the harbor, beneath the palm frond roof, the composite aroma of Vichysoisse: the middleclass marriage, the usual bastard bully, woman-beater, poor devil; the divorce and the whoredom. He wanted to tell it to Xavier, perhaps he ought to. Doubtless it would be difficult to recall the story, because it had gone from Lilia's eyes this afternoon, as though during the morning, the past had left her.

But the present could not flee because they were living it, sitting on woven chairs and mechanically eating a meal he had ordered specially: Vichysoisse, lobster, Côtes du Rhône, Baked Alaska. She was sitting there and he had paid for her. She held the tiny lobster-fork motionless before lifting it to her lips: she was paid for, but she was escaping him. He could not hold her longer. That afternoon, that very evening, she would look for Xavier Adame, they would meet in secret, they had already made their date. And Lilia's eyes, lost in the sleeping water among the passing sailboats, said nothing. He could pull it out of her, of course, make a scene – he felt false to himself, uncomfortable, and went on eating his lobster. Which way now? A chance meeting had defeated his will. Well: Monday everything would end, he would not see her again, would not look for her in the darkness, nude, sure of finding that warmth lying there between the sheets: he wouldn't . . .

'Aren't you sleepy?' murmured Lilia when they were served dessert. 'Doesn't wine make you drowsy?'

'Yes, a little. Take some.'

'No, I don't want any ice cream . . . I want to take a siesta.'

When they reached the hotel, Lilia said goodbye with a little wave of her fingers and he crossed the avenue and told a boy to set a chair under the shade of the palms. He had trouble lighting his cigarette: an invisible wind, difficult to judge in the hot afternoon, kept blowing out the matches. Now several young couples were sleeping their siestas near him, embraced, some with their legs intertwined, others with their heads together under towels. He began to wish that Lilia would come down and lay her head on his skinny, hard, flanneled knees. He felt wounded, disturbed, insecure: he ached with the memory of their immediate and wordless agreement, sealed before his very eyes with actions that in themselves said nothing, but that in his presence, man huddled in the canvas chair, buried behind the visor and dark glasses . . . One of the girls lying near him stretched with a languid movement and began to pour sand on her companion's neck. She yelled when the youth jumped and feigned anger and grabbed her suit. They wrestled in the sand; she got up and ran; the youth chased until, panting and strong, he caught her again and carried her toward the surf.

He kicked off his Italian slippers and felt the warm sand on the soles of his feet. To walk along the beach, all the way to the end, alone. To walk with his eyes fixed on his own tracks, without noticing that the tide erased them and that each footprint was no more than its own unique ephemeral witness.

The sun was at eyelevel.

They came out of the sea, the young lovers, and he, puzzled, could not count the time of their prolonged coitus almost within sight of the beach but cloaked in the sheets of the silvered sea. The brash playfulness with which they had gone down into the surf had become, now, merely two heads together in silence, and that splendid dark young girl's lowered eyes. Young, young. They lay down again, very near him, and covered their heads with their towel. And at the same time night was coming on to cover them, the slow night of the tropics. The Negro who rented the beach chairs began to take them in. He got up and walked toward the hotel.

He decided to take a dip in the pool before going up. The dressing room was next to the pool; he sat on a stool, hidden by the steel lockers, and took off his shoes again. Wet footsteps padded on the rubber mat behind him. Voices laughed, they were drying off. The penetrating smell of sweat, black tobacco, and cologne water. A curl of smoke twisted toward the ceiling.

'Beauty and the beast didn't show up today.'

'No, not today.'

'She's a nice looking piece.'

'A shame. The old goat can't be doing her much good.'

'He'll kill himself trying to keep up with that.'

'Yeah. Hurry up.'

They went out. He put on his shoes and went out too pulling his shirt on.

He went up by the stairs. He opened the door. There was nothing to surprise him. The bed was rumpled from her siesta, but she was not there. He stopped in the middle of the room. The air-conditioning whirred around him. Outside, on the terrace, another night of crickets and fireflies. Another night. He closed the window to keep her smell from escaping. He drank in that aroma of recently sprayed perfume, perspiration, wet towels, make-up. But those things, those smells, had other names. The pillow, still pressed down, was garden, fruit, moist earth, the sea. Slowly he moved to the drawer where she ... He took her silk bra between his hands, held it to his cheek. The stubble of his beard rasped it. He ought to be ready. He had to bathe, shave, prepare for tonight. He let the bra drop and with a new step, at ease again, walked to the bath.

He snapped on the light. Hot water. Shirt over the toilet. He looked at their things: toothpaste, mentholated shaving cream, tortoise shell combs, cold cream, a tube of aspirin tablets, antacid wafers, tampons, lavender water, blue razor blades, brilliantine, rouge, pills to be used for stomach-spasm, yellow mouthwash, condoms, Milk of Magnesia, band-aids, iodine, shampoo, tweezers, manicure scissors, lipstick, eye drops, eucalyptus oil inhalator, cough syrup, deodorant. He picked up his razor. It was clogged with heavy brown hairs between the blade and the guard. He paused. He lifted the razor to his lips, and involuntarily closed his eyes. When he opened them, an old man with sunken eyes, gray cheeks, and withered mouth, an old man who was not his other he, the reflection he had made familiar, grimaced at him from the mirror.

I see them. They have come in. The mahogany door opens and closes and their steps are silent on the thick carpet. They have closed the windows. They have run the gray curtains shut, with a hissing sound. There's a world outside. There's the high wind, wind of the high mesa, wind that shakes the slender dark trees. I have to breathe ... They have come in.

'Go near him, child, so that he can recognize you. Tell him your name.'

Take a good smell. She smells nice. Yes: I can see her, her flushed cheeks, the bright eyes, her young graceful body approaching me with hesitant steps.

'I am ... I am Gloria.'

'That morning I waited for him with happiness. We rode our horses across the river.'

'Do you see how he is ending? Do you see? Just like my brother. He ended like this.'

'Do you feel better? Do it ...'

'Ego te absolvo ...'

The fresh, sweet rustle of new bonds and banknotes taken by the hand of such a man as I. The smooth start of an expensive car, built to order, air-conditioned, with its own bar, telephone, with special cushions and footrests: eh, priest, what do you say, will it be like that up there too, eh? And the heaven that is power over uncounted men with hidden faces and forgotten names, named by the thousand on the payrolls of my mines, my factories, my newspaper: the anonymous face that sang Happy Birthday to me on my saint's day, that hides his eyes under his helmet when I visit the excavations, the faces that duck their heads courteously when I ride through the fields, the face that draws my caricature in opposition newspapers. Heaven that indeed exists and belongs to me. This is to be God, truly, eh? Tell me how I can save all this and I will let you carry out all your rites. I'll beat my chest, crawl to a sanctuary on my knees, drink vinegar, crown myself with thorns. Tell me how to save what I have, because the spirit . . .

'. . . and of the Son, and of the Holy Ghost, amen . . .'

He goes on, on his knees, with his scrubbed face. I try to turn my back to him, but I can't because of the pain in my ribs. *Ayyy.* Now he will have finished, I will have been absolved. I want to sleep. There comes the stabbing pain. There it comes. Aaaah – *aaaay.* And the women. No, not these. The women. Those who rule. What? Yes. No. I don't know. I have forgotten that face. My God, I have forgotten that face. It belonged to me, how am I going to forget it.

Padilla . . . Padilla, call me the information chief and the society editor.

Your voice, Padilla, the hollow sound of your voice through the interphone . . .

Yes, Don Artemio. Don Artemio, we have an urgent problem. Those Indians go on agitating. They want to be paid for their timber.

What? How much is it?

Half a million.

Is that all? Tell the manager of the ejido to clamp down on them. That's why I pay him.

Mena is here. What shall I tell him?

Have him come in.

Ah, Padilla, I can't open my eyes and see you, but I can see your thought, Padilla, through the mask of my pain: the man in pain is called Artemio Cruz, plain Artemio Cruz: only this man dies, you know, no one else. It is a sort of stroke of luck that defers other deaths. This time only Artemio Cruz dies. And his death can substitute for others', perhaps for yours, Padilla ... Ah. No. I still have things to do. They must not be so confident, no ...

'I told you what he was doing.'

'Let him rest.'

'I tell you what he's doing!'

I watch them across the room. Their fingers open the double bottom in haste, twisting it off. Nothing there. But I move my arm now, gesturing toward the oak wall, the long closet that extends the length of that side of the bedroom. They run to it, slide open all the doors, slide the hangers of blue suits, striped suits, two-button suits, Irish linen suits, without remembering that those are not my garments, that my clothes are at my home, the other house: they hurry through the hangers as with two fingers I can hardly move, I indicate that maybe the document is in the right hand inside pocket of one of the jackets. Their haste increases, they thrust their hands shamelessly now, they strew the floor with jackets until all have been checked, and they turn again to me. My face could not be more solemn. I am propped up upon the pillows and I breathe with difficulty, but I miss nothing. My eyes are swift and avid. I gesture for them to come near.

'Now I remember ... in a shoe ... I remember clearly ...'

To see those two women on all fours among the scattered suits, their wide buttocks elevated, their cheeks fluttering with an obscene panting, fumbling through my shoes. Bitter sweetness closes my eyes. I raise my hand to my heart and close my eyes.

'Regina ...'

The women's frantic search and mumbled indignation fade into darkness. I move my lips and repeat that name. Not much time is left for remembering now, for remembering her, her I loved ... Regina ...

Padilla ... Padilla ... I want something light to eat. My stomach is a little touchy. Join me, if that's prepared ...

What? You select, you build, you create, you preserve, you prolong: that is all ... I ...

Yes, see you soon. My respects ...

Well said, señor. It is easy to crush them.

No, Padilla, it is not easy. Pass me that platter ... that one, the little sandwiches. I have seen these people in action. Once they make up their minds, it is hard to turn them ...

How did that song go? Forced from my land I went away to the South, forced from my land by the government, and in a year I came back; *ay* what uneasy nights without you, without you; neither friend nor kin to pine for me; only the love, the love of that woman, made me come back ...

That's why we must act now, while the discontent is just organizing, smash the egg before it hatches. They are not yet organized. They are gambling everything for everything. Dig in, help yourself to the sandwiches, there's plenty for two ...

An egg that will never hatch ...

I have my two ivory-handled pistols to shoot it out with those railroad bastards I'm a railway man I have my Juan and he's my dream and I am all desire: just because you see me in my boots, you think I'm a soldier, but I'm a poor railroad man on the Central Railrooooood ...

An egg that will certainly hatch if they are right. But they aren't right. You, you who were a Marxist back in your wild young days, you ought to understand better. You are afraid of what is happening these days. I no longer ...

Campanela is waiting outside ...

What did they say? A cyst? Hemorrhage? Herniated? Occlusion? Perforation? Strangulation? Inflammation?

Ah, Padilla, I ought to touch a button so that you will enter. I don't see you, Padilla, because my eyes are closed; I have my eyes closed because I can no longer trust the tiny cameras called my retinas: what if my eyes and retinas don't receive anything and send no reports to my brain: what then?

'Open the window.'
'I blame you. As much as I blame my brother.'
Yes.

You will not know, you will not understand, why Catalina, seated beside you, insists upon sharing that memory with you, that memory which she would like to impose upon everyone: you in this land, Lorenzo in that? what is it that she wants to remember? you with Gonzalo in prison? Lorenzo without you on the mountain? you will not know, you will not understand if you are he or if he will be you, if you lived that day without him, or with him, he for you, you for him. You will remember. Yes, that last day you and he were together – therefore he did not live it for you, nor you for him, but you were together. He asked you if you were going to the sea together; you rode your horses; he asked you if you would ride together as far as the sea: he will ask you where you are going to eat and he said – he will say – papá, he will smile, lifting his arm and the shotgun as he comes up from the river with his chest bare and holding the shotgun and the knapsacks high. She will not be there. Catalina will not remember. That is why you will try to remember, to forget the memory she wants you to have. She will live closed in silence and will tremble when he returns to Mexico City for a few days to say goodbyes. If he would only return only to say goodbyes. She believes that, but he will not do that. He will take the steamer in Veracruz, he will go away. She will have to remember that bedroom where the mists of dream struggle to persist although the spring air comes in the open balcony. She will have to remember the separate beds, the separate rooms, the silk headboards, the tangled sheets in the two separate bedrooms, the depressions in the mattresses, lingering silhouettes of those who slept in those beds. She will not be able to remember the mare's black hindquarters, shiny, washed by the river. You will. After crossing the river, you and he will see a spectral land rising out of the misty fermentation of the morning. The battle of dark jungle and burning sun will

141

come together in a double reflection of everything, in a fantasm of water mirror embracing land reflection. It will smell of bananas. It will be Cocuya. Catalina will never know what Cocuya was or is or will be. She will sit waiting on the side of the bed, with her mirror in one hand and her hairbrush in the other, deciding that she will remain like this, seated, gazing vacantly, wanting to do nothing, nothing, saying to herself that scenes always leave her like this: empty. No: only you and he will feel the horses' hooves sinking into the porous earth of the river bank. And only you and he will feel, as you ride up from the water, the freshness mixed with the jungle's seething, and will look back at the slow river that so gently stirs the lichens on the other bank, and farther back, along the path of flowering *tabachines*, to the newly painted buildings of Cocuya Hacienda and the shaded green level where they stand. Catalina will say over and over: God, is this what I deserve? and she will ask herself if this is what Lorenzo will see when he returns, if he returns: that growing shapelessness of her chin and throat: will he notice the powder-hidden wrinkles around her eyes and down her cheeks? She will see another gray hair, and pull it out. And you, with Lorenzo beside you, will ride deep into the jungle. Before you you will see your son's bare back as it catches alternate mango shadow and mottling sun. Knotty treeroots will make the surface of the machete-cut trail uneven, and will appear fierce and twisted. Soon that trail will again be a matted web of vines. Lorenzo will trot along it now erect in the saddle, his head motionless, flicking his quirt over the mare's flanks to keep off the flies. Catalina will tell herself that she will not trust him, will not trust him unless he looks at her as he used to when he was a child, and she will lie back with a whimper, her arms spread, her face clouded, and the silk slippers will fall from her feet as she thinks of her son, so like his father, so slim, so dark. Dry branches will crack beneath the horses' hooves and the flatland will open before you, white with waving cane. Lorenzo will spur ahead. He will turn and look back and his lips will break into a smile as he shouts with joy and raises a strong olive arm: his smile as white as the smiles of your own youth: this place and his youth will let you remember your own youth, and you will not want to tell him how much this land means to you, because to do so might perhaps influence his feeling for it: you will remember in order to remember within your memory. Catalina, on the bed, will remember Lorenzo's baby touch during those bitter days of old Gamaliel's death, will remember the boy kneeling beside her with his head on her lap while she called him the joy of her life because before his coming she had suffered harshly and without the power to say that she suffered, because she had sacred obligations, and the child looked at her blankly and without understanding: because, because, because what? You will bring Lorenzo to Cocuya to live and to learn to love the land for his own reasons without your having to explain why you so lovingly rebuilt the burned-out walls of the old hacienda and brought the savannah under cultivation again. Not because; without because; because. You will emerge from the jungle into the sun and will take the wide-brimmed sombrero hanging at your back and will put it on: the still air will be put into movement by your gallop and the echo of hooves will fill your ears as Lorenzo draws ahead of you raising a cloud of white dust, galloping down the road between the fields, and you, following, will know with certainty that you are both feeling the same opening and sharpening of eyes as you gallop across this wide and sappy land, so different from the plateaus and deserts you know, a land parceled into great red and green and black squares and dotted with tall palm groves, an obscure and deep land smelling of excrement and the husks of fruit, a land that makes your jaded senses fresh while you and your son ride fast and drive the torpor from your nerves and all your forgotten muscles. Your spurs will rake the belly of your mount until it bleeds: you will know that Lorenzo wants to race. His child's questioning stare will cut Catalina's words short: she will stop, she will ask herself what it will lead to and will tell herself that the matter is no more than one of time, a question of unveiling her reasons to the boy little by little until he understands them well. She, seated in the big chair; he, at her feet with his arms around his knees. The earth will shake under the hooves; you will bend your head down, as if you wished to put your mouth to the horse's ear, but there is that weight, the weight of the Yaqui Indian who will be folded, face down, across

143

the back of the horse, the Yaqui who will stretch out his arm to hook it to your belt: pain will make you numb: your arm and leg will hang limp and the Yaqui will go on squeezing your waist and moaning, his face congested with pain: and then the high funeral heaps of mountain stone will stand around you as you ride on, following the canyon into the mountain, discovering inner stone valleys, deep barrancas with their mouths above dry riverbeds, trails of thorns and brambles: who will remember with you? Lorenzo on the mountain without you? Gonzalo with you in the village jail?

[1915: October 22]

He wrapped himself in his blue serape, for the icy wind of these night hours belied, with a rustle of stubble, the vertical heat of day. They had spent the entire night in this open camp, and had not eaten. At less than two kilometers rose the mountain's basalt crowns, their roots buried in the hard desert. For three days the scouting detachment had traveled without track or landmark, guided only by their captain's sense of the tricks and routes likely to be used by Villa's shattered army. Behind, some seventy kilometers away, the main body of their forces waited the arrival of a racing messenger from this detachment, and then would attack Villa's remnants to prevent them from joining fresh troops in Chihuahua. But where were those tattered and defeated rebel remnants? The captain of the scouting detachment thought he knew: hidden in some rough and roadless part of the mountain, following the most difficult trail. On the fourth day, today, the detachment must penetrate the sierra while their comrade loyal Carranzistas would be advancing to the camp they would leave at daybreak. Yesterday they had eaten the last of their toasted cornmeal. Last night the sergeant who had ridden with all their canteens toward the little stream that tumbled through the rocks and was swallowed up the moment it reached the desert, had brought back no water: the little river-bed was pink-veined, clean and wrinkled, perfectly dry. The explanation was that when they passed this way before, two years ago, it had been during the rainy season. Now only a blistering round sun hung over their heads from dawn to dusk. They had camped without campfires: some lookout on the mountain might see them, and moreover, why did they need fire, they had nothing to cook, and in the immensity of the flat desert, a bonfire would warm no one. Wrapped in his blue serape, he rubbed his thin face. The ends of his moustache curled into his two days' beard. Dust crusted the cracks of his lips, his eyebrows, the bridge of his nose. Several meters away from him lay eighteen men: he always slept or kept watch separated from them by such a strip of earth, always alone. Beyond the men, the manes of the horses riffled in the wind and their black silhouettes stood out against the yellow surface of the ground. The captain wanted to get moving: the source of the canyon was among the mountain rocks and it was there that the solitary breath of freshness was born. He wanted to move: the enemy could not be far now. His body was tense in the darkness. Hunger and thirst had honed his senses and deepened and opened wider his eyes, those green eyes that stared so coldly.

He waited, a mask of dust, awake and motionless. At the first line of dawn they would shove off: dawn of the fourth day, as had been ordered. Almost no one was asleep. They sat with their knees drawn up, unmoving, wrapped in their serapes. Those who closed their eyes had hunger and thirst and weariness to fight. Those who were not watching the captain, eyed the line of horses, which were tied to a thick mesquite that stuck out of the ground like a lost finger. The tired horses stared at the ground. It was time for the sun to appear behind the mountains now. It was time.

They awaited the moment when he rose, threw off the blue serape, and uncovered his crossed cartridge belts, the shining buckle of his officer's tunic, his pigskin leggings. Without a word they got to their feet and went to their mounts. He was right: light fanned into the sky behind the lower peaks and threw a faint arch higher. Birds, lords of the vast silence of this abandoned land, had begun to sing somewhere in the distance. He beckoned to the Yaqui, Tobías, and in his Indian tongue said to him:

'You will ride last. The minute we sight them, you will carry the message back.'

The Yaqui nodded and put on his low, round-crowned sombrero, decorated with a red feather in the band. The captain swung up into the saddle and the column moved off at a light trot toward the gateway into the sierra: the canyon, the ocher-colored defile. Three shelves rose from the cut of the canyon. The detachment took the second, which was the narrowest but wide enough for them to follow it in single file, and which led to the canyon's source. Empty canteens banged hollowly, rock fragments kicked off the trail by the horses echoed the echoless sound, like single raps of a taut drumhead. From his position above them, the column looked melancholy. Only he kept his eyes on the mountain ahead, watching the summits, squinting his eyes against the sun, letting his horse pick its way unguided. He felt neither fear nor pride. Fear had been left behind, not in the first engagements but in the repetition of engagements which had made danger the habitual, security the unusual, part of life. The silence of the canyon alarmed him secretly simply because it was silence. He tightened his fingers on the reins and unconsciously tensed his muscles to be ready to draw his pistol quickly. He did not think that he was ever cocky: fear at first and later habit had made such arrogance impossible. He could not feel pride when for the first time bullets had twanged around his ears and his life miraculously managed to make each bullet miss its target; he could feel only awe before his body's blind wisdom in dodging, rising, ducking, stepping just in time behind a tree trunk; awe and also scorn. His body, as tenacious and far quicker than his will, protected him. Nor could he feel pride later, many battles later, when he had become so accustomed to the whistle of bullets that he no longer even heard them. He became anxious, with a dry and controlled uneasiness, only when surrounded by unexpected calm and silence. And now, riding up the canyon, he felt that uneasiness and thrust his jaw forward.

A soldier whistled sharply behind him, confirming danger.

An instant later the whistle was cut off by a volley of shots and the familiar Villista battle howl. Enemy horsemen were making a suicide attack, riding straight down the steep side of the canyon, while riflemen hidden on the third ledge fired into the detachment of scouts and bleeding horses reared and tumbled in a clamor of dust, rolled toward the sharp rocks below. He turned and saw Tobías imitate the Villistas and drive his horse straight down in a hopeless effort to obey orders: the Yaqui's mount lost footing and flew through the air and crashed among the rocks at the bottom of the narrow pass, crushing the rider. The howling grew louder. The rifle fire became intense. He dropped from his horse and slid down the slope of the canyon, slowing his descent with handholds and dug-in heels: in flashes of sight, he saw the bellies of rearing horses above, the ineffectual firing of the scouts, who were unable to defend themselves or to control their mounts. He tumbled down, clawing, kicking, and the Villista horsemen poured down on the second ledge and hand to hand combat began. He reached the bottom and unholstered his pistol. There was new silence. The detachment had been wiped out. With pain in his arms and legs, he dragged himself behind a huge rock.

'Come out, Captain Cruz. Give yourself up now . . .'

His dry throat shouted back: 'To be shot? I'll stay where I am.'

But his right hand, numbed by pain, could hardly hold the pistol. He raised his arm and felt a sharp stab of pain in his belly. He fired, head down, until the trigger merely clicked. Then he threw the pistol over the rock. The voice above shouted again:

'Come out with your hands behind your head.'

He came out around the rock and found the bodies of thirty or more horses, dead or dying. Some were trying to lift their heads; some struggled on a broken leg; most showed bleeding gunshot wounds on foreheads, necks, bellies. And the bodies of the dead from both sides lay in crazy postures sometimes on top and sometimes beneath the horses, faces up as if they awaited a steam of water down the dry canyon, faces down kissing the stone. All dead, except the one who moaned underneath the weight of a sorrel mare.

'Let me get this man out,' he yelled to the group above. 'He may be one of yours.'

How? With what hands, what strength? He bent to grip Tobías' pinned body and a steel bullet sang and struck rock. He looked up. The officer commanding the victors restrained, with a gesture, the man who had fired. Dusty sweat ran down his wrists. He could not move one arm. With the other, he strained until he had dragged Tobías free.

Behind him he heard the hooves of the horsemen who had come down to capture him. By the time he had the Yaqui's legs loose, they were around him. They tore the crossed cartridge belts from his chest.

It was seven o'clock in the morning.

At four that afternoon, when he entered the village jail at Perales, he could hardly remember the forced march Colonel Zagal had ordered. In nine hours down from the mountain ravines and into the little Chihuahua town. His head was racked by dull pain; he scarcely noticed their route. Obviously it was the most difficult route, and for one like Zagal, who had been with Pancho Villa twenty years, crisscrossing these mountains until he knew every recess and trail, every canyon, every short-cut, it was also, doubtless, the simplest route. Zagal's mushroom-shaped *sarakof* hid half his face, but his teeth, set off by his black beard and moustaches, were always smiling. They smiled when the prisoner had difficulty mounting and when the Yaqui's broken, still living body was thrown head down across his pommel. They smiled when the little column moved off, entering a natural tunnel unfamiliar to him or to any Carranzista, that made it possible for them to travel in one hour what would have taken four on the surface. All this he hardly noticed. He knew that like the Federals, the Rebels always shot captured officers immediately. He asked himself why Zagal was taking him, now, to some unknown destination.

Pain made him drowsy. His arm and leg, badly bruised by his fall down the side of the canyon, hung limply, and the Yaqui clung to him and moaned with a congested face. The great piles of sheer rock succeeded one another and they rode forward in the mountains' shadows, toward the foot of the mountains. Inner valleys of stone. Deep barrancas with mouths above dry river-beds. Trails where overhanging shrubs and jutting rocks offered cover. Perhaps only Villa's troops have ever crossed this country, he thought, and their knowledge of it made possible their string of early victories that had broken the back of the dictatorship. They were masters of surprise, encirclement, and swift flight. They were everything contrary to the military school of General Alvaro Obregón, who thought in terms of formal battle, in open field, with precise dispositions and maneuvers over carefully explored terrain.

'Stay together and in file. Don't scatter out,' Colonel Zagal shouted each time he left the head of his column and galloped back, swallowing dust and gritting his teeth. 'We're out of the mountains now and can expect anything. Settle down, everyone alert. Keep a sharp watch for dust. We'll see better with every-one looking instead of just me . . .'

The masses of rock began to thin out. They were on a flat plateau and below them spread the Chihuahua desert, rolling, spotted with mesquite. The heat of the sun was relieved by gusts of high cool wind, a freshness that never touched the burning land below.

'We'll go by the mine, that way is faster,' Zagal said. 'Keep a good hold on your friend, Cruz, it's steep.'

The Yaqui's hand grasped Artemio's belt. But there was more in that grip than the wish not to fall: there was something to be communicated. Artemio leaned forward, stroking the horse's neck, and turned his face toward Tobías' twisted face.

The Indian murmured, in his own tongue: 'We are going to pass by an abandoned mine. When we are close to a shaft open-ing, wheel the horse and break for inside. There are many old cuttings and they probably won't be able to find you.'

He stroked the horse's neck and then sat up straight and tried to see the mine entrance Tobías had spoken of.

'Forget about me,' the Indian muttered. 'My legs are broken.'

Two o'clock? One? The sun was hotter and hotter.

Two goats appeared on a ledge and some of the soldiers raised rifles and fired at them. One escaped, the other dropped from the ledge. A soldier dismounted and brought the goat back across his shoulders.

'Let that be the last hunting anyone tries,' said Zagal, his voice hoarse and smiling. 'Some day you'll miss those bullets, Corporal Payan.'

Then, rising in his stirrups, the colonel addressed the entire column:

'All right, you bastards, understand this. We have the god-damned Carranzistas stepping on our heels. So don't anyone else go shooting up the countryside. What the hell do you think? That we're on a triumphant march south, like before? Well, we aren't. We got our asses whipped and we're running back north where we came from, as fast as we can.'

'But Colonel,' whined the corporal. 'Now we can have a little lunch.'

'What we can have isn't worth shitting,' shouted Zagal.

The men laughed and Corporal Payan tied the dead goat over the back of his horse.

'Leave your water and cornmeal alone until we get down,' Zagal ordered.

Artemio watched ahead. There it was, just around a turn in the trail, the open mouth of the mine. The shoes of Zagal's horse clanged against the narrow steel rails that reached about half a yard from the entrance. Cruz threw himself off and dashed into the mine before the surprised rifles could be aimed. He stumbled to his knees in the darkness. The first shots rang out and the hubbub of voices rose. He was light-headed with the sudden change from desert heat to coolness, and in the dark found it hard to maintain balance. Forward: his legs ran, forgetting pain, until he crashed into solid rock. He opened his arms and found that they reached two separate shafts: through one, a strong draft was blowing; in the other, there was closed-in heat; his stretched fingers felt the different temperatures. He chose the hot shaft, which must be the deeper, and ran again. They were running behind him now; he could hear the ring of their spurs. A match threw a spark of orange light. The ground fell from beneath him and he dropped down a vertical shaft and felt the shock of his body against rotten timbers. Above, the noise of the spurs and voices continued and echoed. He straightened painfully. He tried to see where it was he had fallen, to find a way out to continue flight.

'Better stay where I am ...'

The voices grew louder, as if in argument. Then there was the clear pealing laughter of the colonel. The voices moved away. Far off, someone whistled. He heard other vague muffled sounds that he could not explain. Then, nothing. His eyes began to accustom themselves to the darkness.

'Looks like they have gone. It could be a trick. Better wait.'

In the eyeless heat he touched his chest and felt the rib hurt by his fall down the shaft. He was in a round space with no outlet. Surely it was the bottom of an excavation. Broken and rotting timbers lay on the ground; others propped up the weak clay overhead. He tested the strength of one of the props, and lay back to let time pass. One timber stretched upward at an angle toward the opening through which he had fallen. It would not be hard to crawl up that beam and reach the entrance level. He fingered rips in his pants and tunic. Fatigue. Hunger. Sleepiness. His young body stretched its legs and felt the strong pulse in the thighs. Darkness and rest, the slight panting, and his closed eyes. He thought about the women he would like to know, for he could not remember those he had known. Well, the last, in Fresnillo, a whore, all dressed up, one of those who begin to cry when you ask them where they are from and what they are doing whoring. Just the same old question to start a conversation and give them the opportunity to invent a history. But this one didn't invent anything, she just cried. And the endless war. Clearly it was about over. Mopping up. He crossed his arms on his chest and tried to breathe more regularly. Once they mopped up the scattered remains of Villa's army, there would be peace. Peace.

'What will I do when it ends? And why think now about its ending? I never think about its ending.'

Maybe peace would mean an opportunity to build something. He had traveled the length and breadth of Mexico engaging only in destruction. Destroyed fields would have to be sown again. In the Bajio, once, he had seen a lovely farm where one could build a home of arcades and flowering patios and watch the crops. To see how the seed grows, to care for it, midwife the birth of the plant, gather the fruits. It could be a good life. A good life.

'Don't fall asleep. Stay ready.'

He pinched his thigh. The muscles of the back of his neck drew his head backward.

There was no sound now. He could explore. He climbed on the angled beam and with his feet felt for jutting corners of rock. He moved upward from handhold and foothold to handhold and foothold, his back braced against the beam, until his arms came out on the floor of the upper level. He was in the hot, stuffy shaft. But now it seemed darker and more suffocating than before. He walked toward the entrance, recognizing the main shaft when he came to the fork where the cool air flowed. But light was not entering where the entrance should be. Was it dark outside already? Had he lost track of the hours?

Blindly, he felt for the opening. Not night had closed off the entrance, but a barricade of heavy rocks, raised by his Villista captors before they left. They had sealed him in a tomb.

The nerves in his stomach told him that this was the end. But automatically, his nostrils flared in an effort to breathe, and he raised his fingers to his temples and rubbed them as he thought of the other, the ventilated shaft. That air came from somewhere, it came from outside, it was rising from the desert, whipped by the sun. He ran back. His nostrils led him along the current of fresh air and with his hands following the uneven walls, he stumbled through the darkness. A drop of water touched his hand. He passed his open mouth to the wall, seeking the source of that moisture. Single black drops dropped down one by one from the black overhead. He caught another on his tongue, waited for the third, the fourth. The shaft seemed to end. He lowered his head and sniffed. The air was coming from below, he could feel it around his legs. He knelt and explored with his hands. The stones were loose. An invisible opening. He threw the stones aside until the fissure widened and was finally large enough for him to slip down into a new gallery, illuminated by silvered veins. He could not stand up but had to crawl on his stomach. And so he dragged himself along, with no idea of where his reptile progress was leading him. Gray veins and golden reflections of his officer's braid, only these gave light. His eyes probed the blackest corners of the darkness. A thread of saliva ran down his chin. His mouth felt as if it were full of tamarinds. Even in memory, the fruit made his mouth water: maybe some distant scent, preserved by the still desert air, had stolen this far. His awakened sense of smell noticed something else: unquestionably, that was the scent of earth ... unquestionably, for a man who had been hours locked with the dry smells of rock. A complete mouthful of fresh air, a lungful. The low gallery dipped downward. It ended in an abrupt drop into a wide chamber with a sandy floor. He slid down. There were vines here. Where did they come from?

'Yes, no it goes up again. But can that be light? It looks like only a reflection of the sand. No, it's light!'

He ran with a band around his chest toward the opening bathed in sunlight. He ran without seeing or hearing: without hearing the slow strumming of the guitar and the voice that sang, the lazy sensual voice of a tired soldier:

Las muchachas durangueñas se visten de azul y verde,
de las ocho en adelante, la que no pellizca muerde ...

And without seeing the small fire over which hung the carcass of the goat shot earlier on the mountain, without seeing the fingers pulling shreds of meat from it.

He fell, without seeing or hearing, on the sunlit earth. Three in the afternoon, a westering sun, and the white mushroom of Colonel Zagal's *sarakof*. The colonel extended his hand:

'Come along, Captain, you're going to make us late. Look how your Yaqui friend is feasting. Now you can finally use your canteens.'

Las muchachas chichuahuenses ya no saben ni qué hacer,
pidiendo a Dios que haya un hombre que las sepa bien querer ...

The prisoner lifted his head and let his eyes wander out over the dry landscape, wide and slow, silent and heavy, of jagged rocks and cactus. He got up and walked toward the circle reclining around the colonel. The Yaqui stared at him fixedly. He reached down and pulled a scorched strip from the loin of the goat, and sat to eat.

Perales.

It was an adobe pueblo with little to distinguish it from a thousand others. One block, that which ran in front of the building they called their city hall, was cobbled. The rest of the streets were dust flattened by children's bare feet, by the turkeys that puffed and strutted at intersections, by the paws of the pack of dogs that sometimes slept in the sun and at other times ran, all together, barking. One or two good houses at most, with great entrance doors and iron locks and brass hasps and hinges: the homes of the moneylender and the local political boss (who were usually the same man in these places), both now in flight from Pancho Villa's swift justice. The troops had filled up these two residences, packing into the patios their horses and hay, their cases of tools and ammunition and equipment, everything the defeated Northern Division had been able to save in its march homeward. The pueblo's color was brown; only the front of the city hall shone rose, and its sides and patios were brown too. There was a stream: that was why the town had been established here; town, little more than village, whose wealth was limited to a few turkeys and chickens, a few dry cornfields cultivated in dusty strips, a couple of blacksmiths, a carpenter's shop, a grocery store, and home occupations like weaving. It was a miracle that the place existed. It existed in silence. Like most small Mexican pueblos, its inhabitants seemed to be hiding and one could not say where. In the morning as in the afternoon, in the afternoon as in the evening, you might hear the ring of a hammer on iron or the cry of a new-born child, but you would look in vain for a living soul on the burning streets. At times children appeared, tiny and barefoot. And the soldiers were also hidden behind the walls of the stern houses in the patios of the rose-fronted city-hall, toward which the weary little column rode. When they dismounted, a guard came up, and Colonel Zagal gestured to the Yaqui Indian.

'Put him in the jail. Cruz, you come with me.'

The colonel was not laughing now. He opened a stifling office and wiped sweat from his forehead with his sleeve. He loosened his belt and sat down. Artemio Cruz remained standing.

'Pull up a chair, Captain, and we can talk as comfortably as we wish. Have a cigarette?'

The prisoner took a cigarette. Their faces came together over the match.

'Good,' Zagal smiled. 'This can be very simple. You tell us the plans of the army pursuing us and we free you. I am frank about it. We know we are through, but still and all we want to defend ourselves. You're a good soldier, you understand this.'

'Yes. That's why I'm not going to tell you.'

'It would be very little that we would ask you to tell us. You and all those who died in the canyon were a scouting detachment, that is clear. That means that your main body is not far behind. They even smelled out the route we took north. But as your people don't know that pass through the mountains very well, they will certainly have to go around by the flat, and that takes several days. Now: how many are there, have troops been brought ahead by train, and how many pieces of artillery do they have? What tactics have been decided on? Where are you to be joined by those brigades that have not been following us? Think how simple: you tell me this and you go free. My word of honor.'

'Just what specific guarantees do you offer?'

'Christ, Captain, we're going to lose anyhow. I am frank, we don't have a chance, the Division is shattered and has broken up into small bands that will disappear into the mountains, progressively decimated as men keep dropping out to return to their ranchos, their pueblos. We are exhausted. Many years of hard fighting have passed since we first rose against Don Porfirio. Then we fought alongside Madero, then against Orozo's reds, then against Huerta's bastards, and finally against you sons of bitches in Carranza's army. A long time, we are tired. Our people are like lizards, they are taking the color of the earth now, they are going back to the holes they came from. They are dressing as peons again, to wait the next opportunity to fight, even if they have to wait a hundred years. They know that this time we lost, like the Zapatistas in the South. You have won. Now: why should you die when the battle has been won? Let us go down fighting, that is all I ask. Let us lose with a little honor.'

'Pancho Villa is not in this pueblo.'

'No, he is farther ahead, but not far. And our people keep leaving us.'

'Tell me what guarantee you offer.'

'We'll leave you alive in the jail, to be rescued by your friends.'

'Good if we win. But if we don't ...'

'If we defeat you, I'll give you a horse and you clear out.'

'So you can shoot me in the back as I ride away.'

'It's up to you ...'

'No. I have nothing to tell you.'

'Your Yaqui Indian friend and Licenciado Bernal, an envoy from Carranza, are in the jail. You will join them and await execution.'

Zagal stood.

Neither of the men was a sentimentalist: such feelings had been ground away by each day's exigencies, by the ceaseless hammering of blind battle. They had spoken as if automatically, revealing no emotion. Zagal had asked for information and had offered a choice between freedom and the wall. The prisoner had refused to give that information. But they had acted not as Zagal and Artemio Cruz, but as two gears in opposing machines of war. The prisoner received the news that he would face a firing squad with absolute indifference, an indifference so absolute, indeed, that it forced him to be aware of the monstrous tranquility with which he accepted his own death. He stood up and squared his jaw.

'Colonel Zagal, we have been obeying orders for a long time now without ever giving ourselves a chance to – how shall I say it? – to do something ourselves, something that says: this I do as Artemio Cruz, this I decide myself and for myself, not as an army officer. If you have to shoot me, shoot the man, not the officer. The end is near, you admit, and we are tired. I don't care to die as the last sacrifice in a victorious cause. Be a man, Colonel, and let me be a man. I propose that we meet with pistols. Draw a line in the patio. We come out from opposite corners. If you get me before I cross the line, finish me off. If I cross it without your hitting me, let me go free.'

'Corporal Payan!' Zagal yelled, his eyes glittering. 'Take him to the cell!'

Then he turned to the prisoner. 'I won't tell you when the execution will be. It might be in an hour, it might be tomorrow, it might be the day after. Think about what I've said.'

The yellow light of the setting sun poured through the barred window and silhouetted two figures, one standing, the other lying down. Tobías tried to murmur a greeting. The other, the nervously pacing man in mufti, came up to him as soon as the cell door banged shut and the lock clanged home.

'You are Captain Artemio Cruz. I am Gonzalo Bernal, envoy from Venustiano Carranza.'

He wore a brown suit with a half-belt behind. Artemio Cruz looked at him as he looked at all civilians who from time to time came into the field to observe the sweaty core of a fighting army, with mocking contempt and indifference. Bernal wiped his broad forehead and blond mustaches and went on:

'The Indian is in a very bad way. He has a broken leg.'

Cruz shrugged. 'He will last as long as he has to last.'

'What do you know?' Bernal's hand had paused with the handkerchief over his mouth, so that the words came out muffled.

'They are going to shoot us. But they won't say when. We won't have to die of bad colds.'

Now it was Cruz who stopped. He had been turning, staring, checking the ceiling, the walls, the barred window and dirt floor: the instinctive search for a way to escape: and he had also been seeing a new enemy, the spy planted in the cell.

'Is there any water?'

'The Indian drank it all.'

The Yaqui moaned. He leaned down to the coppery face on the stone ledge that served as bed and bench. For the first time, and with a surprise that made him draw back, he became aware of the reality that previously had been no more than a dark mask, the face of one more soldier, a life more to be recognized by its body's nervous quickness and coordination than by this repose, this pain: Tobías had a face, and he saw it. Hundreds of fine lines, white crevices of laughter and anger and eyes squinted against the sun, radiated from the corners of the eyes and crisscrossed the broad cheekbones. Heavy, protruding lips; brown narrow eyes with turbid light in them.

'So you are here,' smiled Tobías. 'You're really here.' He spoke in the tongue that Cruz had learned in dealing day after day with the troops from the Sinaloa sierra.

He squeezed the Yaqui's strong hand. 'Yes, Tobías. I have to tell you one thing: they're going to shoot us.'

'Has to be that way. You would do the same.'

'Yes.'

They remained silent and the sun disappeared. Presently they prepared themselves for the night. Bernal paced the cell slowly. Cruz rose and then sat down again and with the tip of a finger drew lines in the dust on the floor. Outside, in the hall, an oil lamp was lit. They could hear the corporal of the guard working his jaw. A cold wind came across the desert.

Standing again, he went to the cell door: thick unfinished pine boards, with a little opening at eye level. On the other side of the opening, smoke curled up from the guard's cornhusk cigarette. He gripped the rusty bars and looked at the snub-nosed profile. A black thatch of hair beneath a canvas cap; bare, square cheekbones. Cruz tried to catch his eye and the guard responded with a quick gesture, a silent 'whatyawant' made with his head and free hand. His other hand gripped the carbine.

'Do you have the order for tomorrow yet?'

The corporal looked at him with wide yellow eyes and did not answer.

'I don't know this country. Do you?'

'I'm from up above here,' said the corporal.

'What kind of a place is it?'

'Where?'

'Where they are going to shoot us. What can one see from there?'

He stopped and gestured for the corporal to pass him a light.

'What can you see?' he repeated.

And as he said this, it came to him that he had always, always looked ahead of him, ever since the night he escaped from the ruined hacienda in Veracruz and crossed the mountains: since that time he had never turned his head to look back. Since that time he had wanted to know himself to be alone, with only his own strength to rely upon. And now he could not resist asking what it was like, what one could see from there. Maybe that was the way he concealed his anxious memories, his leaning back toward images of fern fronds and slow rivers, tubular flowers and a tiny hut, a starched skirt and soft quince-scented hair.

'They take you to the patio in back,' the corporal was saying. 'And what can you see? Well, what would you expect? There's a high wall marked up from bullets, for we get such a lot of firing-squad work here ...'

'And the mountains? Can one see the mountains?'

'Well, to tell you the truth, I don't remember.'

'Have you seen many executions?'

'Yes.'

'Maybe the squad see what is happening better than the men who are shot?'

'And you have never been on a firing squad?'

Oh, yes, I have. But without paying attention, without thinking about what one must feel, or that some day it might happen to me. And so I have no right to ask you. You have killed only as I have killed, thoughtlessly. That's why no one knows what it is like and no one can tell us about it. If I could come back, if I could come back and tell what it is to hear the rifles and feel it in the chest and face; if I could tell the truth about that, maybe we would no longer dare to kill, never again; or maybe it would be that no one would mind dying. It may be terrible ... or it may be as natural as birth. What do we know, you or I?

'Say, Captain, you won't be needing those gold stars any longer now. Give them to me.'

The corporal's hand came through the bars and he turned his back. The soldier laughed.

Now the Yaqui was murmuring in his Indian tongue. Artemio Cruz went to the stone ledge and put his hand on Tobías' fevered forehead and listened to his words, a soft singsong ...

'What?'

'I was telling about it. How the government took our land away to give it to gringos. About how we fought to defend our land and then the Federals came and cut off men's hands and chased us through the mountains. How they captured the Yaqui chiefs in a big canyon and tied weights on them and threw them into the sea.'

The Yaqui talked with closed eyes. 'Those of us who were left were lined up in a long column and marched all the way from Sinaloa to Yucatán.

'We had to march to Yucatán and the women and children and old people of the tribe couldn't take it and began to die. Those who survived to get to the sisal plantations were sold as slaves. Men and their wives were separated. They made the women sleep with Chinese, to make them forget the language and breed more workers . . .

'I came back, I came back. I hardly knew that a war had begun, I came back with my brothers only to fight against the persecution.'

The Yaqui laughed quietly. Artemio Cruz felt the need to urinate. He rose and opened the fly of his khaki pants and went to a corner and listened to the splatter of the dust. His forehead wrinkled as he thought about the familiar death of brave men who die with a wet spot on their uniforms at the crotch.

Bernal, standing with crossed arms, seemed to be looking for moonlight, but the night was cold and dark. At times they could hear hammering from the pueblo. Now and then dogs howled. Unintelligible tags and ends of speech outside managed to pass faintly through the walls. Cruz brushed off his tunic and went over to the young lawyer.

'Any cigarettes?'

'Yes . . . I think so. I had them here somewhere.'

'Offer them to the Yaqui.'

'I did. He doesn't like my kind.'

'But you have some?'

'I did. No, they seem to be finished.'

'Maybe the soldiers have a deck of cards.'

'No, thanks. I couldn't concentrate. Sleepy?' said the lawyer.

'No.'

'You're right. Why sleep?'

'Do you think that some day you are going to regret it?'

'What?'

'I mean, having slept before ...'

'You joking?'

'Well, yes. Maybe it would be better to try to remember things. They say it's a good time for remembering.'

'You don't have much life behind you.'

'No. That's where the Yaqui has the best of us. Maybe that's why he doesn't like to talk.'

'Yes ... No, I don't understand you.'

'I mean that he does have a lot to remember.'

'Maybe in his language memory is not the same.'

'Their long march from Sinaloa. That was what he was telling us about a while ago.'

'Yes.'

'Regina ...'

'Eh?'

'Nothing, I was just saying over some names.'

'How old are you?'

'I'll soon be twenty-six. And you?'

'Twenty-nine. I don't have much to remember either. And my life became confused so damn fast.'

'How do you begin remembering? With childhood?'

'You're right, it isn't easy.'

'You know, now, while we were talking ...'

'Yes?'

'Well, I said over some names to myself. They don't mean anything now. They don't say anything to me.'

'It's almost dawn.'

'Don't worry about what time it is.'

'My back is sweating.'

'Give me a cigarette. What happened?'

'Pardon me. Here, take one. Maybe you don't feel anything.'

'That's what they say.'

'Who says so, Cruz?'

'The men who do the shooting say you don't feel anything.'

'Does that matter much to you?'

'Well . . .'

'Why don't you think about . . . ?'

'About what? That everything is going to go on the same, even though we are shot?'

'No, don't try to think ahead, think back. I am thinking about all those who have already died in the Revolution.'

'Yes. I remember Bule, Aparicio, Gómez, Captain Tiburcio Amarillas . . . quite a few.'

'I doubt if you can remember the names of even twenty. And who knows the names of all the others? Not only those in this revolution; those dead in all the revolutions and all the wars, and even those who died in bed. Who remembers them?'

'Look . . . give me a match.'

'Sorry.'

'Now the moon is up.'

'Do you want to see it? I can lift you up on my shoulders, so you can reach the . . .'

'No. It's not worth the trouble.'

'Better that they took away my watch.'

'Yes.'

'I mean, this way I don't keep looking at it.'

'Yes. I knew what you meant.'

'Night used to seem longer . . . much . . .'

'This is a piss lousy place.'

'Look at the Yaqui. He's sleeping. Better that none of us show fear.'

'Another goddamn day stuck in here.'

'Who knows? They may come in any minute.'

'Not these bastards. They want to play with us. They'll shoot us at dawn or not at all. They're going to play with us.'

'What about his being so impulsive?'

'Villa, yes, but not Zagal.'

'Cruz, isn't it damn absurd?'

'What?'

'To die at the hands of one of the leaders, the *caudillos*, yet to believe in none of them.'

'I wonder if we'll go all together, or one by one?'

'I should think it would be easier all together. You should know, you're the soldier.'

'Can't you think of any way out?'

'No. Want to hear something? It will make you laugh.'

'What?'

'I wouldn't tell you if I weren't sure that I'll never leave this place alive. Carranza sent me on this mission for one reason: to have them capture me and be responsible for my death. He decided that a dead hero is worth more than a live traitor.'

'You, a traitor?'

'It depends on how you look at it. You have had to fight. You've obeyed orders and never doubted your commanders.'

'Sure, that's what I have done. You have to, to win a war. What, aren't you with Obregón and Carranza?'

'I could just as well be with Zapata or Villa. I don't believe in any of them.'

'So?'

'So that's the irony. They are the only choices possible. I don't know whether you remember the beginning. It was such a short time ago, but it seems so far away now. Leaders didn't matter then. It wasn't a war to raise up a caudillo, but to raise up all men.'

'Do you expect me to oppose loyalty? This is the Revolution, loyalty to the leaders, just that.'

'Yes, including the Yaqui. He went out at first to fight for his land. Now he fights for General Obregón, against General Villa. No, it was different in the beginning. Then it broke down into factions, but in the beginning every pueblo the Revolution passed through was a pueblo where the campesinos' debts were erased. The money-lenders were put out of business, the political prisoners were released and the old bosses eliminated. Now the men who believed the Revolution's purpose was to liberate the people have been eliminated. The purpose today is to glorify leaders.'

'There will be time to liberate everyone.'

'No, there won't be. A revolution is shaped on battlefields, but once it is corrupted, though battles are still won, the revolution is lost. We have all been responsible. We have allowed ourselves to be divided and controlled by the ruthless, the ambitious, and the mediocre. Those who wanted a true revolution, radical and uncompromising, are unfortunately ignorant and bloody men. And the literate element want only a half-revolution, compatible with what interests them, their only interest, getting on in the world, living well, replacing Don Porfirio's elite. There you have Mexico's drama. Look at me. All my life reading Kropotkin, Bakunin, old Plekhanov, reading since childhood, and discussing, discussing. And at the really critical moment I had to side with Carranza because he is the only one who seems a decent sort of person, a person who won't frighten me. See what a damned effeminacy ... I'm afraid of the tough bastards, Villa and Zapata. "I will continue being an impossible person so long as those persons who today are possible go on being possible ..." Ah, yes. Why not?'

'You'll be a tough bastard yourself when you're up against the wall.'

'"That's the basic defect in my character: a love of the fantastic, adventures never known before, the enterprises that open infinite horizons, unforeseeable horizons." Ah, yes. Why not?'

'Why didn't you say this before you ended up here?'

'I've said it to Iturbe since '13. To Lucio Blanco, to Buelna, to all the honorable soldiers who never tried to become caudillos. And that, incidentally, was why they didn't know how to stop old Carranza, old Carranza who has spent all his life dividing men, sowing discord: because it was the only way he could keep his mediocrity from being thrown to the side. That's why the other mediocrities move up, the Pablo González, those who don't even cast a shadow. And that was how the Revolution was betrayed, split into factions.'

'And was that why they sent you to Perales?'

'I was sent here to convince the Villistas that they ought to surrender. As though we didn't know about the ones who are broken and in flight and in their desperation pass over to whatever Carranza force comes their way. But the old man doesn't like to soil his hands. He wants the enemy to do the dirty work for him. Artemio, Artemio, the leaders haven't measured up to the people and the people's revolution.'

'Why don't you go over to Villa?'

'To another caudillo? To see how long he lasts, and then to join another, and another, until at the last I find myself in another cell awaiting another firing squad?'

'But this time you would save yourself ...'

'No. Believe me, Cruz, I would like to save myself. Go back to Puebla. See my wife, my son. Luisa and little Pancho. And my little sister, Catalina, who depends on me so much. See my father, Don Gamaliel, so noble and so blind. Try to explain to him why I got into all this. He has never understood that there are obligations one must meet even if one knows beforehand that they are going to go smash. For him, the old order was eternal: the hacienda, the disguised usury, all that ... I wish there were someone who could go see them and tell them for me. But none of us will leave here alive. No: it's a crooked game of elimination. We live between criminals and dwarfs, because the big caudillo adopts pigmies who won't show him up and the little caudillo must kill the big one to rise. What a shame, Artemio. How necessary is everything that has happened, and how unnecessary it is to corrupt it. This isn't what we wanted when we made a people's revolution in '13 ... And you, you must decide. As soon as Zapata and Villa are eliminated, only two caudillos will remain, your present leaders. Which one will you follow?'

'My leader is General Obregón.'

'It's better that you have decided. And we will see whether it will cost you your life, whether ...'

'Man, you forget that we're going to be shot!'

Bernal stopped and laughed with surprise, as if he had tried to fly and the weight of forgotten shackles had pulled him unexpectedly down again. He gripped Artemio's shoulder:

'My damn political mania! Or can it be intuition? Why don't *you* go over to Villa?'

He could not see Gonzalo Bernal's face clearly. But even in the darkness he felt the mocking eyes, the know-it-all air of the little lawyers who never fight, who do nothing except talk while men win battles. He pulled brusquely away.

'What's the matter?' The lawyer was laughing.

Cruz grunted and relit his cigarette. 'You don't talk right,' he said between his teeth. 'You want me to speak up? All right: it gripes my ass to have to listen to true confessions I haven't asked to hear, especially when I'm trying to prepare myself for a firing squad. Just keep quiet, Licenciado, say anything you want but say it to yourself, not to me. I'm not going to double-cross anyone.'

Gonzalo's voice became metallic: 'Listen, we're three condemned prisoners. The Yaqui told us the story of his life . . .'

The officer's anger was against himself: he had let himself be carried away into confidences, conversation, and had opened himself to a man not fit to be trusted.

'His life was a man's life. He has the right to talk about it.'

'And you?'

'Fighting, fighting. If there was anything before the fighting, I don't remember it.'

'You loved a woman . . .'

Cruz clenched his fists.

'. . . you had parents. For all I know, you may have a son. No? Well, I do. I agree you have lived a man's life. I think you would like to go on living it. You don't agree? You wouldn't like, this minute, to be making love to some . . .'

His hands found Bernal in the darkness and the voice stopped. He gripped his suit lapels and bellowed and jerked him against the wall. Yet at the same time he knew that the other was merely repeating his own hidden thoughts. What happens after death? And Bernal went on, in spite of the hands that held him:

'If they hadn't killed us before we were thirty, what would our lives have been? I wanted to do so much . . .'

Until he, sweat running down his back and his face very near the other's, also muttered: 'As if you didn't know: everything will go on the same. The sun will rise, kids will go on being born, nothing will change though you and I are dead as mackerel. As if you damn well didn't know.'

He loosened his hands and stepped back and Bernal slid to the dirt floor. He walked to the door of the cell. He had decided. He would give Zagal false information, bargain for the Yaqui's life, and leave Bernal to take care of himself.

As the guard, humming, escorted him to the colonel, he felt

his lost pain for Regina. Bittersweet memories that had been buried deep floated to the surface again and asked him to go on living, as though dead Regina needed to be remembered by her living man, to go on being something more than a decaying body fed upon by worms in a nameless hole, in a nameless pueblo.

'It will be hard for you to fool us,' said Zagal's eternally smiling voice. 'Two detachments are leaving right now to see if what you have said is true. If it isn't, you had better commend yourself to heaven. You will have gained only a few hours, and at the cost of honor.'

The colonel stretched his legs. His boots were off. He wiggled his toes.

'And the Yaqui?'

'That wasn't part of our deal. Look: the night is passing. Why tease those poor bastards with a new sun? Corporal Payan! We're going to send the two prisoners to a better life. Get them out of the cell and take them out back.'

'The Yaqui can't walk,' said the corporal.

'Give him marihuana,' Zagal chuckled. 'Let's see. Put him on a stretcher. Prop him up against the wall as best you can.'

What did Tobías and Gonzalo Bernal see? What he saw too, though he was a little higher than they, for he stood on the roof of the building beside Zagal. The Yaqui was carried out on a litter. Bernal walked with his head down. The two men were placed against the wall between two kerosene lamps.

It was night when dawn was slow, when the outline of the mountains remained invisible. The rifles fired with a red flash as Bernal reached out a hand to touch the Indian's shoulder. Tobías remained propped against the wall, supported by the litter. The lamplight revealed his shattered face. Bernal crumpled and only his ankles were in the light. A little stream of blood began to flow around them.

'There are your dead,' said Zagal.

Other riflefire, distant and heavy, punctuated his words. A shell exploded and knocked off a corner of the building. The Villistas' hoarse shouts rose to the roof while Zagal yelled inarticulate questions.

'They're here! They've caught up with us! It's the Carranzista bastards!' Cruz knocked him down and gripped his hand, which was reaching for the holster, with all his strength. He felt the pistol in his right hand and dug it into Zagal's back and locked an arm around his neck, holding him down. Below, he could see the confusion in the patio. Soldiers were running like chickens, stepping on the bodies of the two executed prisoners, knocking over the lamps. Exploding shells dropped everywhere. Screams, fires blazing up, horses rearing and galloping. More Villistas ran out into the patio buttoning their pants and pulling on their coats. Light from the fallen lamps traced a golden line on every profile and every buckle and metal button. They scrambled for their rifles and cartridge belts. The bar across the stable doorway was hurriedly dropped and the whinnying horses came out into the patio, were swiftly mounted, and cavalrymen raced out the gate into the street. Stragglers followed, and finally the patio stood empty. Two kerosene lamps. The bodies of a Yaqui Indian and an attorney revolutionary. The shouts faded in the distance: they were on their way to meet the attack. Artemio Cruz relaxed his hold slightly. Zagal remained on his knees, coughing, rubbing his bruised throat. He tried, chokingly to shout:

'Don't surrender! I'm up here!'

Morning showed its blue eyelid over the desert.

The confusion had stopped. Villistas hurried through the streets toward the fighting. Their white blouses were tinted with blue. Not a sound rose from the patio. Zagal stood and unbuttoned his grimy tunic, offering his chest. Captain Cruz stepped forward too, the pistol in his hand.

'My offer stands,' he said in a dry voice.

'Then let's go down.' Zagal dropped his arms.

They stopped by the office and the colonel got a Colt that he kept in a drawer. Both armed, now, they walked along cold passages to the patio. They drew a line dividing the patio into halves. Zagal moved Bernal's head out of the way with his foot, while Cruz picked up the kerosene lamps.

Zagal chose a corner. They moved forward.

Zagal fired first and his bullet put another wound in the Indian Tobías. He stopped; hope shone in his black eyes; Cruz advanced without firing. It was becoming a gesture: honor. The colonel held his fire, one, two, three seconds, hoping that Cruz would respect his courage, so that the two men would meet at the dividing line without firing again.

They stopped at the line.

Zagal smiled. Cruz stepped across the line. Zagal, laughing, made a friendly gesture with his hand as two fast shots caught him in the belly. The other watched him double over and collapse at his feet. Artemio Cruz dropped the pistol on the colonel's sweat-soaked head and stood motionless.

The desert wind blew the curls hanging over his forehead, flapped the tatters of his stained tunic, the rips in his leather leggings. A five-day beard bristled his cheeks and his green eyes were hidden behind dusty eyelashes and dry tears. He stood there, solitary hero on the field of the dead. Hero without witnesses. He stood there in the abandoned patio, while a battle was fought outside the pueblo, and drums rolled.

He looked down. Colonel Zagal's dead arm was extended toward Gonzalo's dead head. The Yaqui was still upright, his back against the wall. Artemio Cruz squatted and closed the colonel's eyes.

He stood again quickly and breathed deep of the air of morning. He wanted to find, to thank, to give ... a name to life and freedom. But he was alone, he had no witnesses, no companions. A deaf shout broke from his throat, hushed by the machinegun fire in the distance.

'I am free. I am free.'

He clasped his hands over his stomach and his face twisted with pain.

He looked up and at last saw what a condemned man sees of dawn: the far away line of mountains, the lightening sky, the patio's adobe walls. He heard what a condemned man hears: the chirps of unseen birds, the sharp cry of a hungry child, a blacksmith's hammering. And the steady monotonous roar of the barrage and the riflefire. Anonymous hammering, louder than battle, sure that after battle and death and victory, the sun will always rise again, day after day ...

I no longer desire; I let them do what they will. I try to touch it, I run my hand from my umbilicus to my crotch. Round. Doughy. I don't know now. The doctor has gone, he said he was going to get more doctors. He doesn't want to take responsibility for me. I don't know now. But I see them. They have come in. The mahogany door opens and closes and their steps are silent on the thick carpet. They have closed the windows. They have run the gray curtains shut, with a hissing noise. They have come in.

'Go near him, child, so that he can recognize you. Tell him your name . . .'

Take a good smell. She smells nice. Ah, yes, I can still see her, her flushed cheeks, the bright eyes, her young graceful body approaching me with hesitant steps.

'I am . . . I am Gloria.'

I try to murmur her name. I know they don't hear my words. At least I can thank Teresa for this: to have the young body of her daughter near me. If I could only make her face out better. If I could only be sure of her expression. She must notice this stink of dead skin, of vomit and blood; she has to see my sunken chest, the gray tangled beard, the fluid dripped from my nose, these waxy ears, the saliva dried on my lips and chin, these vacant eyes that must try and try to see, these . . .

They draw her away from me.

'Poor girl, she's too upset to . . .'

'Eh?'

'Nothing, Papá, rest.'

They say she and Padilla's son are sweethearts. How he must kiss her, what words he must tell her, ah, yes, what blushes. They come in and go out. They touch my shoulder, move their heads, murmur words of encouragement, yes, they don't know that I hear them, in spite of everything: I hear the fartherest conversations, those in the corners, not what is said beside my bed.

'How does he seem to you, Señor Padilla?'

'Bad, bad.'

'He leaves an empire.'

'Yes.'

'So many years at the head of his businesses!'

'He will be very hard to replace.'

'I'll tell you: except for Don Artemio himself, no one is as well qualified as you.'

'Yes, I am involved with everything.'

'And in that case, who will replace you?'

'There are competent men.'

'One might expect some promotions?'

'Of course. A complete new distribution of responsibilities.'

Ah, Padilla, come closer. Did you bring the tape-recorder?

'Then you must take the responsibility.'

'Don Artemio ... I brought ...'

Sí, patrón.

Be ready. The government is going to move with an iron fist. And you must be ready to take over the leadership of the union.

Yes, sir.

I warn you that several old foxes are also preparing. I've already indicated to the authorities that you are the man we trust. Have a bite?

Thank you, I've already eaten. I had lunch ju   a little while ago.

Don't let a vote ruin you. Start things moving, but first, to the Secretary, to the CTM, first things first.

Of course, patrón. You can count on me.

Goodby, Campanela. Don't talk. Be careful. Alert. All right, Padilla, let's go ...

There. The tape has ended. Ah. That was all of it. Was that all of it? Who knows, I don't remember. For quite some time I haven't been listening to those taped voices. For some time I've been just pretending. Who's touching me? Who's so close to me? How useless, Catalina. I tell myself: how futile, what a futile caress. I ask myself: what are you going to say to me? Do you think that at last you have found those words you have never dared to pronounce? Ah: you loved me? Then why didn't we say it to one another? I loved you. I don't remember. Your

caress forces me to see you and I don't know, I don't understand, why sitting beside me you share at last this memory, and
this time without reproach in your eyes. Pride. Pride saves us.
Pride kills us.

'. . . for a miserable miserly salary, while he offends us with
that woman, rubs our noses in his luxury, gives us what he gives
us as though we were beggars . . .'

They haven't understood. I did nothing for them. I never even
thought about them. I did it for myself. Their stories don't
interest me: I don't care to remember Teresa and Gerardo's
life; who gives a damn about them?

'Gerardo, demand that he give you your proper place. You
are as capable as he is . . .'

Who gives a damn?

'Easy, Teresa, dear. You must understand my position. I'm
not complaining.'

'Show a little character. He . . .'

'Let him rest.'

'Don't side with him! There is no one he has made suffer
more than you.'

I survived. Regina. What was your name? No: you, Regina.
What was your name, nameless soldier? Gonzalo. Gonzalo
Bernal. A Yaqui. A poor Yaqui. I survived. You others died.

'And me too. How can I forget it: he didn't even come to my
wedding. To my wedding, his own daughter's wedding . . .'

They never understood. I didn't need them. I did it alone.
Soldier. Yaqui. Regina. Gonzalo.

'Even what he loved, he destroyed. You know that, Mamá.'

'Stop, stop. Dear God, don't say any more . . .'

My will? Don't worry: a document exists. Tax-stamped and
notarized. I forget no one: why should I forget them, hate them?
That would please them, secretly. It would give them pleasure
to believe that I thought of them until the last minute only to
make fools of them. No: I have remembered you with the indifference of a cold business matter, dear Catalina, amiable
Teresa, Gloria, Gerardo: I parcel out extraneous wealth that you
will publicly affirm to be the fruit of my effort, my tenacity, my
sense of responsibility, my personal qualities. Be at peace.

Forget that I won that wealth by exposing my hide in a battle I did not know, did not want to understand because it was not convenient to know, understand, because it could be known and understood only by those who expected to gain nothing from their sacrifice. That is what sacrifice is, isn't it? to give everything and receive nothing in return. Then what is it called when you give everything in order to receive everything? But they never offered me everything. She did, everything. I didn't take it. I didn't know how to accept it. What is that called?

Okay, the picture's clear enough. Say, the old boy at the Embassy wants to make a speech comparing this Cuban mess with the old-time Mexican revolution. Why don't you prepare the climate with an editorial . . . ?

Yes. Yes, we could do that. About twenty thousand pesos?

Seems fair enough. Any ideas?

Yes. Tell him to establish a clear contrast between an anarchic, bloody movement that is destructive of private property and human rights alike, and an ordered revolution, peaceful and legal, such as the Mexican Revolution, which was directed by a middle class inspired by Jefferson. The people have short memories. Tell him to deal with us gently.

Fine. So long, Mr Cruz. It's always . . .

Oh, what a barrage of meanings, implications, words. Oh, what fatigue. They won't understand my gesture, my fingers can hardly move: but let it be shut off now, I'm bored with it, it means nothing, just crap, crap . . .

'In the name of the Father, and of the Son . . .'

'I waited for him with happiness that morning. We rode our horses across the river.'

'Why did you take him from me?'

I bequeath them the useless dead, the dead names of Regina, the Yaqui . . . Tobías, now I remember, they called him Tobías . . . and of Gonzalo Bernal, and an unknown soldier. And she? Another.

'Open the window.'

'No. You might be chilled and get worse.'

Laura. Why? Why did everything turn out that way? Why?

You will survive: you will rub the sheets again and know that you have survived, in spite of time and the movement that second by second shortens your fortune: the line of life lies between paralysis and frenzy: adventure: you will imagine the greatest security, never to move again: you will imagine yourself motionless, protected from danger, from chance, unforeseen disaster, from uncertainty: and your immobility will not stop time, it will run on without you even though you concoct and measure it: the time that denies your immobility and subjects you to its own danger of extinction: adventurer, you will measure your speed by that of time:

the time you will create in order to survive, to feign the illusion of greater permanence upon the earth: the time that your brain must needs create to perceive the alterations of light and darkness in the quadrant of sleep; to retain those images of calm threatened by the black cumulous heaping of clouds, by the roll of thunder, lightning's offspring, by pelting explosions of rain, by the inevitable rainbow; to hear the cyclical cries of animals on the mountain; to shout the changes of season, the howls of war, mourning, and fiesta; in order, in short, to say time, speak time, and think the non-existent time of a universe that does not know time because it never began and will never end: it had no beginning, it will have no end, and it does not know that you will invent a measure of the infinite, a rational calipers.

you will invent a time that does not exist, and measure it,

you will know, discern, judge, calculate, imagine, predict, and you will end by thinking that there is no other reality than that created by your mind; you will learn to subdue your violence in order to subdue that of your enemies: you will learn to rub two sticks together until they burn, because you will need to throw a torch into the mouth of the cave and frighten the beasts that see you as no different from themselves, that make no distinction between your flesh and the flesh of any beast; and you will have to build a thousand temples, make a thousand laws, write a thousand books, worship a thousand gods, paint a thousand pictures, build a thousand machines, conquer a thousand cities, split a thousand atoms, in order to throw your lighted torch into the entrance of that cave again;

and all this you will do because you think, because you have developed a neural tangle in your skull, a dense network capable of obtaining information and transmitting it from the front backward; you will survive, not because you are strong, but by the dark chance of a universe growing colder and colder, in which survival is possible only to the organisms that can maintain a constant body temperature in the face of a changing environment, those that can elaborate that frontal neural mass and can foresee danger, seek food, organize their movements and direct their swim through the prolific round ocean, the witness to their origin: the lost and dead species will remain on the bottom of the sea, your lost brothers, millions of brothers whose five contractile stars never emerged from the sea, whose five fingers never gripped the other shore, the solid earth, the islands of dawn: you will emerge with the amoeba, crossed reptile-bird: birds that will throw themselves from the newborn peaks only to smash in the new chasms, learning by failing, while the reptiles already can fly and the earth grows colder: you will survive with birds that are protected by feathers, clothed in the velocity of their warmth, the warmth of their velocity, while the sluggard cold reptiles sleep, hibernate, and finally die; and you will dig your toenails into the solid earth, the islands of dawn, and you will sweat like a horse; you with your constant temperature will climb the new trees and when you come down from the branches, your neural cells will be differentiated, your vital functions will have become automatic, your constants of hydrogen, sugar, calcium, water, and oxygen will have been established: you will be freed to think beyond the limits of immediate sensation and vital needs

you will descend from the branches with your ten million brain cells, with your little galvanic pile in your skull ready, plastic and mutable, to explore, satisfy your curiosity, propose purposes, realize them, avoid difficulties, foresee, learn, forget, remember, combine ideas, recognize forms, and so you will rise by the steps of your emancipation from the necessities of existence, consigning your will to the opportunities and rebuffs of the physical medium, seeking favorable conditions, measuring reality by the criterion of the minimum while desiring secretly the maximum, yet nevertheless not risking the monotony of frustration:

accustoming yourself, molding yourself to the demands of life shared with others:

desiring: desiring that your desire and its object may be one and the same; dreaming of instant fulfillment, of the identification without hiatus of the wish and the wished for:

recognizing yourself:

recognizing others and letting them recognize you: knowing that you oppose all men because every man is an obstacle between you and your desire:

you will choose, in order to survive you will make choices, you will choose from the infinite array of mirrors only one, the one that will reflect you irrevocably and will throw a black shadow over all other mirrors: you will destroy them before they offer you, once again, that infinity of possible paths to be chosen from:

you will sacrifice, you will select one path giving up all the rest: you sacrifice by choosing, you will cease to be the man you might have been, and you will want other men – one other – to fulfill for you the life you mutilated by choosing, by saying yes and when you said no, when you decided it was not your desire, which is one with your freedom, that would be infinitely ramified, but rather your self-interest, your fear, your pride:

on that day you will fear love:

but you will be able to recover it: you will lie with your eyes closed but will not stop seeing, will not stop desiring, because it is thus that you will gain what you desire:

for memory is desire satisfied

today when your life and your destiny are the same.

[1934: August 12]

He chose a match, scratched it on the roughened side of the box, studied the flame, and finally touched it to his cigarette. He closed his eyes and breathed the smoke in. He stretched out his legs and settled back in the velvet armchair. He ran his hand over the velvet and smelled the fragrance of the chrysanthemums in the glass vase on the table behind him, and listened to the slow music from the phonograph, which was also behind him.

'I'm almost ready.'

The open record album was on the low walnut table to his right. He felt the album, labeled *Deutsche Grammophon Gesellschaft*, and listened to the majestic entrance of the cello, which withdrew, returned, and finally overcame the violins' refrain and relegated them to the second ending of the chorus. He stopped listening. He adjusted his tie. His hand lingered caressingly on the heavy silk, silk that whispered lightly beneath his fingertips.

'May I fix you anything?'

He went over to tne cart and poured two fingers of Scotch into a heavy Bohemian-glass tumbler, adding an ice cube and a little plain water.

'Whatever you're having.'

He repeated the operation. Taking both glasses in his hands, mixing the drinks by swirling them, he walked to the bedroom door.

'Just a minute.'

'You chose it for me?'

'Yes. Remember?'

'Yes.'

'Forgive me for holding us up.'

He went back to the armchair, took the album again, lay it on his knees, and read: *Werke von Georg Friedrich Händel.* They had heard the two concerts in that overheated hall and by chance were seated side by side. She heard him in Spanish telling his friend that the room was too hot. He asked her, in English, if he might glance at her program, and she smiled and in Spanish said, with pleasure. They both smiled. Concerti Grossi, opus 6.

They had made a date for the next month, when they would both arrive in the city where they were now, and had met in a café on the Rue Caumartin, near the Boulevard des Capucines, a place he tried to find again years later, without her, and could not locate: wanting to see it again, to order the same drink; and then he did find it again, a café decorated in rose and sepia with chairs of Roman marble and a long bar of reddish wood, not a street café but one open to the street, without doors. They had drunk crème de menthe and water. He ordered the same again. She said that September was the best month, the best time the end of September and the beginning of October. Indian summer. End of vacations. He paid. She took his arm, laughing, breathing deeply, and they crossed the courtyards of the Palais Royal, walking between the galleries and the courtyards, stepping on the first dead leaves, with pigeons following, and then they went to the restaurant with the small tables and the velvet-backed chairs and the walls of painted mirrors, old paint, old gold and blue and brown enamel.

'Ready.'

He looked over his shoulder and saw her come out of the bedroom, putting on her earrings and patting her smooth, honey-colored hair. He gave her a drink. She took a sip, wrinkled her nose, and sat down in the red armchair and crossed her legs and raised the glass to the level of her eyes. He matched her gesture and smiled at her as she picked a speck of lint from the lapel of her black suit. The harpsichord carried the descending melody, accompanied by the violins: he imagined the melody as drifting down from a height, not as a movement forward, a light feathery descent that turned to contrapuntal joy as it touched earth with the edged grave tones of the violins. Only the harpsichord could have done that, dropped the melody so gently down to solid earth. And now the music was dancing upon the earth. They looked at each other.

'Laura . . .'

She touched her fingers to her lips. They went on listening, she seated with the glass between her hands, he standing, spinning the globe of the earth on its pivots, stopping it now and then to look at the figures drawn in silver above the constellations: a raven, a shield, a greyhound, a fish, an altar, a centaur. The needle turned upon silence. He walked to the phonograph and took off the record and put it away.

'The apartment turned out well.'

'Yes. It's curious. But all my things couldn't be used.'

'It's very nice.'

'I had to store the things I couldn't use.'

'If you wished, you could . . .'

'Thanks,' she said, laughing. 'If all I wanted were a great big house, I would have stayed with him.'

'Do you want to listen to more music, or shall we leave?'

'No. Let's finish our drinks and go.'

They had stopped in front of that painting and she had said that she liked it very much and always came to see it because those waiting trains, that blue smoke, those big blue and ochre houses in the background, those erased, scarcely visible figures and Saint-Lazare terminal's horrible iron and glass roof, all these pleased her very much, she liked Monet, he painted the things that she liked in this city where little was lovely if it was seen by itself, in isolation, in detail, but much was irresistible when seen *en masse*, together. He told her that this was an idea to think about, and she laughed and stroked his hand and said that he was right, the picture just delighted her and that was all, everything delighted her, she was contented; and years later, when the painting had been moved to the Jeu de Paume, he returned to look at it and his special guide told him that it was in every way outstanding, that in thirty years its value had more than quadrupled, so that it was now worth several thousand dollars, most outstanding.

He stood behind her chair, ran his hands over the chair back, and touched Laura's shoulders. She moved her cheek against his hand and his fingers stroked her cheek. He sighed a new smile. He sipped a little whiskey. He threw his head back with his eyes closed and swallowed after having held the liquid between tongue and palate.

'Next year we might go back. Don't you think?'

'Yes. We might go back.'

'Often I think of how we used to wander along the streets.'

'So do I. You've never gone to the Village. Remind me to take you.'

'Yes. We could go back.'

'There is something so vital in that city. Remember, you could never learn to distinguish the smells of the ocean and the river. You hadn't quite got them straight. We would walk toward the Hudson with our eyes closed.'

He took Laura's hand and kissed her fingers. The telephone jangled and he went and picked it up. He heard a voice repeating: 'Hello . . . Hello? Hello? Laura?' He put his hand over the mouthpiece and handed it to her. She left her glass on the table.

'Hello?'

'*Laura. It's Catalina.*'

'Yes. How are you?'

'*I'm not interrupting you?*'

'I was just going out.'

'*I won't take a minute.*'

'Tell me.'

'*I'm not keeping you?*'

'No. Go on.'

'*I think I made a mistake. I should have told you.*'

'Yes?'

'*Yes. I ought to have bought the sofa from you. Now that I'm arranging the new house, I realize it. You remember the sofa, the one with the dotted brocade? You know, it would go very well in my vestibule, because I bought some tapestries for the vestibule and I think that the only thing that will go with them is your embroidered sofa . . .*'

'Perhaps. It might be too much embroidery.'

'*No, no, no. You see, the tapestries are a dark tone, and your sofa is light, so there'll be a nice contrast.*'

'But you know I've put the sofa here, in my apartment.'

'*Ay, don't be like that. You have more furniture than you need. Didn't you tell me you had to put half your things in storage? Yes, that's what you told me, isn't it?*'

'Yes. But now I have the living room arranged so that . . .'

'*Well, think about it, won't you? When are you coming to see the house?*'

'Whenever you want me to.'

'*No, not like that, not so indefinite. Pick a day and we'll have tea together and talk.*'

'Friday?'

'*No, Friday I can't. But Thursday would be fine.*'

'All right, Thursday.'

'*But I tell you that without that sofa my vestibule is ruined. I'd almost prefer not to have a vestibule, don't you see? It will just be ruined. And an apartment can be rearranged so easily ...*'

'So, Thursday.'

'*And I saw your husband on the street. He was very pleasant. Laura, it's a sin, it's a sin that you are going to be divorced. I think he is so handsome. You can see that he misses you. Why, Laura, why?*'

'That's all over now.'

'*Thursday, then. Just the two of us, a nice chat.*'

'Yes, Catalina. Thursday.'

'*Goodbye.*'

He had asked her to dance and they had walked along the Hotel Plaza's corridors of potted palms and had entered the ballroom and he had taken her in his arms. She caressed his long fingers and felt the warmth of his palm. She lay her head on his shoulder, raised her head again to look at him and found him staring at her: staring, gazing, his green eyes, her gray eyes, looking at each other alone in a ballroom where the orchestra was playing a slow blues, looking at each other with their eyes and with their fingers and their close embrace, whirling slowly, her batiste skirt, her skirt ...

She hung up and looked at him and waited. She walked to the embroidered sofa and ran her fingers over it and turned and looked at him.

'Want to turn on that light? The one beside you. Thanks.'

'She doesn't know anything.'

Laura moved away from the sofa and looked at him.

'No, that's too much light. I don't have things just right yet. Lighting a big house is not the same as lighting this ...'

She felt tired. She sat on the sofa and took a small leather-bound book from the sidetable and leafed through it. She brushed aside the blonde bangs that covered half her forehead, moved to be in a better light, and in a soft voice read aloud, with her eyebrows arched and a subtle resignation around her mouth. She read almost whispering and closed the book and said: 'Calderón de la Barca.' From memory she repeated: 'Won't there be pleasure some day? Tell me why God created flowers, if smell is never to know their soft fragrance . . .'

She stretched out on the sofa, covered her eyes with her hands, and went on quoting precisely and tiredly with a voice that did not want to be heard either by her or by anyone: '. . . if the ear is not to hear? . . . if the eye is not to see?' She felt his hand touch her throat and the pearls she wore.

'I haven't forced you . . .'

'No, you have had nothing to do with it. It dates from before you.'

'And why?'

'Oh, maybe because I have too elevated an opinion of my own worth . . . because I believe I have a right to be treated differently . . . to be not an object but a person.'

'And with me?'

'I don't know. I don't know. I'm thirty-five. It's not so easy to begin again, unless someone gives us a hand. We talked about it that night. Remember?'

'Yes. We said that we had to learn to know each other . . .'

'That it was more dangerous to close doors than to open them. And do you know me yet?'

'You never say anything, never ask anything of me.'

'I ought to ask something, you think. Why?'

'I don't know.'

'You don't know. You'll know only if I spell it out.'

'Perhaps.'

'I love you. You have said that you love me. No, you don't want to understand. Give me a cigarette.'

He took the package from his jacket pocket. He lit a match as she lifted the cigarette to her mouth. A bit of cigarette paper stuck to her lip and she lifted it off with a fingernail, rolled it into a tiny ball between her fingertips, and flipped it lightly away. And he looked at her.

'Maybe I'll study again. When I was fifteen, I wanted to paint. Later I forgot about it.'

'Aren't we going out?'

She kicked off her shoes, fitted a pillow behind her head, and blew curls of smoke toward the ceiling.

'No, we aren't going out.'

'Another Scotch?'

'Yes, give me another.'

He picked up her empty glass, looked at the lipstick marks, and tinkled the ice cube, still unmelted, as he walked to the bar. He poured whiskey and dropped in another ice cube with the silver tongs.

'No water this time, please.'

She had asked him if he wondered what she was looking at, that girl in the painting, at whom or what she was looking as she stood in the swing dressed in white – white and shadow – with blue bows; something is always outside a painting, she went on, the world represented by a painting must enlarge and extend itself and become filled with other colors, presences, and questions, the reasons why the painting was painted, why it is. And they had gone out into the September sunlight. They had walked, as always with laughter, beneath the arcades of the Rue de Rivoli, and she had said that he should see the Place des Vosges, it was very beautiful. They stopped a taxi. He spread the map on his knees and she ran her finger along the red line, the green line, taking his arm, her breath mixing with his, and she said that the names were charming, one never tired of repeating them – Richard Lenoir, Ledru-Rollin, Filles du Calvaire . . .

He gave her the glass and spun the globe again, reading the names: Lupus, Crater, Sagittarius, Pisces, Horologium, Argo Navis, Libra, Serpens. He spun it rapidly and let his finger ride lightly upon the whirling surface, touching the cold distant stars.

'What are you doing?'

'Looking at this world.'

'Ah.'

He bent and kissed her hair. She moved her head and smiled.

'Your wife wants this sofa.'

'I heard.'

'What do you suggest? Shall I be generous?'

'Whatever you want to do.'

'Oh, you don't care? I may forget that she called? I would like to be indifferent, too. Sometimes generosity is an ugly insult and quite without point. Don't you agree?'

'I don't understand you.'

'Put on a little music.'

'What would you like to hear now?'

'The same. Put on the same record, please.'

He read the numbers on the four sides and put the records on in order. He pressed the button and the record fell with a dry tap on the suede-topped turntable. He smelled a mixture of wax and hot glass tubes and polished wood, and again listened to the wings of the harpsichord, the gentle glide toward happiness, the keyboard's renunciation of air to touch the strings' reality of earth, solidity, the giant's shoulders . . .

'Is the volume all right?'

'A little higher, please. Artemio . . .'

'Yes?'

'I've gone as far as I can, my love. You must choose now.'

'Be patient, Laura. You have to take into account . . .'

'What?'

'Don't try to force me.'

'To do what? Are you afraid of me?'

'Aren't we all right as we are? Is anything lacking?'

'Who knows. Maybe nothing is lacking. Maybe this is all . . .'

'I can't hear you.'

'No, don't turn the music down. Hear me in spite of the music. I'm tired.'

'I haven't deceived you. I haven't forced you.'

'And I have not changed you, which is quite different. You aren't ready.'

'I want you like this, as we have been until now.'

'As we were the first day.'

'Yes, like that.'

184

'It's not the first day now, Artemio. You know me now. Tell me.'

'Be careful, Laura, please. These things can hurt us both. You have to be careful . . .'

'Of what? Appearances? Or of fear? If nothing is going to happen, you can be sure that nothing will happen.'

'We ought to go out.'

'No, not now. Not any more. Make it louder.'

The violins broke against glass: happiness, renunciation. The happiness of her forced smile under her clear and very bright eyes. He got his hat from one of the chairs. He walked to the door. With his hand on the knob, he stopped and looked back. Laura was curled up on the sofa, the pillows in her arms, and her back was turned to him. He went out, closing the door carefully.

I wake again, but this time with a cry: someone has nailed a long cold dagger in my stomach, some stranger: I could never take my own life that way: and someone, someone else has driven a spike in my guts: I reach out my arms, I make an effort to raise myself and there are their hands holding me down, asking me to be calm, telling me that I must stay quiet, and a finger hurriedly dials a telephone number, makes a mistake, dials again and gets it wrong again, and finally reaches the doctor, right away, quickly, because I want to get up and lose the pain in movement and they won't let me – who are they? who can they be? – and the contractions ascend, rings on a snake, they rise to my chest, to my throat, and fill my tongue and my mouth with the bitter ground paste of some meal I have forgotten and that I vomit now, face down, looking in vain for a basin instead of the carpet splotched by the thick stinking liquid from my stomach: it doesn't stop, it tears at my chest and is bitter and scratches my throat with a raw tickling: it goes on, it doesn't stop, it's an old meal mixed with blood and vomited on the bedroom carpet, and I don't have to see myself to know the paleness of my face, my livid lips, the quickened thump of my heart while the pulse disappears from my wrist: they have stabbed me through the bellybutton, the same umbilicus that once fed me life, once upon a time ago, and I cannot believe what my fingers tell me as I touch that belly that is no part of me but must be me: blown tight, swollen, puffed up by the gases I feel moving but that I can't get out no matter how I strain: those farts that rise to my throat and go back into my guts, and I still can't get them out: but I can taste and smell my own fetid breath, now that I manage to lie back, and beside me they are hastily cleaning the carpet, I smell the soapy water, the wet rag that tries to defeat the stink of vomit: I want to get up, if I walk around the room, the pain will leave, I know it will leave:

'Open the window.'

'Even what he loved, he destroyed. You know that, Mamá.'

'Stop, stop. Dear God, don't say any more now.'

'Didn't he murder Lorenzo, didn't he ...?'

'Teresa! I forbid you to talk like this. You hurt me.'

Eh, Lorenzo? It doesn't matter. Doesn't matter to me. Let them say anything. I've known for a long time what they say, without daring to say it to me. Let them say it now. Let them take this opportunity. I give it to them. They never understood. They stand like statues and they look at me while the priest rubs the oil on my eyelids, my ears, my lips, my hands and feet, between my legs, around my genitals. Plug in the tape-recorder, Padilla ...

'We will cross the river ...'

And Teresa stops me and this time I do see the fear in her eyes and the panic in the twist of her pale lips, and in Catalina's arms is the unbearable weight of words she has never uttered and that I keep her from uttering: I try to lie back but I can't, I can't, the pain doubles me up, I have to touch my toes with my fingers to be sure my toes are still there, frozen but not already dead, already dead; and only now it comes to me that always, all my life, there was an imperceptible movement in my intestines, a movement that I recognize now only because suddenly I don't feel it: it has stopped, a movement in waves that was with me all my life, and now I don't feel it, don't feel it, but I see my fingernails when I stretch my hands to touch my numb feet, blue fingernails, blackish, ready to die too: aaah-aaaay, now it won't stop, I don't want this blue skin, this skin dyed by dead blood: no, no, I don't want it, something else blue, blue sky, blue memories, blue horses crossing the river, blue shiny horses and green the sea, blue the flowers, blue me, I blue, no, no, no, no, ahhhhhaaaayyyy, and I must fall backward because I don't know where to move, how to move, where to reach my arms or where to put my numb legs, or where to look, and I don't want to get up because I don't know where to go, all I know is this pain beneath my umbilicus, in my belly, next to my ribs, this pain in my rectum while I strain uselessly, wrenchingly, strain with my legs apart, and now I don't smell anything but I hear Teresa's sobs and I feel Catalina's hand on my shoulder.

I don't know, I don't understand, why you, seated beside me, insist upon sharing that memory with me, and this time without reproach in your eyes. Ah, if you could understand. If we could both understand. Maybe there is another membrane behind our open eyes and only now are we going to break it and see. One can leave one's body only to the extent that one can accept another's look, caress. You touch me. You touch my hand and I feel your hand and not my own. She touches me. Catalina caresses my hand. That will be love. I ask myself. I do not understand: will it be love? We have been so used to each other as we were, to the point that if I had offered love, she would have twisted it into a rebuff; to the point that if she had offered love, I would have twisted it into pride: perhaps two halves of a single feeling, perhaps. She touches me. She wants to remember that with me. Only that. To understand it.

'Why?'

'We rode our horses across ...'

I survived. Regina. What was your name? No: you, Regina. What was your name, nameless soldier? I survived. You others died. I survived.

'Go near him, child, so that he can recognize you. Tell him your name ...'

But I hear Teresa's sobs and I feel Catalina's hand on my shoulder, and the swift creaking step of the man who now feels my stomach, takes my pulse, raises my eyelids and flashes a blinking light into my eyes, on and off, on and off, and then the other eye, and he feels my stomach again and inserts his finger into my rectum, puts a warm thermometer that tastes of alcohol in my mouth, and while the other voices become silent, the stranger says something far away at the other end of a tunnel:

'There is no way to be sure. It may be a strangulated hernia. It may be peritonitis. It may be kidney colic. I tend to think that it's colic. If it is, he should be given two centigrams of morphine. But that could be dangerous. I think we better have another doctor see him.'

Ay, pain that overcomes itself, pain that prolongs until it no longer matters, until it becomes normality: *ay*, pain, now I could not stand it if you were to go away, now I have become used to you, *ay* pain *ay* . . .

'Say something, Don Artemio. Say something, please.'

'. . . I don't remember her, I don't remember her now, yes, how am I going to forget . . .'

'Look: his pulse stops completely when he speaks.'

'Give him the shot, Doctor, so he won't suffer so . . .'

'Another doctor must see him. It's too risky.'

'. . . how am I going to forget . . .'

'Rest, please. Don't talk now. That's it. When did he urinate last?'

'This morning . . . no, two hours ago, without knowing it.'

'Didn't you keep it?'

'No . . . no.'

'Give him the urinal. Keep the urine, I need an analysis.'

'I wasn't there. How am I going to remember?'

Once again the cold metal mouth around my dead penis. I will learn to live with all this. An attack: a man my age can have an attack: an attack isn't so unheard of: it will pass soon, it has to pass: but there is so little time, why won't they let me remember? When my body was young. Once I was young, was young . . . Ah, my body dies of pain but my mind fills with light: they are going to part, I know that they are going to part: for now I remember that face.

'Make an act of contrition.'

I have a son, I sired him: because now I remember that face: where shall I put it, where, so that it won't escape me, where, for God's sake, where, please, where.

You will shout from the depth of memory: you will lower your head as if you wished to put your lips to your horse's ear, and you will spur him with words. You will feel – and your son must also feel – that fierce steaming breath, that sweat, those tense nerves, that glass look of strain. Voices will be lost in the pound of hooves and he will call to you: 'You've never won against the mare, Papá!' 'Who taught you to ride?' 'I tell you, you can't beat the mare!' 'We'll see!' You ought to tell me everything, Lorenzo, as you've always done until now, as you've always ... until now ... Nothing you tell your mother should embarrass you; no, no never be uneasy with me; I am your best friend, maybe your only real friend ... She will repeat those words that spring morning stretched out on the bed, and she will repeat all the words she has prepared for your son since his childhood, stealing him away for herself, taking care of him herself all day, refusing to have a nana for him, sending Teresa, from the age of six on, to a religious boarding school so that all her time could be for Lorenzo, with Lorenzo, and Lorenzo should become forever accustomed to that life of comfort empty of choices. The speed of your gallop will water your eyes: you will tighten your legs around the belly of your mount and will throw yourself forward on his neck, but the black mare will still be three lengths ahead of you. You will straighten, suddenly tired, and pull the horse in, contented to watch the mare and her young rider move away with a drumming gradually lost in the chorus of macaws and the bleating that comes down from the slopes: you will have to narrow your eyes and stare hard not to lose sight of the mare as she leaves the path and slows to a trot and angles through the dense thickets toward the riverbed. No: a life without choices, without difficult decisions, Catalina will describe it, and will remember that in the beginning you helped her by being indifferent, without meaning to, because you belonged to another world, one of work and strength, which she first met when you took over Don Gamaliel's acres and allowed the boy to become, for the time, part of her world of half-lit bedrooms: a natural clinging in a climate of subtle inclusions and exclusions created by Catalina between murmured prayers and quiet dissimulations. Lorenzo will leave the path to angle, at a trot, back through the brush to the riverbed. His raised arm will point toward the east where the sun rose, toward the lagoon separated from the sea by the river-bar. You will close your eyes as you feel warm vapor rise toward your face and shadow fall upon your head. You will let the horse go unguided and will slump in the sweat-dampened saddle. Behind your closed eyelids, the roundness of the sun and the shape of the shadow will disperse in invisible depths, and Lorenzo's young figure will be a blue silhouette. You will have awakened that morning, as every morning, happy for the day to be spent with him. 'I have always turned the other cheek,' Catalina will say, with the boy near her. 'Always. I have always accepted everything. Always. If it weren't for you,' and she will love those shadowed questioning eyes that will let themselves speak: 'Some day I'll tell you.' And when Lorenzo turns twelve you will bring him to Cocuya to live and that, you will tell yourself, will not be a mistake: no, you will repeat, not a mistake. Just for him you will have bought this land and rebuilt the hacienda, and you will leave him there, boy but master, responsible for the crops, exposed to a life of horses and hunting, swimming and fishing. You will see him in the distance now and you will tell yourself that he has become the image of your own youth, well-built, strong, dark, with his green eyes set deep behind his high cheekbones. You will breathe in the muddy stench of the river bank. 'Some day I will tell you about your father . . . your father, Lorenzo . . .' You will dismount together near the rippling sedges of the lagoon. Freed, the horses will lower their muzzles and lap the water and play with each other with their wet muzzles. Immediately they will move off at a slow hypnotic trot,

parting the tall grass, waving their manes, splashing up spray,
letting themselves be gilded by the golden sun and the light
reflected from the water. Lorenzo will place his hand on your
shoulder. 'Your father ... your father. Lorenzo, do you truly
love our Lord God? Do you believe everything I've taught you?
Do you know that the Church is God's earthly body and the
priests are His ministers? Do you believe ...' Lorenzo will place
his hand on your shoulder. You will look into each other's eyes
and smile. You will grab him by the neck; the boy will feint a
blow at your stomach; you will tousle his hair, laughing, will
grapple each other laughing, straining, panting, until you both
fall exhausted on the grass, laughing, gasping, laughing. 'Why
do I ask you this? I have no right, I really have no right. I don't
know ... some of the holy men ... some of the true martyrs ...
Do you think they can approve? I don't know why I ask you ...'
The horses will return, tired in the same way both of you
are tired, and now, leading the horses, you will walk the length
of the sandbar that leads to the sea, the open sea: Lorenzo and
Artemio to the open and unprisoned sea toward which Lorenzo
will run, toward the green tropical sea which will break waves
around his waist and soak his breeches, the sea watched by a
low flight of sea-gulls, the sea that thrusts its tired tongue upon
the beach, the sea that you will impulsively cup in your hand
and taste: sea that tastes like bitter beer, smells of melon, of
apple custard, of guava, quince, strawberry: fishermen will drag
their heavy nets out on the sand; you and Lorenzo will go over
to them, break open oyster-shells with them, eat crabs and
lobsters with them; and Catalina, alone, will close her eyes and
try to sleep as she awaits the return of the boy she has not seen
since his fifteenth birthday, two years ago; and Lorenzo, cracking
the red lobster shell, will thank the fisherman who passed him
the lemon juice and will turn to you and ask if you have never
wondered what lies on the other side of the sea, for to him it
seems that all land is much the same, only the sea is different.
You will say that there are islands. Lorenzo will say that by the
sea so much happens, so that it's as if we must be bigger and
more complete men when we live beside the sea and venture on
the sea. And you, lying on the sand and listening to the fisher-

men's Veracruz guitar, would like only to explain that here years ago, forty years ago, something was broken so that something else would begin, or maybe so that something even newer would never begin. Under early morning's misty sun and in the hard melted sun of noon, on the paths of black earth and beside this very sea, so calm and dense and green, a dream lived for you, not real but real in the sense it was true, that could ... No, it wasn't this – the very truth of those lost possibilities – that brought you back to Cocuya bringing Lorenzo with you; it was something harder – you will say with closed eyes and the taste of shellfish in the mouth and a Veracruz song, lost in the immensity of the afternoon, in your ears – harder to express, to think by oneself: he must understand alone and by himself, for even if you wanted to, you would not dare to tell him: you will listen to him understanding as he kneels with his face toward the open sea and his hands open under the cloaked, suddenly darkening sky: 'A ship sails in ten days. I have booked passage.' The dark sky and your son's hand reaching to receive the first raindrops as if they were alms. 'You would do the same, Papá. You didn't stay out of it, at home. What do I believe? I don't know. You brought me here, you taught me this life ... It has been as though you were living your life over again. Do you understand.' 'Yes.' 'Now there is a front and I think it is the only front left. I'm going to go to it ...' Oh, that pain, *ay* that knifing pain, *ay* how you will want to stand and run and forget the pain by walking, working, shouting, giving orders: but they won't let you, they will hold your arms, they will force you to remain still, they will compel you with physical force to go on remembering; and you will not want to, you do not want to, *ay* you don't want to: you will have only dreamed your days: you don't want to know one day that is more your own than any other, merely because it is the one that someone else lived for you, the only day you will be able to remember in his name: a short, terror day of white poplars, Artemio, and your day too, your life too ...

[1939: February 3]

He was on the roof with a rifle in his hands and was remembering the times when the two of them used to go to the lagoon to hunt. But this was a rusty rifle, no good for hunting: no good. From the roof the façade of the cathedral could be seen. That was all that was left of it, a shell without roof or floor; behind the façade everything had been destroyed by bombs. Half-buried old furniture. And in the street a man with a wing collar and two women in black were walking in file, carrying packages and squinting against the sun. Just to see them was enough to identify them as enemies.

'Hey, over on the other side of the street!'

He shouted from the roof and the man looked up and was blinded by the sun. He waved his arm to warn them to cross over and avoid the danger of the façade of the ruined church: at any moment it might collapse. They crossed, and in the distance sounded the salvos of Fascist artillery, hollow booms in the depths of the mountain, a sharp whine as the shells whistled overhead. He sat down on a sandbag. Miguel was beside him: Miguel would not leave the machine gun for anything or anyone. From the roof they looked out over the town's deserted streets. There were craters below, broken telegraph poles and twisted wires. The interminable echo of the salvos and the poc-poc-poc of rifle fire. The paving stones dry and cold. And nothing standing on this street except the façade of the ancient church.

'We got only one belt left,' he said.

'Let's wait until afternoon,' said Miguel. 'Then ...'

They leaned back against the wall and lit cigarettes. Miguel was so bundled up that his blond beard was hidden. There in the distance, the mountains were snowy, not only on the peaks but also lower, even though the sun was bright. In the morning, the sierra was sharply etched and seemed to move toward them; later it seemed to pull back as the sun rose higher; now, at noon, they could no longer see the trails and pine trees on the slopes;

and at sunset the mountains would be only a distant purple mass.

Miguel looked at the sun and narrowed his eyes and said: 'If it weren't for the artillery and those rifles, one would say we were at peace. These winter days are beautiful. Look how far down the snow has come.'

White deep wrinkles, the snow of his face, ran down from Miguel's eyes to his bearded cheeks. In them Lorenzo had learned to read happiness, bravery, hatred, calm. Sometimes they had won for a while before retreating again. Sometimes they had just lost. Whether winning or losing, Miguel told him with his face how a man should accept things. He had learned a lot from Miguel's face.

He put his cigarette out on the flat rooftop and sparks whipped briefly in the wind. Why are we losing? he said to Miguel. Miguel waved toward the mountains, the frontier, and said: Because our machine guns don't get across. Miguel put his cigarette out too and began to sing quietly:

> *Los cuatro generales, los cuatro generales*
> *los cuatro generales, mamita mía,*
> *que se ham alzado*

and he answered him, leaning back against the sandbag:

> *Para la Nochebuena, mamita mía,*
> *serán ahorcados, serán ahorcados*

They sang often, just to pass time. There were many hours, like this one, when they watched and waited and nothing happened, and then they would sing. They didn't decide to sing, they just began. Neither were they ashamed to sing in front of others. It was the same as with his father, in front of the fishermen on the beach near Cocuya: they had used to laugh without reason, to wrestle in fun, and to sing too. Except that now he and Miguel were singing to keep their spirits up. The words were a joke: the four generals were not going to be hung but, rather, had them cornered in this mountain town with their backs up against the frontier. There was nowhere left for them to retreat to.

About four in the afternoon, sunset began. He rubbed his rusty, yellow-stocked old rifle and put on his cap. He bundled himself up like Miguel. For some days he had been thinking of proposing something. His boots were worn out, but they still hung together; Miguel had only sandals wrapped in rags and tied with string. He wanted to suggest they take turns wearing the boots, one day Miguel, the next day himself. But he didn't dare. Miguel's face told him not to. They blew on their hands: they knew what it is to spend a winter night on a roof.

Then, at the far end of the street, as if he had risen from one of the craters, a running soldier appeared, a Republican. He waved his arms and finally fell face down. Several of his comrades ran along behind him with their boots crunching the broken pavement. The cannonade, which had seemed so far away, came near in one jump. A soldier cried:

'Guns, give us guns!'

'Keep moving!' shouted the man in the lead. 'Don't be sitting ducks!'

The soldiers passed below at a run. Miguel and Lorenzo swung the machine gun toward the far end of the street.

'They must be close.'

'Aim, Mexican, aim carefully,' said Miguel, taking the last belt of ammunition between his palms.

But another machine gun began first, two or three blocks away, concealed, a machine gun that had waited patiently for the moment of retreat and was now peppering the street, killing our soldiers. But not their officer: he fell flat and yelled:

'On your bellies! You never learn!'

Lorenzo shifted the muzzle to bear on the enemy gun, and the sun dropped behind the mountains. The vibration of the jerking weapon shook his body from head to toe. Miguel growled:

'Kidneys aren't tough enough. The blond Moors have better equipment.'

Because overhead, motors were roaring.

They fought side by side, until they could no longer see in the gathering darkness. Miguel put out his arm and touched his shoulder. For the second time that day they were being visited by Italian bombers.

'Let's go, Lorenzo. The Caproni are back.'

'Go where? Do we leave the gun?'

'No good now, we're out of ammo.'

The enemy machine gun was also silent. Beneath them, in the street, a group of women were passing singing aloud in spite of everything:

> *Con Líster y Campesino,*
> *con Galán y con Modesto,*
> *con el comandante Carlos,*
> *no hay milicianos con miedo* . . .

Among the falling bombs, the voices sounded strange, yet stronger than the bombs, which exploded only now and then while the voices sang continuously. 'And their voices were not in battle at all but the voices of women who loved, and there on the roof, as the women's voices sang to their soldiers as if to their lovers, Miguel and I happened to touch hands and we thought the same thought: that they were singing to us, Papá, to Miguel and Lorenzo, and that they loved us . . .'

Then the façade of the cathedral toppled and they were thrown down on the roof and covered with dust, and he thought about Madrid, when he arrived, the cafés packed until two and three in the morning and everyone talking about the war and feeling a great euphoria, a deep certainty that they would win, and he thought how in Madrid they were still holding out, and how with all the bombing the people of Madrid would be all white-haired . . . They dashed to the stairs. Miguel was unarmed. He, Lorenzo, had the orange-yellow rifle. He knew that there was only one rifle for every five men and he decided to hang on to the weapon.

They went down the spiral stair.

'I think a kid was crying in one of these rooms. I'm not sure. The sirens sound like crying sometimes.'

He thought of the child, abandoned there. They felt their way down in the dark. Inside the building it was so black that they emerged on the street as into daylight. 'They shall not pass,' Miguel said, and the women echoed the cry: 'They shall not pass!' The darkness blinded them and they lost their way for a moment and one of the women ran to them and said: 'Not that way. Come with us.'

When their eyes became accustomed to the faint light, they were all face down on the sidewalk. The rubble protected them from the enemy machine gun, which could not reach through the mass of the fallen church façade. He breathed floating dust but also the sweat of the young women lying beside him. He tried to see their faces. A beret, a knit cap. Then the girl lying beside him turned her head and he saw her loose dark hair, whitened by the dust of the fallen façade. She spoke:

'I'm Dolores.'

'Lorenzo. That's Miguel.'

'I'm Miguel.'

'We lost our company.'

'We're from the Fourth.'

'How do we get out of here?'

'Go around, cross the bridge.'

'You two know the place?'

'Yes, I know this town.'

'Where are you from?'

'I'm Mexican.'

'Ah. That's why it's easy to understand you.'

The planes left and everyone stood up. Nuri, with the beret, and María, with the knit cap, gave their names, and they gave theirs. Dolores wore pants and a jacket; the other two were in overalls and ponchos. They went down the deserted streets in file, holding close to the walls, under dark balconies whose windows were open as if it were summer. They could hear the interminable firing, but they didn't know where it was coming from. At times broken glass crunched underfoot, or Miguel, who was leading, told them to watch out for fallen wires. A dog barked at them at a cross-street, and Miguel threw a rock at it. On a balcony an old man was sitting in his rocking chair with a scarf wrapped around his head. He did not see them pass and they did not understand what he was doing there, whether he was waiting for someone to come back, or waiting for sunrise, or what. He did not look toward them.

Lorenzo breathed deep. They left the town behind and came to a field of bare poplars. No one had gathered the dry leaves that fall, and they walked upon a rustling black carpet. He looked at the rags around Miguel's feet and again wanted to offer the boots, but his comrade was walking so firmly, so strongly, that he knew how useless it would be to offer what would not be accepted. Dark slopes waited for them in the distance. Maybe then Miguel would trade with him.

Now he was at the bridge. Swift deep water flowed beneath it and they all looked down.

'I thought it would be frozen.' He made an angry gesture.

'Why?' said Dolores.

'Spanish rivers never freeze,' murmured Miguel. 'They run forever.'

'So we could avoid using the bridge.'

'Why?' said María. The three girls were like curious children.

'Because a bridge is usually mined,' said Miguel.

The little group did not move. The white fast water flowing below them hypnotized them. They did not move. Until Miguel raised his head and looked toward the mountain and said:

'If we cross the bridge, we can get to the mountain and from there to the frontier. If we don't cross, they'll shoot us . . .'

'So?' said María with a suppressed whimper. For the first time the men saw her eyes, glassy and exhausted.

'We've lost,' Miguel said sharply. He clenched his empty fists. 'There's no turning back. We have no planes, no artillery, no nothing.'

Lorenzo didn't move. He stood looking at Miguel until Dolores's warm hand, which had just been removed from her armpit, took his five fingers and he understood. She sought his eyes and for the first time he saw hers. Her lashes fluttered and he saw that her eyes were green, the green of the sea on the coast of Mexico. She was uncombed, without makeup, her cheeks red from cold, her lips puffed and dry. The other three did not notice. They walked out on the bridge hand in hand, he and she. For a moment he hesitated. She did not. Their ten joined fingers gave them warmth, the only warmth he had felt in all these months.

'. . . the only warmth I felt in all those months of retreat toward Catalonia and the Pyrenees . . .'

They heard the river below them, the creaking of the floor-boards. But if Miguel and the two girls shouted from the bank, they were not listening. The bridge stretched long. It seemed they were crossing an ocean.

'My heart beat fast. I could feel its thump all the way to my hand, and so could she, for she lifted my hand and pressed it to her chest so that I could feel the beat of her heart . . .'

They walked on side by side and the bridge shortened.

Near the far side they saw something they had not noticed before: a great leafless elm, huge, white, beautiful. It was not covered with snow but with shining ice. It shone like a jewel in the darkness. He felt the weight of the rifle on his shoulder, the weight of his legs, his lead feet on the wooden bridge. The elm waited for them, white and luminous. He squeezed the girl's fingers. The icy wind blinded their eyes. He closed his eyes.

'I closed my eyes, Papá, and then opened them again afraid that the tree wasn't there . . .'

Then their feet felt the solid earth and they stopped. They did not look back. They ran to the elm, both of them, paying no attention to the shouts of Miguel and the two girls, not noticing them move out on the bridge; they ran to the elm and embraced its bare, white, ice-sheathed trunk and tried to shake it as bits of ice fell upon them like pearls, and their hands touched and they turned suddenly and embraced each other: Dolores, Lorenzo, so that he might caress her forehead and she the back of his neck; she leaned back, so that he might look into her wet green eyes and see her half-opened lips. For a moment she buried her head against his chest. Then her face and lips came up and they kissed, and then their comrades were around them . . .

'. . . How warm, Lola, how warm you are, and how I love you now.'

They were camped on a high saddle of the mountain, below the snow crown. Miguel and the youth had looked for branches and made a fire. Lorenzo sat beside Lola and took her hand again. María took a cracked pot from her knapsack and filled it with snow and set it over the fire, and also produced a slab of goat cheese. Then Nuri laughed and pulled some crumpled Lipton tea bags from between her breasts, and all of them laughed too about the face of the English yacht captain printed on the tea bags' labels.

Nuri told how before the fall of Barcelona there had been packages of tobacco, tea, and condensed milk sent by the Americans. Nuri was chubby and cheerful and before the war had worked in a textile factory. María spoke and recalled her student days in Madrid when she had lived in a dormitory and taken part in the strikes against Primo de Rivera, and had wept over each of Lorca's new works.

'I am writing to you with the paper on my knees while I listen to them talk, and I try to tell them how much I love Spain and the only thing that occurs to me to talk about is my first visit to Toledo, a city that I had imagined to be like the El Greco painting, wrapped in a storm of lightning and green clouds, standing on both sides of the narrow Tajo river gorge . . . a city that seemed, how shall I say it, to be at war with itself. And I found instead a city of sun, of sun and silence and a bombed Alcazar. Because El Greco's painting – I try to tell them – is all of Spain, and if the Tajo's gorge at Toledo is narrow, Spain's gorge opens from sea to sea. This is what I have seen here, Papá. This I try to say to them . . .'

That was what he said to them, before Miguel began to tell about joining Colonel Asencio's brigade and what it had cost him to become a veteran. Miguel said that the popular army was very brave, but bravery was not enough. They also had to know how to fight. And new recruits were slow in learning that there are ways to protect oneself and that if one is going to go on fighting, one must go on living. Even when they learned to defend themselves, they still had to master the art of attack. And when they finally knew all this, they still had to learn what was hardest of all, victory over themselves, over their habits and comforts. He spoke disparagingly of the anarchists, who according to Miguel were merely destructive, and he castigated the arms merchants who had promised the Republic arms which then had been sold instead to Franco. He said that what hurt him most about the collapse was that he could not understand why workers all over the world hadn't risen to help defend Spain, for if we lose in Spain, it is as if they lose everywhere. He said this and broke a cigarette in two and gave half to the Mexican, and the two men smoked, Lorenzo sitting beside Dolores and passing her the butt so that she might smoke too.

A heavy bombardment began in the distance. They could see a yellowish glow, a fan of dust in the night.

'It's Figueras,' said Miguel. 'They're shelling Figueras.'

They looked toward Figueras. Lola was close to him. She did not speak to the others; she spoke only to him, her voice low, while they looked toward the far away dust and noise. She said that she was twenty-two, three years older than he; he added five years and said that he had turned twenty-four. She said that she was from Albacete and had gone to the war to follow her sweetheart. They had been students together – chemistry students – and she had followed him, but he was executed by the Moors in Oviedo. He told her that he came from Mexico and that there he lived in a warm place near the ocean, where there were many fruits. She asked him to talk about tropical fruits and she laughed at the names which she had never heard before and said that *mamey* sounded like the name of a poison and *guanaban* like that of a bird. He told her that he loved horses and that when he first arrived, he had been in the cavalry, but there was no cavalry left now, nor for that matter anything else. She told him that she had never ridden a horse and he tried to explain to her the fun of riding, especially along the beach at dawn when the air smells of iodine and the sky to the north is clearing but there is still a light drizzle and the spray the hooves throw up mixes with the rain mist and one rides with bare chest and lips tasting of salt. This she liked. She said that maybe there was still a trace of salt on his lips, and she kissed him. The others had fallen asleep around the fire and the fire was burning out. He rose to stir it. He saw that they were all asleep, close together for warmth. He went back to Lola and she opened her sheepskin lined jacket for him to clasp his hands inside, on her back, over her khaki blouse, and then she covered his back with the jacket, and they were wrapped together. In his ear she said they must decide where they would meet again, in case they should be separated. In a café I know near Cibeles, he said, when we have liberated Madrid, and she answered that they would see each other in Mexico and he said yes, in the plaza of the port of Veracruz, under the arcade, in the La Parroquia café. They would drink coffee and eat crabs.

She smiled and so did he, and he told her he wanted to tousle her hair and kiss her and so she pressed forward and took off her cap and moved her head around against him as he put his hands under her blouse and caressed her back and groped for her breasts, and then he did not think of anything, nor did she, certainly, for her voice stopped speaking words but emptied everything she thought in a continuous murmur that was thank you I love you don't forget me come ...

They struggled up the mountain, and for the first time Miguel walked with difficulty, not because of the ascent, hard though it was, but because the cold had gotten to his feet, that toothed coldness that all of them felt in their faces. Dolores leaned on her lover's arm and when he saw her out of the corner of his eye she was worried, but when he looked at her directly she was always smiling. He only prayed – they all did – that there would be no storm. He carried their single rifle, and for it he had only two cartridges. Miguel had told them not to be afraid.

'I'm not afraid. The frontier is on the other side of the mountain, we will sleep tonight in France, in beds, under a roof. We'll have a good supper. I think of you and I believe you will not be ashamed of me, that you would do what I am doing. You fought too, and it should please you to know that there is always one who carries on the fight. I know it will please you. But now our fight here is going to end. As soon as we cross the border, the last remnant of the International Brigades will be out of it, and something else will begin. I will never forget my life here, Papá, because here I have learned all I know. It's very simple. I will tell you when I get back home. I can't find the words right now.'

His finger touched the letter in his shirt pocket. In this cold he did not dare open his mouth. He was panting; his breath puffed white from between his clenched teeth. They moved ahead so slowly. The line of refugees was endless; it stretched away out of sight; country people pushing carts loaded with wheat and sausages that they were taking with them into France;

women burdened with mattresses and blankets; paintings, chairs, washbasins, mirrors . . . The peasants planned to go on sowing crops in France. They walked very slowly. There were children, too, some at the breast. The way was dry, cragged, difficult, with many thickets. He felt Dolores's fist pressed against his side. He wanted to save and protect her. He loved her more than last night and knew that tomorrow he would love her more than today. And she him. There was no need to say it. They enjoyed each other: that's it, we enjoy each other. They knew how to laugh together now. They had things to tell each other.

Dolores left him and ran to María. The girl-soldier had stopped beside a rock with her hand to her forehead. She said that it wasn't anything. She felt very tired. They had to move to the side so that the red faces, the frozen hands, the heavy handcarts could pass. María said again that she felt a little dizzy. Lola took her arm and they went ahead together and it was then, yes, then that they heard the roar of the motor and stopped. They could not see the plane. All of them looked for it, but the sky was milky. Miguel was the first to make out the black wings and cross, the first to shout:

'Down! On your faces!'

All of them face down among the rocks, under the handcarts. All of them, except that rifle which still has two cartridges. And it doesn't fire, damned oranged-butted walking-stick, damned rusty blunderbuss, no matter how hard he pulls on the trigger, standing as the roar passes over their heads and fills them with that swift shadow and a machine gun burst patters across the ground and rings on the rocks.

'Down, Lorenzo, down, Mexican!'

Down, down, down, Lorenzo, and those old boots upon the dry earth, Lorenzo, your gun to the ground, Mexican, and a whirling inside your stomach, as if you carried the ocean in your entrails and now your face upon the earth with your eyes green and open and a half dream, between noon and midnight, while she screams and you know that at last poor Miguel will get the boots and his blond beard and white wrinkles and Dolores will throw herself upon you, Lorenzo, and Miguel will tell her that it's useless, beginning to weep too, that they must go on, life is on the other side of the mountain, life and freedom, because yes, those were the words that he wrote: they took the letter from his blood-stained shirt, she pressed it between her hands – how warm! if snow falls it will bury him, when you kissed him again, Dolores, pressed upon his body, and he wanted to take you riding by the sea before spilling his blood and going to sleep with you in his green eyes ... don't forget ...

I would tell myself the truth if it weren't for these bloodless lips, if I weren't doubled up and unable to control my water, if I could stand the weight of the bedcovers, if I didn't keep hanging face down over the edge of the bed to vomit this phlegm, this bile: I would tell myself that it is not enough to repeat times and places, the mere locating coordinates; I would tell myself that something more, a desire I never expressed, made me lead him to – *ay*, I don't know, I don't know – yes, obligate him to find the ends of the thread I had broken, to unite my life again, live out my other destiny, that second part which I was unable to live myself, and she asks me, sitting at the head of the bed:

'Why did it happen that way? Tell me: why? I raised him for something different. Why did you take him from me?'

'Didn't he spoil him and then send him to his death? Didn't he take him from you and from me to warp him? Isn't that true?'

'Teresa, your father doesn't hear you ...'

'He hears me. He closes his eyes, but he hears me all right.'

'Shhhhh.'

'Be quiet.'

I don't know now. But I see them. They have come in. The mahogany door opens and closes and their steps are silent on the thick carpet. They have closed the windows. They have run the curtains shut, with a hissing noise. They have come in.

'I am ... I am Gloria ...'

The fresh, sweet rustle of new bonds and banknotes taken by the hand of such a man as I. The smooth start of an expensive car, built to order, air-conditioned, with its own bar, telephone, special cushions and footrests, eh, priest, what do you say, will it be like that up there too, eh?

'I would like to return there, to the land . . .'

'Why did it happen that way? Tell me: Why? I raised him for something different. Why did you take him from me?'

And she does not know that there is something worse than an abandoned dead body, that the ice and sun buried him, that his eyes, picked out by birds, will be eternally open: Catalina stops rubbing my forehead with the cotton and moves away and I don't know if she is crying: I try to raise my hand and reach her, the effort stabs me with pain from my arm to my chest and from my chest to my belly: in spite of the abandoned body, in spite of the snow and sun that buried him, in spite of his eyes open forever because eaten by birds, there is something worse: this uncontrollable vomiting, this overwhelming desire to defecate without being able to, without even being able to expel the gases that distend my swollen belly, without power to stop the ubiquitous pain, or to find a pulse in my wrist or to feel my legs, with the sensation that my blood is exploding inside me, that it is leaking inside me, yes, inside, I know it and they don't and I can't convince them, they can't see it flowing from my lips, between my legs: no, they don't believe me, all they say is that now I'm not running a temperature, ah, temperature, all they say is collapse, collapse, all they can discover is edema, edema, edema of locked-in fluids, that is what they say as they restrain me, feel me, and they speak of marbling, yes, I hear them, violet marbling on the belly I can't feel now, see now; and in spite of the abandoned corpse, in spite of the sun and the ice that buried him, in spite of his eternally staring eyes, picked out by birds, there is something worse: not to be able to remember him, to remember him only by pictures, the things he left in his bedroom, the notes he made in his books: but how did his sweat smell? and nothing repeats the color of his skin: and worse that I cannot think of him now that I can no longer see him and touch him;

he rode away on horseback, that morning;

this I remember: I received a letter with foreign stamps but to think of him ah, I dreamed, I imagined, I knew those names, I remembered those songs, *ay* thanks, but to know, how can I know? I don't know, I don't know what that war was like, with whom he spoke before he died, what the men's names were who were killed with him, nor the names of the women, what he said, what he thought, how he was dressed, what he ate that day, I don't know: I make up a countryside, I invent cities, I imagine names, and now I don't remember: Miguel, José, Luis? Consuelo, Dolores, María, Esperanza, Mercedes, Nuri, Guadalupe, Esteban, Manuel, Aurora? Guadarrama, Pirineos, Figueras, Toledo, Teruel, Ebro, Guernica, Guadalajara: the abandoned corpse, the sun and ice that buried him, the eyes open forever, pecked out by birds:

ay, thank you, because you taught me what my life could be,

ay, thank you, for living that day for me,

there is something worse, more painful:

eh, eh? This does exist and is really mine. This is to be God, isn't it? to be feared and hated, this is indeed to be God, isn't it? Tell me how I can save this and I will let you carry out all your rites, I'll beat my chest, crawl to a sanctuary on my knees, drink vinegar, crown myself with thorns. Tell me how to save what I have, because the spirit ...

'... and of the Son, and of the Holy Ghost, amen ...'

There is something worse, more painful:

'No. In that case there would of course be a soft tumor, but also a dislocation to some extent of the viscera, perhaps a partial herniation ...'

'I repeat: there is an obstruction as a result of a twisting of the intestine. An obstruction. This pain can be caused only by a twist or kink, and there we'll find the obstruction ...'

'In that case, he should be operated ...'

'It may be that gangrene is developing, and unless we ...'

'The cyanosis is already obvious ...'

'Observe the facies ...'

'Hypothermia ...'

'Lipothymia ...'

Be quiet ... Be quiet!

'Open the window.'

I cannot move. I don't know where to try to look. I don't feel warmth or cold except the cold that comes and goes in my legs, not the warmth or cold of the rest, inside, the parts of me I have never seen . . .

'Poor girl, she's upset to . . .'

be quiet . . . I know what I look like, you don't have to tell me . . . I know that my fingernails are dark, that my skin is blue . . . be quiet . . .

'Appendicitis?'

'We must operate.'

'It's risky.'

'I repeat: nephritic colic. Two centigrams of morphine and he will feel better.'

'It's risky.'

'There is no bleeding.'

Thank you. I could have died in Perales. I could have died with that unknown soldier. I could have died in that empty room, in front of that fat man. I survived. You died. Thank you.

'Hold him. The basin.'

'Do you see how he is ending? Do you see? Just like my brother. He ended like this.'

'Hold him. The basin.'

Hold him. He is going. Hold him. He vomits. He vomits that taste which before he had only smelled. Now he can't roll over. He vomits face up. He vomits his shit. It runs out over his lips, down his jaw. His excrement. They cry out, the women cry out, though I don't hear them. It doesn't stop. It isn't happening. They have to cry out because nothing is happening. They hold me down, press down on me. No. He is going. He is going naked and alone. Without anything. Hold him. He is going.

You will read that letter, postmarked from a concentration camp, stamped with foreign stamps, and signed Miguel, the letter that will enclose another letter signed Lorenzo, you will receive the letter and will read: 'I'm not afraid . . . I think of you . . . You will not be ashamed . . . I will never forget my life here, Papá, because here I have learned all I know ... I will tell you when I get back home ...' you will read and you will choose again: you will choose another life:

you will choose to leave him in Catalina's hands, you will not take him to Cocuya, you won't push him to responsibility for himself, to that fatal destiny which could have been yours: you won't force him to do what you did not do, rescue your lost life: you will not allow, this time, that you die on a rocky path and she be saved:

you will choose to embrace the wounded soldier who came into the providential thicket, to lay him down and clean his shattered arm with water from the desert-burned spring, to bandage him up and stay with him and keep him breathing by breathing yourself, to wait there, wait to be found and captured and executed against a wall in a peublo with a forgotten name, a dusty little town of adobe and stubborn life: rifles leveled at him and at you, two nameless nude corpses buried in the common ditch used for executed rebels, without a headstone: dead at twenty-four, no more roads to follow, no more labyrinths to thread, no more choices to make: dead hand in hand with the unknown soldier whose life you saved: dead:

you will tell Laura: yes

you will tell the fat man in the blue room: no

you will elect to stay in the cell with Bernal and Tobías, to share their fate, not to go to that patio made bloody in order to justify yourself, not to think that by killing Zagal you wash your hands of the deaths of your comrades

you will not visit old Gamaliel in Puebla

you will not take Lilia in your arms when she returns to you that night, you will not think that now you will never be able to possess any other woman

you will break the silence that night and will speak to Catalina asking her to forgive you; you will tell of those who have died for you to live and will ask her to accept you as you are, with those crimes upon you; you will beseech her not to hate you, to accept you as you are

you will stay on with Lunero at the hacienda, you will never leave your place you will stay with your teacher Sebastián, as he was, as he was and will not go to join the revolution in the north

you will be a peon

you will be a blacksmith

you will keep out of it, with those who kept out of it

you will not be Artemio Cruz, you will not be seventy-one, you will not weigh a hundred and seventy-four pounds, you will not be five feet eleven and a half, you will not use false teeth, smoke black cigarettes, wear Italian silk shirts, collect cufflinks, order your neckties from New York, wear three-button blue suits, prefer Irish cashmere, drink gin and tonic, own a Volvo, a Cadillac, and a Rambler wagon; you will not remember and love that Renoir, you will not breakfast on poached eggs with Crosse and Blackwell marmalade, you will not every morning read the newspaper you own, you will not look over *Life* and *Paris Match* in the evening, you will not hear at your side that incantation, that chorus, that hatred which would tear life from you before your time, which invokes, invokes, invokes all that you could have imagined with a smile so short a time ago but now will not tolerate:

De profundis clamavi

De profundis clamavi

See me now, hear me, light my eyes, let me not sleep death/ For the day when you eat of him you will assuredly die/ Take no joy from another's passing, for all pass/ Death and hell were thrown into the fiery pit, and this was the second death/ What I fear comes to me, fills me with terror, possesses me/ How bitter is the memory of the man who feels himself satisfied with riches/ Have they opened death's gate to you?/ Sin began with the woman and because of the woman we all die/ Have you seen the door into the dark room?/ Clear is your judgment of the needy and those whose strength is spent/ And what fruits did they gain then? Those of those who are now ashamed because their end is death too/ Because the hunger of the flesh is death:

word of God and of life, profession of death,

de profundis clamavi, domine

omnes eodem cogimur, omnium vesatur urna

quae quasi saxum Tantulum semper impendet

quid quisque videt, nunquam homini satis cautum est in horas
mors tanem inclusum protrahet inde caput
nascentes morimus, finisque ab origne pendet
atque in se sua per vestigia volvitur annus
omnia te vita perfunta sequentur

chorus, sepulcher, voices, pyre: and you will imagine in the forgotten region of consciousness the rites, the ceremonies, the endings: burial, cremation, embalming: exposed upon the height of a tower, so that it be not the earth, but the air itself will rot you; sealed in the tomb with your dead slaves; wailed by hired mourners; buried with your most valuable possessions, your company, your black jewels: death watch, vigil,

requiem aeternam, dona eis Domine
de profundis clamavi, Domine

Laura's voice, which used to speak of such things; she is seated on the floor with her legs doubled under her and the little bound book in her hands, which says that everything can be fatal to us, even what gives us life; that only sudden death is to be feared, which is why the powerful keep confessors always at hand; that as we cannot do anything about death, misery, and ignorance, we would do well, for our happiness, not to think about such things; which says I know man: he fears not danger but death without danger; which says that the premeditation of death is the premeditation of freedom; which says, what mute footballs you have, oh cold death; which says that your hours will forgive you evil, the hours that are pitiless are your days; which says show me the hard knot cut; which says my door is built of strong metal; which says that a thousand deaths will be made for me, for my life is one with my hope; which says that man decides to live when God commands him to die; which says: to what end your treasures, vassals, servants?

to what end and to what end? let them chant, sing, plaint: they will not touch the sumptuous relief-work, the opulent marquetry, the gold and plaster mouldings, the bone and tortoise-shell chests of drawers, the escutcheons and knobs, the coffers with iron panels and keyholes, the benches of scented *ayacahuite*, the choir chairs, the baroque cowls and robes, the curving chair-backs, the twisted chair-legs, the polychrome masks, the bronze nailheads, the tooled leather, the castered ball and claw feet, the filigree chasubles, the damask chairs, the velvet sofas, the refectory tables, the urn cylinders and jars, the pie-crust tables, the canopied curtained beds, the striated posts, the shields and ribbons, the merino carpets, the iron keys, the framed paintings, the silks and cashmeres, the wools and taffetas, the mirrors and chandeliers, the hand-painted glasses, the warm ceiling beams: this they will not touch, this will be yours:

you will reach out your hand:

on an ordinary day, that nevertheless will be an exceptional day, three or four years ago; you will not remember it, you will remember by remembering; no, you will remember because the first thing that you remember, when you try to remember, is a day set apart, a day of ceremony, a day marked in red: and this will be the day – you yourself will think then – when all the names, people, words, and deeds of a full cycle will ferment and break the crust of the earth; it will be a night when you will celebrate the new year; your arthritic fingers will grasp the iron banister with difficulty; you will bury the other hand deep in the pocket of your robe and you will descend the stairs heavily:

you will reach out your hand:

[1955: December 31]

He grasped the iron banister with difficulty. The other hand he dug deep into the pocket of his robe and he descended the stair heavily, without glancing at the wall niches dedicated to the Mexican Virgins: Guadalupe, Zapopan, Remedios. The setting sun came through the slit windows and gilded the quilted robes and full skirts of the images, reddened the burned finish of the beams, lightened half of his face. He was dressed formally, dark trousers, a stiff shirt and black tie; covered by the red robe, he looked like an old and tired magician: and he thought now of the repetition tonight of a scene which once had been able to give him singular delight: tonight he would recognize with boredom the same faces, the same words that year after year had set the tone of the fiesta of St Sylvester in his enormous residence in Coyoacán.

His steps dragged hollowly on the tezontle-stone floor. Lightly squeezed in their black patent leather pumps, his feet moved with the tottering heaviness he could no longer avoid. Tall, rocking on his uncertain heels, with his chest gray and his hands hanging distended with gray veins, he walked slowly through the white-washed passages, over the deep wool carpets, catching glimpses of himself in the antique mirrors and the small glasses of the colonial commodes, brushing his fingers over locks and knobs, the coffers with iron corners and keyholes, the fragrant benches of *ayacuahuite* wood, the rich marquetry. A servant opened the door to the great salon; the old man stopped for the last time in front of a mirror and adjusted his bow-tie. He smoothed his still curly thin gray hair back from his high forehead. He clenched his jaw to settle his false teeth well in place, and stepped onto the polished salon floor, a vast expanse of brilliant cedar, rugless now for dancing, that opened upon the garden and tiled terraces. Paintings from the colonial period were hung around the walls: St Sebastian, St Lucia, St Jerome, St Michael.

At the far end of the room beneath a chain-suspended chandelier of fifty lights, the photographers were gathered around the green damask chair waiting for him. The clock on the fireplace struck seven. The leather chairs were drawn close to the hearth these cold December days. He nodded and sat in the big chair, straightening his shirt-front and piqué cuffs. Another servant came up leading two pink-lipped mastiffs with melancholy eyes, and placed their leashes in their master's hand. The dog's collars had bronze spikes that glittered in the light. He raised his head and tightened the teeth again. Flashbulbs whitened his gray head. As the photographers asked for new poses, he smoothed his hair again and ran his fingers down the dewlaps that hung from the corners of his mouth and lost themselves in his collar. Only his high cheekbones maintained the old hardness, and they were webbed with wrinkles that spread from his eyes, every day set deeper as if to protect their half-bitter, half-amused expression, the green irises hidden under the loose lids.

One of the mastiffs barked and tried to free himself. A flashbulb went off at the instant the old man was jerked from his chair by the dog, with an expression of rigid surprise on his face. The other photographers glared at the one who had taken the picture. The guilty one pulled the plate from his camera and handed it wordlessly to them.

The photographers finished and departed. He reached out a trembling hand and took a filter cigarette from the silver box on the table. With some difficulty he caught his light at the fireplace, and slowly moving his head, he inspected the thick-varnished old hagiographic painting; it was splashed with glare that eliminated the central details but, in recompense, gave a dark relief to the corner tones of yellow and rosy shadow. He touched the damask of his chair and inhaled the filtered tobacco. A servant came silently and asked if he wanted something to drink. He nodded and said a very dry Martini. The servant slid open the carved cedar panels of a mirrored niche, a showcase of colored labels and decantered liquids: opalescent, emerald green, red, crystalline: Chartreuse, Peppermint, Acquavit, Vermouth, Courvoisier, Long John, Calvados, Armagnac, Beherovka, and Pernod: rows of crystal glasses, thick and stubby, thin and ringing. He took the glass, and told the servant to go to the cellar for the three brands that would be served at dinner. He stretched his legs and thought of the care with which he had rebuilt and furnished this house, his true home. Catalina could live in the Lomas mansion, a place barren of all personality, not different from any millionaire's residence. He preferred these old walls with their two centuries of sandstone and tezontle. In a strange way they took him back into their own past and reflected a land that did not want everything to be transient. Yes, he was quite aware that there had been a process of substitution, the waving of a magic wand. And there was also no doubt that the old timbers and stone, the ironwork and mouldings, the refectory tables, the cabinets, the grainwork, the inlays, that these conspired to bring back to him, with a faint perfume of nostalgia, the scenes, the smells, the tactile sensations of his own youth.

Lilia complained. Lilia would never understand. What could a ceiling of antique beams possibly say to such a girl? A window with iron tracery? The sumptuous touch of the chasuble, rich with gold and bordered with silver thread, over the mantelpiece? The scent of the great chests of drawers? The scrubbed cleanness of the Puebla tiled kitchen? The archbishop's chairs in the dining room? The possession of such things was as rich and magnificent as the possession of money and equally blatant marks of wealth. Yes: what a whole and perfect pleasure, what a refined sensuality these inanimate objects provided: what pleasure, what free and self-contained delight. And once a year – only once, at the framed reception on the day of St Sylvester – did he permit guests to participate in his pleasure. Day of compounded delights, because he forced those invited strangers his guests to accept this as his true home while remembering Catalina the solitary who, joined for the New Year occasion by Teresa and Gerardo, would be dining at the house in the Lomas. While he presented his Lilia and opened the doors of the blue dining room upon the blue china and the blue linen, the blue walls, upon flowing wines and platters heaped with rare meats, pink fish, fragrant shellfish, secret herbs, tall desserts . . .

Was it necessary for her to interrupt his meditation? Lilia's heels clicking indolently. Her unpainted fingernails scratching the salon door. Her grease-plastered face. She had come to inquire whether her rose dress would be appropriate for tonight? She didn't want to wear the wrong thing, like last year, and provoke his irritation and anger. Ah, he was already drinking! Why not invite her to join him? She was getting damn tired of the way he mistrusted her, keeping the bar locked. That impertinent servant denying her the right to go to the cellar. Was she bored, then? As if he didn't know! She almost wished she were old and ugly so that he would throw her out once and for all and let her live as she wanted to. He wasn't stopping her? And then where would she have such luxury, this big house, his money? Plenty of money, almost too much luxury, and no happiness at all, no fun, not even free to have a little drink, if you please, damn it. Well: of course, she loved him very much. Hadn't she said it a thousand times? Yes . . . women grow accustomed to anything: it all depends upon the affection shown them: they can become accustomed to paternal love as to juvenile. Yes: she had affection for him, and that was enough. It was almost eight years that they had lived together and he never made scenes, rarely reprimanded her. No, but just the same, he made her very ... But how fortunate, he smiled, that she had discovered another gray hair. What? Did he think she was that absurd? Now, now ... you have never been able to take a joke ... All right, but don't make silly jokes ... No one lasts forever: crowsfeet around her eyes already ... Their women's bodies ... only he was also accustomed to her. Yes, at his age it would be troublesome to start over. For all the millions, it takes work and time to find a woman ... wicked creatures, so slippery, always elaborating the simple and obvious, dragging out courtship ... the negative, the doubt and uncertainty, the wait. The temptation. *Ay*, all those tricks. And they make fools of old men. Clearly it was more convenient to hold on to her ... Well, she wasn't complaining, gracious no. Even to flattering his vanity of having that crowd come every New Year's eve to ruin her evening ... She loved him, yes, she swore it, she was much too used to him to ... but how often and how terribly she was bored! Look, what harm would there be in letting her have a few close women friends, in letting her go out once in a while to have a little fun, in allowing her just one tiny drink once a week?

He sat there, motionless. He had never extended her the right to harass him, but a tepid lassitude, a spiritlessness that was completely foreign to his character obliged him to stay where he was and listen to her inanities, a woman who daily became more common. She was no longer even appetizing. She had become unbearable, indeed, for how was he going to continue to control her? All that obeyed him now he controlled by a certain inert extension of the force of his younger years. Lilia might leave him. His heart tightened. No need to bring that up, that fear. Perhaps he would never have another: he would remain alone. He moved his fingers stiffly, then his forearm and elbow, and knocked the ashtray on the rug. Moist yellow butts spilled out, gray ashes, black ashes. He leaned over to clean up, and his breath came short.

'Don't bend down. I'll call Serafín.'
'Yes.'

Perhaps . . . Tedium. But nausea, revulsion . . . still imagining doubts. An involuntary tenderness made him turn his head and look at her.

She watched him, spiteful, sweet, from the doorway, her hair dyed ash blonde, that brown skin. She could not go back either. She would never have what she had lost, and that evened the score between them, and made them, in spite of the years and character that separated them, almost equals. Scenes? What for. He felt tired. Nothing, nothing more. No more memorable places, no more memories, no names other than those already known. Will and fate deciding. Nothing. He ran his fingers over the damask again. The cigarette butts on the floor had an unpleasant smell. And Lilia, standing across the room with her greased face.

She on the threshold. He sitting in the damask chair.

Then she sighed and went clicking off to the bedroom and he sat there and waited and thought of nothing at all, until darkness surprised him: darkness outside, he saw himself reflected sharply in the glass doors that opened on the garden. The houseboy came in bringing his jacket, a handkerchief, and a bottle of cologne. The old man stood and let the boy put the jacket on him, and then he opened the handkerchief so the boy could sprinkle a few drops of the lotion on it. As he adjusted the handkerchief in his breast pocket, his eyes met the boy's eyes. The servant at once looked down. No: why had he been about to wonder what the houseboy could be feeling?

'Quickly, Serafín, these ashes . . .'

He stood, rising by supporting himself with both hands on the arms of the chair, and walked to the fireplace and touched the Toledo irons and felt the heat of the flames on his face and hands. The first voices, enchanted, admiring, in the hall. He leaned to hear them while Serafín finished cleaning up the ashes. He ordered the fire to be stirred.

The Régules came in. From the door that led to the dining room, another servant advanced carrying a tray. Roberto Régules took a drink from it while the young couple, Betina and her husband, the Ceballos boy, strolled about the salon holding hands and praising the old paintings, the gold frames, the rich hangings, the baroque miters and chasubles, the polychrome masks. A glass smashed on the floor with a sound like a broken bell, and he turned. Lilia's voice shouted jocosely. The old man and his guests stared at her face, bare of makeup, as she leaned, hung, upon the doorhandle.

'Hallooo ... ! Happy New Year! Don't worry, old man, I'll be ready in an hour or two. And I'll act as if nothing ... I just wanted to tell you that I've made up my mind to have a won-der-ful New Year ... but super-duper-won-der-ful!'

He went toward her with his difficult, faltering pace. With every step he took, her voice fluted higher. 'I'm sick of watching TV all day, little old manny-man! I already know all those cow-boy stories. Bang-bang-bang! the marshal of Arizona, camp of redskins. Bang-bang! I dream about their damn voices, old man! Have a Pepsi ... and that's all, old man. Security with comfort. Policies ...'

His arthritic hand struck her and the dyed curls fell over her eyes.

She held her breath. Then she turned and slowly left, a hand to her cheek. He returned to the group of the Régules and Jaime Ceballos. He stared at them, first one and then the other, for a moment, his head high. Régules drank his whiskey, hiding his expression behind his glass. Betina smiled and went up to her host with a cigarette poised, as if she were looking for a light.

'Where did you find that chest?'

The old man stepped back and Serafín, the servant, held a match to the girl's face and she had to move her head from close to the old man's bosom and turn away from him. At the rear of the hall, the musicians were coming in bundled up and shivering with cold. Jaime Ceballos snapped his fingers and spun on his heels like a flamenco dancer.

On the dolphin-legged table, in the light of bronze candle-sticks: partridges in a sauce of bacon and old wine; cod wrapped in leaves with tarragon mustard; wild ducks à l'orange; carp flanked by roe; Catalan *bullinada*, heavy with the scent of olives; coq-au-vin, flaming, swimming in Macon; doves stuffed with artichoke purée; plates of little white eels, on crushed ice; broch-ettes of lobster decorated with lemon spirals, mushrooms, and sliced tomatoes; Bayonne ham; stuffed beefsteaks sprinkled with Armagnac; gooseneck stuffed with pork pâté; paste of chestnuts and appleskins sautéed with nuts; onion, orange, garlic, and pistachio-nut sauces. He opened the door carved and painted in Queretaro with cornucopias and fat-buttocked little angels. He opened the doors two at a time and chuckled drily, hoarsely, when each Dresden plate was offered. A hundred guests. The rattle of silver on the blue dinnerware. Servants tipping bottles to glasses. He ordered that the curtains be opened to reveal the garden shaded by cherry trees and fragile bare plum trees, the clean shapes of monastic statuary: lions, angels, monks from the palaces and convents of the Viceregency. Fireworks rose, great castles of fools' fire clear and distant in the center of the garden grove. White sparkling crossing the red flight of a fan of fire edged with serpentine yellows: the night's open scars, festive monarchs glittering gold medallions against night's curtain, rocket lights racing toward the arch of night's darkness. Behind his closed lips, he chuckled. Empty plates were refilled with more game birds, more fish, more rare meat. Bare arms fluttered around him, old man sitting heavily in a corner of the ancient choirchair that was exuberantly inlaid with a caprice of miters and robes. He looked, smelled: the swelling of their low-cut dresses, their shaved armpits, their jeweled ears, white throats, small waists; their perfume, their cloth: silk, taffeta, gold lamé. He breathed in the smells of lavender and tobacco, lipstick and mascara, spilled brandy and the fine leather of expensive shoes, nail polish. He raised his glass and stood. A servant put the leashes of the mastiffs in his hand; they would accompany him the rest of the evening. New Year shouting began. Glasses shattered on the floor. Embraces, squeezes, women held high to celebrate the season, this funeral, this pyre of memory, this resurrection and fermentation of all his history, while the orchestra played *Las golondrinas*, all the dead events and dead words and dead things that had lived during the closing cycle: celebration of these hundred lives who suspended their men's and women's questions to say to each other, with damp looks sometimes, that there is no other time than this time of vivid stretched moments while rockets soar and bells ring wildly. Lilia stroked his neck as if to ask forgiveness. He knew, perhaps, that many things, many little desires, must be repressed if in a single moment of sensual plenty one is to know complete enjoyment unmarred by previous indulgence: she ought to thank him for such a moment: he said it in a low voice. The violins in the great salon took up the tune *Poor People of Paris*. With a familiar gesture she reached for his arm but he shook his white head and walked, preceded by the dogs, to the big chair he would occupy, facing the dancing couples, the rest of the evening. He amused himself watching their faces: sweet, feigning, malicious, intelligent, faces of idiots, faces of rogues, thinking about their luck, the good luck they had all had, he and they. Faces, bodies, beings free like him, dancing ... They made him secure, they reassured him as they moved lightly upon the waxed floor; they loosed his memories into obliteration and forced him, perversely, to retreat into the identity by which they knew him, his freedom and power. He was not alone now; he was companioned by the dancers; this was what the warmth, the satisfaction in his belly told him ... black honor guard and carnival troopers for a white-haired, arthritic, dignified VIP, they were the echo of his persistent hoarse smile reflected in the movement of his green eyes. Men of the new order, like himself, sometimes of an order even newer than his. Whirling, whirling, whirling. He knew them: industrialists, businessmen, agents, sycophants, agitators, ministers, deputies, newspapermen, wives, sweethearts, procuresses, lovers. Their snatches of conversation whirled as they passed before him, dancing, dancing:

'Yes ...' 'We'll go afterward ...' '... but my Papá ...' 'I love you ...' '... free? ...' 'That's what they told me ...' '... we've plenty of time ...' 'And then ...' '... like this ...' '... I'd like to ...' 'Where?' '... tell me ...' '... so, I won't go back there ...' '... did you enjoy it?' '... difficult ...' '... that's a lost ...' 'darling, ...' '... delightful ...' '... went under last ...' '... most deserving ...' 'hmmmm ...'

Hmmmm! He knew how to read their eyes, their lips. He could tell what they thought even when they were silent. He could tell who they were, remember their real names ... phony bankruptcies, preknowledge of monetary devaluations, price speculations, banking manipulations, fat new agricultural acreage, newspaper fame at so much a line, inflated contracts for public works, highlife on political junkets, the family fortune squandered, wheeling-dealing tenpercenters ... fictitious names: Arturo Capdeville, Juan Felipe Couto, Sebastian Ibargüen, Vicente Castañeda, Pedro Caseaux, Jenaro Arriaga, Jaime Ceballos, Pepito Ibargüen, Roberto Régules ... And the violins played and the skirts and coat-tails whirled. That would not be what they talked about. No, they would talk of trips and love affairs, houses and cars, vacations and parties, jewels and servants, illnesses and priests. But there they were, there, in the court of the most powerful of them all, who could make or break them with one line in his newspaper, impose Lilia's presence upon them, insist, in a secret voice, that they dance, eat, drink. And sense them when they came near ...

'I had to bring him, just so he could see that painting of the Archangel. That one. Divine ...'

'I've always told him: just having Don Artemio's taste ...'

'How can we ever repay you?'

'I can see why you don't accept invitations.'

'Everything is so magnificent that I am speechless, completely speechless, Don Artemio. What wines! And those magnificent ducks!'

... or turn away and turn them off like faucets. The vague distant sound was enough for him, he didn't like to focus, he preferred the murmur of the moving crowd. Textures, scents, flavors, images. Between laughs and chuckles, they call him the Mummy of Coyoacán. They mock Lilia with little hidden smiles. And there they were, dancing before him, as he pulled their strings.

He raised an arm, a signal to the orchestra leader. The music ended in mid-note and the dancing stopped. An oriental melody was picked up by the strings. Guests made way and a dancer stepped through the doorway, semi-nude, arms and legs undulating, and moved to the center of the floor. Cries of delight. The dancer knelt to the rhythm of the drums that controlled her panting body: oiled skin, orange lips, white eyelids, blue eyebrows; standing, dancing around the circle, moving her belly in faster and faster contractions: she chose old Ibargüen and pulled him out by the arm, sat him on the floor, fixed his arms in the pose of the god Vishnu, and danced around him as he tried to imitate her movements: she went up to Capdeville and made him take off his coat and dance with her: from the depth of his damask chair, he toyed with the mastiff's leashes and laughed, laughed: the dancer jumped on Couto's shoulders and sat there and inspired several women to imitate her: piggy-back, they mussed their steeds' hair and spotted their faces with sweat: skirts rose, sliding above knees: some of the younger girls stretched their legs long to put spurs into their apoplectic chargers, who galloped around the woman with open thighs and the two elderly men dancing with her. Guffaws, shrieks.

He looked up as if removing himself from the hubbub by force of will, looked up above the tousled heads and serpentine arms, the seventeenth-century paintings and the walls and the little carved angels, up to the clean beamed ceiling: and in his sensitive ear heard the secret shuffle of immense rats, black fanged and sharp muzzled, that lived in the ceilings and cellars of this old Hieronymite convent and at times scurried impudently across the corners of the room, and that waited, in the darkness, above the heads and beneath the feet of the dancers, by the hundreds and thousands waited, perhaps, for an opportunity to take them by surprise, infect them with fevers and aches, nausea and palsy, hard painful swellings at groin and armpit, black splotches, bloody vomit ... if he raised his arm again for the servants to drop the iron door-bars, the ways of escape from this house of urns and scrolls and chamfered panels and canopied beds and great iron keys and riveted doors and elaborate choirstalls and figures of monks and lions; and then his retinue would find themselves obliged to remain with him, unable to abandon ship, forced to join him in sprinkling the corpses with vinegar and lighting perfumed faggots, in hanging rosaries of thyme around their necks, in brushing away the green buzz of flies, while he commanded them, compelled them, to dance, dance, live, live, drink. He looked across the clamor of the crowd for Lilia. She was drinking, all right, alone and silent in a corner, her back to the dancers and the mock jousting. Men were leaving to urinate, their hands already at their flies; women to powder, their evening bags already open. His hard smile was the only stone in this stream of hilarity and munificence. He chuckled silently. He was imagining them, all of them, lined up before the two toilets on the ground floor, pissing from taut bladders charged with those splendid liquids, crapping the remains of that meal which had required taste and days of exacting care; the final destiny of the ducks and lobsters, the sauces and purées: the greatest pleasure of the whole evening. Ah, yes . . .

They tired quickly. The dancing girl stopped and stood there surrounded by indifference. Conversations sprang up again. Women asked for more champagne, couples sat down in the deep sofas. Others were returning from their journeys, closing trouser flies, putting compacts in purses. It was dying, dying. The foreseen, foreplanned brief orgy, the punctual, programed excitement. Voices returned to their usual sing-song, to the pretenses and open blankness of the Mexican highland. Their usual concerns returned as if in revenge for the moments now passing, the fleeting

'. . . no, because cortisone makes me break out . . .'

'. . . haven't you heard about the spiritual exercises Father Martínez is giving . . .'

'. . . look at her. Who said it . . . ? And they say that they were . . .'

'. . . Luis comes home so tired that all he wants is . . .'

'. . . No, Jaime, he doesn't like his . . .'

'. . . to watch TV for a while . . .'

'. . . with servants the way they are today, one just can't do a thing, not a . . .'

'. . . lovers, about twenty years ago . . .'

'. . . how can he give suffrage to that gang of Indians . . .'

'. . . and his wife alone at home, never . . .'

'. . . questions of high politics; we received the . . .'

'. . . that the PRI continue electing by nomination, and now . . .'

'. . . sent by the President to the Chamber . . .'

'. . . well, I'm not afraid to try . . .'

'. . . Laura . . . I think her name was Laura . . .'

'... we'll work for a few ...'

'... if they mention that *income tax* again! ...'

'... for thirty million lazy bastards ...'

'... right away my savings go to Switzerland ...'

'... the Communists understand only ...'

'... no, Jaime, no one ought to disturb him ...'

'... it's going to return a fabulous profit ...'

'... by the barrelful ...'

'... they're investing a hundred million ...'

'... it's a heavenly Dali ...'

'... and we'll get it back in a couple of years ...'

'... the people at my gallery sent it over ...'

'... or less ...'

'... in New York ...'

'... she lived several years in France; deceptions ... they say ...'

'... let's get together, just us girls ...'

'... Paris is the city famous for noms d'amour ...'

'... to have fun just by ourselves ...'

'... if you want, we can leave for Acapulco tomorrow ...'

'... makes you laugh; the wheels of Swiss industry ...'

'... the American ambassador called to tell me ...'

'... it's moving along, thanks to the ten million dollars that ...'

'... Laura, Laura Rivière; she married again over there ...'

'... in my small plane ...'

'... that we Latin-Americans have deposited ...'

'... that no country is free of subversions ...'

'... sure, I read it in *Excelsior* ...'

'... I'll tell you: he dances divinely ...'

'... Rome is the eternal city par excellence ...'

'... but he hasn't got a nickel ...'

'... I made my pile by hard work ...'

'... oh, you, if he tastes that divine egg-dipped ...'

'... Why should I pay taxes to a government of gangsters? ...'

'... they call him the Mummy ... the Mummy of Coyoacán ...'

'... Darling, a sensational modiste ...'

'... credits for agriculture? ...'

'... I tell you, he still falls down on his putting ...'

'... poor Catalina ...'

'... and then who controls the droughts and the frosts? ...'

'... can't make it any longer: without American investments ...'

'... they say she was his great love, but ...'

'... Madrid, divine. Seville, precious ...'

'... we'll never get out of the hole ...'

'... but as Mexico ...'

'... they could have been plus the profits. Get me? ...'

'... the lady of the house; if it weren't ...'

'... I pull back forty cents on the dollar ...'

'... they give us their money and their *know-how* ...'

'... before lending it ...'

'... and we still complain ...'

'... it was twenty-odd years ago ...'

'... agreed: local machines, crooked union leaders, and everything else ...'

'... I did it all in white and gold, marvelous! ...'

'... but a good politician doesn't try to change reality ...'

'... The President honors me with his friendship ...'

'... instead of taking advantage of her and working with her ...'

'... as for the arrangement he has with Juan Felipe, of course ...'

'... does thousands of works of charity, but never speaks of them ...'

'... all I said was you're welcome ...'

'... we all owe each other favors, don't we? ...'

'... what she would give to leave him ...'

'... of course he cut me. Poor Catalina ...'

'... he took them, but for less than ten thousand dollars ...'

'... Laura. I think her name was Laura. I think she was quite good-looking ...'

'... but what's a poor girl to do? ...'

They moved far away, came nearer again, the tide of the dance and their conversations. But now, this youth with the open smile and the light hair had squatted down beside him, balancing a champagne glass in one hand and holding to the arm of the chair with the other, and was asking if he, the young man, had put a great distance between them? and he, the old man, replied, 'You have done nothing else the entire night, Señor Ceballos,' and did not look at the young man but kept his gaze fixed on the crowd. The unwritten law: guests were never to come near him except to speak some hasty praise of the house or the dinner. They were supposed to keep their distance, indeed, and to express their gratitude by enjoying themselves. They were the players and he was the audience, and vice versa. Obviously young Ceballos wasn't aware. 'You know, sir? I admire you.' The old man searched his pocket and pulled out a crumpled pack of cigarettes. He lit one, lifting the match slowly, and did not look at young Ceballos, who was saying that only a king could show the contempt he showed when he looked at them. The old man asked if this was his first time tonight, and the young man said yes. 'Your father-in-law didn't tell you that I ...' 'Oh, yes, of course.' 'Then?' 'That rule was made without consulting me, Don Artemio.' He did not struggle against the young man. His eyes were languid. The smoke curled. He turned to Jaime and the youth looked at him, almost roguishly, without blinking, moved his lips and jaw ... a game that he remembered, ah ... that disconcerted him, ah ... 'What, Señor Ceballos ... ?' what had he sacrificed ... 'I don't understand you ...' he didn't understand, he said he didn't understand him ... 'The hurt that makes us betray ourselves ...' who did he think he was talking to? Did it occur to him that he, an old man, might be deceiving himself? Jaime moved the ashtray nearer. Ah, they rode their horses across the river that morning ... '... by justifying ourselves ... ?' ... he watched without being watched ... 'Surely your father-in-law and the others with whom you are concerned ...' across the river that morning ... '... that our wealth is its own justification, for we worked to gain it ...' '... our recompense, eh ... ?' he asked him if they would ride together as far as the sea ... 'Do you know, young man, why I stand above all these little men and women ... and control them like puppets ...?' Jaime pushed the ashtray near him and he gestured with his cigarette. He came up from the river with his chest bare ...

'Ah, you came over to talk with *me*, I didn't summon you ...'
Jaime half closed his eyes and drank from the champagne
glass. 'You are losing your illusions ... ?' She said over
and over, God, is this what I deserve? lifting the mirror,
asking herself if this is what he would see when he returned ...
'Poor Catalina ...' 'Because I don't deceive myself ...' after
crossing the river they saw a spectral land, a spectral, yes ...
'What do you think of this party ... ?' *vacilón, qué rico vacilón,*
cha cha cha It smelled of bananas. Cocuya ... 'It makes no
difference to me ...' He spurred ahead. He turned and looked
back and his lips broke into a smile. '... my paintings, my wines,
my comforts. I control them, just as I control you my guests ...'
'Does it seem so to you ... ?' this place and his youth let him
remember his own youth ... 'Power is worthwhile in itself, this
I know. And to get it, you have to do everything ...' but he did
not want to tell him how much this land meant to him, because
to do so might perhaps influence his feeling for it ... '... as I
have done and your father-in-law and all those people dancing
out there ...' that morning he waited for him with happiness ...
'... and as you will have to do yourself, if you want
to ...' 'To work with you, Don Artemio, to see if one of your
businesses, you can ...' His raised arm pointed toward the east
where the sun rose, toward the lagoon. 'As a rule, these matters
are arranged rather differently ...' The horses moved off at a
slow hypnotic trot, parting the tall grass, waving their manes,
splashing up spray. '... the father-in-law calls me and insinuates
that his son-in-law is ...' They looked at each other's eyes and
smiled. 'But you see, I have other ideals ...' to the open and
unprisoned sea which broke waves around his waist ... 'You
accepted things as they are; you became realistic ...' 'Yes, that's
it. Like you, Don Artemio ...' He asked him if he had never
wondered what lies on the other side of the sea; for to him it
seemed that all land was much the same, only the sea was
different. 'Like me ... !' He said that there are islands ... '...
did you fight in the Revolution, risk your hide, to the point that
you were about to be executed ... ?' Sea that tasted like bitter
beer, smelled of melon, quince, strawberry ... 'Eh ... ?' 'No,
I ...' A ship sails in ten days. I have booked passage ... 'Come

to banquet before it's over, eh? You hurry to gather up the crumbs ...' You would do the same, Papá ... '... on top for forty years because we were baptized with the glory of that ...' 'Yes ...' '... but you, young man? Do you think that that can be inherited? How are you going to continue ... ?' Now there is a front and I think it is the only front left. 'Yes ...' '... to hold our power ... ?' I'm going to go to it ... 'You yourselves, sir, taught us how ...' 'Bah! You're too late, I tell you ...' He awaited him with happiness that morning ... 'They may try to fool others; I have never fooled myself, that's why I'm where I am ...' Rode their horses across the river ... '... hurry up ... stuff yourself while you can, for it's ending ...' He asked him if they would ride together as far as the sea ... 'It doesn't matter to me ...' the sea watched by a low flight of gulls ... 'I will die and I'll laugh about it ...' the sea that thrust its tired tongue upon the beach. '... and I will laugh to think ...' sea which broke waves around his waist '... I keep a world alive for someone who no longer exists ...' The old man put his lips near the Ceballos youth's ear ... sea that tastes like bitter beer ... 'Would you like to hear a confession ... ?' sea that smells of melon and guava ... He tapped the champagne glass lightly ... fishermen who drag their nets out on the sand ... '... true power is always born of rebellion ...' What do I believe? I don't know. You brought me here, you taught me this life ... 'And you, all of you ...' with his face toward the open sea and his hands open under the cloaked, suddenly darkening sky ... '... all of you, you don't have what it takes ...'

He looked across the salon again.

'So ...' Jaime murmured. 'May I come to see you ... one of these days?'

'Talk with Padilla. Good night.'

The clock struck three times. The old man sighed and shook the leashes of the sleeping dogs. They pricked up their ears and stood when he stood. With an effort, pushing against the arms of the chair, he lifted himself. The music stopped.

He crossed the salon to the low buzzing of thank yous from his guests' inclined heads. Lilia walked before him

'Excuse me ...'

and then took his rigid arm. He with his head high (Laura, Laura); she with her eyes down and reflective; they passed through the lane opened for them, past the elegant hangings, the rich inlays, the gold frames, the bone and tortoise-shell chests, the locks and hasps, the metal-cornered coffers, the fragrant ayacahuite benches, the choir boxes, the baroque miters and robes, the polychrome masks, the bronze nailheads, the tooled leather, the castered ball-and-claw feet, the cloth of silver cassocks, the damask chairs, the velvet sofas, the scrolls and urns, the chamfered panels, the merino carpets, the framed oils, beneath the crystal chandeliers, the warm ceiling beams, to the first step of the stairway. Then he touched Lilia's hand and she helped him up the stairs, taking his elbow, half bending, the better to support him. She smiled.

'You didn't tire yourself out?'

He shook his head and touched her hand again.

I have wakened ... again ... but this time ... yes ... in this car, in this hearse ... no ... I don't know ... it runs so quietly ... I can't really be awake yet ... I open my eyes wide but I can't make them out, things, people ... white luminous eggs that wheel before me ... a wall of milk between me and the world ... between me and what can be touched and from the voices beyond ... I am shut off ... I die ... I separate myself from ... no, an attack ... a man my age can have an attack ... not death, not separation ... I don't want to say it ... I would like only to ask it ... but I say it ... if I make an effort ... yes, now I can hear something above the siren ... it's an ambulance ... the siren and my own throat ... my throat, narrow and closed ... saliva dripping drop by drop ... a bottomless well ... will? ah, don't worry ... it's written, stamped, sealed, notarized ... I don't forget anyone. Why should I forget them ... ? hate them ... ? It would give them pleasure to believe that to the last minute I thought about them only to make fools of them ... ? ah, what a laugh, ah, what a joke ... no ... I remember them

with the indifference of a cold business matter ... I parcel out
this wealth that they will publicly attribute to my strength ...
my tenacity ... my sense of responsibility ... my personal
qualities ... do it ... be at peace ... forget that I won that wealth,
I risked it, I won it ... giving everything in exchange for nothing ... what is it called when you give everything in order to
receive everything ... call it what you will ... they came back,
they wouldn't admit they were beaten ... yes, I think about it
and smile ... I mock myself, I mock all of you ... I mock my
life ... isn't that my privilege? isn't this the last moment to do
it ... ? I couldn't mock while I lived ... now, yes ... my
privilege ... I will leave them the will ... I will bequeath them
those dead names ... Regina ... Tobías ... Páez ... Gonzalo ...
Zagal ... Laura, Laura ... Lorenzo ... I can think about it and
ask myself ... without knowing ... so that they may not forget
me ... why these last ideas ... this I know, I think, I think ... why
they pass distant from my will, ah, yes ... as if the brain ... is
asking ... and the answer comes to me before the question ...
probably they are both the same ... to live is to find separation
... with that mulatto and the hut and the river ... with Catalina,
if we could have spoken ... in the town jail that dawn ... don't
cross the sea, there are no islands, I deceived you ... with my
teacher ... Esteban? Sebastián ... ? I left him and went to the
North ... ah, yes, yes ... yes, my life would have been different
... but only then different ... not the life of this dying man ...
not dying, no ... I tell all of you, no, no, no ... an attack, an
old man, an attack ... convalescence, that's it ... but not
another's ... not that of another ... different life but ... also
separated ... ay, deceptions ... in the land of men ... life
hidden ... hidden death ... alloted fate ... without feeling ...
my God, ah ... that may be my last undertaking ... who is
putting his hands on my shoulders ... ? believe in God ... good
investment, so why not ... ? who is forcing me to lie back, as if
I could possibly want to rise ... ? can there be another possibility,
even if one does not believe in it, of believing that one continues
being ... God God God ... just to say a word a thousand times
is to make it lose all meaning ... not even a rosary of hollow ...
syllables ... God God ... my lips are dry ... God God ...

illumine those who remain ... make them think of me once ...
in a while ... let my memory ... be not lost ... I think, I think
... but I can't see them clearly ... I don't see them ... mourning
men and women ... the black egg breaks from ... my eyes and
I see ... that they go on living ... back to their occupations ...
their lounging ... intrigues ... without remembering ... the
poor dead man ... who hears the shoveled dirt ... wet ... on
his face ... the crawling ... crawling, crawling ... luxurious ...
worms ... my throat drips ... an ocean ... a lost voice that
wants ... to speak again, speak ... continue living ... continue
life from where the other cut it off ... speak again ... be born
again ... go back and start over from the beginning ... revive ...
be born ... revive ... choose again ... revive ... decide again ...
no ... ice at my temples ... blue fingernails ... belly distended
... swollen up with nausea ... of shit ... there's a reason for
death ... no, no ... ah, the women, the impotent women ... who
have had everything ... wealth ... but the hearts of mediocrity
... if at least you had used ... your advantages ... what wealth
is for ... while I have had everything ... do you hear me ...?
everything that can be bought and also what cannot be bought
... I had Regina ... hear me ... I loved Regina ... her name
was Regina and ... she loved me ... loved me when I had
nothing ... followed me ... gave me life, down ... there, below
... Regina, Regina, how I love you ... love you today ... without
needing to have you near ... fill my heart with content ...
warmth ... wash over me ... with your forgotten perfume ...
forgotten, Regina ... see, I remembered you ... look well ... I
remembered you before I could ... remember ... just how you
are ... how you love me and how ... I loved you in that world
and no ... one can take that away from us ... Regina, from you
and from me ... I carry and cherish it ... protecting it with
both ... hands like a flame small ... alive ... that you have
given me ... that you said ... to me you said to me ... I must
have lost ... but I gave you ... *ay*, dark eyes, *ay* brown fragrant
flesh, *ay* sable lips, *ay*, dark love I cannot touch, name ... *ay*,
your hands, Regina ... your hands upon my throat ... and forgotten your meetings ... forgotten all that was ... beyond you

and me ... *ay*, without thought, Regina ... without words ...
living in your dark thighs' timeless ... abundance ... ah, my
pride then, pride ... in having loved you ... challenge without
reply ... what can the world say ... to us, Regina, and what
could I add to what ... we had, how could I speak of ... our
madness ... in having loved each other ... what ... ? dove,
carnation, moonflower, foam, trefoil, key, arch, star ... phantom
flesh, what shall I call ... you love how will ... I come again to
you ... by my breath ... will beg ... surrender ... I will caress
you ... your cheeks ... and kiss your ears ... open your lips
between ... your thighs ... and will say ... your eyes your eyes
... taste your taste ... leave behind my solitude for ... our
solitude ... tell you again and ... again that I love you love you
... how shall I revive ... your memory to await your ... return
Regina Regina ... the stabbing comes back, I'm waking ... the
half-dream of the sedative ... I am waking ... with the pain in
my guts and ... Regina, give me your hand, don't ... leave me
I don't want to wake without you ... at my side, my love, my
Laura, woman adored, savior ... memory, percal skirt, Regina,
I ... hurt my forever tenderness, little turned-up nose, I hurt ...
Regina, I discover that I hurt ... Regina, come so that I may ...
strive one more time ... Regina, change your life, give it to me
and I will give you mine ... die again, Regina, so that I may ...
live ... Regina soldier Regina hold me. Lorenzo. Lilia. Laura.
Catalina. Hold me. No. My temples are ice ... don't die, brain,
mind, reason ... I want to find a reason ... I want ... I wish
to ... the place of my birth ... my country ... I love you, I
wanted to go back ... reason beyond reason ... to watch life
lived, from a high place, very high, and not see ... and if I see
nothing ... why die ... why die ... why die suffering ... why
not go on living ... dead life ... why pass from living ... nothing
to dead nothing ... it's ending ... ending panting ... howling ...
howl of the siren ... pack of hounds ... ambulance stops ...
tired ... never tireder ... where I come from ... light in eyes ...
voice ...

'Doctor Sabine is operating.'

Reason? Reason ... ?

The stretcher runs out of the ambulance on little wheels.
Reason?
Who is alive?
Who lives?

You could not be more tired than you are, more exhausted. It's
that you have traveled a long way, footback, walking, on the old
trains, and the country never ends. Remember this country?
You remember it. It is not one; there are a thousand countries,
with a single name. You know that. You will carry with you the
red deserts, the hills of prickly pear and maguey, the world of
dry cactus, the lava belt of frozen craters, the walls of golden
domes and rock thrones, the limestone and sandstone cities, the
tezontlestone cities, the adobe pueblos, the reed-grass hamlets,
the black mud paths, the roads across the drought country, the
lips of the sea, the thicketed forgotten coasts, the valleys sweet
with wheat and corn, the horse pastures of the north, the Bajio
lakes, the slender tall forests, the boughs laden with hay, the
white peaks, the asphalt flats, the ports with malaria and whorehouses, the bony skeleton of sisal, the lost rivers hidden in cliff-
walled canyons, the tunnels that burrow for gold and silver, the
Indians who lack a common tongue: Cora, Yaqui, Huichol, Pima,
Seri, Chontal, Tepahuana, Huasteca, Totonaca, Nahua, Maya;
the native fife and drum, the group dancing, the guitar and
cithern, the head-dresses of plumes, the delicate-boned men of
Michoacan, the squat bodies of the men of Tlaxcala, Sinaloa's
light eyes, white teeth from Chiapas, the *huipiles*, the Veracruz
combs, the Mixtec braids, Tzotzil belts, Santa María rebozos,
Puebla marquetry, Jalisco glass, Oaxaca jade, the ruins of the
serpent, of the black head, the great nose, the churches and altar-
pieces, the colors and reliefs, the pagan faith of Tonantzintla and
Tlacochaguaya, the old names Teotihuacan and Papantla and
Tula and Uxmal: you will carry these with you and they are
leaden, they are stone heavy for one man: they have never moved
and you have them bound to your neck; they weight you down,

they have entered your guts, they are your bacilli, your parasites, your amoebas ...

the land of your birth

you will think that there is a second conquest of this land in that soldiering across its length and breadth, the first foot to tread mountains and gorges that stand like challenging fists before the helpless, desperate, slow advance of roads and rails and dams and telegraph poles: nature that refuses to be compared or controlled, that wants to live on in harsh loneliness and has granted men only a few outlying valleys and rivers for them to cling to her skirts; nature that goes on ruling the smooth unattainable peaks, the flat burned deserts, the forests and the deserted coast; men, fascinated by such arrogance, keep their eyes fixed upon her, and as nature turns her back on them, they turn their backs to the wide forgotten sea, boiling with fecundity, with ignored riches

you will inherit the land

you will never again see those places and faces you knew in Sonora and Chihuahua, the faces of soldiers that you saw sleeping and enduring today and tomorrow enraged, thrown into battle with neither reason nor palliative, into the embrace of the killers, the set-apart, the next day thrown into the cry of here I am and I exist with you and with you too, with all our outlawed hands and outcast faces: love, a strange common love that will die away of itself: you will tell yourself about it, because you lived it and while you lived it did not understand it: but dying you will accept that love and will admit openly that even without understanding, you feared it all the days of your power: you will be afraid that those love-filled meetings between men of hatred will explode again; and now you will die and no longer fear: but you will tell others that they had better be afraid: distrust the false tranquillity you bequeath them, the fiction of concord, the magic formula, the sanctioned greed: let them fear this injustice so pervasive it does not even know its limits: so habitually injust it no longer knows itself as injust at all:

they will accept your legacy: the decency that you acquired for them: they will offer up thanks to bare-foot Artemio Cruz because he made them people of position: they will give thanks to him because he was not content to live and die in a Negro hut; they will thank him because he ventured away and gambled his life: they will justify you because they will not have your justification: they will not be able to speak of their battles and captains, as you can, and shield themselves behind glory to justify rapine in the name of the Revolution, self-aggrandizement in the name of working for the good of the Revolution: you will think about them and will wonder: what justification will they find? what wall will they oppose? but they will not think about it, they will merely enjoy, while they can, what you leave them: they will live happy, show themselves, in public, and you ask no more, to be mourning and grateful, while you wait with three feet of earth above your head, wait until you feel the tramp of feet over your dead face, and then you will say

'They have returned. They didn't give up,'
and you will smile, mocking them, mocking yourself, which is your privilege: nostalgia will tempt you to make the past more beautiful but you will refrain:

you will bequeath the futile dead names, the names of so many who fell that your name might stand: men despoiled of their names that you might possess yours: names forgotten that yours might be remembered:

you will bequeath this country: your newspaper, the hints and the adulation, the conscience drugged by lying articles written by men of no ability; you will bequeath the mortgages, a class stripped of natural human affection, power without greatness, a consecrated stultification, dwarf ambition, a fool's compromise, rotted rhetoric, institutionalized cowardice, coarse egoism:

You will bequeath them their crooked labor leaders and captive unions, their new landlords, their American investments, their jailed workers, their monopolies and their great press, their wet-backs, hoods, secret agents, their foreign deposits, their bullied agitators, servile deputies, fawning ministers, elegant tract homes, their anniversaries and commemorations, their fleas and wormy tortillas, their illiterate Indians, unemployed laborers, rapacious pawnshops, fat men armed with aqualungs and stock portfolios, thin men armed with their fingernails: they have their Mexico, they have their inheritance:

You will bequeath them their faces, sweet, far away, bereft of tomorrow because they do everything today, say everything today; they are the present and they live in the present: they say tomorrow because they don't give a damn about tomorrow: you will be their unwilling future, you will consume yourself today, thinking about tomorrow; but they will be tomorrow because they live only today:

your country

your death, animal who foreseeing your death, sings your death, talks it, dances it, paints it, remembering, before you die, your death.

the place of your birth:

you will not die without returning to it:

village at the mountain's foot, inhabited by three hundred souls, barely distinguishable, by a few splashes of roof, in the foliage that clings to the rock mountain and grows thick on the smooth slope that accompanies the river on its course to the nearby sea: like a green half-moon, the arc from Tamiahua to Coatzacoalcos will gnaw the white face of the sea uselessly – for the arc will be consumed in turn by the misty ring of mountains, seat and limit of the Indian plateau – in an attempt to join the tropical archipelago of graceful undulations and broken bodies: Mexico's dry languid hand, sad and immutable, reaching from the barrier of rock walls and dust, yet locked in the highlands or the Veracruz half-moon would have a different history and be tied by threads of gold to the Antilles, to the Atlantic, and eventually to the Mediterranean, which in truth will never be conquered except by the counterpush of the Eastern Sierra Madre: where the volcanoes stand naked and silent shapes of the maguey rise, there will die a world which sends its sensual crests in repeated waves from the Bosporus womb-way and the teats of the Aegean, sends a splatter of grapes from Syracuse and Tunis, a profound birthcry from Andalusia and the gates of Gibraltar, adulation of the trod-upon black from Haiti and Jamaica, carnival of dances and drums and silk-cotton trees and corsairs and conquistadores from Cuba: and the dark land absorbs the ocean swells: upon iron balconies and in arcade coffee shops the waves from afar become still: the emanations die between

the white columns of country porticoes and in the voluptuous
tonalities of bodies and voices: then the gloomy pedestal of eagle
and flint will be raised upon the limit, the border, a frontier no
one will ever defeat: not the men from Estremadura and Castille
who were lost in the first building and afterwards were unknow-
ingly conquered as they climbed to the forbidden platform that
destroyed them yet deformed only their appearances, victims,
at last, of the concentrated hunger of the dust statues, victims at
last of the blind suction of the lake that had swallowed their gold,
the limed cements of how many foundations, the faces of how
many violating conquerors: no, not they, and not the buccaneers
who piled their brigantines with coins thrown, with bitter
laughter, from the summit of the indigenous mountain; no, nor
the friars who crossed Malinche Pass to deliver new disguises to
imperturbable old gods imaged in stone but resident in the air;
no, nor the Negroes imported to tropical plantations and there
seduced to languidness by the advances of Indian girls whose
downy cunts soon conquered a race of curly fuzz; no, nor the royal
princes who came ashore from imperial sailing vessels and let
themselves be deceived by the sweet landscape of Palm of Christ
and hanging fruit, and who with their trunks of lace and lavender
climbed to the highland and the bullet-pocked execution wall;
no, nor the tricorned epauletted caciques who in the mute opacity
of the highland finally met exasperating defeat before mere
reticence, deaf mockery, and indifference.

you will be the boy-child who goes to the land and finds the
land, who leaves his beginnings and encounters his destiny, today
when death is the same as beginning and ending and between
the two, in spite of everything, is strung the thread of freedom:

[1903: January 18]

He heard the mulatto Lunero grumbling: Ah, drunk again,
drunk again, and woke as the cocks – mournful fowls fallen into
sylvan captivity, once they had fought the spurred favorites of
the region's great man and had been the pride of the hacienda,

but that was more than half a century ago – cried greeting to a quick tropic dawn which to Señor Pedro, embarked, there on the red stone terrace of the ruined building, on one more splendid solitary binge, was no more than the end of night. Señor Pedro's drunken song reached the palm-thatched hut where the boy was rubbing his eyes and Lunero stood sprinkling the earth floor with water from a jar that had come from some other region and whose decorations of ducks and red small blossoms had shone, in another time, with brilliant lacquer. Lunero lit the brazier and put the minced charal fish, yesterday's leftover, to heating. He squinted as he examined the fruit in the basket and picked out the darkest skins, the fruit that must be eaten quickly before rot, fecundity's sister, made it wormy and mushy. Then a little later, as the smoke from the brazier brought the boy fully awake, the phlegmy singing stopped and the stumble of heels could be heard, and finally a door slammed, prelude to Señor Pedro's morning of insomnia lying there without sheets on the bare woven mattress of his great mahogany bed, desperate because his liquor was all gone. And in the old days, Lunero recalled, when the spread of the hacienda had been from the mountain to the sea, the Negro huts had been built far from the big house and no one knew what was happening there, for the fat cooks and the young half-breed girls who swept the rooms and starched the shirts carried no tales back to the hacienda's other world of brown-skinned men in tobacco fields. The boy came to the fire in his short camisole, showing the first shadows of puberty, and Lunero tousled his head. Yes, that was what it had been like in the old days. But now no land was left and everything was close and squeezed together and there were no secrets. Of the big house there remained only fire-blackened walls with glassless windows and the one room in back where the grandmother, Ludivinia, lived. The memory of many servants was kept alive by a single Indian servant woman, Baracoa. And there was only one workers' hut, and he and the boy were the only workers.

The mulatto sat on the smooth earth floor and divided their fish, emptying half into a clay pot and the rest out on the iron sheet. He offered the boy a mango and peeled a banana, and they ate in silence. The little mound of coals burned out. Through the hut's one opening – door and window too, threshold for sniffing dogs, barrier for red ants stopped by a line painted with lime – came the heavy scent of the moonflower vine Lunero had planted years ago to conceal the brown adobe walls and to wrap the hut in the fragrance of the tubular nocturnal blossoms. Neither man nor boy spoke. But both were feeling the same grateful joy at being together, a pleasure they never expressed, not even in a mutual smile, because they were not there to talk or smile but to live in the hut and every dawn to go silently out in the dampness-laden tropical air and perform the toil required for them to go on living and providing Baracoa with the money that bought food for the grandmother every Saturday, and demijohns for Señor Pedro. They were pretty, those demijohns, fat blue bottles fitted with leather handles and insulated against the heat by reed basketwork. They were pot-bellied, squat, and narrow-necked. And Señor Pedrito went on leaving them thrown helter-skelter about the door to the house, and every month Lunero went to the village at the foot of the mountain carrying the long pole used for carrying buckets of water, and returned with the pole across his shoulders and the demijohns hanging from its ends. The village at the foot of the mountain was the only nearby settlement. It had a population of three hundred and was barely distinguishable, by a few splashes of roof, in the foliage that clung to the mountain rock and grew thick on the gentle slope that accompanied the course of the river to the sea.

The boy went outside and ran along the path past ferns that grew thick around the gray, smooth trunks of mango trees. The path was muddy and roofed with sky-concealing pink flowers and yellow fruit, and it led to the clearing Lunero's machete had made along the bank of the river, which here was still turbulent and swift but had begun to widen. Lunero arrived fastening his bell-bottom denim pants, relic of some forgotten sailor style. The boy took the short blue pants which all night had been drying on the rusted iron circle from which candle-wicks were suspended. Strips of mango bark, open and rough, lay with their ends soaking in the water. Lunero stopped in the ooze for a moment. This near the sea, the river spread and brushed against the masses of ferns and banana trees. The jungle seemed higher than the sky, which was low and flat, a mirror.

Each knew what to do. Lunero took sandpaper and with powerful strokes began to polish the bark. The boy brought up a lame, rotten stool and set it inside the iron ring, which was suspended from a central wooden spindle. From the ten holes in the ring, as many wicks hung down. He gave the ring a spin and squatted to light the fire under the kettle of myrtle. The melting myrtle bubbled out its thick vapor. The ring turned, the boy poured the wax into the evenly-spaced holes.

'The Feast of Purification is coming soon now,' said Lunero with three nails between his teeth.

'When?' The small fire and the sunlight shone in the boy's green eyes.

'The second, Cruz lad, the second. And then we will really sell candles, not only around here but to people up the river, too. They know ours are best.'

'I remember from last year.' Hot wax splashed out now and then; the boy's forearms were spotted with little round scars.

'It's the day the groundhog looks for his shadow.'

'How do you know?'

'A story from far away. The old people told it.'

Lunero reached for his hammer and his dark forehead frowned.

'Cruz lad, do you think you can make a canoe?'

The boy smiled broadly with a show of white teeth. Green light reflected from the river and the damp ferns accentuated the pale, bony outline of his face. Combed by the river, his hair curled down over his broad forehead and brown neck; sun had burned tones of copper in his hair, but the roots were black. All the hues of green fruit were reflected from his thin arms and hard chest, made to swim against the current. His laugh was that of a boy acquainted with the freshness of the grassy-bottomed river.

'Yes, I can make a canoe. I watched you so much.'

The mulatto lowered quiet wary eyes. 'Then if Lunero goes away, you will be able to handle things?'

The boy stopped turning the iron wheel. 'If Lunero goes away?'

'If he has to go.'

I ought to say nothing at all, the mulatto was thinking. No, he ought to say nothing, just go, as others of his people had gone, saying nothing because they knew and accepted destiny and sensed an abyss of reasons and memories between their knowledge and acceptance and the knowledge and rejection of other men. Without saying anything, because they knew nostalgia and wandering. But although he knew that he ought to say nothing, he also knew that the boy – his constant companion – had cocked his head with curiosity yesterday when the man in the tight sweaty frockcoat had come looking for Lunero.

'You know what I mean, handle things. Sell candles in the village and make extra when the Feast of Purification comes around. Take back the empty bottles every month and leave Señor Pedrito's liquor at the door. Build canoes and every three months take them down river. Hand the money you earn over to Baracoa, you know, holding back one gold piece for yourself. Fish for charal . . .'

The rusty candle wheel and the hammer were motionless now. Boxed in by the green growth, the murmur of the swift water grew louder. Patches of bagasse and trees torn up by the nightly storms swept by, and cut grass from upriver fields. Black and yellow butterflies drifted across the clearing. The boy's arms dropped and he stared at the mulatto's fallen eyes.

'You're going away?'

'You don't know the whole story. At one time the land here from the mountain to the sea belonged to the family. Then they lost it. The old master died somewhere far away. Señor Atanasio was badly wounded, by treachery, and everything went to pieces. Or went to others. I was the only worker left. For fourteen years they let me be in peace. But my time had to come, too.'

Lunero stopped because he did not know how to go on. The silver edges of the water distracted him; his muscles wanted to continue their toil. Thirteen years ago, when the boy had been left in his care, he had thought of entrusting him to the river to be reared by butterflies, and to return some day powerful and famous. But the death of the young master, Don Atanasio, had made it possible for him to keep the boy safely with him, with no objections from Señor Pedro or from the grandmother, who was already living locked up in the blue room with the lace curtains and the chandeliers – one could hear their prisms tinkling during storms – and who never became aware, sealed in her madness, of the boy growing up just a few yards away. Yes, Don Atanasio had died opportunely; he would have had the child killed. Lunero saved the boy. Then the last tobacco fields passed out of the family – only Señor Pedro and the old grandmother Señora Ludivinia were left of them – into the hands of the new great man of the region. There remained only the ruined big house like a cracked old kettle, and this tiny strip of land along the river. Workers departed to sweat for their new master. Other workers began to arrive, brought in from up river. Old hands were pulled off their places on ranches and in the pueblos and sent far away to the south. He, Lunero, began to make a living for the family, candles and canoes. And he believed that hidden there on that tiny fingernail of land between the house and the river, he would be overlooked by the sign-up men. So, for fourteen years, it had happened. But the sign-up men's obstinate raking of the whole region was bound to root him out sooner or later. That was why the man in the black frockcoat had come yesterday with sweat streaming down his face: to tell him that tomorrow – today now – he would have to go away to the señor cacique's hacienda down in the southern part of the state. God damn it, good tobacco workers were hard to find, and for fourteen years he had been sitting on his ass here beside the river looking after a damn drunk and a crazy old woman.

Lunero did not know how to explain all this. He felt the boy would not understand. But the mulatto's real reason for silence was the fact that if he began to trace one thread of the story, the whole story would have to come out. He would have to explain the beginning, and he would thereby lose the boy. And he loved him, the long-armed mulatto said to himself as he knelt beside the strips of sanded bark; he had loved him ever since they had run his sister off beating her with sticks, Isabel Cruz, the boy's mother, and he had been left with the baby and had fed him with goat's milk and taught him the alphabet by drawing in the mud the letters he, Lunero, had learned when as a child he had been a servant for the French in Veracruz; and had taught him to swim, to recognize and enjoy different fruits, to use a machete, to make candles, to sing the songs Lunero's father – as much the boy's grandfather as Señora Ludivinia was his grandmother – had brought from Santiago in Cuba when the war began and the families fled, with their Negroes, to Veracruz. And that was all Lunero wanted to know about the boy. Maybe it was unnecessary to know more, except that the boy loved him too and did not want to live without him. But if he went away, those shadows lost to the world, Señor Pedro, the Indian woman Baracoa, and the grandmother, would move to the foreground and become real and sharp, with all their strangeness, their apartness from the ordinary world, and it was then that the boy would begin to think and understand.

'We won't have enough candles if you don't get at it. The priest will be sore.'

A breath of wind shook the suspended wicks. A macaw gave its noon-day scream.

Lunero stood and walked to the river. He dove and came up in the middle with the small net hanging on one arm. The boy Cruz took off his short pants and threw himself into the water too. He submerged and opened his eyes. The clear undulations of the swift upper layer flowed over a green and muddy bottom. He let himself be carried by the current. There, above and behind him, were the big house he had never in all his thirteen years entered, the man he had seen only at a distance, and the old woman he knew only as a name. The boy's head rose and he looked ashore. Lunero was already frying the fish they had netted, and opening a papaya with his machete.

It was a little after high noon. Rays of sun filtered through the dense roof of tropical leaves, striking hard before they began the descent into the west. Branches were motionless and even the river seemed not to move. The Cruz boy hung from the solitary palm, whose shadows, the trunk and plumed crown, were lengthening minute by minute. Slanting light climbed his body as he leaned against the trunk: first his feet, then his bare legs and limp penis, his flat belly, his water-hardened chest; the long neck, the square jaw with two deep sutures rising like arched supports to the sharp high cheekbones; the clear eyes which later that afternoon were closed in deep tranquil siesta.

He slept. Lunero lay stretched out face down and was drumming on the wax-making kettle. Gradually the mulatto began to feel the rhythm he was beating. His body seemed lax but was not. His moving arm was full of tension as it rang clear tones from the side of the kettle. It was an often remembered melody, always accelerating, and he began to hum it: song of his childhood, of the long ago life when his forebears were crowned, near a silk-cotton tree, with rattles-decorated caps and their arms were anointed with aguardiente and a man, the man, sat on a chair, his head covered by a white cloth, and they all drank the mix of hot corn and bitter orange to the syrupy bottom of the jug, and they told their children that at night they must never whistle:

> *tó...*
> *la hija de Yeyé...*
> *le gusta mario...de otra mujé...*
> *tó, la hija de Yeyé, le gusta mario, de otra mujé...*
> *tóla hijaeyeyé legusta.*

The rhythm continued to accelerate. He stretched his arms out and touched his fingers to the damp earth and beat the rhythm with his palms slapping the earth. His belly was muddied. A wide smile broke on his face. His cheeks were tight across the wide cheekbones ... *legustamariodeotramujé* ... The afternoon sun fell leadenly upon his round fuzzy head. He could not get up, sweat ran from his forehead, over his ribs, between his thighs. The sound of his voice became deeper and softer, the beat of his hands and body harder and louder. He was pounding the earth as if he were having sexual intercourse with the earth. *Tólahijaeyeyé*. His smile spread. He forgot the sign-up man who was coming after him this evening, the man in the black frockcoat. He was lost in his song and his prone dance.

Yes, and on this same heat-stifled afternoon, while the boy slept and the mulatto beat out the rhythm of his unforgotten song, old Ludivinia, the grandmother, locked forever in her bedroom with its absurd chandeliers – two of them, hanging from the plain white-washed ceiling, one in the corner near the four-poster bed – and its yellowing lace curtains, old Ludivinia lay with her eyes wide open, fanned by the Indian woman Baracoa, and tried to remember another song. She could hum the melody but she could not recall the words, and she would have liked to repeat them, for she did remember that they made sardonic mock of General Juan Nepomuceno Almonte. General Juan Nepomuceno Almonte had for years been a friend of the family. He was even god-father to Ireneo Menchaca, Ludivinia's dead husband. And he had been a member of Santa Anna's court, but later, when Mexico's savior the Menchaca's great protector – of lives and haciendas – had wanted to return from banishment abroad, had disembarked and recovered from an attack of dysentery, Almonte had thrown over loyalty and had had the old General detained by the French and made to take the ship again. She remembered Juan Nepomuceno Almonte's dark face, and now the words of that damned Juarista song came back: *y qué te lo pareciera que llegaran los ladrones, se robaran a tu vieja y le bajaran los calzones*; and she twisted her sucked-in toothless mouth and with an impatient movement of her palsied hand, shaking the black silk sleeves of her dress, its cuffs of ruined lace, told the Indian servant woman to work the palm-leaf fan faster.

The room was hot and musty and smelled of the tropics, a muffled smell that moved while the air remained still. There were great moisture stains on the walls. Lace windows, crystal, elm-wood tables with heavy marble tops upon which stood the glass-bell clocks with ball feet. Wicker rockers on the tile floor, with cushions that would never be used again. Chamfered panels, bronze nailheads, coffers with iron corners and lock escutcheons; oval varnished portraits of unknown rigid Creoles with spongy sidewhiskers or high bosoms and tortoise-shell combs. Wrought tin frames for saints and for the Christ-child of Atocha, the latter image in the old quilted style and now so rotted that scarcely any gold leaf remained. The carved foliage of the four-poster bed with its canopy and striated posts: resting place for her bloodless body, nest of closed-in smells, of stained sheets and straw humps and lumps in the mattress.

'Indian, bring me a jar of water.'

The old woman waited for Baracoa to leave and then broke all the rules by moving toward the window. News of the birth of the child had never reached her in her seclusion, but a presentiment had. She had watched, secretly, the unknown boy grow; she had spied through the lace window. She had seen those green eyes and had cackled with pleasure to know that her blood had been born young again in other flesh: she who carried a century of memory and, in the lines of her wrinkled face, the marks of winds and suns long disappeared. She had lasted, she had survived. It was hard to reach the window. She almost crawled, humped over with her eyes fixed on her knees and her hands clutching her thighs, her white head drawn down between her shoulders.

Yes: she had survived. She had lived on at Cocuya trying to maintain, from her rumpled bed in the forgotten back room, the breeding and manner of the lovely pale young wife who had opened the hacienda's doors to the long parade of Spanish prelates, French businessmen, Scotch engineers, British bond salesmen, and agitators and adventurers who had passed by on their way to Mexico City, city of young and anarchic opportunity, of baroque cathedrals, of mines of gold and silver, of carved stone palaces, of business-wise clergy, of political carnival, of perpetual governmental indebtedness, and of easy concessions that could be quickly won by a foreigner's smooth tongue. Those had been glorious days in Mexico City. And they, Ireneo and Ludivinia Menchaca, had left their hacienda in charge of their elder son, Atanasio, so that he would become a man dealing with laborers and bandits and the Indians, and with their pleasure-loving younger son Pedro had themselves traveled up to the highland capital. There they had glittered in the make-believe court of His Most Serene Highness, General Santa Anna. For how could the General live without his old war comrade Colonel Menchaca at hand, brave man wise as to fighting cocks and theater pits who could spend a whole night drinking and remembering the Casamata campaign, Barrada's expedition, the Alamo, San Jacinto, the War of the Cakes, and all the rest, including their defeats at the hands of the invading Yankees, a catastrophe to which the General referred with cynical hilarity as he tapped the floor with his wooden leg and lifted his glass high and stroked the long hair of the Flower of Mexico, the child-bride who had been carried to his bed at the last death-rattle of his first wife.

Then had come days of difficulty. The General was expelled from Mexico by the Liberals and the Menchacas had to go back to their hacienda to defend their own: the thousands upon thousands of acres that had been granted them by Santa Anna, just appropriated with no questions asked or answers given to the Indian farmers, who had either to stay on as peons or retire to the foot of the mountain. Rich land worked now by the new black labor, so cheap, brought in from the Caribbean islands. Wide land enlarged by the foreclosure of mortgages. Heaps and piles of tobacco. Carts loaded high with bananas and mangoes. Herds of goats that grazed in the Sierra Madre foothills. And in the center of everything, the two-story big house with its red tower and whinneying stables, its carriage and launch pleasure rides. And green-eyed Atanasio, the young master, dressed in white and riding a white horse which was another gift from his father's old friend the cock-fighting tyrant, Atanasio galloping across the fertile land quick to impose his will and quick to satisfy his gross appetites upon the young country women, quick and strong to defend the land with his band of imported Negroes as the incursions of the Juarez partisans became ever more fervent. *Viva México primero, que viva nuestra nación, muera el príncipe extranjero* . . .

And those last days of the Empire, when old Ireneo, advised that Santa Anna was returning from abroad to proclaim a new Republic, went in his black carriage to Veracruz and waited at the dock, while on the deck of the *Virginia*, in the darkness, the General and his German free-booters made signals to the Fort and received no reply: the port garrison was loyal to the Empire and sneered at the fallen tyrant, who paced the deck under the pennants and spat curses from his fleshy lips and was totally helpless. Then the *Virginia*'s sails filled again and the two old comrades, the General and the Colonel, sat in the Yankee captain's cabin and played cards together while the ship sailed south across a warm slow sea from which they could just discern the heat-veiled coastline. They came to Sisal's white silhouette. Santa Anna went below accompanied by his friend and issued a ringing Proclamation to the People of Yucatán, and once more lived his dream of greatness. Maximilian was dead in Queretaro; the Republic had the right to count upon the patriotic return of its true and natural leader, its uncrowned monarch. But Sisal's commander merely arrested the crippled old soldier and sent him to Campeche along with Ireneo Menchaca. There, with their hands chained, jabbed by bayonets, they were driven through the street like common criminals, and afterward thrown in a dungeon. Colonel Menchaca died that summer, swollen by putrid water, and was buried in a nameless grave without a headstone in the Campeche graveyard. American newspapers announced that Santa Anna had been executed by the Juarez troops. But no: the old man merely left for new exile abroad, wearing the permanent grin of madness.

Atanasio had told his mother. And since that day Ludivinia had not left her room. Here she had brought her best jewels, the dining-room chandelier, the veneer chests, the varnished paintings. Here she had secluded herself to await the death that her romantic indignation had told her was imminent. Imminent now meant thirty-five years, lost years but as nothing, nothing, to a woman of ninety-three born in the year of the first Revolution, brought into the world behind doors battered by terror. She had lost her calendars. The year 1903 was no more than another mockery of the quick death that ought to have followed the death of her colonel husband.

And in '68 the Liberals had come through on their last campaign against the Empire and had burned the hacienda that had opened its doors to the French marshal and its storerooms to the Conservative troops, who had loaded mules with preserves and beans and tobacco and marched off to destroy the mountain lairs from which Juarez guerillas – outlaws, outlaws! – had swept down to harass French flatland encampments and the garrisons of the Veracruz cities. At Cocuya the Zouaves had discovered cithern and harp musicians who sang *Balajú se fue a la guerra y no me quiso llevar* and Indian and mulatto girls who soon were giving birth to blond mestizo babies and chocolate mulatto babies with light eyes, children named Carduño and Alvarez when their names should have been Dubois and Garnier.

The Liberals had fired the big house but the flames had stopped at the doors of the sealed bedroom while her sons – there were two of them but she loved only Atanasio – shouted for her to save herself and she piled the tables and chairs against the door and coughed in the thick smoke. And afterward she had wanted to see no one except the Indian woman Baracoa who was there because someone had had to be there to bring her her meals and mend her black clothes. She wanted to know nothing except the room and her memories, for within these four walls she had lost the reason for everything except what was essential: her widowhood and the past and then, suddenly, the green-eyed child running in the distance on the heels of an unknown mulatto.

'Indian, bring me a jar of water.'

But instead of Baracoa returning, a yellow specter stood in the door.

Ludivinia shouted without voice and retreated. Her sunken eyes grew wide with fear and it seemed that the shell of her face was cracking apart. The man on the threshold stretched out a trembling hand:

'I am Pedro.'

She did not understand him. She could not speak, but she managed to make a gesture that was an attempt to exorcize, to deny. The pale phantom came forward with his mouth hanging open.

'Pedro ... eh,' he mumbled, rubbing his light, unclean beard. 'Pedro.'

Her eyelids twitched and she did not understand what he was saying. He stank of sweat and cheap liquor. 'Eh,' he was going on, 'nothing left, you know. Everything gone ... to the devil ... and now ...' He stopped, stammering. His voice became a dry whisper. 'Now, they're taking the Negro. Mamá, you don't know ...'

'Atanasio.'

'No, Pedro.' He fell drunkenly into a wicker rocker and opened his legs, as if he had come to the port of departure. 'Now they are taking the Negro who ... provides food for ... you and me ...'

'No,' she said. 'A mulatto and a boy.' She was listening, but she did not look at him. A voice might be heard in the forbidden cave, but it must not have a body.

'All right, a mulatto. And a boy ... eh?'

'A boy who runs out there sometimes. I've seen him. He pleases me.'

'The sign-up man came. Woke me up in full daylight ... they're going to take the Negro ... what will we do?'

'They're taking a Negro? Pah, the plantation is full of Negroes. The colonel says they are cheaper and work harder. If you want to keep him so much, raise him to six reales.'

And thus they remained, statues of salt, thinking what later they would wish they had said, later when it was too late and the child was no longer with them. Ludivinia tried to make herself look at the spectral presence she refused to acknowledge. Who could he be, this man who quite on purpose had raised the dust upon her best jewels by trespassing her room? Yes: his stiff shirt-front of holland, spotted by the mildew of tropical storage; the narrow too-tight trousers, too small for the little pot-belly of his wornout body; the tobacco and alcohol sweat, the transparent eyes that were far from the self-affirmation and borrowed presence of his clothing. Eyes of a drunkard who was beyond malice and equally beyond doing anything at all. Ah, Ludivinia sighed, lying back in her mussed bed again and finally admitting that the voice had a face – ah, that was not Atanasio, so like her in his virility: this one had the same mother but a white beard and white balls. He was not the man she would have been if she had been a man: that man was Atanasio, and this was why she had loved one son and not the other, the son who had remained rooted to the place that had been theirs on earth and had not lived where this one, even in their defeat, had wanted to go on enjoying life, the high place among the palaces, the place that had been given to them which had never, she was sure, been theirs by right. And now nothing was theirs and her own place was within these four walls.

They looked at each other, mother and son.

Are you here, she said to him silently, *to tell me that we no longer have land or greatness ? That others have taken from us what we took from others ? Have you come to tell me what I have always known would happen, since my first night as a wife ?*

I came with a pretext, he replied with his eyes. *I didn't want to be alone any more.*

I would like to remember what you were like as a child, she went on. *I loved you then. When a mother is young, she loves all her children. As old women, we know better. No one has a right to be loved without a reason. Blood ties are not reason enough. The right reason is blood loved without reason.*

I have wanted to be strong like my brother. For example, I have treated that mulatto and the boy with an iron hand. I have forbidden them ever to set foot in the house. Like Atanasio, remember ? But in those days there were so many workers. Now there are only the mulatto and the boy and the mulatto is being taken away.

You have remained alone and now you seek me out merely to escape loneliness, the old woman understood. *You think that I am alone, too, I see it in your little dead eyes. Fool, still, and weak ! You are not the son who asked pity of no one; but you are myself as I was when I was a young wife. Not now, though, not any more: now my whole life goes with me and I don't need to be an old woman. You old man, you who thinks that everything has ended because of your gray hair and your drunkenness and your lack of will. Ah, I look at you and see you . . . fuck you ! You're the one who went up to the capital with us and thought that our power was reason enough for you to waste our power on women and liquor, instead of something to be made deeper and stronger and used like a whip. You're the one who thought that he had inherited everything effortlessly and that therefore he would always be on top, even when we had to come back to this burning land, this fount of all we were, this hell out of which we had risen and into which we had to fall again. Smell ! There's a smell stronger than horsesweat or fruit or gunpowder. Have you ever smelled the smell of a man and woman copulating ? That's what the earth smells of here, a love sheet, and you have never known it. Listen . . . ah, I petted you when you were born, nursed you and called you my own, my son, but all I remember is the moment when your father created you with the blindness of a love that intended not your creation but my pleasure. And that has remained, and you have disappeared out there, outside, do you hear me? . . .*

Why don't you say something? said her son, without words. *That's all right, it's all right, don't speak. It's something at least to see you there looking at me. It's better than my bare bed and those unsleeping nights . . .*

Do you search for someone? asked the old woman. *And that boy out there, isn't he alive? I suspect you. You must think I see nothing, know nothing. As if I couldn't feel his flesh, my flesh, moving about, another life like Ireneo and Atanasio, another Menchaca, another man like the men they were . . . I have known that he is mine when you have not even seen him. Blood understands . . . without eyes, touch . . .*

Lunero,' said the boy when he woke and saw the mulatto lying exhausted on the damp ground. ' I want to go in the big house.'

Afterward, when it was all over ánd the son was dead and the grandson was gone, old Ludivinia would break her silence and come outside to scream, like a wingless crow, down the aisles of ferns; she would lose her vision in the thick underbrush, and at last she would raise her arms toward the mountains. She would reach out her arms to find the human form which, blinded by the night of her permanent mourning, she hoped to discover behind every twig that struck her face. And she would smell the earth and in a muffled voice shout the forgotten names and the names learned only today, and would gnaw her hands with fury because something in her chest – years, memory, the past that had become her whole life – would tell her that there would still exist a shore of life beyond the river of her century of memories: that something lived that had not died with the deaths of Ireneo and Atanasio.

But now, facing Pedro in the bedroom, she could believe that this moment and place were the center and united memory, now, and others. Her son rubbed his sharp chin and spoke, this time aloud:

'Mamá, you don't know . . .'

Her look froze his voice.

Know? she snorted silently. *Know what? That nothing lasts? That power founded on injustice must perish at the hands of in-*

justice? That the enemies we shot, whose tongues we cut out, whose arms we cut off, whose lands we raped so that we could be the great family ... that someday they would find revenge and destroy us, take from us what was never really ours, what we held by strength and not by right? That in spite of everything your brother refused to give up and went on being a Menchaca, not far from the scene, as you did, but here below, among the workers facing danger, raping mulatto girls and Indian girls and not, like you, merely seducing willing women? That from his thousand fornications there had to remain at least one proof that he had existed in this land? That of all the sons he sprinkled over the countryside, one at least had to be born close by? And that on the same day that his son was born in a Negro hut – on the bottom, where he should have been born, to prove again his father's strength – Atanasio himself was ...

She knew that Pedro did not divine her unspoken words. Her gaze moved from his spent face and floated in the liquid heat of the bedroom.

Don't reproach me for anything, he was thinking, *I am also your son. My blood is the same as Atanasio's ... Then, why, that night ... they told me: Sergeant Robaina, who was with Santa Anna in the old days, has found what you and your brother have searched for so long, your father's body. He was buried in a cemetery in Campeche. A soldier who was there at the burial showed the sergeant where to dig, and the sergeant recovered the Colonel's remains and now, passing through on transfer to Jalisco, would like to deliver them to you and your brother tonight. I will expect you after eleven in the clearing two kilometers from the village ... the clearing where the gallows used to stand. So I wasn't very smart? Atanasio believed it too. His eyes filled with tears and he never doubted the message. Ay, why did I have to come back to Cocuya that season? Only because my money had begun to run out, and Atanasio never denied me anything. He would even have preferred for me to stay away, he wanted to be the only Menchaca here, your only guardian. Under the hot red moon we rode to the clearing. There was Sergeant Robaina, whom we remembered from childhood, leaning against his horse. His teeth and his white mustaches shone like rice. We knew him, he had always accompanied the General and he had been famous as a horse-breaker. He had always had a way of laughing as if he were part of some colossal joke. And there was the bag, dirty, hanging across his percheron's rump, the bag we had come to receive. Atanasio embraced him and the sergeant laughed as always. He laughed until his laughter became a whistle, and four men came out of the brush, four men in white, very white in the moonlight. These blessed souls, said the sergeant in a pleasant voice, these blessed people who are not satisfied with having lost everything but must try to come back. His voice changed and he too moved toward Atanasio. No one paid any attention at all to me. They just came forward staring at him, as if I didn't exist. I don't know how I managed to mount and gallop away as they came forward with their machetes in their hands, and Atanasio yelled at me, in a voice half hoarse and half serene: Come back, brother, remember what you're carrying! I felt the butt of the shotgun slapping against my knees, but I couldn't go back. They swung at his legs first and cut the tendons so that he couldn't move, and then they chopped at him there under the silent moon. What good would it have been for me to get help here ... when he was already dead? And when he had been killed by a cacique who had to kill him, if he was going to be the real cacique here? What could I do? I didn't even want to know about the fence they put up the next day, robbing us of our fields. We had been beaten. Our workers went over to the new man thinking how unfortunate it was that Señor Atanasio had tried to fight him. And as if to tell me to keep quiet, the platoon of Federals patrolled the new fence line for a week. I was grateful that they hadn't killed me, too. And a month later, General Porfirio Díaz visited the new man in his new big home. Nor did they forget to mock us. When they sent me Atanasio's mutilated body, they sent along a bag of cow bones, a great horned skull, the remains that the Sergeant had brought us. I just hung the loaded shotgun over the front door. Who knows why? An act of homage to poor Atanasio? Really, that night it never occurred to me that I was carrying a gun, even though the butt kept slapping my knee all the long way home, the long way, so long, Mamá, I swear ...*

'No,' said Lunero, standing up. 'No one is allowed in the big house.' His prone dance of anguish and terror had ended, his silent farewell to the boy on their last afternoon together. It must be half-past five by now. The sign-up man should be along soon.

D.A.C.—16

253

'Try to hide from us,' the sign-up man had said yesterday. 'Just try. We have something better than bloodhounds. Plenty of bastards who are happy to turn a poor peon in just because they know they have to go themselves.'

Lunero thought of the sandy coast. As he stood there, he looked enormous to the boy. He stared at the current flowing so swiftly toward the Gulf. How tall he seemed, with his thirty-three years and his cinnamon skin and his pink palms! He stared toward the coast and his eyes were white with nostalgia for another, older age across the Gulf, beyond the sandbar that broke the river's mouth and stained the edge of the sea brown. Farther, farther, the world of the islands; and farther, farther, to the continent where a man like himself could hide forever and say that he had returned. Behind him was the sierra, the highland, the Indian country. He did not want to look that way. He drew a deep breath and gazed toward the sea, as if toward a vision of freedom and plenty.

The boy ran to him. His embrace reached no higher than the mulatto's ribs.

'Don't go, Lunero.'

'But, my God, Cruz lad, what can I do?'

The mulatto rubbed the boy's head. He was filled with happiness and with gratitude for a moment he had always feared would be painful. The boy looked up at him.

'I'm going inside to tell them you can't go ...'

'Inside?'

'Yes, inside the big house.'

'They don't want us there, young Cruz. Don't ever bother them. Come on, let's get back to work. I'll be here for quite a few days yet. Who knows, maybe I'll never have to leave.'

The noisy afternoon river opened and closed around Lunero's body as he dove to avoid the boy's words and touch. The boy went back to work at the candle ring. He smiled as Lunero swam upstream imitating the thrashing of someone drowning. Lunero did a cartwheel in the water and came up with a stick between his teeth. On the bank again, he shook himself like a dog and made funny noises and sat down with the hammer and nails and went to work. But he could not stop thinking about it: the man in the black frockcoat would not be long now. The sun was already below the tree tops. He resisted but it was too late, the thread of his happiness had been cut bitterly short.

'Bring me some sandpaper from the cabin,' he said to the boy. He was sure that these were his farewell words.

He would go just as he was, in his work shirt and work pants. Why change? Now the sun was out of sight. A guard would be standing at the end of the path now, so that the man in the frockcoat would not have to come all the way to the hut.

'Yes,' said Ludivinia, 'Baracoa has told me everything. How we are supported by the labor of a mulatto and the boy. That we eat thanks only to them. And you don't know what to do?'

The old woman's real voice was hard to hear, it was so accustomed to muttering in solitude.

'Pah! Do what your father or your brother would have done! Go out and protect that mulatto and that boy and keep them here! And if you can't, then give up your life trying! Are you going, fuck-up, or am I? Bring me that boy, I want to talk with him ...' With a gesture of impatience, she ordered him to light the candles.

The boy saw only vague outlines through the lace veil. He could not be sure of the voices or the faces either. He left the window and tiptoed to the front of the house, to the tall sooty columns, the forgotten terrace where the hammock Señor Pedro used for his solitary drinking hung. And something more: above the lintel, supported by two rusty hooks, was the shotgun Señor Pedro always kept oiled and ready, the last defense against cowardice. Its double barrel shone white in the twilight. The boy passed beneath. What had been the living room had lost both roof and floor. Green evening light poured in from above and revealed weeds and ashes and, in the corners, stagnant pools of rain water. Frogs were croaking. A patio opened ahead of him, rank with brushy growth, and beyond it, at the back, a thin line of light showed beneath the door of the old grandmother's room. The voices from the room were louder. The Indian woman Baracoa appeared from the other side, where the kitchen had been, and looked toward the door with incredulous eyes. The boy stepped back into shadow. He went out on the terrace again and by stepping on broken adobe bricks climbed high enough to reach down the shotgun. Now the voices were very loud, a repeating stammer and a thin-toned fury. A tall shadow came out of the bedroom wearing a frockcoat with swinging tails. Boots rang on the square tiles. The boy did not hesitate: he knew the path those boots would take. With the gun in his arms he ran toward the hut.

Lunero was already waiting, far from hut and house, at the place where the red earth roads crossed. It was about seven now. The sign-up man would be along any minute. He looked down the road in both directions. The horse would raise dust, he would have warning. But he had no warning for the sudden double crash of the shotgun. For a moment he could neither move nor think.

For the boy had crouched in the ferns cradling the shotgun. As the man's steps neared him, he felt afraid. Then he saw the tight boots pass, the tails of the frockcoat, flapping. He had no doubts: it was the same frockcoat as yesterday. He had no doubt when the man whose face he could not see went into the hut and shouted 'Lunero!' in an impatient voice, a voice in which the boy recognized the threat he had seen yesterday in the man's manner, movements. Why had they come looking for the mulatto, if not to take him by force? And the shotgun was heavy with power that gave weight to the boy's silent fury. Fury because now he knew that life had enemies and was no longer the smooth flow of the river and their work. Fury because now separation was about to begin. The tight trousers came out of the hut. The frockcoat. He raised the shotgun and aimed the double barrel and squeezed the trigger.

'Cruz, my boy!' Lunero cried as he stood over Señor Pedrito's destroyed face. The stiff shirt was stained with blood, and he wore the false smile of sudden death. 'Cruz!'

And the boy, coming tremblingly out from the ferns, could not recognize that bloody gunpowder-marked face of a man he had always seen at a distance, usually half naked, a patched shirt over his hairless chest and the demijohn in his hand. This was not that man, nor was it the elegant gentleman Lunero remembered from years ago, nor was it the spoiled child Ludivinia had briefly loved. This was only a face lacking its nose, eyes, and mouth, and a bloody shirt and a stupid grin. Lunero and the boy were motionless. Cicadas trilled. Lunero understood what had happened.

And Ludivinia opened her eyes and wet her index finger with spit and pinched out the candle beside her bed. She made her way, almost creeping, to the window. Something had happened out there. The chandeliers had tinkled. Something had happened forever, been taken away by that double crash. She heard faint voices. Then they faded and there was nothing except the whir of insects. The cicadas trilled.

Baracoa, in the kitchen, let the fire go out and poured the wrong liquid into the wrong pot and told herself with a tremor that the bad times of shootings had returned.

Ludivinia did not move for several minutes. Gradually the silence became too much for her and she was overcome by a thin fury that four walls could not confine. She stumbled out into the darkness, dwarfed by the night sky. She was a small wrinkled white worm reaching out her arms in the hope of touching a human form she had known, for thirteen years, to be near, but that only now she wanted to hold and call by name rather than merely embracing him in her presentiments. Cruz: Cruz without given name, without the right surname, baptized by the mulattos with the syllables of Isabel Cruz or Cruz Isabel, the mother who had been run away with a stick by Atanasio: the first woman there who had given him a son. The old woman had forgotten what night was like. Her legs trembled, but she walked on, hunched over, crouching, pushing her spraddled legs forward, reaching for the last embrace she would ever know. But she found only a pounding of hooves and a cloud of dust, a sweat-lathered horse that reared when her bent form crossed the road, and the voice of the sign-up man yelling:

'Where did the black and the boy go, you old bitch? Where are they, before I send the hounds and the men after them?'

Ludivinia knew how to reply with a shaky fist raised in the darkness, and her natural curse:

'Fuck you!' She could not lift her head high enough to see his face. 'Fuck you!' The horse whinneyed.

His whip slashed her shoulder and she fell to the earth as the horse whirled and galloped away, raising dust that folded gently down.

I know that a needle is piercing the skin of my forearm. I cry out before I feel pain: the news of the pain travels faster than the pain itself, to prepare me for the pain ... to alert me against it so that I will be more sensitive to it ... for awareness ... weakens us ... makes us ... victims ... awareness ... of pain ... that never consults ... being unaware ... of us ... now: pain that is no more ... the injection ... but the other, the pain I know ... they are feeling my belly ... carefully, swollen belly ... clammy, blue ... they touch it ... I can't stand it ... they touch it with ... that soapy razor ... shaving my belly, my pubis ... I can't stand it, I scream, I have to scream ... they hold me down ... my arms, shoulders ... I yell for them to let me alone ... to let me die in peace ... don't touch me ... that inflamed stomach ... sensitive like a sore eye ... I can't stand it ... I don't know ... they hold me ... they hold me up ... my intestines don't move, they ... aren't moving ... I know ... gases blow me up ... don't come out ... paralyze liquids that ought to flow ... don't ... puffy ... I know it ... I don't have any temperature ... I don't know where to go ... who to ask for help ... so I can get up ... and walk ... I strain, I strain ... the blood doesn't ... I know the blood ... doesn't go where it's supposed to ... it ought to pour out ... of my mouth, my anus ... it doesn't ... they don't know ... guessing ... palp me, palpating my racing heart ... they feel my pulseless wrist ... they bend me, bend me in two ... they lay me back ... I'm going, going ... to sleep ... I tell them ... I don't know who they are ... I ought to tell them ... before I go to sleep ... we crossed, we rode ... our horses across the river ... I smell my own breath ... fetid ... they lay me back ... the door opens ... the windows are opened ... I'm rolling along, they're pushing me somewhere ... I see the ceiling ... the hazy lights that pass ... I

feel ... smell ... taste ... hear ... taking me ... passing ...
close by a decorated corridor ... taking me ... pass close touching, smelling, tasting, smelling the sumptuous robes – the rich
marquetry – the gold frames – chests of bone and tortoise-shell –
locks and hasps – coffers with iron corners and key escutcheons –
fragrant benches of ayacahuite wood – choir benches – baroque
robes and miters – worked chair backs – polychrome masks –
bronze nailheads – tooled leather – castered ball and claw
feet – damask chairs – chasubles of cloth of silver – velvet sofas –
refectory tables – vases and urns – chamfered panels – four-
poster beds – striated posts – shields – the merino carpets – the
great iron keys – the framed oils – the silks and cashmeres –
the crystal and the candelabras – the hand-painted dinnerware –
the warm ceiling beams – they will not touch this ... this will
not be theirs ... my eyelids ... I must raise ... open the windows
... wheel ... my huge hands ... enormous feet ... I sleep ...
lights that pass before ... open eyes ... ceiling lights ... open
the stars ... I don't know ...

You will be there on the first crest of the mountain that behind
you rises higher and higher into thinner and thinner air. At your
feet, foothills will fall away wrapped in tropical foliage and
nocturnal chirruping, until they are lost in the steaming flatland,
blue carpet for night. You will stop on the first rock platform,
lost in your quaking incomprehension of what has taken place,
the end of a way of life that you secretly believed to be eternal:
your life in the hut that was wrapped in bell-like flowers, your
life swimming and fishing in the river, making candles, living
with Lunero. But despite your internal convulsion, vibrating
from one pin in memory and the other in your intuition of the
future, the new world of the mountain and the night will open
before you with a dark lighting of a new path for your eyes –
which are also new and still blurred by what has ceased to be
life and has become only the memory of a boy who now belongs
to the indomitable and to what is beyond his own strength, to

the breadth of the wide world. Freed from the destiny of birth and birthplace, bound now to a new fate, a fate unknown that impends beyond the starlit mountain, as you sit and catch your breath that vast panorama will spread around you, the light of the star-thronged sky will fall upon you. The earth will follow its uniform flight spinning on its own axis while circling a controlling sun; the earth and its moon will whirl about each other and both around the common field of their masses. All the court of the sun will move within their white belt, and the current of liquid powder will flow in front of the external conglomerates in the wheeling of the clear arch across the tropical night, a perpetual dance of interlaced toes, the limitless and directionless dialogue of the universe. And the twinkling light will bathe you, upon the plain, upon the mountain, with a constancy most unlike the movement of the star and the whirling of the earth, its satellite, the sun, the galaxy, the nebula, most unlike the frictions and cohesions and elastic comings and goings that press together the forces of world, stone, and your own hands, and unite them. You will want to fix your eyes on just one star, to gather in all its cold light, which is as invisible as the color of the light the sun gives. You will squint and in darkness as during the day will not perceive the true color of the world, for that is prohibited to human vision. You will lose yourself in the contemplation of the thin white light that will enter your pupils with a sharp discontinuous rhythm. From billions of billions of beginnings, the light of the universe will fly its rapid curved course bending past great fleeting sleeping bodies; on across the mobile concentrations of the tangible, the arcs of light will circle, adapt, confine themselves, and separate, creating in the permanence of their velocity the contour of the whole. And you will feel the light arrive and at the same time will experience the scents of the mountain and plain: *arrayan* and papaya, the smells of darkness and tabachin, pine and tulipan laurel, vanilla and *tecotehue*, cimarron violet, mimosa, tiger flowers. You will see clearly how the light recedes dizzily farther and farther from the frozen islands, and farther and farther from the first opening and the first explosion. As the light will race to meet your eyes, it will at the same time race to the most remote edge of space. You will

press your hands down on the stone where you sit and will close
your eyes and hear again the cicadas and the bleating of lost
goats. In that instant when your eyelids are down, everything
will seem to move forward and backward and toward the supporting earth. The dark wings of the buzzard that flies chained
to the deep bend of the Veracruz river, and that later will pose
in immobility on a crag, will cut the even insistence of the stars.
And you will feel nothing, will not know that anything moves;
not even the buzzard will interrupt the silence; you will not feel,
neither with your eyes nor your feet nor the skin of your neck,
the infinite race and spin of the universe. You will contemplate
the sleeping earth. The whole earth of rocks and veins of
minerals, of humped mountains, of the weight of a plowed field
and the current of a river, of man and his dwellings, of beasts
and birds, and of stone shells ignorant of the inferno at their
core. And everything will oppose, without managing to resist,
the irreversible movement. You will play with a little rock as you
wait for Lunero to come with a mule. You will throw it from the
cliff so that for one moment it may attain a swift, energy-laden
life of its own; a small errant sun and brief kaleidoscope of
reflected stars, almost as swift as the light that reveals it, it will
become a tiny mite lost down the mountain, while the starlight
will continue to flow with an imperceptible and absolute velocity.
Your sight will turn back from the lower precipice where the
rock disappeared. You will prop your chin on your fist and your
profile will be sharp against the night horizon. You will be that
new element in the landscape which will go away to seek, on the
other side of the mountain, your life's uncertain future. But here
and now your life will be the moment just at hand and will cease
to be what has passed. Your innocence will die, not at the hands
of your guilt, but before your enormous surprise. You are high
above the world, you have never been so high before, and cross-
roads of such breadth you have never seen before: here the
familiar narrow world beside the river would be only a tiny pinch
of the unaccustomed immensity. And yet you, looking and looking in this moment of contemplative calm, will not feel small.
The distant piling of clouds. The long sweep of the undulant
earth. The vertical leap of the sky. You will feel not small but

better, more in control of your life and more serene. You will not suspect that you stand upon new land risen from the sea only a few hours ago to crash against wall after wall of mountains and wrinkle them like a parchment. You will feel yourself to be high upon the crest, perpendicular to the flatland, parallel to the horizon. In darkness, the sun's lost angle, and in time. Are the faraway constellations side by side, as they appear to your naked eye, or are they separated by incalculable epochs? Another planet will spin above you and its time will be identical to itself: perhaps that dark and distant rotation will be consumed in a single instant, the unique day of its unique year, a mercurial measure eternally strange to the days of your years. Its hour will not be your hour, just as the present moment of the stars which you are now contemplating will not be your present moment. Their light will be that of a time far away and possibly dead. The light you see will be only the specter of the light that began to journey years and, by your measure, centuries of centuries ago. Does that star still live? It will live so long as your eyes see it. And you will know that it has died only when on some future night you look for it and its light will no longer be there for your same eyes. Perhaps the light too will have ceased to exist. At any rate, the light you view is ancient, not that which in the now of star-time is racing away from the star: you have baptized the star with your stare. Dead in origin, it will still be alive in your eyes. Lost, calcined, fountain of light that now has no place of birth yet will nevertheless go on traveling toward the eyes of a boy who will live in the night of a different time, another time. Time that fills itself with vitality, with actions, ideas, but that remains always the inexorable flux between the past's first landmark and the future's last signpost. Time that will exist only in the reconstruction of isolated memory, in the flight of isolated desire. Time that, once it loses the opportunity to live, is forever wasted. Time that is incarnate in the unique being called you, now a boy, now a dying old man, a being who in a mysterious ceremony links together tonight, the little insects glowing against the dark cliff, and the immense stars whirling in silence against the infinite backdrop of space. Nothing will happen in this silent moment belonging to the earth, the sky, and to you. Everything will exist, will move and be moved, will form and conform, a river of change that in another instant will dissolve, age, and corrupt everything without a single voice being raised in alarm. The sun burns out its living days, iron sifts down as ubiquitous dust dissipates itself circling space, masses slowly come apart as radiation, the earth chills toward extinction, and you will sit there waiting for the mulatto and a mule with which to cross the mountain and begin to live, to fill up time, to execute the steps and poses of the macabre dance in which your life will leap before you at the same time it falls dying behind you, a mad dance in which time devours itself and no one can hold back, without destroying it, the irreversible flow toward disappearance. The boy-child, the earth, and the universe: one day there will be no life left for any of them, no warmth, nothing except forgotten nameless unity ... when no one will be alive to speak a name: fused space and time, matter and energy. One day everything will have the same name: nothingness. But not yet. Men are still being born. You still hear Lunero's 'Halooo' and the clang of mule-shoes on stone. Your heart will still quicken inside you as you become conscious at last that from this day on – this night – an unknown adventure begins, the world opens to you and offers you its time. You exist. You stand on the mountain. You answer Lunero's hoot with a whistle. You are going to live. You are going to be the point of encounters, and the reason for the universal order of things. Your body has its reasons. Your life has its reasons. You are, you will be, you have been the universe incarnate. For you galaxies will flame and the sun will burn. So that you may be, may live, and may love. So that you may find the secret and may lie helpless to participate in it, for that is a power you will possess only when your eyes are forever closed. You, standing, Cruz, thirteen years old, on the edge of life. You, green eyes, thin arms, hair coppered by the sun. You, friend of a forgotten mulatto. You will be the world's name. You will hear Lunero's call. You engage the infinite depthless freshness of the universe. You will hear the clang of mule-shoes. In you the earth and the stars touch. You will hear a rifle shot behind Lunero. Upon your head will fall, as if you were returning from a journey with neither beginning nor end in time, the promises of love and solitude, hatred and power, violence and tenderness, friendship and dis-enchantment, time and forgetfulness, innocence and surprise. You will hear night silent and empty of Lunero's cry and the sound of the mule-shoes. In your heart, open to life, this night, in your open heart . . .

[1889: April 9]

Drawn up, doubled upon himself in the middle of those con-tractions with his head dark with blood hanging by the most tenuous of threads at last open to life while Lunero held Isabel's arms and closed his eyes and did not want to see what was happening between her spread legs and asked her, his face turned, did you count the days? and she could not answer be-cause she was screaming with her lips closed inside and her teeth clenched and was feeling the head come out now while Lunero held her by the shoulders Lunero all alone and a pot of water boiling over the fire and the knife and the rags ready and he was coming out between her legs now coming coming coming out pushed by the contractions of her belly, contractions always harder and sharper, and Lunero had to let her shoulders go, Cruz Isabel, Isabel Cruz, to kneel between her legs and receive that black wet head the sticky little body still tied to Cruz Isabel, Isabel Cruz and the woman stopped moaning and sighed heavily and wiped the perspiration from her face with white palms, trying to see him, reaching her arms for him while Lunero cut the cord and tied the end and washed the body and face and petted him and kissed him and wanted to give him to his sister Isabel Cruz, Cruz Isabel, but now she was moaning with a new contraction and the sound of boots came toward the hut where she lay on the earth beneath the palm roof as the boots came closer and Lunero held his head down and struck him with his open hand to make him cry while the boots came closer and he cried and cried and began to live.

I don't know ... don't know ... I am he or if ... you were he ... or if I am the three ... You ... I carry you inside me and you will die with me ... God ... He ... I carry him inside me and he will die with me ... the three ... who spoke ... I ... I will carry him within me and he will die with me ... alone ...

You will not know: you will not know your open heart tonight, your open heart. Scalpel, they say, scalpel. I hear it, I who continue knowing when you no longer know and before you know. I who was he, I will be you. I listen in the depth of the glass, behind the mirror, at the very bottom, below and above you and him. Scalpel. They open you and cauterize. They open the walls of your abdomen. The thin cold knife separates the tissues. And they find that liquid in your abdominal cavity, and inflamed twists of intestine swollen and tied to your mesentery, swollen hard, full of blood. They find the area of gangrene bathed in fetid liquid. Infact, they say, and repeat: mesenteric infarct. They look at your dilated intestine, deep scarlet, almost black. They say: pulse, respiration, temperature, punctiform perforation. Eaten away, corroded. Hemorrhagic fluid drips out of your open belly. Hopeless, they say, hopeless, they repeat. The three. The clot breaks loose. Black blood is thrown out. The blood will flow and then it will stop. It stopped. Your silence and open eyes, sightless eyes. Your icy unfeeling fingers. Your blue-black fingernails. Your quivering jaw. Artemio Cruz ... Name ... hopeless ... heart massage ... hopeless ... You will not know now. I carry you inside and with you I die. The three, we ... will die. You ... die, have died ... I will die.

Havana, May 1960
Mexico City, December 1961

MORE ABOUT PENGUINS, PELICANS
AND PUFFINS

For further information about books available from Penguins please write to Dept EP, Penguin Books Ltd, Harmondsworth, Middlesex UB7 ODA.

In the U.S.A.: For a complete list of books available from Penguins in the United States write to Dept DG, Penguin Books, 299 Murray Hill Parkway, East Rutherford, New Jersey 07073.

In Canada: For a complete list of books available from Penguins in Canada write to Penguin Books Canada Ltd, 2801 John Street, Markham, Ontario L3R 1B4.

In Australia: For a complete list of books available from Penguins in Australia write to the Marketing Department, Penguin Books Australia Ltd, P.O. Box 257, Ringwood, Victoria 3134.

In New Zealand: For a complete list of books available from Penguins in New Zealand write to the Marketing Department, Penguin Books (N.Z.) Ltd, P.O. Box 4019, Auckland 10.

In India: For a complete list of books available from Penguins in India write to Penguin Overseas Ltd, 706 Eros Apartments, 56 Nehru Place, New Delhi 110019.

KING PENGUIN

A selection

WHERE I USED TO PLAY ON THE GREEN
Glyn Hughes

Embittered by the death of his wife, William Grimshaw becomes a fanatical evangelist. Creating a terrifying vision of demons and eternal damnation he struggles to bring the 'barbarous' people of Haworth into total submission to God and ultimately the factory bell. But amidst the fire of conversion he is fighting an inner battle against loneliness and the torment of repressed sexual desire . . .

'Glyn Hughes presents all the tensions without for a moment losing sight of the humanity of his characters or the landscape in which they live . . . We can only praise the author for his complete imaginative command over a whole period of time' – Hilary Bailey in the *Guardian*

'Convincing, alarming and memorable. It seems to me a real book, full of truth, vividly imagined and felt' – Ted Hughes in *Arts Yorkshire*

WINNER OF THE GUARDIAN FICTION PRIZE 1982 AND THE
DAVID HIGHAM PRIZE FOR FICTION 1982

KEEPERS OF THE HOUSE
Lisa St Aubin de Terán

Since the eighteenth century the eccentric and flamboyant Beltran family have ruled their desolate Andean valley. Now they are almost extinct.

At seventeen, Lydia Sinclair, newly married to Diego Beltrán, the last of the line, arrives at the vast decaying Hacienda La Bebella. As her husband retreats into himself, Lydia takes refuge in learning of his ancestors' tragic history. Benito, the family's oldest retainer, relates tales of splendour and romance, violence and suffering and from these she weaves a rich Gothic tapestry in which the fantastic legends of the past are mingled with the present necessity for survival in a harsh, drought-ridden land.

'A spellbinding storyteller . . . the book enthrals' – John Mellors in the *Listener*

Danny Abse	Ash on a Young Man's Sleeve
Paul Bailey	At the Jerusalem
	Old Soldiers
Caroline Blackwood	The Stepdaughter
Jorge Luis Borges	Labyrinths
Jocelyn Brooke	The Image of a Drawn Sword
	The Orchid Trilogy
A. S. Byatt	The Game
	The Virgin in the Garden
Angela Carter	The Bloody Chamber and Other Stories
	Heroes and Villains
	The Infernal Desire Machines
	of Doctor Hoffmann
John Cheever	Bullet Park
	The Stories of John Cheever
J. M. Coetzee	Waiting for the Barbarians
David Cook	Walter
	Winter Doves
Robertson Davies	The Deptford Trilogy
	Rebel Angels
Nigel Dennis	Cards of Identity
Anita Desai	Fire on the Mountain
	Games at Twilight
G. V. Desani	All About H. Hatterr
David James Duncan	The River Why
Wessel Ebersohn	Store Up the Anger
Shusaku Endo	The Samurai
James Fenton	The Memory of War/Children in Exile:
	Poems 1968–83
John Fuller	Flying to Nowhere
James Hanley	The Furys
Tony Harrison	Selected Poems
Shirley Hazzard	The Transit of Venus
R. C. Hutchinson	Rising
	Testament
	The Unforgotten Prisoner
Kazuo Ishiguro	A Pale View of Hills
Robin Jenkins	The Cone-Gatherers
B. S. Johnson	Christie Malry's Own Double-Entry
George Konrad	The Loser

Denton Welch	Maiden Voyage
	A Voice Through A Cloud
William Wharton	Dad
	A Midnight Clear
Patrick White	The Twyborn Affair
Marguerite Yourcenar	Memoirs of Hadrian
Alexander Zinoviev	The Yawning Heights